12th and Bruce

A story of a neighborhood, one street corner,
two friends traveling opposite sides of the law

TOM MacGEORGE

Omni Publishing Co.

2017

This is a work of fiction. Names, characters, businesses, places, events and incidents are either the products of the author's imagination or used in a fictitious manner. Any resemblance to actual persons, living or dead, actual events or locales is purely coincidental.

Published by
Omni Publishing Co.
www.omni-pub.com

Library of Congress cataloging-in-publication data
MacGEORGE, TOM
12th and Bruce
ISBN: 978-1545500507
Printed in the United States of America
October 2017

For Mom,

known to many as Nana,

one of Roscommon's finest.

La Cosa Nostra (Mafia)

La Cosa Nostra, or Mafia, is a secret, criminal society ruled by a commission made up of the bosses of the five New York families:

Bonnano
Columbo
Gambino
Genovese
Lucchese

"Made" men are inducted members. Before a man is accepted he "must do the right work." They are untouchable in the criminal underworld. Each family has the same strict organization:

BOSS   Head of the family; Godfather; Don; Receives a cut of every operation taken on by each member of his family

UNDERBOSS   Appointed by the boss; second in command. Usually first in line to become acting boss and logical successor to the boss

CAPOREGIME   Capo; Skipper; Captain; Leads a crew of soldiers

SOLDIERS   *Made* members of a family. Follow directions of their Captains and usually have upwards of ten associates working for them

ASSOCIATES   Not soldiers. Earners under the protection of a *made* man

CONSIGLIERE   Advisor to family. Boss's "right hand man" and moderator of disputes

Chapter One

The Mass

The celebration of Mass took place on a blustery cold day, the third week of March 1988. It started promptly at noon in Saint Joseph's Catholic Church, located in the Central Ward section of Newark, New Jersey.

A veteran of the corner of 12th Avenue and Bruce Street, Blackie Capone spoke. "Where else? This is where Gabe is from, where he grew up. For chrissakes' he was an altar boy, right? Besides, we get a chance to look at his friends from New York."

Gabe Randinoli, age fifty, went missing four months ago. No one doubted he was dead. Not that long ago, Gabe was hanging out with his friends on the corner of 12th Avenue and Bruce Street. The corner, located a few blocks up the hill from "Saint Joe's," would be empty today. Situated in the heart of Newark, the corner held lots of memories for many of the congregation.

Capone's partner, Tony Quinn, agreed. "You're right Blackie, Gabe's father and the rest of his family deserves closure. The odds of his body showing up are slim to none, maybe even a hundred to one. If they did the job, those people are experts, they kill you and the body disappears." Like others, Capone and Quinn never approved of the way Randinoli left his roots. That was all history now and they would do whatever it took to make things easier for Randinoli's father, a neighborhood icon known as "Cuban Pete."

After leaving the neighborhood, Randinoli went to New York City and became a "made" member of the Brooklyn-based Bonanno La Cosa Nostra crime family. Now he was dead, presumably at the hands of his associates.

The law enforcement community in New York—local, state, and federal—did not expend resources looking for the perpetrators. For police veterans, a missing member of the Mafia is not cause for alarm. A Brooklyn homicide detective who spoke with experience said, "Randinoli apparently made the hit list. He's gone for good. Another case closed."

Earlier in the week, Brad Mason called Mr. Randinoli. "I spoke with Father Luiz. He assured me of the details for the Mass. Everything will be as you requested. Suppose I pick you up at ten o'clock?"

"That would be just fine. I will be ready." Always happy to hear Mason's voice, the old man smiled as he hung up the phone.

Inside St. Joseph's, they sat together in the first pew; Cuban Pete and Brad Mason, Randinoli's best friend. The elder Randinoli always dressed immaculately, featuring shiny black patent leather shoes with two-inch heels. The Cuban heels accounted for the lifelong nickname.

All of the neighborhood people were proud of Mason's accomplishments as a *federale*. Capone said, "Look at our man Brad. Who would have thought we all would get together for this?" Mason dressed appropriately, trying not to look too much like the poster boy for a federal agent's get-together.

Quinn added, "They certainly traveled different roads. Brad will miss his buddy but he's not surprised. Gabe made his decision and lived and now died with it."

Light conversation filled the church as the attendees waited for Mass to begin.

"Things get crazy Brad, don't they?" Mr. Randinoli stared straight ahead at the statue of the Blessed Mother.

"What's that, Mr. R?" Mason turned to look at the older man.

"I mean you two growing up here, two peas in a pod. Now my Gabriel is lying dead somewhere. Who knows where? I pray he'll meet up with his mother. And thank God you are safe, my other son." As he smiled, a tear rolled down his cheek.

Mason could not find words to speak. He thought, "*Okay Gabe, we will see what needs to be done. You never made things easy.*"

Chapter Two

We will not be so noticeable

Earlier that same morning, another group was gathering at the Bonanno headquarters, the luncheonette on 4th Avenue in Brooklyn. The underboss, Carmine Cuccio, put out the word. "The boss wants fifteen guys, looking good, to go to Jersey to pay our respects for Gabe. It looks bad if we don't show." The boss earlier selected only made men to attend the Mass. Don Giuseppe "Joe" Nittoli had an ulterior reason for the trip to Newark. He wanted to meet a certain individual face-to-face.

Nittoli was the man who gave the order to murder Randinoli. He told his underlings, "We go to Jersey and act like we are angry that Gabe is missing. We are bewildered. Remember, most important, we are respectful. Do not get involved in awkward conversations. Listen closely, if asked, this is what we say: God knows what happened to our friend. We pray he will show up some day and say he lost his memory or some such thing."

Nittoli was very serious and everyone nodded in agreement. "Do not be concerned with FBI and police presence. We have every right to pay respects to an old friend." The boss always admired Randinoli's ability to earn money for the family. "Gabe was a model citizen, a few minor pinches, never served serious time. He was a businessman."

It was a most difficult decision for the Don. Nittoli was certain he made the right pronouncement the past December. He believed he did what was necessary when he gave the order to kill his favorite capo. The Don invested much thought before he issued the order. *"Gabe had balls and did the right work, but he became too careless on a few occasions. It was not good for the family's reputation. He had to go."* And, most importantly, the decision would solidify Don Nittoli's leadership. The members must never doubt that the boss acts for the benefit of the family. Nittoli's predecessor, Sal Cassando, would have handled it in the same manner. Nittoli spoke with reverence whenever he spoke the name of his mentor and friend.

Former FBI Assistant Director Todd Price would not be at the service. Price, a man obsessed with inhabiting the office of Director of the FBI, met Randinoli on one occasion in New York. The AD also journeyed to New York to meet with Don Nittoli.

Nittoli disliked Price. He did not believe the words mouthed by Price concerning Randinoli and Mason. Still, because of Price's distinguished position within the FBI, Nittoli used the lies in support of his declaration to have Randinoli murdered.

The members of the hit team that put three rounds into the back of Randinoli's head received a special warning from the boss. "You guys could get careless since you were the last to see him alive. After a few drinks, you might slip and say something stupid. Again, remember we are going to Newark to pay our respects, to give his father our sincere condolences." He added, "I have put ten grand in an envelope with a sympathy card. His father will appreciate the remembrance."

"*Marone!* Boss that's a very generous chunk of dough. His father will be happy and his friends will know we are good people." Jimmy Palmeri was always the one to blow smoke up the rear end of the boss. Nittoli ignored the comment.

The New York entourage of sixteen mobsters, traveling in Cadillac Eldorados, left the city at 9:00 a.m. After a leisurely drive up the Hudson River into Manhattan, they drove through the Holland Tunnel and followed a westerly direction toward Newark, arriving at the church at 10:40 a.m. There were lines of people outside making their way in to the old, gray brick structure. Palmeri said, "Geez look at the crowd. Gabe sure knew a bunch of people."

The boys playing box ball by the firehouse across from the church stopped to stare at the visitors. "Look at the size of those wheels." Tommy Penn never saw anything like this. As the men exited the cars, Penn counted aloud. "Let's see, twelve, thirteen … sixteen of them. Gabe must have been a big shot in the Big Apple." The boys resumed the game.

The Bonanno people appeared very submissive. They parked in the church parking lot and slowly walked into the church with Nittoli in the middle of the pack. As they entered the timeworn building, Nittoli observed that both sides of the center aisle were already half-filled with what looked like Randinoli's family and neighborhood friends. He nodded toward a few empty pews midway up the center aisle. "Sit there, we will not be so notice-able. You two get in the pew behind," he said. Both guns understood and settled in directly behind their leader. Church or not, the boss always re-quired as much protection as possible.

A sixteen by twenty-four-inch color photograph of Randinoli, set off in a gold-plated frame, adorned the top step of the red-carpeted altar. The pic-ture showed a smiling seventeen-year-old wearing the gold and orange col-ors, the uniform of the Saint Joseph's Drum and Bugle Corps. The two tenor drum mallets he held rested on the mother of pearl drum. The drum rested just above his left knee. The young man in the photograph stood at attention with his feet at a forty-five degree angle. A tape recorder now played from the sanctuary. Throughout the church echoed the drum line, remembered as one of the best in the country. The former corps members in the congregation could pick out the clean snare, tenor and bass drums, each recalling a happy time.

Brad Mason owned the picture and kept it in his home for many years. He knew that Randinoli's father was unaware of its existence. Mason gave him the remembrance a few weeks after his son was declared missing. The day he presented this photograph to the elder Randinoli, the old man could not speak at first. Instead he wept and stared for several minutes at the pho-tograph of his young son.

"You should have this. Gabe wanted you to have it." Mason placed his hand on the elder Randinoli's shoulder. "I printed the date on the back. The photographer picked Gabe out of a whole bunch of drummers. It was taken in 1954 at the National Championships in Minnesota. Gabe was seventeen. He looks great." The truth was that the entire drum line had individual pic-tures taken. "*So what,*" Brad thought, "*the old man will cherish a memory that his son was special.*"

"It makes me so glad to remember my son as a happy young man. It will rest on the mantle in the living room. God bless you, I treasure it already."

After the recording ended, Jack "Professor" Murphy, the church organist of many years, began to play soft and somber church music.

At precisely 11:00 a.m., Father Luiz Alfonso, the new, young Cuban priest, entered the altar from the sanctuary directly behind the four steps leading to the pulpit. The bright sun shone through the three huge, plate-glass windows directly atop the rear of the altar. The bright colored glass, high above the main altar, depicted the Holy Family. Two teenage acolytes, a boy and girl, accompanied the young priest as he proceeded to the middle of the altar.

Sister Francis, Randinoli's favorite nun, sat in one of the front pews. She whispered, "I have never seen the church look so beautiful."

The congregation rose as Father Alfonso faced the congregation in the middle of the altar. He raised his arm and smiled. "Welcome, everyone, to Saint Joseph's." He adjusted his miniature microphone and began. "In the name of the Father, and of the Son, and of the Holy Spirit." The ceremony proceeded without incident. The homily delivered by the priest was short and to the point. Earlier, Randinoli's father had made a request to the priest, saying, "Father, please say some nice things about my son, but we know he was no saint."

The young priest smiled as he nodded. "Mr. Randinoli, God will look out for Gabriel, he is in good hands."

The New York visitors appeared quite at home. They joined the line of communicants, received the Eucharist and drank the wine distributed by one of the deacons. Nittoli and his people returned to the pews with heads bowed, with a couple of them reverently making the sign of the cross. Randinoli's friends watched closely from the other side of the church.

Johnny Zatz could not hold back. Not very quietly, he said, "Those bums are too much. You would think that they go to St. Joe's every morning. It is better than Hollywood, they look like saints who lost their best friend. They did the work and now it's like, we are so sorry for your loss. You gotta be kidding me. I don't think I can hold back when we go to the club."

Always the calming influence at the famous schoolyard crap games at 12th and Bruce, Tony Quinn whispered to his friend. "Zatzie, remember what we all agreed to with Brad. Let them have their day. Brad will figure out if we need to do anything and it will be taken care of the right way. Besides, what do we really know? We heard Gabe bought it in New York. Then we heard his own people whacked him. We do not know anything for sure. We go to the club after Mass, have a few drinks, something to eat and call it a day. It will work out the right way." He smiled at his friend and said, "Zatzie, the Volpe's are catering. You can have extra eggplant, you okay with that?"

Zatz respected his friend for many reasons. "Anthony, you should have been a lawyer, you know that?" Across the aisle, one of the women from the Rosary Sodality placed her index finger to her lips and "shushed" him. The other women gave out "the stare." The conversation ended abruptly. It was from another never-to-be-forgotten lesson learned at an early age. *Do not mess with the girls from the RS.*

At the request of the Randinoli family, Mae Johnson, a black parishioner of many years and choir member, sang a beautiful rendition of "Amazing Grace." Quinn could not resist, saying, "I told you, only a black woman can sing that song. Remember, Gabe used to tell her that he wanted to manage her career."

"Right," he would say, "Mrs. J. we will make millions. With your voice and my business expertise, we can't miss." Danny Sherman could be counted on to remember prior conversations, word for word.

Sister Francis wept. "It seems like yesterday Brad and Gabe volunteered at Saint Michael's." She spoke of the High Street Shelter for homeless men. The women in the church, along with a few men, shed tears thinking of the young man who attended Saint Joseph's Elementary School.

The Mass concluded with Father Alfonso saying, "Go, the Mass is ended." The assembly responded, "Thanks be to God," with the hungry attendees responding louder than necessary. "Gabriel's family has requested that I make the following announcement." Father stretched his right arm and pointed in the direction of the club, saying, "Everyone is invited to Saint Joseph's Club, just down the block at the corner of Hartford and Hudson Streets. There will be food and liquid refreshments for all to enjoy. Thank you for attending this Mass in remembrance of one of our finest altar boys."

Chapter Three

Everyone pays in the end

Approximately two hundred and fifty people leisurely walked the one block from the church to the club and entered the old, reddish-gray, brick building. The women from the RS moved quickly up the stairs to the second floor.

Sister John, the optimist, said, "It will be much warmer up here."

"Right Sister, if Dutch ever gets the bloody heat working," said Mrs. Sherman, who, like many of the RS women, had often experienced the failure of the furnace.

Mrs. Donato said, "We'll have access to the kitchen. We won't smell the alcohol, or inhale cigarette and cigar smoke."

Sister John added, "Or listen to the colorful language."

The mourners were greeted by mountains of hors d'oeuvres, set up earlier on the twelve-foot-long folding tables. The RS women had made sure to include a neighborhood favorite: ginger fruit cocktail, featuring bananas, fresh strawberries and melon balls, all covered with chilled ginger ale. A large punch bowl held the Italian cookies requested by the senior Randinoli.

Mae Johnson filled a plate with food and said, "Everyone will be relaxed as soon as the beer and wine kick in. Pray to God there will be no trouble."

Many were concerned someone from the corner might cause a scene with the visitors from New York. Johnny Zatz, the most unforgiving of the neighborhood group, came prepared to do whatever it took to make a point. More than once, Capone and Quinn reminded everyone they needed to hide their true feelings. Quinn put it best, saying, "Brad asked that we show the respect Cuban Pete and his family deserve. Remember, no matter what we really believe, the New York visitors are guests. As far as we know, they too are here to pay their respects. Don't jump to conclusions."

Zatz spoke to his partner Joe Simpson, saying, "Jump to conclusions? I may decide to jump down somebody's throat."

Simpson did not offer a response. If Zatz decided to take action, Simpson would be close by. This meant some of the guests would be hurt.

After expressing his condolences to Cuban Pete Randinoli, the boss of the Bonanno family sought out someone in particular and extended his hand. "Special Agent Brad Mason, I have heard much of you, and all good, I might add." Nittoli wanted to meet Randinoli's boyhood friend and judge for himself if the stories were true. He pointed to one of the small tables in the corner by the cigarette machine. Several sets of eyes watched with curiosity.

Earlier, one of the club's renowned bartenders, Dutch Bauer, was smart enough to remove the power cord to the jukebox. "This is the only record player in the city to play the same records from thirty years ago. I love Crosby and Sinatra as much as anyone, but this crowd might not appreciate the repetition."

Mason looked the mobster directly in the eye and shook his hand firmly, saying, "Mr. Nittoli, thank you. Your reputation is also well regarded." Mason then nodded and said, "My pleasure, indeed." He realized this was the most powerful LCN member in the country. The FBI agent now assigned to the Boston FBI Office was determined to be the perfect host and obtain whatever information was offered. The two occupied the only corner table of the first-floor bar area.

Nittoli said, "Please Brad, call me Joe. I would like to be your friend."

Mason thought of the crap game in the schoolyard. One of the regulars was popular with everyone. He often said to a newcomer, "Welcome, I am Victor Finocchi. I am everyone's friend." He offered a huge smile, as big as his bankroll that increased repeatedly, a result of money taken from the inexperienced newcomers to the game.

Not a surprise to the locals, the meal catered by the local Volpe family restaurant was a masterpiece. Peter Volpe wanted to impress the guests from New York. He never involved himself in politics, including local disputes. He immersed himself solely in preparing good food. He loved all the kids in the neighborhood, including Gabe. "Gabe was a good kid. Who knows why he wanted something else. He made a decision. I cook, that is what I do," he said. The Italian food was plentiful: antipasto, linguini, meatballs, sausage, veal piccata, eggplant, mussels and calamari. The Volpe family secret-recipe marinara sauce, as always, received many kudos.

Nittoli sipped red merlot from a large, twenty-ounce goblet and smoked a long, green Bering cigar. "I ate too much, but I hate to admit the meal even surpassed some of our fine New York Italian restaurants," he said. He paused and smiled toward his new acquaintance. "Now mind you, Brad, *some* of our restaurants, not all. You and your friends must be my guests at one of my fine restaurants in Manhattan." After another drink from his tall wine goblet, the older man seemed to be thinking of a memory. One of the young girls helping with the over-generous brunch removed a large bowl of mussel shells. He smiled as he spoke. "I am sure you know how much Gabe enjoyed mussels."

Mason surprised himself, growing more comfortable with the big boss. Perhaps he wanted to believe Nittoli owned no responsibility for Gabe's departure. "Oh for sure, especially served Fra Diavolo." He now relaxed just by mentioning an Italian dish he and Gabe often shared. "It was a mandatory dish for the holidays. Mrs. R would always add extra red pepper for Gabe and me. Cuban Pete would say, 'The more you sweat, the better the mussels,' and we would all laugh."

Joey Coughlin, sitting at the bar with a few of the old corps members, nodded toward Mason and Nittoli. "I think that's peachy, two street guys hanging out and shooting the shit."

Bauer said, "No more for you. Keep your voice down before all hell breaks loose." Bauer knew what would result if the locals went into action.

Mason and Nittoli drank more wine and spoke of many things. They discovered they both attended night school before becoming college graduates; Nittoli at New York University, and Mason at New Jersey's state school, Rutgers University. They talked of the important things of life, Nittoli's Yankees versus Mason's Red Sox, and two of the greatest of the game, Joltin' Joe DiMaggio and Teddy "Ballgame" Williams. With DiMaggio and Williams as subjects, baseball aficionados were never at a loss for lively conversation. The good guy-bad guy personas disappeared.

The mob boss, now on a roll, spoke slowly. "Of course you realize that Joe D. was the reason for most of the Bronx Bombers' accomplishments; ten pennants, nine World Championships, 361 lifetime home runs, and finishing lifetime with a .325 batting average. "Di Mag definitely was the greatest." Nittoli did not hold back, and demonstrated he was truly a fan of the Yankees and, in particular, Joe DiMaggio.

Mason nodded and smiled. "There is no argument, DiMag was very good." He paused for effect. "However, no hitter ever came close to the Thumper. The records do certainly speak volumes. Williams was a two-time most valuable player, six-time AL batting champion, named to seventeen

All-Star teams, a two-time Triple Crown winner, and a lifetime .344 batting average." He knew Nittoli was probably aware of the stats. The mob boss grinned widely and Mason continued. "Not to mention that he finished his career with 521 home runs and a .482 on-base percentage, which as you know is still the highest of all time." Mason sipped the wine and waited for the next barrage.

Instead, Nittoli said, "Bravisimo! You have out-statisticed me. Okay, we will agree they were two of the best of all time." Nittoli would love to discuss baseball more frequently but none of his associates shared his love of the game. The boss enjoyed the sparring match. He honestly felt at ease, even though they only just met. He held a high opinion of the FBI agent sitting across the old battered table. He thought, *This man is someone I could admire as a friend. Not now, but I will give him a real gift. Does he have any idea of the scumbag in the big-shot position in the FBI? He is smart, he must know."*

Not a traditionalist, Nittoli enjoyed a reputation of being the new generation of Mafioso boss. Certainly not cut from the old-school of well-known "mustachio Pete" mobsters. Over the years things change, including organized criminals. Unlike Mafia leaders of the past, such as Charley "Lucky" Luciano and Al "Scarface" Capone, Nittoli systematically relocated much of the Bonanno family assets into legitimate businesses as quickly as possible. Mason was already aware of the mobster's educational background and astute business prowess. Still, he knew the mobster would do whatever it took to keep his power.

The wine was having a relaxing effect on Nittoli. "I believe profits are available in many ways, some of them legitimate."

Nittoli was also a fight fan and up-to-date with Mason's successes as an amateur boxer, in particular the New Jersey Golden Gloves championships. "I never got to see you fight but am told you hit as hard as anyone—maybe good enough to turn pro."

Mason accepted the mobster's compliment, saying, "I have to hit hard, I don't run very fast. I never considered the fight game as a career. You know better than I the people that run the boxing business can be difficult to deal with."

Nittoli owned a percentage of an up-and-coming middleweight contender from Queens. He understood what the agent opined. "You are correct, stay the hell away from it, a very dirty game."

Both determined to lead by example, to honor Randinoli's memory without shouting, swearing or offering theories concerning his disappearance. Their demeanor rubbed off on the others. Men who never met behaved like old friends. There were no war stories coming from the cops or the robbers. Jimmy Palmeri said to no one in particular, "I can't believe it. This is just like Brooklyn. I feel at home."

Nittoli steered the conversation back to Randinoli. "Of course, you know Gabe was no dummy. I will never admit it in public, but in our business, we do not employ the smartest people in the workforce. Gabe was a street guy who spoke intelligently and possessed the ability to deal with people. He even worked at improving his English." This was an honest observation by the boss. However, he left out the parts where Randinoli stopped speaking and became very physical when certain folks did not cooperate.

Mason agreed, saying, "We used to talk about education just hanging on the corner. Gabe did not have the time." Mason smiled as he thought of his friend. "He would use one of his favorite sayings: 'I am a very busy man.'"

Mason noted Nittoli's earlier comment. The boss used the past tense when speaking of Randinoli. He said, "Gabe *was* no dummy" and "*was* a street guy." Now, there was no longer any doubt in his mind. "*My friend is dead.*" It was worth the cost of the expensive wine; even a Mafia boss has loose lips. Mason believed for some time that his friend was murdered. Now he was certain. As for becoming an employee of La Cosa Nostra, Mason was well aware that academia was not a requirement. A street education was necessary. The most important requirements were to always be present, always be prepared to break the law, and always be ready to "do the right work"— to kill someone.

"I admire his father. He decided that his son is dead and he wants closure, today he gets that." Nittoli's comment was right on the mark.

Mason agreed. "He is a wonderful man, and did everything he could possibly do. After Mrs. R passed, the old man became . . ." Mason paused as he searched for the right words.

"More than a father, if that's possible." The mob boss seemed to understand.

Mason continued, "Yeah, he was a strict taskmaster yet the kindest, gentlest man I ever knew." He grinned, "I guess the taskmaster stuff only worked for Gabe when it fit his program.

Nittoli nodded in agreement. He noted the noise level increasing at the bar. After another hour of what turned into an enjoyable meeting for both, Nittoli looked over at his men. This was the sign it was time to go. He moved away from the table, saying, "Brad, I will be sending you something you can use." Not waiting for an answer, with the palm of his right hand he gently squeezed Mason's left forearm. "For what it is worth, in my own way I too loved Gabriel Randinoli." He rose from the table and extended his hand. Mason reached out and the two men smiled and shook hands.

Mason was certain a slight tear appeared on the boss's face. "I believe that, but things happen and there are consequences. I have learned and I believe we are all responsible for our own actions. You can call it a code of belief. The wonderful nuns at St. Joe's have taught us in school and at the church we just left. I believe what they explained, that everyone pays in the end." Not waiting for a response, he led Nittoli to the front door, placed his hand on the Don's shoulder and said, "I wish you safe passage out of the great state of New Jersey." *What the hell, take one last parting shot.* He smiled and said, "And Joe, I wish your Yankees success as they fight for second place."

The boss smiled broadly, "We should make a small wager, maybe a bottle of great single malt scotch. But, since I am not a gambler, we have a gentleman's bet, okay?"

Mason enjoyed the humor. The boss of New York's biggest illegal gambling operation does not gamble. He thought, "*Makes sense, the house does not gamble, the house never loses.*" The two joined again in a firm, parting handshake.

The New York crew circled around their leader and exited out of the building onto Hudson Street. They crossed to the other side of the street, half of them still puffing on cigars as they walked back to their expensive Cadillac sedans.

Johnny Zatz looked out a window. "Look at that beauty parade. The neighborhood is forever blessed, the freakin' heavyweights of the New York Mafia walkin' down Hudson Street. Between them, they whacked enough people to fill both cemeteries, Holy Sepulchere on South Orange Avenue and Gate of Heaven in Hanover." Zatz's mind was made up. The outsiders killed one of the kids from 12th and Bruce. "One grenade and it would be over," suggested Zatz.

A few of the 12th and Bruce people silently prayed that the New Yorkers would walk faster and get the hell out of the neighborhood and the city. It was no secret that in an instant Zatz could get his hands on a grenade and whatever else he required in the way of heavy artillery.

Chick Rozella showed his crooked smile and whispered, "I think that went well. Thank God we promised to keep things peaceful."

Chapter Four

Not a typical fed

The crisp March air felt good after eating and drinking all afternoon. The New York crew enjoyed the slow, one-block walk from Saint Joseph's Club to the church parking lot.

Out of the ear shot of the boss, Palmeri said to no one in particular, "We'd never do this in Brooklyn. The other families would be using us for target practice."

The box ball participants were now in the middle of an intense argument. The popular street game was played throughout the city streets. The rules were very close to baseball. It required a pitcher, catcher, batter, first, second and third basemen, and a shortstop. No outfielders, six players to a side. The pitcher usually spun the rubberized ball so when it hit the ground it was more difficult to hit. The ball bounced once before getting to the batter who swung at the ball with a clenched fist. The idea was to hit the ball somewhere between the infielders and run like hell to first base. Each team was allotted three outs per inning. A game lasted seven innings.

"Foul my ass, that was inside the line by two inches." The smallest kid of the lot was adamant. His face was as crimson as his wavy red hair.

The New Yorkers stopped to enjoy the confrontation. Before he entered the big car, Nittoli said, "Let us prevent a war. Give those kids a twenty. Thank them for watching the wheels. Tell them to invest it wisely." Nittoli was in a good mood. He truly enjoyed the time spent with the old friend of a former employee.

One thing was certain: Palmeri's reputation as the cheapest bastard in the outfit continued. He became deaf when anyone mentioned parting with money, especially his own. Dinny "Specs" Buchanan, an associate member of Randinoli's crew, once told Palmeri, "Jimmy, you suffer from acute, terminal frugality."

Frank Sassano, a capo, peeled off a twenty-dollar note from a thick wad of bills and waved it to the young boys. He yelled across the street as he waved the twenty, "Hey kid, c'mere."

Quick to react, Tommy Penn raced to the church parking lot and accepted the crisp bill. He made a lame attempt at justifying the mobster's kindness. "Thanks, we made sure no one messed with your wheels."

"Right, and invest it wisely. No dice game at Bruce Street, right?" Sassano smiled as he spoke.

Penn could keep up with the best of them. "Are ya kiddin' Mister? As soon as Wall Street opens tomorrow we drop it all on GM, win, place, and show."

Sassano got in the car and reported his conversation. "Man, those kids are really sharp, I never even heard of GM at that age."

The Bonanno family members looked forward to a relaxing ride back to Brooklyn. The boss occupied the passenger seat, Palmeri was the driver, and Frank Sassano and Stephen Lombardi sat in the back. Earlier, Nittoli ordered that the cars not travel in tandem and arrive back in the city at intervals. His reasoning simple, he explained, "There's no need to bring attention to ourselves in and out of the city. The cops and the other families have enough to do without wondering about our travel arrangements." The others smiled.

Sassano was curious. "Boss I couldn't help but notice. It looked like you and Gabe's friend the fed were having a good time. Did he say anything about Gabe going missing?"

Nittoli answered, "His name is Brad Mason. We did have an enjoyable conversation. We discussed many subjects, especially sports, baseball in particular. He spoke of him and Gabe growing up in the city, holiday meals and that sort of stuff." The Don thought out loud. "But never fool yourself. Mason knows the business Gabe chose. He knows we hit his friend. Will he make it his mission to find out what happened? I do not think so. I believe he understands our business and accepts Gabe's situation for what it was— a business decision. Still, we need to keep track of him." That ended the explanation.

After a few blocks heading out of the neighborhood, Lombardi said, to no one in particular, "Ya know, I liked those people. For a while, I thought I was back in our own neighborhood. I mean the food, the good wine, it was just like home."

Before Nittoli responded, Palmeri said, "You're right Stevie. At first, I didn't know what to expect. Everything turned out great, they thanked us for being there and I believe they really appreciated that we showed up." He turned to Nittoli. "Boss, you were a hundred percent correct. We acted respectful and they fell for it."

The two guns in the back seat immediately recognized the *faux pas*. Nittoli did not speak immediately. He looked straight ahead and spoke evenly. "Jimmy, you never heard me say anything about having anyone fall for anything . . ."

Palmeri started to speak, "No, I didn't . . ." Don Nittoli waved him off. "If you listened, you would have heard we would be respectful because it was proper. We were not *acting* in a respectful manner. We were truly respectful. Gabe was one of us. His friends are not our enemies. They do not interfere in our business. Louie expressed it correctly. He liked them. They appear to be good, hard-working people. Gabe's father, as we learned firsthand, is a fine man. You ate his food and drank his wine." Nittoli's voice heightened. "Now you say, "They fell for it." Palmeri's hands moistened on the steering wheel, "I didn't . . ."

"Do not talk and drive. Keep quiet and listen. If you paid attention the first time, there would be no need to go over it again." He had the full attention of the others and Nittoli never wasted time making a point.

"First of all, Gabe was a captain, a highly-respected member of the family. He was human and he made some errors that he paid for with his life." Don Nittoli turned slightly toward the driver. "As the boss, I am expected to make decisions. My order to attend the funeral service was the result of a well thought-out decision. Who knows when next I will face the same set of circumstances?" The car stopped at a red light, and Nittoli turned toward Palmeri. "It could be for your funeral."

Palmeri felt himself losing saliva as he attempted to speak. "Boss, for God's sake, I . . ."

"Did I not just tell you to keep quiet?" Nittoli, now almost whispering, said, "You are a good *soldato*. However, you have a very distasteful habit of speaking when told to shut up! What will I do with you? Do not answer. Today we did the right thing and now it ends. Now!"

Nittoli settled in his seat and closed his eyes. The other three did not speak. The boss no longer questioned his decision of ordering the murder of Randinoli. He thought, "*I will have no problem with the FBI over the capo hit. Brad Mason will enjoy the gift I will give him. He is not a typical fed. He comes from the streets and he does not forget.*"

Chapter Five

God will reward you

1950 was a memorable year for many folks. The population was growing at a record-setting pace. The world war that ended in 1945 left people with a desire for lasting peace. However, the United States and Russia became entangled in what was to be known as the "cold war." North Korea invaded South Korea, and both the U.S. and Russia raced to develop a hydrogen bomb. Political tensions were high.

There were important events happening in Newark's Central Ward, as well. Reaching the eighth grade at St. Joes' was not an easy task for a few of the 12th and Bruce members. Gabe Randinoli, not stupid by any stretch of the imagination, considered it beneath him to work at studying or take school seriously.

"Gabe, you made it, good stuff." Brad Mason truly meant it. He was proud of his friend. "Now one more year of keeping our noses clean and just doing the drill and like magic, we're in high school."

Randinoli was not one to accept praise graciously. "Brad, my man, do not lay the odds on the high school career. I stayed here for eight years to keep an eye on you and some of the other bums. Without me, you would still be chasin' the girls in kindergarten. I believe that as the eldest, I have responsibility." Although both were now thirteen, Randinoli never failed to remind his friend he was a few months older.

The summer flew by for the soon-to-be eighth grade "upperclassmen." Mason received a nice chunk of dough from the parish pastor. He and Jimmy Coughlin spent their summer painting inside the parish buildings. Randinoli received money from the crap game operators for picking up the beer and soda, icing the drinks, sweeping the schoolyard area for the game and whatever needed attention to keep the crapshooters reasonably happy. Both looked forward to their new status. Now the younger students would treat the elder classmen, who comprised two eighth grades, with great reverence. It was tradition; the "seniors" expected the respect. Even Randinoli became anxious for his final year to begin. He planned to order a few people around.

"I will straighten out those lowlifes. Of course, a little extra lunch money will not hurt." His scheme involved "asking" the younger kids for a few cents so that he could buy lunch. "Hey, I only need eight cents to buy milk." Randinoli never mentioned he had no intention of paying back the loan. By the time he concluded his rounds, he always had more than enough change to cover his lunch bill. He explained, "The trick is to time your collections. Never hit the same kid two days in a row. It's all in the planning."

During the first week of the new school year, their favorite nun, Sister Francis, suggested that Mason and Randinoli volunteer to work for a few hours on weekends at Saint Michael's Men's Shelter on High Street. "The people down there can certainly use the help. The place is a beehive of activity on the weekends."

Sister Francis assured the boys when she said, "I think you will both benefit. It will be an experience." All through elementary school, this caring nun watched her two favorite students growing into adulthood. She saw something special in them and always steered them in a good and orderly direction.

Randinoli was not so sure of the nun's suggestion. "Sister, how much do we get paid?" The young nun feigned deafness. Mason slowly shook his head.

Mason smiled. "We do it for charity Gabe, because we are good people. No pay." He knew that Randinoli respected the nun more than any teacher in the school. "And Sister Francis thinks it's a good idea."

Randinoli answered, "Right, I realize that. But a few bucks wouldn't hurt."

Sister Francis truly enjoyed the boy's exchange; she smiled and said, "Gabriel, God will reward you."

The Saint Michael's facility gave refuge to over two hundred men, the largest shelter in the state of New Jersey. If anyone other than Sister Francis had asked for their help, the boys would likely have refused. They agreed to give it a try and began the new adventure at the shelter as all-around helpers.

After a few weeks of volunteering, Randinoli wondered aloud, "When do we get promoted on this job?" He believed that sweeping floors, washing dishes, pots and pans was well below his station. The supervisor put them on the chow line. Now, they worked the real deal, placing food on the well-worn plates as the men of all colors, ages, shapes and sizes shuffled through the chow line.

Sister Francis spoke the words of a prophet. Volunteering at the shelter became a rewarding encounter. They listened to the stories of homeless men speak of how they each lived on the streets prior to arrival at St. Mike's. Each day, the residents were bused to job sites, hopeful to obtain any type of available work. Most of the men were addicted to alcohol and some were dealing with the ever-growing drug scourge. Many lost their families, homes, businesses—all their worldly possessions. One counselor summed it up, saying, "More than any of the *stuff,* these men lost their self-worth."

Men belonging to the fellowship of Alcoholics Anonymous attended AA meetings each morning after breakfast. They loved to sit around after the meetings and talk with the St. Joe's youngsters about their road to recovery. They spilled out real-life accounts of what life was like when they were drinking, what happened to them, and then described their present lives. They had changed and were now able to put down the bottle and live meaningful and productive lives.

The boys were curious and attended one of the AA open meetings. One of the members, a former college professor, spoke to the attendees. "You fellows have a chance to turn your lives around. Most of you have made a good start. Keep praying, asking for help, and going to meetings and you will reach your own conclusions."

The boys knew of men and a few women in the neighborhood who drank a lot more than they should have. Later Randinoli asked an AA member how someone becomes an alcoholic. "You may have a tendency to be an alcoholic. Do not test it. Do not take that first drink my young friends. That's the one that leads to problems."

He told a story of how bad life got for him before he found AA. "Living on the streets, I paid daily visits to Tony's barbershop on Mulberry Street. Tony was a real good guy, he let me drink from the hair tonic bottles. Tony was a recovering alkie himself and knew that alcoholics have an uncontrollable obsession to drink alcohol. He understood that we craved alcohol and would do anything to get it. The barber was sober for twenty-plus years and grateful for the way his life turned around. Tony had a weird sense of humor. After a close shave, the customer came to expect what came next. Tony would place a hotter-than-hell cotton towel on the poor guy's face, and enjoy a loud belly laugh when he heard the 'Yah!' scream. Oh right, the good old days. Vitalis was my favorite drink at the barber shop." He explained how, before joining AA, he had an obsession to drink from any bottle containing alcohol.

Family members often visited their sons, husbands, and fathers at the shelter and expressed gratitude to the staff. The volunteers, as well, received kudos from the administration, the residents and the families.

Mason thought that his friend might be another type of addict, abusing people and believing he was entitled to things not his. Mason commented, "I got a good feeling when the woman thanked us for volunteering and helping her husband. You too?"

Randinoli appeared embarrassed. He said, "I guess so, but I would not say no to a little *spondulix* for all my hard work."

Mason smiled and asked, "Where were you when Sister Joan talked about character and conscience?" Finally—no response from Randinoli.

Chapter Six

Early fifties—Newark's Central Ward

In 1952, Gabe Randinoli, at the age of fifteen, was the elder. He was five months older than his friend Brad Mason. Their physical characteristics also differed. Mason, of Scotch-Irish ancestry, stood an inch or so taller, with a full head of wavy, dirty-blonde hair and hazel eyes. Gabe's tan skin, jet-black hair and deep-brown eyes were suggestive of his Italian heritage. How could they remain friends through the years when they were so different concerning things that truly counted? It is what the nuns called "character and conscience."

Both boys lived in the same neighborhood, attended and graduated from elementary school together, and were taught by the same nuns and teachers. Now a high school sophomore, Gabe had no intention of graduating. "That's it, I got plans." He would quit high school after completing his second year. He never discussed his choice with his counselor or any of the teachers. Gabe decided that school was a waste of time. He wasn't making enough money even with his "lunch money" scam. "I know lots of guys who never went to school and drive big cars," he'd often say.

Mason, unconvincingly, would say, "So, you'll take some time off and then go back. Okay, that sounds like a plan."

Randinoli answered, "No way. The crap game's as busy as ever. Blackie and Tony promoted me. I'm now the official eyes and ears of the Bruce Street dice game. They've been takin' more time off and I sit in for who-ever's missin'. If TJ wasn't so tough about stayin' in the corps, I would be gonzo with that, too. I guess you'll finish school and then go to some college.

The guys think you stand a good chance of grabbin' a sports scholarship. Wadda ya think?"

"No, if I go to college it will be local, like Rutgers or Seton Hall. And I'll take night classes," replied Mason, who had given the matter much thought.

Randinoli asked, "Why nights?"

"I need to work days and save some money. I can't count on scholarship money—the competition is too heavy. It's a crapshoot. Besides, many of the companies pay college tuition expenses for employees. I'll find time to stay involved in sports, but first things first. Boxing at the club and the drum corps will take up many hours, as well." Mason believed he had the goods to compete at a smaller college, but not at the level required to move up to professional sports. His desire was to enter law enforcement. He would receive a quality education and still be able to stay at home and work during the day. He knew he would pick up some weekends working the roofs.

The corps was the real problem requiring attention. The older boys wanted to leave, but were brainwashed into believing it would be unconscionable to leave TJ and everyone connected with the organization. But the time required for drum and bugle participation had reached an impossible level. It was too much for the young men to endure, yet the thought of leaving the corps created an empty feeling. Although Mason and Randinoli and their peers graduated from St. Joe's and were now in high school, staying with the corps was an issue of loyalty to the parish. For the past six years, the boys worked hard at becoming primary additions to the fast-growing drum and bugle competition circuit. The sacrifices for membership included valuable time away from school and other normal social activities. Everyone enjoyed the bragging rights. The corps brought credit not only to the parish and the neighborhood, but to the entire city. But how much longer Mason and Randinoli would stick it out remained to be seen.

The National Weather Bureau got it right. The temperatures dropped to near freezing during the night. Neither of the boys wore gloves, stuffing their hands deep in the pockets of their jackets.

A homeless man sat curled in a side doorway to the Bruce Street School for the hearing impaired. His head was covered with a black-wool ski cap and a two-week old beard, chilled and soggy from the freezing temperature. Wrapped in an old, dirty blanket, his face appeared wet and crusty. He seemed to be sleeping.

As they got closer, the man opened his eyes but did not speak. Looking at the man, Mason said, "Hey pal, we'll make a call to Saint Mike's. They'll send the van around and get you into the shelter. A warm meal and you'll feel great."

"Thank you." It appeared a strain to speak. The boys later agreed that he showed a slight smile.

The four inches of December snow, which fell during the night, covered the streets and sidewalks with blankets of white. A few hearty souls along 12th Avenue struggled as they shoveled the heavy snow from the steps in front of their houses and small shops. The city truck snowplows moved huge amounts of black slush and sleet, making room for the city buses traveling east and west on 12th Avenue, from downtown Newark to the west end. Now the relentless northeast wind howled through the New York–New Jersey metropolitan area. The forecast for the next few days predicted continued, below-average temperatures and high winds to go along with the blustery weather.

They were at the usual corner of 12th Avenue and Bruce Street. Today Randinoli was even more antsy than usual, the cold air elevating from his mouth, visible as he spoke. "Let's go downtown and do some Christmas shopping."

Friends since the fifth grade, Mason read his friend like a book.

"We don't have any money Gabe, what can we buy?" Mason jumped up and down in an attempt to keep his blood circulating. He knew just where Randinoli was proceeding with this latest resolution.

"You should've seen Bamberger's the other day. Man, you could walk away with that place and no one would bother you. I picked up a real cool leather wallet for my old man and a silk scarf for my sister. Ho, Ho, Ho!" A local plumbing contractor drove by and waved to the boys, his truck exhaust forcing black smoke into the cold air.

Mason clapped his hands together trying to stay warm. "I've got some more money coming from TJ for the last paint job. I'm getting some real cool stuff for my mother and grandmother." He and Jimmy Coughlin occupied their time for four-and-a-half weeks painting the interiors of St. Joseph's school, rectory and the club. "My shopping can wait 'til then." This was the second painting job they had landed. TJ convinced the pastor to hire the youngsters, saying, "They are good at it and the church will save money hiring them in place of a painting contractor." The parish pastor was unsure at first about hiring non-professionals.

TJ Finneran, a parish priest and moderator of the Saint Joseph's Cadets, the parish drum and bugle corps, struck a fair deal with Mason and Coughlin. Of course, the agreement included 12-inch grinders and a quart of cold milk from McGarry's sandwich shop on West Market Street. The boys responded by showing up every day and providing a near-professional job. Father William Bradson, the parish pastor, was ecstatic. He joked with the boys. "Finally, the old structures look refreshed. There will be places for you two in heaven."

Coughlin didn't let the comment go unanswered. "Okay Father, but no hurry, right?"

Mason knew it would be to no avail to lecture his friend on visiting the department store. Mason and Randinoli retained completely opposite positions on the subject of stealing. Mason remained hopeful that Randinoli would straighten out before it became too late. He often prayed on it. The two friends were so close except when it came to certain rights and wrongs. Was Mason so naïve to believe that his friend would come to a realization of what was in store for him? "Gabe, it's freezing out, let's go over to the club and work out for a few hours, take a hot shower and be ready for the shelter."

"You always want me to sweat." He quickly changed the subject. "Hey, notice no curse words today. I'm a regular saint. Not easy Brad, my man, f'n hard." He laughed aloud at this attempt at humor. Whenever Sister Francis heard one of the students use foul language, she would hold them by the ear and strongly urge, "Lock your lips and throw away the key."

Randinoli admired Sister Francis. She made him promise to work on his language. "No more swear words Gabriel. You can communicate much better using the mouth God gave you, not the filth you hear at the schoolyard." The nun sounded much like his mother; there was even a slight physical resemblance. Mrs. Randinoli died last winter from an undiagnosed illness. None of the adults spoke of the cause, as if keeping a deep, dark secret. The women spoke of it at the Rosary Sodality meetings, whispering, "The poor woman, so young. I'll bet it was cancer, mother of God, how awful."

Randinoli did not give up easily; he was not yet finished. At his young age, he believed himself invincible. His personal philosophy was that if you're smart and unafraid to take chances, no one can touch you. He enjoyed gambling with his nerve. It was fun, even gave him a little high. It mattered not what anyone said, once he made a decision. His gut took care of the rest. "Okay, spend your hard-earned dough. I'll invest my extra cash in the schoolyard. Tomorrow I break the crap game."

"Good luck with that." Mason smiled, not impressed and present many times when Randinoli participated in the crap game. Mason was certain the game would survive. The Bruce Street crap game, never canceled or postponed, continued despite inclement weather. Shovels and brooms, always at the ready, cleared the way for the dice to roll without a lengthy delay.

"I made a decision. Brad my man, we are in the holiday season. First, I do a little more Christmas shoppin'." The freezing temperature, the added snow on the ground would not deter him from following yet another of his choices. Randinoli offered a weak giggle and struggled to button his green corduroy jacket as he moved with his cocky walk down the slippery 12th Avenue hill on route to downtown Newark and his destination, Bamberger's department store. He turned and shouted to Mason, "You should see the cool jewelry." After a few steps, he turned again and yelled louder . . . "on display *outside* of the showcases."

As he walked into the corner candy store, Mason shouted back, "If you're still a free man I'll see you on the corner at three o'clock. We can walk to the shelter from here." His friend waved back in acknowledgement.

Inside Chick's Palace, Mason stopped and listened as the juke box played an ancient version of a Christmas favorite, "Jingle Bells." The customers enjoyed Bing Crosby and the Andrews Sisters' recording of the 1943 classic. The sound of the scratchy record always put people in the Christmas spirit.

Chapter Seven

The corner

12th Avenue ran east and west from West Market Street to Newark's Vailsburg section, twenty-six city blocks. Bruce Street intersected with West Market Street to the north and ran southeast until reaching Springfield Avenue, fourteen city blocks in length. It was located almost dead center in the heart of the Central Ward, the corner of 12th Avenue and Bruce Street. The number fifty-four West End bus transported neighborhood residents at both sides of 12th Avenue and ran downtown—moving people to work, shopping, perhaps a movie—then westbound into the Vailsburg section. Weather notwithstanding, number fifty-four was never empty and most times crowded. A veteran driver commented, "I think half of them just get on to chew the fat with their fellow passengers. It is really an inexpensive way to spend time and stay current with the Central Ward news." The well-known driver was appropriately named Smiley.

A few mothers traveled this route to reach their domestic jobs in the Vailsburg section, and even as far as the Oranges. The pastor at Saint Joseph's, Father William Bradson, often said, "Some families might go hungry if not for the working mothers' financial contributions to the family budget." Like much of Newark, the Central Ward was classified as a low-income community. Most men worked construction or factory jobs. A few were fortunate enough to have a connection at city hall and became part of the city payroll—maintenance workers in a public school or at the city hospital on Fairmount Avenue. A job at the hospital was considered prime employment because the head of the household could walk to work, saving bus fare or gas money, although family automobiles were rare. One of the old timers observed, "The wise guys running the crap games own more vehicles than half the people in the ward."

The corner of 12ᵗʰ Avenue and Bruce Street is where Brad Mason and Gabe Randinoli spent many days and nights growing up with their friends.

The two spent most of their time in the Bruce Street school playground. The school was locally referred to as "the deaf and dumb school," but an article in the Newark Evening News spoke highly of the institution. "Actually, the school enjoys a reputation in academia as the finest school in the state where children experiencing speaking and hearing deficiencies receive the best-available care and education. The neighborhood community enjoys a healthy relationship with the students."

The Bruce Street playground was a playground in name only when compared to other areas in the city. The asphalt surface consisted of one dilapidated steel basketball backboard and a rim that hung a few inches lower at the front end. There were some real high jumpers playing "hoops" at Bruce Street. A few of the black guys could actually dunk the ball.

"Yo Joey, now you gettin' up there. I bet you wuz at least fo' inches offa da ground." Joe Deylan was one white dude who would give anything if he could only leap. Big Roland, a huge black guy, was born in the same house his family still lived in on Bergen Street. Roland taught science at Central High public school. He loved to get on Deylan, using his best "po' boy" impersonation. "Joey boy, stop tryin' to get a rebound. I done told you several times now, you ain't black, stop that jumpin' stuff fo' you hurt y'own self. Remember where you at, you be playin' at 12ᵗʰ and Bruce, where the moose run loose."

Deylan always smiled and took it in stride. He made up for his rebounding shortfall with the best jump shot in the playground, from any part on the small court. As he threw one in from thirty feet, he yelled to Roland, "No need to rebound that baby, Roland my man. If we had a net, that sweet thing would say nothing but *swiiissshh*." The games spirited when he and Roland played. They were close friends and both loved the game.

The area for basketball was small. No more than six players—three on three—could get on the court at one time. Most of the games were two on two. Skins against shirts was the uniform du jour with the exception of Meryl Sweeney, who was always in the same attire; shorts and one of her brother's shirts, loose and baggy, that reached her knees. During the hot and humid summer months, the three-man, on occasion a girl or two, basketball games were an all-day activity. Sweeney was the one girl good enough to compete with any of the boys, and she played a rough game. She won more than her share of the competitions. "I have to win. Once you lose it may be an hour before you get back on the court."

On exceptionally hot and humid days the crapshooters would surprise the basketball participants with ice-cold bottles of Pepsi. "Tell 'em where you got it." Whenever one of the degenerate gamblers went broke and had to leave the game, Quinn or Capone gave out carfare and reminded the unfortunate gambler to spread the word of the game. While walking the treats to the basketball court, the crap game operators, either Tony Quinn or Blackie Capone, would parrot this much-used phrase.

No one acted surprised when Meryl received a full-boat basketball scholarship to a prestigious, suburban Catholic high school. Roland put it best. "She's as quick as a rabbit, and one determined girl."

Mason often took part in one of the highly competitive basketball games. Not so for his friend. "Man, why run and sweat and stink? I understand the need for runnin' when the cops are after you, but a basketball game, no way."

Although there was one memorable day when they were short one player and Randinoli was asked to play. "We need someone." Bebba Kaskie, a daily player who loved the game, joked, "Get in here Gabe, you can pace yourself, probably won't break a sweat."

"Okay, but one game and that's it," Randinoli said, adding one of his favorite sayings, "I am a very busy man." Basketball was certainly not his forte, but he wiped out at the crap game so it would give him something to pass time.

The game became heated and very competitive. Randinoli knew he was out of his element and created the excuse that Kaskie was taking advantage of him. He claimed imaginary fouls. "Once more Bebba and you get popped." Kaskie wanted the game to end as it was no longer fun. With Randinoli guarding him, Kaskie feigned left, dribbled to his right and again scored an easy lay-up.

One more basket and the game would be in the record books.

Randinoli wasted no time, saying, "I told you about the fouls." From behind, he grabbed the shoulders of the unsuspecting Kaskie, threw him on the ground and before anyone could react, kicked Kaskie on the side of his shoulder and upper arm.

Kaskie screamed, "You snake, you rat bas…" He rolled over on the asphalt pavement and held his shoulder obviously in pain.

The crap game in full stride, Tony Quinn noticed the problem and went after Randinoli before he did any more damage. "I'm outta here, but he pounded me with his elbow, foulin' all over the place." Randinoli sauntered out of the Morris Avenue side of the schoolyard and picked out a Lucky Strike from his shirt pocket.

Later, when Mason heard about the latest episode, he asked Randinoli, "Kaskie, one of the nicest guys on the corner, what the hell was that all about?"

"Let me tell you Brad, the guy was killin' me, fouls all over the place. I made a decision."

"You don't know a foul from third base. They said you kicked him when he was on the ground."

"Brad, you weren't there. He's a big guy, if he gets up, who knows?" Randinoli now embellished some more, convincing himself the action was justified. "He really started it, with all that stuff with the elbow." He lied defending another decision—and escaped without a scratch.

Rain or shine, the schoolyard boiled over with activity. The remaining space on the Bruce Street side saw stickball, occasional softball and, of course, the daily and nightly crap games.

The Bruce Street stickball guru was a black dude named Harold Lee, a stickball addict. Lee moved with his family from South Carolina at the time the Korean War broke out. He was always hustling up a game, at the ready with the required half of an orange rubber ball and his favorite bat, a four-foot stick, three inches in diameter. He wrapped black adhesive tape around the bottom of the stick, which made for a better grip. Lee loved the game and was adept at the finer points of pitching wide, roundhouse curve balls. Lee had other talents. He owned an outstanding alto voice and sang lead with the Fairmounts, the neighborhood rock n' roll quartet. When he wasn't playing stickball, Lee was on the corner rehearsing with the other three members of the a cappella group.

"Brad, no more heat for you, from now on you get the smooth, fast-breaking curve ball." The half-ball showed different movement when tossed side-arm. Mason often played a few innings and loved to hit Lee's attempt at the high, hard one.

The crapshooters became annoyed when an errant ball settled in the middle of the crap game. There was instant shouting from the crapshooter losing the most money at the time. Blackie Capone calmly issued the usual friendly reminder. "Harold, next time that ball comes over here, it goes up someone's black ass."

"Yessuh, mista' Blackie suh." Lee never paid attention to the warnings and continued with his passion.

"This neighborhood would make the United Nations people happy." William Bradson, the pastor of Saint Joseph's Church, spoke the truth. The neighborhood was as diverse as any in the city. The UN could not have put together such a concoction of people. A variety of skin colors and religions were all represented in the Central Ward. "The Catholics may be the largest but the others are well represented. We have many denominational Protestants, Jews, Southern Baptists, and a sprinkling of Jehovah's Witnesses. There may be some Muslims but I am not sure, they may keep low profiles. This is definitely a working-class neighborhood, yet it's never necessary to lock doors. The only time you see the police is when Blackie and Tony forget the cop's end and the crap game is raided."

The corner emptied when someone shouted, "Jimmy Buff's." Fat Barteck loved to jump in one of the cars, travel across town to Fifteenth Avenue and Jimmy Buff's for the city's best hot dog, served with greasy potatoes and peppers and onions. If pizza was the choice, then the caravan headed to the Comet Pizzeria in Hillside to enjoy the thin crust and the tastiest homemade sauce in the area. When Fat would say, "Let's go to the ward," this meant north to the First Ward. Here were not only the beautiful Sacred Heart Cathedral and Barringer High School, the oldest school in the state and one of the oldest in the entire country, but some of the best Italian restaurants found in the metropolitan area.

"I don't care where I eat. Please get me the hell away from Chick's sandwiches. I think the stale bread is eating a hole in my stomach." Not a food connoisseur, yet Barteck drew the line when his stomach was under attack.

Mason asked, "Fat, what is your problem with the corner, the view is fantastic?"

Randinoli, never to let an opportunity pass, said, "Brad, my man, you are right. Here on our right we have the latest in automobile design." They viewed what remained of a 1946 Ford, windshield smashed, tires missing, and rust and dents throughout. It remained parked on 12th Avenue for two months, the result of a near fatal crash. "Take notice of the clean bullet holes. In addition, directly across the street we have the Point Tavern and liquor store, open to all. Its motto, 'In God we trust, all others pay cash.'" The Point, a leftover from prohibition, looked sadly in disrepair, paint peeling, "Schaefer" and "Ballantine" beer signs sometimes blinking. A venture inside was only for those with very strong stomachs and stout hearts. "How could anyone even consider leaving this portrait of paradise?"

The others were surprised with Randinoli's depiction of the neighborhood. Mason earlier complimented his friend on his use of the English language. What they did not know was that Randinoli had made another decision. When he became a big shot Mafiosi he would command more respect by using bigger words and pronouncing each adjective with the proper ending. "Right Brad, I decided to speak like Sister Francis says we should. If anyone says anything about it, I will just hurt them."

Barteck said, "Brad, I'll bet the Point looked better during prohibition when your uncle Mike owned it. Man, the stories they tell about that place. There were always cops, fights, shootings, and your uncle throwing the troublemakers out the side door."

Mason answered, "My mother said her brother Mike was quite the businessman, he did very well when he came to this country from Ireland. He operated two or three speakeasies in Newark and one somewhere in Philadelphia. I heard more than once it was near Shibe Park on West Lehigh Avenue. One day Uncle Mike took me there. The old speakeasy is now a very busy tavern owned by one of the former Philadelphia Athletics. My uncles say in its day Uncle Mike's place was even rougher than the Jersey bars. He fought in several bare-knuckle bouts at the Newark Armory and Laurel Garden in the Central Ward."

Mason thought about it and smiled. "No one knows what happened to all the dough. At least if they do, no one in the family ever mentions anything about it. Uncle Mike only tells great stories about the goings on during Prohibition. He is one entertaining man. And he would give you the shirt off his back." He paused again and laughed. "Hell, maybe that is where all the bread went, he gave it all away."

Randinoli joined in. "You know, I think Uncle Mike can still kick ass. He looks like he could still throw a few people around. I wouldn't want him pissed at me."

Mason said, "That's funny. He's probably the most serene of the entire family. My parents say he made a bundle of money 'in the day' but they said he was too generous with it, an easy touch. Anyway, he told me that he regrets nothing, it was a real-life experience operating the Point during those heydays, as he calls them." Mason appeared deep in thought as he spoke of his uncle. He loved to hear the stories of his mother's brother, and the adventures he experienced when he fled Ireland as a young boy. Like so many other Irishmen, forced to leave their native land because of English tyranny and the brutality of the feared Black and Tans. Like so many immigrants, he loved the opportunity the United States offered, became a legal citizen, worked hard and made a place for him and his family in his adopted country.

Chick Rozella chimed in. "That's the right way for sure, the American way, the way so many other immigrants made it happen. They all worked hard and followed the rules. Look at the Irish, Italians, Polish, Germans, and all the rest. Where would we be without them all?" Chick Rozella always fought off emotion when speaking of what he called, "the greatest freakin' country on the planet." He always added a little humor, "and that includes North Dakota."

Barteck wanted to get back to the neighborhood tour, gesturing in the direction of Bruce Street. "And finally, if you gaze in a southerly direction, you see the valued city employees keeping our city clean." The men working on the garbage trucks were always fun to watch. Everyone enjoyed seeing the cans filled with garbage dumped on the back of the truck. The man assigned to the back, without looking, flipping the now empty can to the "walker" who caught it without missing a beat, and set it down in its original place. Barteck said, "Poetry in motion." The entertainment included loud music coming from the truck's cab. It was usually blues or jazz broadcast from a New York station. The men smiled and kept beat with the sounds. The guys on the corner all snapped their fingers and sang along with the "professionals."

One of the men would yell, "Okay young people, make room for the sanitary engineers."

Weather permitting, two-hand touch football, on the Morris Avenue side of the school, filled in much of the summer seasons. Although the bloody wrought-iron fence never moved, it resulted in many visits up the hill to the City Hospital Emergency Room. The perimeter of the grounds contained a solid, cast-iron fence with slanted supports. It did not make any sense to attempt end sweeps, as the fence prevented many touchdowns. A game seldom ended without at least one bloody shin requiring a trip to Fairmount Avenue and stitches for the wannabe athlete. There were permanent bloodstains on most of the wrought-iron support posts. For some, it became a mark of honor to point out the dry bloodstains where a player was injured.

Danny Sherman was fond of showing off the exact location of his battle scene. Touching his forehead, he said, "See, that's where I went head first into the fence, but I kept going and scored the winning touchdown. When I turned on the speed burner no one could ever catch me—a cloud of dust."

"Right, Danny—great job!"

Chapter Eight

Billy the Hat

After an afternoon at the Central movie house, a few neighborhood guys walked down Central Avenue heading back to 12th and Bruce. Earlier, in the Central men's room, Deltucci argued with Lamont, a black guy from Bergen Street. Lamont was a few years older and much bigger but Deltucci, at age sixteen, was not intimidated. They called each other a few unacceptable names. The theater manager, Mr. Rothstein, heard the shouting and told them to "take it outside or go back to your seats and enjoy the show." When he returned to his seat, he never mentioned the encounter to his friends; as far as Deltucci was concerned, the matter ended. No one from the corner expected the troubles that followed outside the theater. The Bergen Street crew, all a few years older, had different thoughts. As it turned out, they were not only bigger and stronger but also much better equipped to do battle.

After the movie concluded, the Bruce Street contingent separated into two groups when they reached the bottom of the Five Corners hill. A few of them headed down Central Avenue and the others toward West Market Street. They were unaware they were being followed by the Bergen Street people, now close behind and waiting until they reached the right time and place. The stalkers did an outstanding job of quietly concentrating on Deltucci. They wanted to be certain he got a beating. Unfortunately for Mason, he was one of those heading down West Market Street, also unaware of the tail. In an instant, Mason had his back to a wall outside the Five Corners Tavern, with a cold knife blade resting at his throat. His arms pinned behind him, he never forgot the words. "You ain't in no ring now. Move mudda-fucka' and you get cut straight down." Next, he received a whack to the side of his head with an unknown object.

Years later, as new agents at the FBI Academy, Mason and his class-mates learned that certain rules were necessary for victory over the bad guys. The four S's included safety, security, surprise and, most importantly, fire-arms superiority. On this occasion, the 12th and Bruce guys were four short of these essentials.

The black crew had knives and long leather belts with thick weighted buckles at each end. One guy had a club. Later, Randinoli, Mason and the others joked about how much weaponry they had. Jimmy Coughlin said, "We had zip. Those guys could have beaten the New York Giants." Deltucci required a few stitches to his ear after taking a smack from a leather belt. Before the short skirmish was over, Randinoli landed the only good punches of the night, leaving one of the Bergen Street people lying in the gutter half unconscious and bleeding heavily from the nose. He did remember to kick him in the back as hard as possible.

"Where the hell was Jimmy Cagney when you need him?" Coughlin said later, jokingly referring to the James Cagney movie they had just seen, "Kiss Tomorrow Goodbye." Coughlin was one of the first to run from Central Ave. across to West Market and immediately caught a belt buckle across the back of his head, leaving an ugly welt on the side of his face, very close to his eye.

The incident was certainly not the norm. People usually got along in the ward. There were few racial problems in the community; everyone was busy, struggling to make life work. The fight that took place at the Central that day in October 1953 surprised a lot of people and was unacceptable to everyone. However, now the score appeared lopsided and needed adjusting.

Two weeks after the incident, Coughlin, his five brothers, three cousins, and a few of the older people from 12th and Bruce visited "The Ranch House," a three-decker dwelling on Bergen Street where Curtis Farmer lived. Farmer, the leader of the Bergen Street gang, was the ringleader at the Central movie ambush. The younger guys from the corner received orders to "stay clear of the Bergen Street area." Coughlin immediately recognized the belt buckle dude and challenged Farmer to come out of the three-decker to fight one-on-one. Farmer was familiar with the Coughlin's family reputa-tion, thought about it and declined to participate. By this time the entire area filled with friends, family, onlookers—everyone in Newark seemed to be present for what they thought would be a small war. The number three Ber-gen Street bus stopped so the passengers could see the action. Most of the bus drivers considered themselves comedians, this one no exception. He called out, "Ladies and gentlemen, your friendly transit company offers this entertainment free of charge." After a few minutes' pause he added, "It appears there will be no show today so we'll move along before the city's finest lock us all up. Maybe next time." The crowd booed as the bus continued its journey.

Later, Johnny Zatz said, "It's a damn good thing that didn't get started. Bergen Street would have been in flames with a few dead bodies in the streets, us and the blacks." Zatz was in his early thirties, an old 12ᵗʰ Ave. leg breaker who served a few stretches in prison for various crimes. Near six-feet tall and close to two hundred pounds, many rightfully viewed Zatz as being crazy as a loon. Zatz never traveled without his five-shot S&W Colt, and, on occasion, took some target practice in the schoolyard. Behind his back, even his friends said he was completely whacko—an asset in this particular situation. The Bergen Street crew did not want any part of Mr. Zatz.

Before evacuating Bergen Street, one of Coughlin's older brothers challenged a few of the Bergen Street people, but no one accepted the offer. This brother had returned from Korea wounded and highly decorated. Everyone in the Central Ward knew of his reputation, both in and out of the ring. Farmer said, "You must be crazy man. No one is nuts enough to go with that dude. He will hurt you."

The visit to "The Ranch House" ended peacefully. Later in the evening, a few of the Bergen Street people were welcomed in the schoolyard crap game. Blackie Capone said, "Hey, no harm no foul, a good crap game soothes a lot of animosity."

Weeks later at the Second Precinct Police Athletic League Boxing Club, Mason, a PAL member for three years, worked out on the heavy bag. He and Coughlin often stopped for a workout and shower after a long day on the hot roofs. One of the black guys who jumped the 12ᵗʰ and Bruce people a few weeks back was sparring in the ring with one of the detectives who helped train many of the young fighters. No one ever knew the real name of the Bergen Street boxer. His first name was Billy and he was known as "Billy the Hat" for obvious reasons. At the Central movie fight, Randinoli dropped Billy with two quick punches to the head. Billy the Hat, recalling the incident, said, "Let me tell you Brad, Gabe knocked my ass down and out. Man, I saw me some shiny stars. I never want to get hit like that again. And the sucker kicked me." He never mentioned the serious damage to Coughlin and Deltucci, both injured with thick belt buckles.

No one mentioned the reason for the fight, but both knew that a few stupid remarks caused the melee. It only took a day for the Bergen Street people to return to the schoolyard and, in a matter of weeks, everything was "hunky dory"—as Zatz described it. The roughhouse may have escalated in the basketball games but, overall, things were back to normal.

A few years older, Billy was an exceptional boxer but not a hitter. He was aware that Mason boxed out of the club at St. Joe's. Since he was in jail at the time, Billy was not aware that Mason won a Golden Glove championship as a middleweight in the open class. Billy saw an opportunity to get even for what happened to him with Randinoli. "Hey man, you wanna go a few rounds, maybe a little sparrin'?" They were both middleweights. Billy believed he would handle the kid from the corner without breaking a sweat. He wanted to get even for the beating he received in the Central deal.

"Let's do it," Mason said.

"No sparring with this crumb, make it the real thing." Coughlin knew this from experience.

Billy had no intention of sparring on this day. He sauntered directly to the center of the ring and started with a straight right, which landed squarely on Mason's chin. He danced away and started to come forward again. Billy was showing a wide smile on his face. He intended to do damage in a hurry. Billy faked a left jab and started with the straight right, which he figured would end the sparring session. This time Mason saw the right hand coming, so he crouched while sliding to his left and let go with a wicked left hook to Billy's body. Then he followed with a light, left jab followed by a powerful right hook to the jaw that Billy never saw coming. The referee, Detective Jake Rabshore, stood over Billy and counted the mandatory ten. It was over in a minute and a half. Billy the Hat lay motionless, flat on his back.

Mason felt good about the victory. He believed that dropping Billy was pay back for the belt buckle attack after the Central movies. It was bad luck for Billy that he was put down by both Randinoli and Mason.

When Randinoli heard of the fight in the ring he said, "I told Brad more than once that's why I hate that ring shit. You can't show the dude the latest dance step."

Chapter Nine

Wild Bill

The corner of 12th Avenue and Bruce Street, and the Bruce Street schoolyard, were the gathering spots for so many characters.

Had Damon Runyon cast the neighborhood players, he certainly would highlight Bill Kennedy as one of the stars. Kennedy was right out of "Guys and Dolls." With slicked-back, pitch-black hair and blue eyes, he stood over six-feet tall and weighed just north of two hundred and fifty pounds. The big man's wardrobe seldom changed and consisted of a blue pin-striped suit, white shirt, near shiny black leather shoes and a small, black fedora that sat atop his bigger than average head. His reputation for poor choices and losing money were both well known. Kennedy would wager on anything, not just dice. If he bet on a pro football team to win, everyone else would go with the opposing team. Big in stature, Kennedy owned a heart of gold, and often gave his last dollar to help a friend. Some people referred to him as "Wild Bill," the exact opposite of his demeanor.

Kennedy, like many of the neighborhood men, worked as a roofer out of the Newark Local Roofers Union. At lunchtime, he scurried off the roof to call Jimmy Contino, the local bookie who operated his business out of Duffy's Tavern, a neighborhood watering hole. Most of the time, Kennedy avoided visiting Duffy's. He was constantly behind paying his gambling debts. Contino was not one to allow too many late payments. "Bill, I have bills to pay as well—get the money." Everyone knew Contino worked for and had the muscle of the Battiato family, now Newark's major crime syndicate.

Kennedy on occasion petitioned the bookmaker for a slow payment. "Jimmy, we had a slow week, just two days of good weather." He told the truth. While the pay was better than other construction specialties, when bad weather prevailed the roofers didn't work except for an occasional inside waterproofing job. "Ringers"—five consecutive days of work—were few and far between.

"Bill, I love you like a brother but this work shit only goes so far. I've got bills to pay and bosses who hold me accountable. How many times have you heard me tell people, 'you don't play if you can't pay.' Friday night, I'll be at the crap game at the hall; you need to bring the whole deal, two hundred." Contino emphasized the exact night so there would be no chance of a misunderstanding. Somehow, Kennedy usually found a way to get the money and pay his debt.

Contino was another businessman Randinoli admired. "Is that a great way to make a living or what? Sit on your ass at Duffy's all day and wait for the bread to come in. If you get a slow payer you beat the crap out of him, case closed."

Stories of Bill Kennedy were easily enough to fill a novel. The legendary handicapper anecdote took place in May 1953. Kennedy, with three of the schoolyard crapshooters, drove his black 1948 Caddy to Louisville, Kentucky, to be present at the greatest racing event of the year, the Kentucky Derby. Leading a field of outstanding thoroughbreds was the greatest thoroughbred of them all. Native Dancer, the undisputed favorite after impressive victories at the Wood Memorial and the Gotham Mile, was picked by the majority of horse racing analysts.

The ultimate sports authority, Bill Kennedy, direct from the famous Bruce Street crap game, was certain to have his name engraved in the gambler's history book. He planned the trip for weeks. Everyone knew of his master plan. "Bet the mortgage on Native Dancer. The odds don't matter. Even if he goes off at even money, it's a lock, a guaranteed sure thing." This would be the first sure thing of his brilliant gambling career. Someone asked if Kennedy was drinking too much. When the big person heard this, he let out with that infectious laugh. "As my dear uncle Pat would say, 'Tis true that too much alcohol is not good for one. But the same goes for milk.'"

Kennedy was not alone with his handicapping. The world of racing kept presenting evidence of how the big horse would glide across the finish line ahead of the field. No matter how short the odds, Wild Bill could live off this sports story for the rest of his life. He was destined to be the wagering genius of the Central Ward. People would seek his counsel whenever the topic of conversation touched on sports wagering.

The Bruce Street contingent of Wild Bill, Danny Sherman, Joey Cough-lin and Shadow Deltucci found inexpensive accommodations about a mile from the track. They then filled the motel rooms with the necessities—ice, beer, pretzels and more beer.

Kennedy, proud of his research, asked, "Did you guys know the first Kentucky Derby took place in 1875? The first horse to win was named Aristedes."

Deltucci was not impressed with the sports history lesson. He said, "That's great, Bill."

Sherman never expected an answer to his question when he asked, "You don't happen to know the name of the owner, do you Bill?"

Kennedy never hesitated, the information was all memorized. "I do. The man's name was H. P. McGrath." Now on a roll, and before any more ques-tions, Kennedy added, "Interestingly enough, the horse was trained and rid-den by two black guys. Ansel—that's A-N-S-E-L, last name Williamson, usual spelling—and Oliver Lewis."

Coughlin, the least impressed, said, "Shadow, get me a cold one outta the cooler."

Kennedy never felt this much excitement in his life. He continuously filled his companions with the latest race updates. Adding their own money to what they collected from the investors from the corner, they managed to scrape together from the neighborhood just north of $5,200. It was guaran-teed, the four Newarkers would leave Kentucky with somewhere between $5,200 and $6,200 net profit, a respectable return on their investment and a chance to witness the historical race. Even more importantly, they would be legends in the Central Ward.

The much-disciplined Newarkers behaved admirably. They never placed any wagers on the other races, waiting for the big one. On the first day in May 1953, they were thrilled to be part of "the longest, continually running sporting event in America." The one hundred and forty-seven acre setting at the Churchill Downs racetrack filled with race enthusiasts from all over the world.

Native Dancer, known as "The Grey Ghost," was a magnificent speci-men. Horse of the Year in 1952, he well deserved the title. Before they left the corner, Randinoli told the four friends to look for a way to fix the big race, saying, "A long shot will pay millions." After listening to a few more of his hare-brained ideas, the others nodded their heads. The odds on Native Dancer changed ever so slightly; at race time he was the 3-5 favorite.

Deltucci said, "Hey, at these odds we will be lucky to get our money back."

Kennedy kept up the positive, reassuring analysis of the expert equestrian. "The big races never show the real odds. He's probably 2 or 3 to 1. Stay focused on the big picture. The reality of the situation is that today we're sitting on the only sure thing in the entire world."

Every nickel the 12th and Bruce bettors had in their possession went on Native Dancer's nose to win. Although not quite every nickel, since Sherman, the true doubting Thomas in the crowd, wisely stashed enough dough to pay for petrol for the gas-guzzling Caddy's return trip to Jersey.

The historical moment arrived. One could feel the electricity in the air, the crowd of one hundred and sixty-five thousand waiting in anticipation of something monumental to happen.

The public address announcer bellowed, "And they're off!" Kennedy moaned a bit; the favorite appeared uncomfortable, the start of the race not smooth. The big horse was bumped twice as he tried to get outside and secure some running room. Later, experts agreed that Native Dancer was fouled twice during the race. The race aficionados were not worried; this was a mile-and-a-half track and the great horse had plenty of time and speed to make up for a horrendous start.

Dark Star at 25-1 had jumped out to an early lead and looked very relaxed. The rest of the field were bumping and jostling for position. "What the hell is he waiting for? Run, you big shit, run!" Coughlin, getting impatient, looked as he might be having a coronary.

The heavy favorite was at the back of the pack as the horses headed for the last turn. At the turn for home, the great horse finally found some outside room and ran after the leaders. Dark Star still led, with the other horses desperately in pursuit.

Native Dancer put on a burst of speed down the stretch, moving in and out of open chutes. The 1953 "Run for the Roses" finish was nothing short of spectacular. The "Wild Bill" Kennedy group was among the loudest in the park. It was total hysteria. Would Native Dancer be the first to the finish line?

It was clearly a Wild Bill Kennedy finish. Despite a great effort, Dark Star held on to win by a head. The record-breaking crowd was completely silenced. Kennedy's reputation remained intact. He backed another loser. The great horse would finish his illustrious career with twenty-one of twenty-two first place finishes. It turned out to be the only loss of Native Dancer's distinguished twenty-two-race career. Kennedy et al wagered on the one loss.

The tote board was quick to post the painful official results. Dark Star the winner paid $51.80 for every two-dollar wager. The investors from the corner would have received $134,680 had they bet on the winner.

It took the rest of the day to sink in. A single tear trickled down Deltucci's cheek. "I bet Blackie could have fixed the crummy race." Back at the motel, he tried to sound upbeat. Despite the heart-breaking loss and being broke, the sportsmen from the corner could brag for the rest of their lives. "We were there and witnessed the historic sporting event." Wild Bill was not thinking of bragging about any historic event. He sat in quiet shock.

However, life goes on. The ride back home was mournful for the most part. When the radio aired gorgeous Julie London's "Cry Me a River," someone humanely put an end to that tune. Wild Bill pretended sleep. His pain was indescribable.

Weeks following, the sports pages filled with accounts of the race. The jockey Eric Guerin received most of the heat. One sportswriter wrote, "He took that colt everywhere on the track except the ladies' room." The curse of Wild Bill Kennedy never reached the public—except in the Bruce Street schoolyard. The group stayed ruthless. Quinn announced that the Bruce Street tabloid would be unrelenting. He said, "The headlines will scream, 'Great Colt Succumbs to Wild Bill Curse.'"

All, except for one individual, enjoyed the sarcasm.

One night the corner was filled with advice and sympathy for the "Derby Dudes." Randinoli, never bashful regarding his take on any issue, said to Kennedy, "Bill, not your fault. If you guys took my advice and fixed the damn race everything would be perfect."

Fixing the Kentucky Derby was not at all a realistic solution. Outsiders hearing his advice would view Randinoli's comments as a joke and simply a foolish statement. Yet those who knew him well held no doubt that the wannabe wise guy was deadly serious.

Mason, tired of his friends' half-baked advice, spoke to Kennedy. "Bill, you did your thing, everyone supported you, and you made a decision. Fixing the big race was never an option." Everyone agreed and enjoyed this dialogue as Mason looked at Randinoli, then continued, "In spite of the advice given by some people."

Randinoli was now in the minority but not finished by a long shot. "That's the problem with you people. You think small, never the top rung of the ladder. You're satisfied with second place. Someday you'll see the big picture."

The day when I'm the top dog.

Chapter Ten

Marching and maneuvering

Brad Mason and Gabe Randinoli, both students of the same parochial elementary school located "on the hill" in Newark's Central Ward, were integral parts of the nationally known St. Joseph's Cadets Drum and Bugle Corps. The parish organization, nicknamed the "Hilltoppers" because of the location of the church property, was under the watchful eye of its moderator, the Rev. Timothy J. Finneran, more commonly referred to as "TJ." The priest, a tough, young Irish-American, founded the corps in 1946. Father Finneran transferred to St. Joseph's from St. Vincent's Parish in Bayonne, New Jersey. The hierarchy in the diocese enthusiastically supported the transfer. The rational at the crux of TJ's relocation, as expressed by the bishop, was that "the boys at St. Joe's need an alternative to loitering around the streets. The city is changing and they are headed for trouble. More important, they need discipline. Father Finneran is the man to deal with the situation."

While assigned to St. Vincent's, TJ became involved with the rapidly-growing popularity of drum and bugle corps in the 1950s. Now a fast-growing form of entertainment throughout the country, people of all ages attended the drum and bugle competitions, which featured precision marching and maneuvering, military-linked color guard, intricate drum selections, and the always-entertaining brass presentations. Unfortunately, it quickly became evident that TJ could be a sometimes out-of-control disciplinarian.

Before his arrival at St. Joe's, the rumor circulated that TJ was a talented amateur boxer before entering the seminary. His pug nose supported the story and enhanced his reputation with Mason and Randinoli as well as the rest of the neighborhood boys.

Randinoli echoed the sentiments of the rest of his friends. "I don't think I'll be messin' with this guy."

From the very first day TJ came to the hill, he impressed the boys with his philosophy. Wearing a slight smirk, he said, "Only one person can be in charge here. That would be me."

To his credit, TJ began the organization with two objectives. The first was to get boys from an inner-city neighborhood off the streets, and second, if possible, was to win a national championship. For the most part he succeeded with his first goal, although the latter eluded him. "Mighty St. Joe's," as they became widely known, did win several state championships in New Jersey and a few major competitions throughout the country, including the nationally known Dream Contest and the Northeast Open Championship. TJ and many of the boys who had been in the corps for several years never accepted this very well. It was always a sore spot, and everyone retained his own reasons for never winning a national championship, "the big one." Without expressing it, many of the members blamed TJ for never winning a national title—attributing it to his refusal to play politics. A little schmoozing with the American Legion, VFW, and other organizations sponsoring the competitions was required for the corps to have a fair shot at victory. It was well-known that other group moderators did whatever it took to gain favor with the judges who either made it happen or ignored obvious talent. The Hilltoppers' bus driver once remarked, "It'll be a cold day in hell when TJ kisses ass to win a contest. Maybe he's right, but the kids work their butts off and he should bend a little and play ball once in a while."

At first, the young men respected him because of the collar he wore—as a priest he represented a higher authority, deserving the respect of the members. The years went by and now many of the boys were entering high school—some even graduating—and finding it difficult to fulfil the requirements for membership in the corps. Separate from his duties as a parish priest, TJ labored long hours to keep the group operating. The more time the youngsters spent at rehearsals and on road trips to competitions, they recognized how much time and effort it took and how hard TJ worked for the good of the corps. In the beginning, the members liked him despite his mood changes and offensive temper. Still, he embodied the first adult the young men actually feared. They kept their concerns private, never discussing anything outside the corps. They knew not to bad-mouth a member of the clergy, especially one who was looked on by the community as doing a great job keeping the young men in check. TJ screamed and occasionally added physical abuse to his repertoire. The boys stayed alert to the fact that a drum stick could sail in anyone's direction when his temper soared.

Over the years, the makeup of the corps changed dramatically. In the early days, it varied between one and three majors, between ten and twenty color guardsmen, twenty to thirty-six horns, and eight to eighteen percussionists. The horn line started with small brass G-bugles, and the uniform consisted of long-sleeve white shirts with green cummerbunds, black pants and green overseas caps. In summer months, the long sleeves took their toll during lengthy, often-delayed parades. In later years, after several championship victories and the expansion of competitions throughout the country, the uniforms graduated to more of a military look—blue and orange, with tall shakoes and white plumes. The equipment became very modern, with the horns—sopranos, French horns, baritones and bass—all consisting of two vertical pistons. The percussion included snare, tenor and bass drums, and four styles of cymbals. The lines were augmented with a sideline pit of timpani, traps, vibes, marimbas and chimes.

It did not take very long for "Mighty St. Joe's" to gain a reputation for having one of the finest horn lines in the country. One follower of the competition circuit said, "The other side of the reputation is one of toughness, for occurrences that take place off the field of competition." Through the years, the members took part in more than one scrape. The skirmishes most often were with other corps or with locals who wished to test the reputation of the Hilltoppers. Within the corps, Randinoli's brutality became evident early on. With each brawl, he increased his reputation for kicking people. "Big Jack" Olson, a baritone player, spoke the undeniable truth. "No matter the opponent, Gabe's reputation for brutality spreads with each fight."

Mason and Randinoli were nine years old when they *joined* the corps. As teens, the schedule—including the three-a-week music and M&M rehearsals, parades, special events for the city, and steady diet of appearances and competitions—became monotonous. As days passed into months then into years, it became painfully apparent to the corps members that TJ's active temper was unacceptable.

The current schedule included an appearance at the 1954 New Year's Day Gator Bowl in Jacksonville, Florida. The older members talked of making the event their last. Jimmy Coughlin, one of the senior members of the Hilltoppers and a recent Golden Glove champ, was not happy with TJ's behavior. "Priest or not, if someone takes a stick in the eye, then what? Maybe someone needs to have a talk with him."

TJ more often than not was quick to smack someone around whenever he got the notion. One day he went after the wrong horn player. A few from the brass section horsed around and Mason and Randinoli sparred while waiting for both the percussion and horn instructors to agree on the next phase of music. The competition season starting soon, the corps was rehearsing entirely new music and marching presentation. TJ never asked why they were not practicing the new number. He mistakenly presumed they decided to goof off.

"Mr. Mason," he smiled as he yelled, "you think you're a real tough guy. A golden glover this year, right? I spent some time in the ring. Maybe you and me should mix it up?"

Between working as a roofer and steady workouts on the heavy bag at the club, Mason kept in excellent physical condition.

The school auditorium went still. Everyone waited for the response. Mason actually looked for a reason to leave the corps—and now he had it. Not at all happy with being made the center of attention, he said, "I never think of myself as a tough guy, Father." Now eighteen, Mason surprised the priest and everyone else with his next statement. He later said he even surprised himself. Mason said, "No not with you, but I'll mix it up with your brother." The boys would never fight with nor hit a priest, but a priest's brother was a different story. TJ's younger brother, who visited the music rehearsals on occasion, also had experience in the military and as an amateur boxer.

Randinoli did not like the brother and once commented, "That guy bothers me. If he ever says a word I'll drop the turd. No questions, the jerk goes down—and stays down."

Joe Deylan, the corps major and now a freshman in college, observed the potential confrontation and, before TJ could respond, moved between TJ and Mason. "Father, we're waiting for a decision on the new stuff." He gestured toward the sheet music resting on the stands.

"When I want an opinion from the peanut gallery, I'll ask for it," TJ said as he gestured toward Mason and Randinoli. "Get back to rehearsal, both of you—now!" He offered no comment on Mason's alternative offer.

Everyone present in the auditorium breathed a sigh of relief. "Deylan saved a very bad situation." Big Jack Olson spoke the truth.

After rehearsal the rain came down in buckets. Randinoli, Mason and a few others jogged up the Cabinet Street hill en route to the corner and Chick's Palace. He queried his friend. "I have a feelin' you would've accepted his invitation if he pushed it and took off the collar. Am I right or am I wrong?"

Mason answered, "We'll never know. Deylan did the right thing. The truth is I never before got so mad at him. I think being tired had something to do with it, but that's no excuse." *I wonder—TJ was wrong, but still he wears the collar.* "There's no doubt I've had enough of TJ and the time it takes to be in the corps. We gave it more than enough of our time and energy. For myself, after Jacksonville, I need to move on."

Randinoli said, "Amen brother, I hear you loud and clear. I still think Deylan saved the padre from gettin' a beatin'. We never quit on anything, but this is out of control. TJ needs to retire before someone gets hurt. I've had enough tenor drummin' to last a lifetime. I'm startin' to look like Louie Prima. Besides, I have plans. You and me need to get our own crap game goin'."

Mason answered quickly. "You don't quit with that stuff. The crapshooting business is for people with few options. We're young enough to do whatever we want. You can run a number of legitimate businesses. I'm going into law enforcement. Let Blackie and Tony take care of the dice."

The tenor drummer needed the last word. "Man, that would have been more than awkward. I never kicked a priest."

Chapter Eleven

1954 Gator Bowl

Mason's senior high school year proved to be stressful. The Hilltoppers' growing popularity resulted in many invitations to perform around the country. Abe Saperstein, the owner and manager of the internationally known Harlem Globetrotter basketball team, contacted TJ with an offer for the boys to perform halftime shows during a ten-game Globetrotter swing covering the entire east coast.

"Father, my team loves to listen to your music. It would be a first— never been done before. The crowds will love to watch the Globetrotters play while your boys play 'Sweet Georgia Brown.' It will be great. I'll pay the union price plus ten percent, and your people travel first class."

TJ never shared the details of the offer with anyone. He turned Saperstein down. "Mr. Saperstein, we're honored but I must refuse your generous offer. The boys can't afford to miss more school days." The priest realized that Mason and Randinoli and a few of the others were seriously thinking of leaving the corps. The Globetrotter owner accepted the refusal and the two stayed in contact through the years.

TJ had committed to an offer for a halftime performance at the January 1954 Gator Bowl held in Jacksonville, Florida. The football game featured the Auburn Tigers and the Texas Tech Red Raiders.

Due to cold weather, the bus trip entailed four days of treacherous roads for the experienced driver. TJ's temper targeted Leo, the driver, for anything that delayed the trip schedule. If Leo took a wrong turn at an unfamiliar area, TJ screamed, "Can't you even read a map?" He never offered to look at the map and act as navigator while the driver maneuvered through difficult and unfamiliar roads. It was seldom Leo's fault, but TJ vented his anger if the bus happened to be in the wrong place. Leo, a quiet man, never retaliated. He was a very spiritual, church-going individual and would never get into a confrontation with a priest. The boys noted how TJ treated the well-liked driver, and this added to their decision to leave the corps after the Florida trip.

Randinoli never hesitated with his commentary. "I'll drive the freakin' bus and see how he screams. He'll be too busy wiping his butt to say anything. Leave Leo alone and we get there in good shape with time to spare but no—TJ has to let everyone know he's the boss."

The boys previously read accounts of bias toward blacks and heard stories of life in the Deep South. The nuns prepared them for what might be waiting for them. Now they possibly would experience first-hand the treatment of their black friends. After the trip, the other corps members learned the parents of the black members were very reluctant to allow their children to make the trip in the first place. Some parents were born in the South and they retained unhappy childhood memories. They did not want the young boys mistreated or possibly physically injured. TJ convinced the parents that all would be well. "The boys themselves desperately desire to make the trip with their friends. It may be a once in a lifetime experience for them." So it was resolved that they would embark on the adventure.

The bus filled with gas at a scheduled stop in the state of Georgia. While the white members were having lunch at the roadside restaurant, two Georgia State Troopers exited their vehicle and approached the bus. One of the officers reached in the driver's window and released the front door. Without warning, they opened front door and walked on the bus. The four black members remaining on the bus were talking and joking.

Mason and Joey Coughlin were bringing a lunch of sandwiches, snacks and sodas back to their friends when they noticed the state police officers entering the bus. Earlier, the northerners discussed the situation concerning the restaurants. Randinoli asked aloud, "How the hell can this be? Who came up with these rules?" He and the rest could not understand why the restaurants remained off limits to their black friends, who were forced to stay and eat on the bus. The white guys had heard some things were different in the South, but never expected to be separated from their friends in the restaurants.

The boys could not believe how imposing the two troopers looked, standing in the aisle wearing wide-brimmed black and navy-blue hats, military-like jackets with shiny gold buttons on the lapels and sleeves, and striped pants neatly stuffed into black shiny leather boots that climbed to their kneecaps.

The two youngsters could not alter their gaze from the size of the guns sticking out of the black leather holsters.

One of the troopers growled, "Hey boy, whose gonna eat that food?" The cops, now blocking the aisle, appeared even bigger.

Mason and Coughlin knew the state troopers were up to no good. For some reason they were not afraid but also did not trust the so-called law enforcers, and were definitely concerned for the welfare of their friends. Mason looked out the side windows and spotted Mr. Bloom, one of the volunteers, hurriedly heading toward the bus. Mason said, "The sandwiches are for our friends, officer. Is that a problem?"

At that moment Edward Bloom stepped up the stairs and onto the bus. A tenacious lawyer, Bloom had been in many courtroom battles. He served as a county prosecutor for five years prior to moving to the defense bar. Now a senior partner of a respected Newark law firm in the Central Ward, Bloom enjoyed a well-deserved reputation as a tough, no-nonsense litigator. The lawyer quickly appraised the situation and stepped in front of Mason. "Excuse me officers, my name is Edward Bloom. I practice law in New Jersey and I'm accompanying these young men on a business trip to Jacksonville. May I ask what you're doing on our bus?" Go on the offense, short and sweet, but to the point.

The troopers lost some of their bullying stature. They really did not want to mix it up with some big shot northern lawyer, especially since they had no police business on the bus. The ranking officer said, "We wanted to make sure the food was paid for, just about to ask to see the receipt."

Mason could not stay quiet. He waved the receipt from the restaurant, and said, "Sir, you were on the bus before we came on with the food."

An awkward silence followed for the troopers. Before either of them could follow up with another lie, Bloom decided to take them off the hook. "Well, I suppose you entered this bus without a warrant or a legitimate reason, so why don't you leave and we'll forget what happened."

The senior of the two troopers did not like the way their authority was threatened in front of the young travelers, especially the black teens who were quiet but paying attention to every word. This northern piece-of-shit lawyer was disrespecting the troopers in their own territory.

The senior officer regained his composure. This wiseass lawyer required a reminder of exactly where he was. "You must think you're scarin' someone. You bein' a Yankee Jew lawyer don't cut it down here. You are south of the Mason Dixon, Mr. big shot, lawyerin' in our jurisdiction." The huge trooper smiled at his partner. "As far as we're concerned we got all the legitimate reasons in the world to make sure your niggas ain't up to no good. Their kind is always pullin' somethin.'"

Coughlin opened his mouth to speak, angry at the trooper's language. The lawyer waved him off.

Bloom heard enough. He walked forward until he was now eyeball to eyeball with the talker. He spoke slowly, "I will say this once. You are correct. I am Jewish and I most certainly practice law. You will have the opportunity to see me in a courtroom and it will be something neither of you will ever forget. So let us proceed. We are most certainly south of the Mason Dixon line, which as I recall is still part of the United States of America. You have no legitimate reason to be on our property. You broke the law when you illegally entered our bus. There has not been a complaint registered regarding food not being paid for. You lied about that. You have been shown proof of payment. I will shower you both personally with a blizzard of litigation. Your superiors will think you tried to initiate another civil war." Bloom's voice quieted as he said, "For the last time, remove your sorry asses from our bus—do it now!"

The trooper hesitated, and then stole a contemptuous peek at the boys sitting in the back. "Shit, we got more important things to do." Both troopers walked off the bus, stepped into their cruiser and raced out of the parking lot.

Coughlin lightened the mood. "Man, they were lucky I went easy on those turkeys." Now shadowboxing, punching and dancing, bobbing and weaving, he said, "I was ready to put both those dudes down. I'm talkin' down." Everyone, including the lawyer, laughed at the show.

"You tell 'em, Coughy," laughed Gerald Border from the back of the bus.

Mason smiled. "Mr. Bloom, 'Shower you with a blizzard of litigation?' I'm thinking, over the top, no?"

Bloom, happy for the quote, said, "Brad, I use that line often—it always gets attention."

Mason never forgot the encounter with the state police and the way Mr. Bloom responded. He often thought of what the cops would have done to him, Coughlin, and their black friends if given an opportunity to be alone with them. This would not be the last time Mason would confront people in authority, supposedly on the right side, wearing shiny badges and carrying big guns.

The bus arrived safely at the Gator Bowl without further incident. The corps members quickly prepared for the halftime performance. Does it ever end? High up in the stands sat a group of Georgia high school football players. The Georgia footballers were special guests of the management since recently winning the Georgia State High School Football Championship.

The Georgia team, occupying the top rows of the south grandstands, began shouting derogatory names to the "Yankees" and bombarding them with peanut shells. Some names were very unkind toward the black members. One of St. Joe's baritone players, Jack Olson, known as "Big Jack" for good reason, became very pissed. For Olson, the quiet person from a New Jersey suburb, this was a very uncharacteristic reaction. Big Jack raised his heavy muscular arms out wide as though he was about to deliver a fire and brimstone homily, and addressed the football team. "Excuse me fellows, we are playing at halftime. Let us meet right after the show and continue this discussion." It was obvious that Olson was educated and from a very superior school system. The Georgia boys continued with their insults but agreed to the proposed meeting. Big Jack's diction only fueled the fire. The football team interpreted his manner of speaking as an insult. The footballers now screamed not only would they meet, but that the "Yankee band fairies" would learn a hard lesson from real southern football players. The deal was set.

The public address announcer introduced Mighty St. Joe's. "And now on the starting line, it is my pleasure to present to you all the way from Newark, New Jersey, the world-renowned championship drum and bugle corps, the St. Joseph's Cadets. Ladies and gentlemen—the Hilltoppers."

On the starting line awaiting the major's command to start the show, Billy Washington, a flag bearer said, "World renowned? What the hell is that guy smokin'?"

After an extraordinary rendition of the "Madame Butterfly" overture, the Hilltoppers owned the crowd and proceeded to glide through fifteen minutes of precision marching and maneuvering, great scores of music featuring a lively concert highlighted by the upbeat "The Continental." Now at the apex of their performance, the Hilltoppers concluded with the always popular "Brazil" that brought the entire stadium to its feet. Even a few of the Georgia footballers applauded.

As the corps exited the field, stepping to the single beat of Randinoli's tenor drum, the crowd continued to demonstrate their appreciation and treated the boys to a raucous round of applause lasting minutes after the show ended.

This turned out to be a historic day for the world of drum and bugle. Now exposed to this form of entertainment, the southerners loved the entire show. TJ was crowded with individuals interested in organizing groups of their own, asking all the right questions. It would not take long for churches and other organizations to establish drum and bugle corps throughout the South. In a few years, they could boast of some of the very best contingents in the country.

The warm and appreciative crowd numbered over sixteen thousand. A local newspaper reporter covering the halftime show called it, "Love at first sight," saying "the youngsters from New Jersey made a lasting impression on the record crowd." Later, Deylan said of the article, "It was good he didn't interview the state football champions."

The dozen men who travelled with the corps, including the drivers of the bus and equipment trailer, were all aware of what was in progress. They realized it fruitless to do anything to stop the meeting between the two groups. Mr. Walsh summed it up. "We are handcuffed, it is a done deal. We can at least steer TJ away from the stands and keep him occupied with spurious issues. He will have a nutty if he learns of the scheduled extracurricular activity."

The Yankees had discussed the situation. The older members decided to play it low key. Jimmy Coughlin said, "It makes no sense to bring unwanted attention to ourselves." They quietly stripped off their uniforms and placed them neatly on the hangers provided. They positioned the uniforms on the equipment truck with all the instruments and color guard paraphernalia. There was no further talk. They did not know how close TJ was and did not want him to suspect anything.

The football team assembled exactly where Big Jack directed, and close-up they looked bigger than life. Each wore a red and gold jacket with the school name and a patch that said "Georgia State High School Football Champions" on the back. The jacket sleeves listed all the opponents and scores of each game during the year. They enjoyed an undefeated season.

When the dust settled, it was clear that the championship football team had suffered its first defeat of the season. This was the first time that anyone had seen Big Jack in action, himself a standout high school football player at Union High School. A few of the St. Joe's people watched in awe. Usually a reserved individual, perhaps Jack felt responsible for the melee. He threw football players in every direction.

As the footballers launched an embarrassing retreat, you could hear Big Jack offer a heartfelt invitation. "Come back lads, let's see how much you like peanuts."

Of course, a few comedians aided the one-way conversation. Shadow Deltucci yelled, "Yo guys, no one's perfect. One loss for the year ain't all that bad."

Border, at least for the moment, forgot where they were, and added his very loud version of one of Hoagie Carmichael's greatest hits, "Georgia on my Mind." "I said Georgia, oh Georgia, no peace I find, just an old sweet song keeps Georgia on my mind." A few others supplied the background chords. His black skin and huge sunglasses gave the Ray Charles effect. The on-looking crowd cheered and applauded.

The long journey to Newark, far from boring, was filled with exaggerated versions of Big Jacks' single-handed victory. The big guy showed a sincere smile, munched on potato chips and continued adjusting his glasses while reading an engineering textbook. "Please gentlemen, I had adequate assistance."

There was one dark cloud to disrupt the cheerful atmosphere. It was not a secret. Randinoli kicked one of the Georgians who lay face down on the ground. Apparently, he completed yet another of his decision-making exercises and exhibited the infamous mean streak, which was unmistakably growing meaner by the day. Everyone was unhappy and embarrassed but they all knew it was a lost cause talking to Randinoli about his latest action.

Randinoli sloughed it off and tried to get support from Mason. "Hey, he was getting up. He belonged on the ground, right?"

Mason tired of the same routine; he was ready to give Randinoli a beating right on the bus. He never felt this much anger for his friend. Tired of explaining Randinoli's actions to others, he yelled, "Wrong! You didn't have to kick him. He was out of it and injured, finished. How many times have we been through this, the choices we all have to make? We had those southern spectators on our side, they loved the show. We get in a fight with some of their people, so okay—they don't find too much wrong with that. They understand these things happen. Now the word spreads that one of the southerners takes a kick for no reason. He's dealing with at least one broken rib and on and on." Mason realized he was in the middle of a sermon. "Why pursue it?" His voice steadied. "I get a little tired of making excuses for you. Just forget it. It's over."

Randinoli got on the bus. He was thinking about what his friend said, *"The choices we all have to make."* Maybe the next time he will make a different choice—then again, maybe not. His friend always told it like it was, never held back. No one else ever escaped after correcting Randinoli's actions. The violence escalated after his mother died at such an early age. He was aware that Mason had many discussions with his father, Cuban Pete Randinoli, who worried about his only son. He saw the anger in his son. The senior prayed that his son would grow into a decent person. Randinoli

53

thought that he would try a little harder to control his temper. Then the thought crossed his mind, *"but what if the prick got up?"*

The New Jersey travelers were glad to be heading home. After a few days back in Newark, Joe Deylan, the corps major, wrote a letter of apology to the high school principal in Georgia. Deylan attempted to downplay Randinoli's action and the letter characterized the entire incident as something that just happens in such a situation. Surprisingly, Deylan heard back from the football team captain and apparently there were no hard feelings on their side. It was a good way to end.

TJ never learned of the fight. If he did, he never mentioned it.

The historical game was the last Gator Bowl played in January. Texas Tech finished on top 35-13. Soon after, a new stadium was constructed holding a capacity of 36,000. In years to come, major D&B competitions filled the beautiful stadium with corps from the entire country. The 1954 Hilltoppers received much credit for the rising popularity of drum and bugle corps in the South. The meeting with the boys from Georgia was never mentioned.

Chapter Twelve

The crap game

It was summertime 1954. *The* crap game as always was in full swing in the midst of all the other Bruce Street schoolyard activities. The game, under the supervision of Blackie Capone and Tony Quinn, generally operated without a hitch. The two founded the gambling operation soon after an armistice ended the Korean War on July 27, 1953. While serving in the military, both young men were decorated for bravery in the face of danger. They were under enemy fire more than once. Johnny Zatz put it simply. "Those guys had real bullets coming at them. Conflict my ass, that was no *conflict*. Korea was the real thing, a real war."

After being awarded honorable discharges from the U.S. Army within days of each other, Capone and Quinn returned to their old stomping grounds at 12ᵗʰ Avenue and Bruce Street and followed up on plans they talked of while in the service. Although he had a sense of humor, Capone seldom smiled, never told a joke or funny story, and was always strictly about business. "Tony, like we talked about so many times. We're in this to make money. The time is ripe in the city for a high-class, well-run game. The guys back from the "conflict" are looking for some action. They have money to gamble. We do whatever it takes to be successful. Keep the players happy, but keep everybody in line." They would take a percentage of every bet made. Win or lose—it made no difference. Capone and Quinn took their cut whether the dice were "right" or "wrong."

Quinn, more of a thinker than his partner, agreed. "Amen. If I learned anything in the military, the operation runs smooth when the generals agree on the goals. We've gone over everything. We'll be fine."

They opened the game and built it to be the best in the area. The two friends furnished the dice, the police protection, cold water, beer and soda, and pretzels. They also supervised the lighting of the candles when darkness came. The game must go on. None of the other crap games offered night services. This was no social club where a few select people played. The Bruce Street game was high action day and night, with heavy hitters crowding the back of the schoolyard. The game enjoyed a well-thought-of reputation throughout the New York–New Jersey metropolitan area.

Capone and Quinn sustained excellent physical condition, utilizing the facilities at St. Joe's Club to keep fit. Capone always sported a deep tan, the result of his daily use of a very expensive "sunning machine." His closest friend and partner Quinn, a handsome and rugged looking six-footer, was always well-dressed no matter the weather. His smile became an integral part of the game.

Randinoli worshipped Capone and Quinn since making his first visit to the game. He told Mason, "Tony is the sharpest dresser of all. He could be in the movies. Blackie is as smart as they come and tough as nails. He got that scar on his neck when he was in Korea. They run a smooth operation and take no shit. They make a lot of scratch."

It appeared to most that the only thing in life that mattered to Capone was protecting the solid reputation of the Bruce Street crap game. Those close to him never gave him an opportunity to anger. He was viewed as a quiet person, definitely not someone to disrespect. There were a few incidents through the years, with one episode of Capone losing his temper taking place during the second year of the game's existence. Mason and Randinoli were present for the occasion.

A degenerate crapshooter from nearby Irvington showed up one Saturday afternoon for his first visit to the schoolyard. He gave the impression of a guy who had been around, and certainly sounded tough. The visitor stood slightly over six-feet tall and weighed north of one hundred and ninety pounds, most of it fat. His nose gave the appearance of taking a punch or two.

The new player introduced himself, although no one asked. "They call me Timeserved." He appeared very serious, so Capone, Quinn, and the other players called him Timeserved when they required his attention to advance the game. The other players were quite familiar with the term. When a convict is in custody awaiting trial and sentencing, he sometimes earns an early release, receiving credit for time already served.

Quinn said, "Is this guy for real? Timefreakinserved? He is a big one. We better not call him late for dinner."

Capone laughed and said to his partner, "We call him whatever he wants. His money is good so long as he follows our rules." Quinn agreed.

It was a scorcher in the middle of July. The younger kids sucked on ice popsicles and Italian ice cups while the crapshooters drank gallons of water, soda and cold beer. This particular day, it was Quinn's turn as the pit boss. His job: assign the dice to the next shooter after the dice showed seven and out. "The dice are yours Mike, good luck." Without this direction, arguments over shooting the dice threatened the organization of the game. He always performed this task masterfully, without a mishap.

On this particular day, the 'do' bettors, those betting with the dice, held their own. Not the case for Timeserved, who alternated his bets— some with the dice and others, wagered that the dice would be wrong. His system did not work well. The other players noticed his bad luck increasing as the game progressed. Every bet went sour. Now down about six hundred dollars, he became unruly. "Where'd the beer come from, a steam room?" He had polished off four or five complimentary twelve-ounce bottles provided by his hosts. The Ballantine Ale bottle he held came from the same fifty-gallon ice-filled trashcan. His turn to roll the dice; his number five, he threw seven. Now "tap city," gambling for the big man ended for the day.

Timeserved nodded toward Quinn and, without looking up, he barked, "Give me five hundred."

Hearing this more as a demand than a request, Quinn said, "Not today, we have rules. One is that we do not lend money during the game."

"Hey, I'm good for it. I'm down over a grand and I want a chance to win it back." Now he sounded more threatening.

Still calm, Quinn made it clear. "When you leave the game, you'll be given carfare. That's been our policy since day one. Now, why not call it a day." As Quinn started to peel off bills from a thick wad of twenties, the visitor became angry.

"Those dice do not feel right, who buys them?" He focused on Quinn as he spoke, never noticing that Capone observed the entire scene as he sat on the top step leading into the rear of the school building. Quinn started toward the newcomer, but before he could say anything, his partner spoke.

He appeared interested and spoke quietly as he smiled. Capone said, "I buy them, do you have a question?" He came across as though he was actually concerned about Timeserved's observations.

The alcohol offered a little encouragement. "Not a question—a complaint! The dice are loaded. I want my grand back." Timeserved dropped the beer bottle to his right side, holding it by its neck in a threatening manner. This being his first visit to the game, he was not familiar with the reputations of the two in charge. He figured they would fear someone who had spent time in jail. Quinn took a step toward the visitor. The other players placed their folded money in their pockets and moved back.

Capone slowly reared himself while offering his partner a friendly wave. "Tony, take it easy." He reached the bottom of the steps and stood a few feet from Timeserved, smiling at his partner. "You've been working hard all day, relax."

Capone continued, still speaking in a friendly tone. "Now Mr. Time-served. That is your name right, Timeserved?"

Timeserved positioned the bottle further to the back of his leg. "That's right, I got it in the joint. They thought . . ." Capone waved him off and looked directly into the complainer's eyes. "That's all fine. There's no need to explain. It doesn't matter to us. Your name is your business." Capone gestured toward the ground where the dice lay. "This game is our business. My partner and I make no apologies for the game. However, let me be sure I have the facts right."

Capone motioned toward the ice-filled bucket holding the water, soda and beer. "One, the free beer you've been guzzling has been sitting in ice since eight a.m. You say it's warm. Two, the provider of dice for the last decade is now selling us faulty merchandise. Finally, number three, you demand that we return money you lost to other players because of your ridiculous play. That, incidentally, by my count is closer to six hundred than a thousand. That about cover it?" One needed to strain to hear the last of what he said, as he spoke more softly than usual.

Randinoli whispered, "Brad, look at Tony."

Quinn showed a slight smile. Not a soul alive understood Capone like his partner. Quinn thought, *"This turd thinks Blackie is actually negotiating."* Judging from the softness of Capone's voice, the Irvington crapshooter believed he would come out smelling like a rose.

The coddling quickly ended and, before he got an answer, Capone said, "You have two choices. One, you turn around and run, not walk, to your car and drive away. Or two, I hurt you very badly."

Randinoli struggled to keep from having an orgasm.

"You son of a . . ." In spite of the alcohol, Timeserved moved fast, but not quickly enough.

Capone let go with two straight punches to the face, first a solid left followed by a lightning quick right. The beer bottle shattered as it fell to the ground. His knees wobbled, then the startled Timeserved fell straight back onto the concrete, landing with a thud.

One of the schoolyard comedians, Shadow Deltucci, shouted through cupped hands and offered his imitation of radio announcer Don Dunphy doing the blow-by-blow on Friday night fights. "Fight fans, I can say without any doubt that the Irvington heavyweight will not get up for the next round. It's in the record book. This fight is ovaaah." This professional observation supposedly coming from a ringside broadcast at Madison Square Garden. Not his first time with this performance, Deltucci then gurgled through his cupped hands and mimicked the sound of a cheering crowd.

Blood squirted from Timeserved's nose and flowed down, covering his lips and chin. His eyes quickly swelled, and, as he turned to one side, the big man coughed up more blood.

Quinn quietly spoke to the teenagers. "Brad, how about you and Gabe carry him to his vehicle. Soak that towel with the cold water from the bucket and splash it on him. Make sure he's awake before he drives out of the neighborhood. Now, get him out of here before the blood stains our runway." This was not the first time Capone and Quinn trusted the two young guys to act on their behalf. Quinn later remarked, "So long as Gabe doesn't make one of his decisions. We'll be transporting crapshooters to the City Hospital Emergency Room. I feel better when Brad is around to keep an eye on his pal. They are both dependable but when Gabe loses it the whole deal can turn sour."

The two friends lifted the still-drowsy visitor by his feet and arms, carried him through the schoolyard and out to his new white-over-blue Buick Super Riviera Coupe, parked on the south side of Bruce Street. Life went on. The basketball game resumed play and Harold pitched a high, hard one. The batter belted the half-ball high in the air, sending it onto the school roof.

They gently settled the big man behind the steering wheel of the Buick Riviera, and Randinoli slammed the front door. "You come back again, Mr. Timeserved. We love visitors to our game." He spotted what looked like a new, navy blue sharkskin suit hanging in the back seat.

"Just my size!" He opened the back door and reached in. "Man, I'll look so cool in school. This should help my business."

Mason grabbed his friend's outstretched arm before it reached the new suit. "You quit school remember? We need to get back to the schoolyard."

Timeserved muttered something barely audible, found the ignition, started the car and drove erratically down Bruce Street, steering with his right hand, using the left to shove a bloody handkerchief into his nostrils.

Mrs. Sweeney leaned out of her second story window and said, "I see another happy investor is escorted out of the neighborhood." She smiled at the crowd standing outside the schoolyard gate.

A few corner people started to cheer and Deltucci yelled, "Way to go Mrs. S, everybody's a comedian."

Capone and Quinn asked the younger guys to stay vigilant in case Time-served decided to return with an army. Capone said, "Brad, you both know what he looks like, sound the alarm if he's crazy enough to come back with reinforcements." Quinn added, "Go fill Zatzie in."

Newark icon Johnny Zatz, the bookie and part-time leg breaker who sometimes did some collecting for the Battiatos, grew up in the neighborhood and loved being around the crap game. Some of the crapshooters also bet the horses, baseball, basketball, football, and any other sporting event taking place. When the game first opened, Capone said, "What the hell, Zatz is right here, might as well give him the action." Everyone knew that losing wagers never went outstanding for long periods. When Zatz wasn't bookmaking or leg breaking he engaged himself in his favorite hobby—explosives. An expertise carried over from his years in the military, Zatz stayed current and his small Bergen Street warehouse stored more weapons of mass destruction than several small countries. From time to time, it became necessary to hear a loud noise or view a small fire. Zatz welcomed the opportunity "to serve humanity."

A little crazy when necessary, the stories of Zatz's achievements were endless. Some might debate the word *achievements*. One could not take issue regarding his love of the community and the lengths he would go to protect the people of the neighborhood. The most recent of his activities occurred six months ago, when seven-year-old Talia Jones was lured into a strange car as she played with friends in front of her house on Bergen Street. The kidnapper, a white male in his thirties, sped away in the direction of Central Avenue and Branch Brook Park. Before the police arrived, the people in the schoolyard were in action.

Following Quinn's direction, Mason and Randinoli, now seventeen, raced three-and-a-half city blocks to where the girl was abducted. People in the neighborhood speak freely to neighbors they know. Without hesitation, an elderly gentleman sitting on his porch provided them with the license number of "a fairly new green foreign baby." He said, "It had a white stripe along the sides. I yelled out but too late, the dude was truckin'. I could see little Talia's head stickin' up."

The number was phoned in to one of the neighborhood cops working in the second precinct and in a matter of minutes the posse had hold of a name and address.

Zatz, along with his partner Joe Simpson, Capone and Quinn, assembled in Simpson's white international truck. "The name that came up is Stewart

Reid, 1135 Beechnut Court, Essex Fells, New Jersey. I know the area." Zatz, not wasting a second, was now all business. "Joe, head over First Street to Interstate 280 west, I'll fill you in from there." In the passenger seat, he looked at his friend and said, "No stops, no nothing, all forward." Simpson, a part-time roofer and full-time weight lifter, understood the necessity; he would get to the Essex County high-end suburb in record time. Simpson broke many traffic laws—speeding, running red lights and stop signs, swerving in and out of lanes—what some might identify as reckless driving.

There were few large dwellings scattered throughout the wooded landscape. The upper-class neighborhood was quiet. The four former servicemen exited the truck and, with Zatz leading the way, walked directly toward number 1135 Beechnut Court. They thought it bigger than any private residence in the Central Ward, at least room for four cars in the garage on the side of the house. If the visitors held an interest in real estate they would be impressed with the colossal, Tudor-style building, maybe more accurately described as a mansion. The medieval era attention-getter showed massive roofs with cross gables and three chimneys capped with chimney pots. Tall windows, each with small, rectangular panes, were arranged in groups of three. The manicured landscaping challenged the most picturesque part of Branch Brook Park, cherry blossoms included. As they agreed to earlier, each of the group remained silent. There was no sign of a foreign car.

Zatz stepped aside as he nodded to Simpson. The twelve-foot cedar door shattered as Simpson brought the forty-pound sledgehammer down in the direction of the doorknob and lock. The collision shook the Tudor arch over the door. Capone's combat boot kicked in the remaining bulk and, in a matter of seconds, Zatz and Quinn quickly entered the home.

The apparent occupant stood in the middle of a large entry and living room area. "What's the meaning of this? Who are you?" The startled resident was a white male in his middle thirties, athletic-looking, clean-shaven, with wavy black hair and piercing blue eyes.

Zatz appeared calm and said, "Stewart Reid. Do you know him?"

Reid looked annoyed at the stranger and said, "That's me. What are you doing in my house? Are you the police? How dare you! What do you want with me?"

"I'm going to kill you. Real slow. Where's the girl?" He walked closer to Reid. Zatz held a twenty-two revolver in his right hand.

Capone and Quinn were already hurrying up the stairs, and Simpson headed for the kitchen and the back end of the house. The three carried pieces.

Reid tried to decide what to do. He heard the pounding footsteps ascending the steps and then sounds coming from upstairs. Next, the voice of a frightened little girl was crying out, "Mommy, please . . . I want my Mommy." As he listened, Reid stared at Zatz and said, "Listen to that, will you? I should have killed the little bitch."

Zatz holstered his twenty-two. He walked toward the kidnapper, reached out and, using both hands, cupped Reid's ears and lifted him off his feet. He then slammed him on his back and forced a knee into his stomach. Reid struggled for breath. He needed oxygen. "No please, please . . . I'll pay you . . . I have money . . . I own many businesses . . . please." He reached for Zatz's knee, trying to release the pressure. The weight increased as Zatz leaned forward on his chest and squeezed Reid's ears.

Reid's eyes teared as he gasped for air. Next, he yelled something indistinguishable. "Agh! Ogh! I beg . . . no more . . . ." Blood stained mucus leaked from his nose.

Two minutes passed and his two friends tiptoed past Zatz and Reid. Capone sounded almost polite. "Excuse us, we have the girl. She's good, we'll be in the car." Quinn followed, gently carrying the seven-year-old as he headed for the smashed front door. "It's okay Tania, like I told you, we're going home and you can see your Mom and all your friends." He looked at Zatz and Simpson with a reassuring look. *"Nothing happened. The scum never had the chance. We got here in time."*

Still carrying the sledgehammer, Simpson stared down at the frightened man. "I hate maggots who take kids from their mothers." He pushed the heavy tool over his head with one muscular arm and said, "I have to finish him, pal."

Reid screamed out, "Oh God . . . no don't let him hurt me . . . anything you want . . . I'll give you anything." Simpson pointed at the pedophile with his left fist taking aim as he turned slightly to his right, as a batter would do in the batter's box. He held the pose. "What about it, I get to smash his head in, right?"

Zatz never took his eyes off his prisoner and said, "Some other time. I promise. I'll be out in a bit. Give the kid the chocolate ice cream in the cooler, and the cookies."

"Okay, not too long, right? We need to be history before our friends arrive." Simpson stared directly down at the pathetic man on the floor. "I hope we meet just one more time." He leaned over and let the weight of his weapon rest on Reid's forehead. "I'll have this with me, that's a promise." He left without getting to use his sledgehammer.

With his left hand, Zatz pulled his captive up by the hair and slammed his head down on the oak floor. "Your thing is to harass defenseless little girls and force them to accompany you to your mansion. You get off on that. Or do you need more?" He pushed down harder with his knee. It drew the same response, but now Zatz was not listening.

"What is your business?"

Reid could hardly speak, "I own all . . . the Upper Claz hair salons . . . in the New York, New Jersey metropolitan area. There are forty-six . . . no make that forty-seven . . . Agh!" The pain was unbearable.

Zatz looked and sounded maniacal. "Don't give me a story. A short answer or I'll finish you now. Understand?"

"Yes, yes."

"Who lives here?"

"Me, just me."

"This is what you need to know. Your family, friends, pets, no problem. We find all of them. All in wheelchairs and other stuff. When the cops get here, confess to what you did. Tell them exactly what happened, how you planned it, your target, how long you've been doing what you do, everything. Understand?"

Reid stared, as if he were deep in thought.

"I can see your sick mind working. You think when we go you can tell the police anything you want. I will see the reports, every word you utter. I will know if you've been truthful. With your money and lawyers, it's possible you will get away with a slap on the wrist. You agree? Yes or no."

"Yes."

"You need to make sure that doesn't happen—if you want to live. If you walk from this, I will be back. I will not kill you immediately. First, I will ensure you never hurt a little girl again, especially one from the Central Ward. The sledgehammer will be used to break most of your bones. You will never walk again. Nod your head if you are listening."

Reid lowered his head and let it hang still.

"You will be a vegetable forced to eat from a straw. Then I will deliver you across the street in your wheelchair so you can see this big playhouse burn to the ground. You will then make a full circle tour of your businesses, and watch as each of the forty-six, make that forty-seven salons, turn into parking lots."

Zatz heard the light tap of the truck horn. He heard the sound of police sirens in the distance. "I've made myself clear. I'm leaving now. You make sure you receive a prison sentence. I almost hope you ignore my orders. I will enjoy ending your sorry life—real slow."

Zatz kept close track of Reid as he served eighteen months in a Midwest prison. Upon his release, Zatz paid a visit reminding him of the sledgehammer and the bad things that happen to people messing with kids. They never heard from Reid again.

Simpson speculated about the situation. "Who knows with those people, maybe we straightened him out and he'll get some treatment. If it happens again, Doctor Zatz will end the patient's rehabilitation sessions."

Now that Timeserved was escorted out of the neighborhood, Randinoli still had something to say. "Blackie, I carried the prick under his arms, way heavier than Brad's end. I know the extra casheroo goes to the guy who did the most work."

Everyone laughed, and Mason said, "Gabe, you almost dropped the poor guy on his head. We came close to having a medical emergency on our hands."

Danny Sherman followed. "I can see Hatlas's column in the Star-Ledger now. 'A distinguished Irvington resident, while visiting the Bruce Street crap game, suffered mysterious head injuries.'"

Enough fun, always covering all the bases, Capone added, "Brad, he may sober up a little and come back. If he is alone and just wants to play again, you and Gabe search his sorry ass before he gets near the game. You know what to do if he brings back the cavalry from Irvington."

Mason and Randinoli walked away from the game and out of the schoolyard. Mason said, "If we see the British coming, you go to Chick's and get Zatz and Simpson, and anyone else in the store. They can come in the schoolyard behind Timeserved's crew. I will give Blackie and Tony the word."

Randinoli agreed and said, "My man, all this extra work and shit, this is gonna turn into a nice payday for us." He loved the thought of fighting and beating the crap out of someone—anyone. Getting paid was icing on the cake.

Quinn was as equally devoted to the business as his partner. He viewed the game as something sacred, like Capone, and he treated the participants with respect but never hesitated to heave an unruly player out of the schoolyard on his ass. The two entrepreneurs were friends since first grade at Saint Joseph's. Quinn, who kept his GI crew cut, always had a kind word and a smile for the gamblers.

Together they made a great team. They were excellent business executives for the particular business they chose. The losers always received a few bucks for carfare before leaving the game. The operators shared this theory with the younger guys on the corner. "We never let anyone leave broke."

Quinn said, "It's good business and the players show their appreciation by returning to invest again and most likely lose more money." Of course if a player won money, as he left the game, either of the two partners would remind him, "Tell 'em where you got it."

Later in the year Quinn injected some humor into the game. "Ya know Blackie, this business is getting more challenging. Ya think we should go back to the car parking racket?"

There were shouts of, "Great. Yeah, that's the ticket. Do it, do it. Now we're talkin' real dough. Drive right in."

Capone and the rest of the schoolyard understood his partner's question. The car parking story was well known. "Not a bad idea, we've been on the outside for too long. A few years in a gated community will do us good, improve our outlook."

Quinn's reference concerned a two-year period, which ended the previous fall, during which the two friends operated a downtown parking lot located behind the Prudential Insurance building. They came upon the idea of going into the parking lot business when they noticed that the lot filled with vehicles every day, yet never saw anyone collecting fees and never noticed any signs of security. They correctly surmised that the property owner was absent, and that no one was paying for the parking privilege. Capone and Quinn changed that scenario.

"This is an opportunity to utilize some of Newark's prime real estate," Capone observed.

"Absolutely, it is sinful to let the property go dormant," Quinn fully agreed.

Wearing official looking, dark green collared shirts with white "Park'n Go" logos on the sleeves, the entrepreneurs raked the leaves and paper from the dirt and gave the area a general sprucing up. They were ready for business in their prime location. The lot soon displayed a freshly painted six-by-eight wooden shed with asphalt roof shingles, compliments of a friend from the roofers' local. They included a small, painted, black-over-white sign displaying the new owners' hours and rates: "Parking All Day—9 a.m. to 6 p.m.—$1.00." Now they were ready for business in their prime location, and worked the lot together.

The questions raised by a few regulars were handled in a courteous and professional manner. "Sir, we purchased the property and you can be sure your vehicle will receive maximum security." "Madam, while you shop you will be happy to know that half your parking fee is going to a deserving local charity."

After the operation began running smoothly, with fewer questions from the customers, Capone and Quinn split the shifts—each working three days a week. They decided to work Saturdays to handle the busy shopping traffic, but would not charge for Sunday parking. Showing compassion for the churchgoers, Quinn said, "After all, Sunday is the Sabbath so we will allow free parking. We will be in church as well."

For two years, the cash poured in. They prepared for the cold winter months with the addition of a new oil heater placed in the cashier's shed. Whenever the entrepreneurs took time off, Mason and Randinoli filled in. However, all good things eventually end.

One day, a distinguished-looking man driving a shiny new model Mercedes-Benz showed up unexpectedly. He glanced at the cars on his property and took note of the sign nailed to the shed. He turned off the engine, buttoned his cashmere overcoat and walked in the direction of the shed. Without hesitation, he said, "My name is Waltham Breckenridge and I own this property. What the hell do you two think you're doing here?" The 12th and Bruce residents both sensed it was time to pack and close up shop. Randinoli nodded toward the lot, covered his mouth and whispered, "I'll be ready to roll." Mason picked up on the signal and walked toward the well-dressed gentleman.

Mason, feigning innocence, slowly explained. "We work for Mr. Smith. I'll go across the street to the luncheonette and tell him you would like to speak with him. If you'll give me your name again, you two gentlemen can work it out." While Mason stalled, Randinoli quickly emptied the shed, walked to his car, started the engine and waited for his partner. Mason, seeing it was time to vanish, walked away from the bewildered Mr. Breckenridge, jumped in the waiting car and took off—waving goodbye to a very lucrative enterprise. When they explained to the crap game operators what happened, Capone and Quinn understood and took it in stride. Quinn, the philosopher, said, "That's the way business goes, like a toilet seat, up and down, up and down."

Capone added, "I hope Mr. Breckenridge appreciates all the effort that went into getting his business off the ground. We'll have to stop by and see how he's doing."

The crap game grew in reputation, becoming the most visited game in Newark and the surrounding area. Neither partner concerned himself with the cops. Both had minor rap sheets. Shortly after honorable discharges from the military, the two friends each served short stints resulting from gambling charges. Since they opened the game in the schoolyard, it operated as smooth as silk. If matters got out of hand, a couple of bangers were always at the ready at the schoolyard or within close proximity. The heavy artillery was called in on very rare occasions. In addition to short stretches for bookmaking, both rap sheets included a few minor assault charges. Capone and Quinn personally addressed ninety-nine percent of the disagreements.

It's no secret that Capone and Quinn kicked back a percentage from the crap game revenue to the Louis Battiato family, who controlled all gambling enterprises in the city. In addition, a few of the Newark Police detectives working the second precinct took a piece and looked the other way. Capone and Quinn never discriminated. Both the cops and the robbers were welcome to the game. Several police officers often appeared off duty to try their luck with the dice.

"We don't give a shit who plays. Good guys, bad guys, so long as they follow the rules. Business is business." Capone repeated this mantra more than once.

A cast of characters from far and near found their way to *The Game,* the label describing the 12th Avenue and Bruce Street attraction. Players from New York were especially familiar with the Battiato name and regarded the action as lucrative and safe from the law. No one worried about surprise raids by the police or robberies by adventurous "lone rangers."

The atmosphere on a warm summer's day was near-festive. The sounds blended—music from the basketball court, a basketball game, a pitch quarter game, stick ball and the sometimes-noisy crap game—and put nearly everyone within earshot into a relaxed frame of mind.

The big boss, Louie "The Boss" Battiato, made an appearance with a few of his guns every few weeks, the time never advertised. The always-present smile on the face of the big man did much to disguise the unchecked killing and bloodshed that raged during his twenty-year reign as the leader of his family.

Congenial as always, Battiato sounded like the "Man of the Year" during a recent visit. "Tony, Blackie, you are both looking well. Life is still agreeing with you," he said.

Showing mutual respect, Capone and the boss shook hands, hugged each other, and kissed each other's cheeks. Capone said, "Always good to see you Louie, you look better than ever." The boss, still smiling, shook hands with and hugged Quinn in the same fashion. "Hello Louie," Quinn said. It was a short greeting but said with respect. Quinn never liked to socialize during business hours. He and his partner viewed the relationship with Battiato as strictly business—they never considered themselves as part of any family or criminal enterprise. They were independent businessmen operating a successful crap game. Quinn paid his respects and returned to his top priority, that being the business of operating the crap game.

The respect went both ways. Battiato admired Capone and Quinn for their service to the country and for the way they planned and now operated the most successful gambling operation in the city. He valued their business sense and was well aware of their personal toughness, as well as the support they received from people like Zatz and Simpson. It was a mutually-favorable business arrangement for all parties. He liked to say, "If it isn't broke, don't fix it."

If Randinoli was absent when Battiato showed up, someone searched for him. "Come get me when Louie is in the neighborhood."

"Gabe idolizes Louie Battiato, never takes his eyes off the big guy." Shadow Deltucci was not the only one to notice the obvious.

Mason had heard it many times before. One hot and humid weekend, the younger guys from the corner drove to the Jersey Shore. The two were lying on the beach at Seaside Park, drinking cold beer, when Randinoli said, "Louie is the real deal. I would do anything to be in his shoes—someday."

Mike Cooper, a well-known pimp, operated his stable of high-class prostitutes from the plush surroundings of the Addison Hotel on Park Place in Newark. He played craps very conservatively, did not bet heavy. Win or lose, he always managed to schedule a few of the crapshooters to an evening of booze and depravity. He'd say, "If you behave, Connie may be available."

Connie Turner, a tall, strikingly beautiful and shapely woman, was rated as the most desirable and proficient prostitute in the city. Her clientele paid extra. The johns never complained of the price. The rumor attached to Turner was that most of her money went to the support of a bedridden brother. Her sibling, a former Newark cop, was shot two times while apprehending a couple of lowlife B&E perps in the Vailsburg section. He would never walk again. Much of her customer base came from cops and lawyers.

Each night when dark settled, Capone and Quinn supervised the lighting of the candles. They directed one or two of the young guys to place the thick, ten-inch candles in strategic places outlining the area of the "shooting alley." An ingenious idea, it served its purpose since the introduction of the game in the schoolyard. The flickering candles emitted an ethereal presence. When the candles glowed, the kibitzers mocked the church's Latin refrains, singing, "Yo Danny, "Who's got the dominoes?" The reply, always the same, "Benny's got the dominoes." Quinn shouted, "You jerks will burn in hell making fun of the Mass."

"Tony, we were first team altar boys at St. Joe's, we dig that Latin music." Danny Sherman and Joey Coughlin never missed an opportunity to perform for the players. They chanted in solemn, two-part harmony, "Who's got the dominoes? Benny's got the dominoes"—their version of *Benedictus Dominos*. They figured it was safe since TJ was not around to smack them for bastardizing the Latin.

Every day the schoolyard, which featured many Damon Runyon-type characters, promised some level of controversy. Joey Coughlin always said, "On Bruce Street, you ask the question, there's always someone with an answer, always something to learn. The wrong question, watch out!" One overcast Saturday afternoon, Jack Tocco asked what he believed to be a legitimate question. "How come Blackie still gets unemployment checks?"

Quinn overheard the question. He waited to see if Tocco's query would start an unnecessary discussion among the small group. He walked up to Tocco. "What is your problem?"

"No problem, I was just wondering, I mean, he never worked, right?" Tocco was now entering uncharted waters. Everyone on the corner was aware that Capone cashed his monthly checks at Chick Rozella's Palace, the "candy" store at the corner of 12ᵗʰ and Bruce. The checks arrived like clockwork on the first of the month. No one ever dared raise the subject.

"You were just wondering." Tony was not pleased with anyone asking questions concerning his partner. He spoke slowly and clearly. "Maybe he is just a very deserving American. Maybe he's being rewarded for his exemplary military record. Maybe you have never heard his philosophy concerning his business." His voice became a little louder as he got in Tocco's face.

"Whoa Tony, I meant no disrespect, I . . . ." He never finished the sentence.

"So, I will bring you up to date. Mr. Capone believes and very strongly, I might add, that there are two kinds of business. One, there is his business, and two, there is none of your fucking business."

His eyes squinted as though he just walked into bright sunlight. Still by no means a slouch, Tocco understood that this was Tony Quinn speaking. "Okay Tony, I apologize. It won't happen again." The others enjoyed a sense of relief.

Zatz was dead right in assessing the situation. "He showed good sense, dropping the topic in a hurry. Tocco would have been dropped in a hurry."

The subject never surfaced again. Tony's explanation was sufficient to end the matter and more importantly, Capone was unaware of the incident. There was speculation about what would happen if Capone learned of Tocco's inquiry.

Capone held the most interesting opinions on a myriad of subjects. He once explained to the younger Mason and Randinoli his philosophy on forgiveness. Capone said, "It is okay to forgive your enemy, but remember the asshole's name." Capone and Quinn, both voracious readers, let go with one-liners on a daily basis, one of the reasons the two were inseparable.

The crap game progressed to become the biggest in the New York-New Jersey metropolitan area. Thousands of dollars changed hands each day. The game boasted the most people participating, the largest amount of money exchanging hands, and the fattest amount of "hush" paid to the cops. It was common to see two lines of ten or more players on either side of the player with the dice, the shooter. Most of them "do" bettors, betting the dice will stop at the number they bet, before the shooter throws a seven. The wise guys, backed mostly by Battiato family money, more often than not covered the action betting against the dice. The wise guys did very well, especially when the game attracted outside-the-neighborhood participation. Zebep Fabrizio represented the Battiato interest and became an ever-present participant at the 12th and Bruce crap game.

Fabrizio, a Sicilian immigrant and built like a fire hydrant, won accolades from Quinn. "The man is incredible. He can cover eight to ten bets at a time. Zebep never misses a beat. No one has ever witnessed a mistake by the guy and he never sleeps—he can stand day and night covering the action. Maybe it's the never-ending supply of Pepsi and Devil Dogs that keeps him going."

Capone agreed. "The guy stands on his feet for six or eight hours, never pees, and for his main meals he eats Chick's greasy sausage and meatball sandwiches loaded with peppers and onions, and he's back bright and early the next day."

The police took payoffs to stay out of the playground, although on occasion an enthusiastic young Newark detective would appear unexpectedly, break up the crap game and book a few of the better known Battiato members. Someone forgot to inform the new cop of the rules.

The mobsters usually returned to the schoolyard within a few hours. Phil Battiato took a bust in stride. "Hey, did I miss anything? I would have been back sooner but the desk sergeant is a friend. He wanted me to look at a ton of pictures of his new grandson—one ugly little shit."

Humor was always present in the schoolyard. Throughout the crap game, the operators always laid out a few bucks to two of the younger kids whose assignment was to have a good view of all of Bruce Street and Morris Avenue. They reported to Capone and Quinn unrecognized cops or first-time visitors. The operators paid extra to one of the more agile youths to shimmy a drainpipe up the school's three stories to the roof. Most times this worked just fine, although some nights the cops were too quick and on top of the crapshooters in a flash. Louie Doherty and Bebba Kaskie were the top two climbers. Of course, night duty cost the operators a little more. The "youths" were not yet thirteen but did not lack street smarts. They put a fair value on their athleticism and charged accordingly. Quinn often said, "You two squirts are well on your way to successful political careers. You squeeze every nickel you can from the poor working man."

With few exceptions, everyone gambled on something in the schoolyard. The choices were many: craps, cards, checkers, basketball, softball, pitching nickels or quarters, and even stickball.

There was gambling on guessing closest to the time of day the forecasted rain would start. "I felt a drop, I win."

"That's sweat, you moron."

Mason did well at craps, and one of the few who won a little more than he lost. He discovered early on that for him it paid to be a "don't" bettor. Louie Battiato liked him and schooled him on the subtleties of the game. "Remember Brad, betting against the dice is the way to go." The "do" bettors outnumbered the "don'ts" which meant that betting against the dice required a formidable bankroll.

Mason picked his spots. When the game was small, then he would cover all the action laying the odds against the dice. During one summer, he and Randinoli decided to join forces. Mason made clear the business plan. "We are equal partners. We'll spend time at only three games; Bruce Street of course, 8ᵗʰ Street and the warehouse on Central Avenue. No branching out, right?"

"Okay, that will keep us busy enough." Surprisingly Randinoli lived up to the agreement and the young syndicate enjoyed a financially beneficial summer—without getting locked up. His behavior was near normal until the end of the summer. The business enterprise ended when Randinoli, working alone, got upset with a player at the warehouse. He arrived at one of his decisions and the crapshooter arrived at the emergency room at City Hospital. When Mason heard of the incident he ended the partnership. He was certain that his ex-partner would provide a very convincing story for the latest action. The poor victim probably took too long to pay the twenty dollars he owed—that certainly validated the beating.

Once asked to describe the two friends, Quinn said, "Brad is this guy and Gabe is that guy. Period. They are friends but with very different personalities and heading in totally different directions."

His partner the philosopher agreed. Capone said, "It may be more than their personalities that differ. However they wind up, they'll take with them the lessons learned at 12ᵗʰ and Bruce."

Randinoli admired Quinn and Capone—and their lifestyles. "Man, they are so cool. They always look good. They have big cars and plenty of money." He laughed aloud. "And they never have to work. They run the crap game, man that's livin'."

Mason also liked the two older crapshooters, but believed that both might serve more jail time. This also made him question the future of the neighborhood. "The game cannot go on forever. Do they go back to old habits, get pinched and do more time or get real jobs? They both tried a few days on the roof. The money was good but that was hard work and not their cup of tea."

Randinoli said, "Hey, do not start with that law and order shit, please. You make more scratch shootin' dice than anyone in the schoolyard does. We need someone to organize, set the times, and handle the cops so Brad can play craps, right. You have no place to complain." Randinoli was pleased with his commentary.

Mason knew his friend was making sense as far as the game goes, but not for his hero worship of the organizers. "And I am glad the game is available. I like Blackie and Tony. I just don't want to end up like any of those guys, Capone or Quinn or the Battiatos, or anyone who makes a living without working a real job." He paused, "I look up to my father and to Cuban Pete Randinoli and the men in the neighborhood who do real work." *That should shut him up.*

Not a chance. "You are a real pain in the ass. I've told you a hundred times, with my brains and good looks and your lengthy sermons and right hand, we could own this city. We could muscle every one of the wise guys out, and operate the biggest games in the city." He wrinkled his forehead, feigning deep thought. "Make that the state!"

Although Randinoli sounded as though he was half kidding, he would try anything once. Mason was now dead serious and he made sure his friend heard every word. "Keep it up long enough, you get to the point where you believe it, you act on it, and you're history."

The conflict continued. This was not the first time the two friends had this conversation, and likely not the last.

Capone liked Mason since the kid first came to the corner. Now it was time to think about where the game would move once the inevitable happened to the city. One late Monday evening while he was taking a break from the game, Capone motioned to Mason. He wanted to speak with him.

They walked around the Morris Avenue side of the school and sat on the concrete stairs of the building.

Capone lit a stogie. Capone loved smoking the short, inexpensive cigar, and was always a good bet to have an ample supply of the terrible-smelling smokes. Quinn loved to tease his partner. He would say, "My God Blackie, it's a miracle we still have players returning to the game. Those things smell worse than Dutch Bauer's only undershirt." This comment— a friendly shot at the popular bartender at the club.

Capone said, "Brad, I think everyone knows that someday you will be a cop and a good one. You won't take advantage of people."

Surprised at this cop talk from a guy who seldom speaks, Mason said, "I don't know Blackie, but it's on my mind. What do you think?"

Capone felt honored—the kid he watched grow up was asking for his opinion. "I think you should go after it, you would be a good one. You would bust the real bad people, leave the crapshooters alone, right?"

"Of course, a friendly crap game keeps the kids off the street." They both laughed.

"Okay, now listen to what I say. This city is getting ready for a big explosion. You need to get out of the neighborhood as fast as possible. When the time comes, go into law enforcement someplace else, not in Newark." Capone paused to draw a big pull on his withered stogie.

Mason was confused. "Why not work in Newark? God knows we need cops."

Capone had been preparing for this conversation for some time. "Listen, Newark is going to go through real tough times. It's time to move on. Block busting is a well-organized method for moving white people out and blacks into the city. Look around the ward, poor blacks are moving in by the busloads. A lot of them are coming from the South because of bullshit promises that life here will be a whole lot better. Many of the people living here now will not move out without a fight. The NAACP is determined to force the whites out to make room for their people. It's already started. There will be real trouble, maybe riots. In a few years, you'll be getting married. Cops working in the city will be forced to live here. Newark will not be a good place to raise a family. It will happen fast. We won't recognize this place. Sad to say, the game will be history as well. Tony and I have been looking at options." He offered a little smile. "We will relocate to some godforsaken place like Hillside." Not any too happy with his words, Capone was dead certain of his position.

Less than a decade later, Capone's prophesy materialized. In 1967, the riots that took place in Newark lasted from July 12 to July 17. The five days brought killings, beatings, looting and all the mayhem that goes with it. Even Capone was shocked at the human suffering. In the end, there were twenty-six dead and hundreds injured. One of his friends, a Korean vet, said, "Korea was bad but this is the United States of America. This is Newark, New Jersey. The world is going crazy."

Chapter Thirteen

Newark's worst ghetto

After serving two turbulent terms, Newark's mayor, the Honorable Marshall P. Creedon, planned on seeking an unprecedented third term in office. The goal was to finish out the decade as the longest serving mayor in the city's history. And, of course, steal as much money as possible before exiting the office. However, the Creedon political machine could not ignore the facts. They were well aware that the incumbent would face a bloody battle to secure another term in the upcoming 1954 elections. Creedon's performance in office, even more importantly his lack of performance, was now noticed by more and more of the voters. His machine, comprised of no-show city hall employees, would do whatever it took to keep their man in power.

Creedon's opponent, Robert Q. Blango, a young black man from the Central Ward, appeared to be a more than worthy adversary. Blango articulated a well-planned agenda that included ridding city hall of the lifelong hacks.

A desperate incumbent, Creedon would say anything to ensure re-election. In the middle of a ragged re-election speech to non-Central Ward folks, the mayor forgot his survival required a large surplus of votes from the Central Ward. The press covering the campaign salivated at his faux pas when, referring to the Central Ward, Creedon said, "It is the worst place in the city, an absolute disgrace." Rambling on, he said, "Our city is plagued with five ghettos and the 12th Avenue and Bruce Street section of the Central Ward is by far the worst."

Ghetto was a word heard for the first time by many of the voters. Hanging on the corner, Fat Barteck said, "Whatever happened to the slums? Ya know, I think I like ghetto better, more class."

The mayor did not stop there. Sounding as though he possessed firsthand information, Creedon, for some unknown reason, targeted the corner. "12th Avenue and Bruce Street is the center of Newark's worst ghetto area and when I'm re-elected, I'll continue with my determination to clean it up."

Martin Hatlas, a product of 12th Avenue and Bruce Street and a confidante of Mason's, knew more about corruption at city hall than any of the other investigative reporters. Hatlas's ambitious election coverage in the Star-Ledger sustained the heat on the entire Creedon corrupt political machine. It appeared his FBI and Newark Police Department sources provided Hatlas with names and just enough information to draw attention to the politicians and their benefactors. The pressure later paid off. Employees not pleased with the idea of doing jail time came forward and testified in the "Newark's Disgrace" cases in federal court. Hatlas came up with the headline title as an added hook for his readers. Unfortunately, the defendants were city employees caught using their positions to grant favors in return for money. Anything they could say regarding Creedon was hearsay, so His Honor continued to escape indictment.

On two occasions during his time in office, Creedon came close to answering federal indictments. Mason followed the coverage closely, impressed with the FBI's investigation.

During his senior year in high school, Mason got into a spirited and near-heated discussion with Mrs. Oliver, the popular history-civics teacher. The topic centered on the mayor and his performance. She, an obvious supporter, believed the public always gets what it deserves. "The citizens remain on the sidelines and do not give enough credit for those who seek elective office, campaign hard, and serve the people." This was her opinion even though she was well aware that Creedon won the last election virtually unopposed, receiving the strong support of an entrenched and powerful political machine.

The teacher went further. "If more people became involved in everyday politics, Mr. Mason, don't you think the system would work better?"

Mason replied, "I certainly do. But I believe that once elected, politicians do not own the right to take advantage and abuse the system. Serve the people? It makes no difference whether the public official is elected or appointed. They accept the big paydays to take on the responsibility to do a job. Mayor Creedon's responsibility is to do the best he can for all the citizens. It's no secret that he takes care of himself and his cronies." This encouraged a few others to participate in the discussion.

"Why hasn't he been indicted?" This from a cheerleader not usually involved in class discussion.

Mrs. Oliver said, "There have been allegations but he has not been found guilty of any crimes. And we are all aware that in this country a person is innocent until proven guilty. There is no evidence of wrongdoing."

The largest member of the football team could not resist. He said, "Mrs. O, that's what they said about the Correlones." This drew a round of laughter.

"Don't you think the mayor could avoid all the hoopla by just answering the allegations without hiding behind a truckload of lawyers—all paid for by the taxpayers?" Mason was aware that his reporter friend from the Star-Ledger was positive Creedon was hiding a bunch of wrongdoing.

Before the teacher responded the bell sounded, signaling the end of the period. There was a slight moan. The class enjoyed the give and take. Mrs. Oliver said, "Okay, maybe we will pick up on this another time." She looked at Mason, smiled, then said, "Or maybe not." The teacher and student enjoyed taking part in the joust. Mrs. Oliver once confided as much to Mason. "Mr. Mason, it's discussions like these that add to making my class one of the most popular in the school."

Unable to resist, Mason said, "As any good politician would say, 'Where's my end? I don't get a piece of the action?'"

Mrs. Oliver, who truly liked her student, said, "An A is more than enough pay off. Don't push your luck."

Mason realized that teachers were required to communicate the mandatory school committee agenda. He always wanted to hear what teachers believed personally, in particular when it came to the law, law enforcement, politics and politicians. He utilized the Blackie Capone approach. "Know your subject then stay on the offense." His sometimes over-participation in class contributed to excellent grades in high school.

Mason's school routine seldom altered, consisting of classes, after-school sports, and an occasional dance in the gymnasium. He was always accompanied by his now-steady girlfriend, Ann Murphy, a pretty brunette he met at a dance at Saint Charles Academy earlier in the year. The academy was large by Newark standards, occupying an entire city block in the Central Ward. Beautifully landscaped in the spring and summer months, the big structure was located across the West Market Street side of St. Joseph's property. Mason and Randinoli spent time doing odd jobs, including cutting grass in the summer and shoveling the winter snow.

 Like his friends, Mason also spent too many nights at boring music rehearsals in St. Joe's hall or marching and maneuvering drills at the local armory. In contrast, Randinoli was completely finished with his high school education. He spent time hanging out on the corner and would sneak into a downtown movie or, if he had some money, would try his luck at one of the other crap games in the city. He also made a few trips to Atlantic City or to Yonkers Raceway to bet on the trotters. He could not find enough to do and had too much idle time on his hands. Still, he said it often—*I am a very busy man.*

Mason always talked to his friend about staying in school, but Randinoli would cut it short. "Let it go, I made my decision. I wasted enough time in school. I have things to do."

After one of the sessions with Mrs. Oliver, Mason stopped by the schoolyard. He and Capone talked about the press coverage of the mayor's problems. Mason said, "Creedon knows how to use his media hacks. I like the way the bureau deals with the press. They hold back on the statements. They have a standard "no comment" response regarding a pending investigation, period. I suppose they don't want to give out anything to help the perp during trial."

Capone was not surprised. "Holy shit, you sound more like an FBI agent every day."

The Newark FBI agents who were assigned the political corruption case continued to search out a cooperating witness—a person having firsthand knowledge of the shady dealings of the mayor, and/or his bagman. It was common knowledge that the bagman was the infamous Eddy Creedon, the mayor's smooth-talking brother. The media, in particular Martin Hatlas's column, hammered away at the Creedons' reputation for ties to city building contractors as well as their obvious close cooperation with crooked union bosses. A few of the so-called leaders in the black community stirred up the neighborhoods by shouting that the mayor's dirty politics caused people to feel left out and that rioting would be a justified response.

The handful of instigators blamed this type of *quid pro quo* political corruption as the contributing factor to the mid-sixties arsons and riots throughout the city.

Hatlas loved the neighborhood and the variety of people. Unlike his friends Mason and Randinoli, the reporter, as a young man, was too busy with school work to participate in the drum corps or gambling activities. He had a short, stocky, yet well-defined physique and handled himself on the streets when necessary. The reporter became a regular at the basketball and softball games in the schoolyard. The two often discussed what they wanted to do with their lives. Mason would seek a career in law enforcement while Hatlas would write at some level.

"Brad, you will be a great cop or "statey" or fed, whichever you choose," Hatlas said. As a young student at St. Joe's, Hatlas possessed and demonstrated a knack with words. It was a gift. He, the editor of the school paper in high school and college, always questioned political decisions and had an aptitude for describing people, places and things on paper. His writing covered other areas of interest, as well. When a few of the 12th and Bruce people fought in the Golden Gloves, he accepted the extra assignment, covered the bouts for the Star-Ledger, and received kudos from his boss.

Tony Quinn once said to Hatlas, "Someday you'll contribute to make things better in our neighborhood and the city and," pumping a fist in the air, "perhaps even the world."

"Tony, maybe I'll write a novel dealing with the art of crapshooting." Hatlas was only half serious.

"That's fine, but no pictures."

Mason was proud of Hatlas's investigative reporting. Mason could hear his friend's voice when he read his words in print. In one column titled "A Done Deal," Hatlas wrote, "With Mayor Creedon and his brother in control, Newark will never be short of quid pro quos. If you need something to happen in Newark, take care of the Creedons and it's a done deal. The man is a dealer." Hatlas never concerned himself with possible lawsuits. Over a few beers at the club, he once told his friends, "I report what I can back up—at least most of what I can back up. My boss never complains. Anyway, can you imagine the number of Ledgers we'd sell if Creedon brought legal action against the paper?"

The Hatlas columns never failed to point out that "His Honor now spends more time at his palatial estate in Margate than his mansion in Vailsburg." Each story included pictures of the huge home at the Jersey Shore, depicting the mayor's "guests" coming and going. They included some shady businessmen and even a few known local gangsters. The stories of the corrupt administration continued to fill major newspapers, radio and television.

The neighborhood residents, particularly the more senior ones, were both angry and disgusted by the mayor's words. The shoe cobbler on the corner of Bergen and Cabinet Streets, Vito Moreno, angrily asked, "What the hell is that bum talkin' about? No one's ever seen his sorry ass up here. Our people work hard when they can find work. We pay taxes, keep our homes clean, some even go to churches and synagogues. That jerk doesn't understand the most important thing, we all watch out for each other." The more he spoke, the angrier Moreno became. "Ghetto? This is where we live and raise our families. This is not a ghetto but a good place to live. Will that moron come here lookin' for votes and say that garbage in front of us who call this home? You can bet your ass he won't. The guy stinks!" Moreno's outrage mirrored the perspective of the entire Central Ward community. They were as one when an outsider focused on their neighborhood.

Anthony Washington, a parishioner at St. Joe's and one of a dozen attorneys with offices in the Central Ward, remarked, "Creedon must be smoking something. We thought we had it made and His Honor is telling everyone we live in the worst ghetto in the city of Newark." Washington, a black man, wrote a strong letter to Creedon demanding an apology. Not surprisingly, the mayor ignored Washington's understandable outrage. Hatlas made sure the letter was published in the weekend edition.

The Central Ward residents took the mayor's political cheap shot personally. The less educated on the corner of 12th and Bruce, and those in the schoolyard, each spoke of Creedon's remarks. Even the crap game was included in the outrage. A few of the older crapshooters talked about paying "Marshy Boy" a visit to his home in the Vailsburg section, or to city hall.

Mayoral candidate Robert Q. Blango, known as "Bobby Q," would have the support of the Central Ward. A lifelong parishioner of St. Joe's, he was well known in the neighborhood, a frequent visitor to the crap game and well-liked by the 12th and Bruce residents. Blango attended college with Martin Hatlas at Seton Hall and would likely gain the support of the influential newspaper.

Randinoli attempted to form a group from 12th and Bruce to visit the mayor at the Jersey Shore. "I can't stand meatheads that talk about somethin' they don't know nothin' about. We move a couple of carloads down the Garden State Parkway and pay the shithead a visit. Zatzie can fix me up with the necessaries. A little house fire always gets attention." The others knew he meant every word.

Cooler heads prevailed. Tony Quinn, always the voice of reason, said, "No one visits His Honor. The bum is not worth any of our people going to the joint. The payback will have to wait until the next election. Bobby Q. deserves a shot. We make sure the ward comes out strong."

On a positive note, the mayor's slurs caused people to pay attention to what was happening at city hall and they began to engage themselves in local politics.

During a summer session his senior year in high school, Mason became friends with Barbara Creedon, who was also a senior at the very private and prestigious St. Charles Academy and a friend of Ann Murphy's. He and Creedon were in the same biology class that offered extra credit. He found her to be a quiet person and difficult to engage in conversation. The two never discussed politics.

Barbara Creedon's father, His Honor Marshall P. Creedon, was now getting hammered by both Newark's newspapers. The mayor's wish to serve an unprecedented three terms as Newark's number one politician started to fade. Thanks to Martin Hatlas and his coverage in the Star-Ledger, it was now more fact than rumor that Creedon's machine was an out-of-control corrupt organization. In one column, he compared the Creedon political machine to those of Chicago, Detroit and other large urban cities. "The Creedons would do well in these cities. The mayor makes the corruption in New York look like stealing from a cookie jar."

Mason made the mistake of telling his friends on the corner about his platonic relationship with the mayor's daughter.

Unrelentness with the cheap shots, Randinoli fired the first round, saying, "Brad, how you can date that broad, after what her old man said about the corner?"

"Date? I'm working undercover for the FBI, getting first-hand information of the crooked deals at city hall." Mason would attempt anything to keep Randinoli quiet. It never worked.

Capone and Quinn usually found Randinoli to be helpful. They could take time off knowing that business would not suffer. The high school dropout surprised his father on a few occasions by visiting the Randinoli tailor shop on Clinton Avenue. One of the elder statesmen of the neighborhood, Cuban Pete was always happy to see his only son, yet sad to know that he would not graduate from high school. "Maybe you go back next year and you like it."

"Maybe Pop, we'll see how things go." This said more to appease his father than anything else.

Randinoli was involved in other adventures that no one heard about. He was in and out of trouble, but never serious enough to spend time in jail. Now exposed to new people showing up at the crap game, Randinoli met a guy who claimed to be an automobile mechanic. It turned out that "Wrench" operated a chop shop for stolen cars. Nothing to do with mechanics, the nickname was the result of slugging a guy with a lug wrench. He let people believe what they wanted to. Car thieves brought him the stolen vehicles; he disassembled the parts and sold everything a la carte. His business boomed. One day he took Randinoli aside and offered a proposition.

"Gabe, you look like you can handle yourself. You do a good job of filling in and running the game. I won't waste your time. There's a 1951 black Super Estate on the Buick parking lot on Halsey Street. It'll be there for a few days, I don't know, in for some small leak problem. Anyway, my source says it came in last night and it'll drive out without a problem. If you think you can handle it, your end is two C notes. Cold cash on delivery. You drop it off, you get the dough. That's if you're interested."

Randinoli heard the cold cash part, and said, "Sure, maybe tonight. Will you be at your garage?"

"I'm there all night." He asked, "No problem with the ignition wires? This ain't your first boost, right? No problem crossing the wires? I ask just to be sure."

"No, that year and model should be a piece of cake." Randinoli sounded convincing. He didn't have a clue. It would be no problem; he watched the wire thing in the movies plenty of times.

Later, Tony Quinn asked, "What did Wrench want?"

Randinoli sounded casual. "Nothin'—he was tellin' me about his business. He may need some help sometime and said he would keep me in mind." He didn't mention the two hundred dollars he would get for lifting a car.

"Forget that guy. You'll wind up in jail in a heartbeat. He has people who take all the risk while he grabs the big money. Stay here where you know what's going on. I'm not kidding with you. You hear me?" Quinn made it clear that Wrench was bad business.

"Tony, I hear you." Randinoli laughed. "I think they heard you downtown."

He waited until it was dark and Randinoli walked the ten blocks to the Buick dealership on Halsey Street. It was a quiet evening, minimum bus traffic. Of course he was prepared. His tools included a screw driver and pliers he borrowed from the back of Deylan's pickup truck.

There it sat, just as Wrench described. He walked slowly to the Buick and found the driver side door open. Randinoli figured Wrench was responsible for this stroke of luck. He got in and sat in the driver's seat and closed the door. The soon-to-be car thief bent over and picked at a couple of wires with his handy tool, the screw driver. He ignored what he thought smelled like gasoline. *Car lots are supposed to smell*. He reached in his jacket pocket and removed the pliers. The car thief had made a decision. He yanked at the wires until some were loose, then he rubbed the ends together. He heard the spark and felt the fire on his hands.

The explosion was audible for blocks. Randinoli rolled out of the car and ran as fast as he could and did not stop until he reached the schoolyard. The crapshooters were doing their thing, some cheering and others moaning. The candles flickered a little from a slight breeze. His mind raced. He would tell Wrench the car was afire when he arrived at the lot. He would say, "I didn't stay around to see what was happening." His short-lived career in the car theft industry ended on a sour note. Randinoli snuck out of the darkened schoolyard and went straight home. He bathed both hands in ice water and felt better. The damage was not so bad; he got away before the entire car erupted in flames.

Maybe the gasoline was the problem.

Chapter Fourteen

Goodbye Hilltoppers

TJ near did everything in his power to keep the boys in the Hilltoppers for at least one more year. He promised to reduce the required rehearsals, which he never did. The following year—1955—the corps travelled to Miami to participate in the Orange Bowl halftime show. The older members, anxious to move on to other interests, were asked by TJ to show up for this contract. He knew their days with the corps were short lived and needed them to make this one last show.

The previous summer, at the VFW State Championships in Asbury Park, New Jersey, a group of local toughs picked the wrong bus to raid. They expected to walk away with money and maybe some valuable equipment. Many people often grouped drum corps personnel with a derogatory term, "raggedy ass bands," and wrongly classified them as lightweights off the field of competition. In this instance, the locals made a big mistake. After the performance, the members physically removed the intruders from St. Joes' bus. The town ambulance squad transported a few of the surprised gang to the emergency room at the local hospital.

Mr. Meade helped restore order and commented, "Well, it would have been a lot worse if Mr. Randinoli made it to the bus."

During the announcement of the competition results, the VFW commandant bellowed into the public address microphone. "Ladies and Gentlemen, the ambulance wasn't here for any member of any of the competing corps." The explanation was clear to the spectators that understood the lingo. Often in hot and humid weather, marchers dehydrated and "went down" in the stress of competition, which was how they described that a marcher had fainted. Scully summed up the situation. "Everything is fine folks. Some people inadvertently selected the wrong bus and were strongly asked to leave." The other corps and many in the crowd of spectators grasped exactly what he said.

Big Jack said, "The Orange Bowl, definitely my last gig." He echoed the feelings of many of the "old-timers." Some had spent nearly ten years as members of the Hilltoppers.

The bus journey was extra-long because of accidents and unusually heavy traffic on interstate highway I-95. The hot August summer did not help the moods of the passengers. TJ ordered Leo the driver to stop at a Miami Shores roadside restaurant. The bright orange and green sign invited customers to enjoy cold, fresh-made Florida orange juice. The humidity rose to a new high, and the northerners looked forward to the break away from the monotonous bus trip.

The drum and bugle presence added to an already crowded restaurant. Every booth filled quickly. Nick Macaluso, a soprano horn player from Queens, found the last seat at the thirty-seat counter and, without delay, placed his order. Nick's physique featured big broad shoulders, the result of his weight-lifting regimen. Recruited last year by the St Joe's horn instructor, Macaluso fit in immediately and got along with everyone. The big horn player joined St. Joe's after spending several years in a top-notch New York outfit and was a welcomed addition to an already nationally-acclaimed brass section.

Macaluso gulped down half of the fresh-squeezed, cold orange juice then left to use the restroom. When he returned, Randinoli occupied his seat.

Nick smiled. Obviously the tenor drummer made a mistake. "Gabe, that's my drink and here comes my lunch." The young man behind the counter placed Nick's cheeseburger and French fries on the counter.

Randinoli had already reached a decision. He mumbled a lame excuse and suggested Macaluso find another seat as he perused the menu. Macaluso was no less tired and hungry than everyone else. The very capable New Yorker was in no mood to take crap from anyone, including the tough Randinoli. He knew some of Randinoli's reputation but was not intimidated. He had been tested in New York on a few occasions and finished in good shape. Many customers and corps members now paid attention to the discussion. Still on the bus and unaware of the potential confrontation, Mason slept soundly.

His crimson hair hanging over bright blue eyes, the young, freckled-face soda jerk sensed trouble brewing. He politely announced, to no one in particular, "I told this gentleman that the seat was already occupied and I had placed the food order." The clerk hoped this attempt would convince Randinoli to relinquish the seat. He smiled and continued. "You may not have seen the juice. It really is this gentleman's seat." For some reason, the young southern gentleman presumed he was speaking with a fair and reasonable person. Randinoli ignored the clerk, continued reading the menu, and became angrier as the horn player and the employee pursued the matter. Not interested in fairness or the gist of the discussion, Randinoli heard only bothersome noise.

Macaluso felt obligated to speak and offer Randinoli an out. "Gabe, tell you what, I'll gobble it down, you'll be eating in a few minutes."

The other diners offered comments as they became more aware of the situation. If a majority vote counted for anything, the tenor drummer would come in second. Randinoli's always-present mean streak readied itself to rear its ugly head and explode.

Randinoli had definitely arrived at another of his decisions. Without looking around at Macaluso, he stared down at the place setting and slowly said, "Okay, you're tellin' me to get up." He turned around to face the New Yorker. "If I get up, you go down. Which is it?"

A few of the diners within earshot tried to calm things down. An elderly woman said, "Now boys, you act nice now."

Macaluso had hoped that a reasonable approach would end it. He was not going to back down. "Gabe, you know this is my seat. Why act like a jerk?"

Randinoli placed the menu on the counter and, without looking up, said, "So I get up, right?"

Nick answered, "Right, that would be the…" He never finished the sentence. As he turned and looked in the direction of the young man behind the counter, Randinoli spoke.

"I get up, you go down." Randinoli spun around on the stool, and in one motion—Boom! The straight right hand landed on the side of Macaluso's chin, bone-on-bone resonating throughout the restaurant. The horn player fell down sideways, landing on his right side and shoulder. He did not move. One big groan came from the spectators.

Amidst the vocal protests from the startled diners, Randinoli said nothing, looked straight ahead and made his exit. The choice made, the action taken, and the mean streak got meaner. Still within hearing distance of the diners, he said, "I wouldn't eat that slop anyway." He reached in his shirt pocket for a cigarette as he left the restaurant.

For Randinoli, that was his last act of brutality as a member of St. Joe's. He had things on his mind—very important things. He smiled as he thought, "*anyway, Brad can't lecture about kickin'.*" The trip continued without any further distraction. Mason did not learn of the stopover in Miami until days later. He elected not to comment on the incident to anyone, including Randinoli. The others knew how Mason always tried to get through to Randinoli but the tenor drummer still increased his sadistic behavior. *Why talk? He made a decision.*

Mason, Randinoli and a few close friends followed through on their resolves and left the corps and all the memories after the Miami trip. The time-consuming rehearsals, competitions, occasional long parades and grueling bus rides all interfered with their plans for the future. In recent years, TJ spoke only the same mantra—"for the good of the corps." He was not concerned with any individual's plans for the future. Mason and others regretted they did not leave years earlier. There were many things they wanted to do but had felt an obligation, even pressure, to remain with the corps. A few parishioners were more than upset at their departure. One of the women from the Rosary Sodality said, "After all that man has done for you, and now you're just up and leaving. You all should be ashamed of yourselves."

When Randinoli heard of the comment he went ballistic, totally forgetting his promise to Sister Francis regarding use of the "f" word. "That old broad should mind her own fucking business. We put the time in for near ten years, not that old hag. Let her stand out in the fucking rain for an hour waiting for a fucking rinky-dink parade to start or sit on a hot fucking bus listening to TJ rant and rave about somethin' that no one gives a fuck about. Shove it lady!"

His friend said, "Don't hold back. Tell us what you really think." He laughed with his friend. "I think you got your quota of fs in. That should do it for the rest of the year."

Mason, still working as a roofer during the summer, had plans to enroll in night classes at Rutgers, majoring in accounting with a minor in psychology. He knew that the FBI accepted only candidates with degrees in law or accounting.

He understood Randinoli's anger. It was tough during their teenage years, attempting to attend all the drum corps rehearsals while at the same time finding time to study and take part in sports and other extracurricular activities. TJ never said much about school. His focus was always a one-way street. The corps—period.

In Newark, many families now formed an exodus and "getting the hell out of the neighborhood, the Central Ward, and the city" was the objective. Mason fully realized that if he were to follow his dream of entering law enforcement, he needed more than a high school education. He told Capone,

"Blackie, you were right on the money about the demise of Newark. It is time to move on. 12th and Bruce was great growing up, but now it's history."

Randinoli had very different thoughts on his mind. He would take the corner experience with him to greater heights. His gambling experience, coupled with his guts, would aid him in his chosen career. There are wise guys and there are real wise guys. Gabe Randinoli would climb to the top of the gangster hill.

During the autumn of 1955, TJ was killed as the result of a terrible automobile accident. Alone in his vehicle, the car overturned on a busy New Jersey highway and he died instantly. Most of the corps alumni attended the funeral service at Saint Joe's and later reminisced over a few beers at the club.

Dutch Bauer was always happy to see the club filled with the old crowd. "I never get to see my boys unless someone dies, gets married, or gets out of the slammer."

Joey Coughlin sputtered, "Dutch, your boys are getting older. Some of us even vote. And more than one time, for the right price."

"I wish you could vote one more time for the soldier, General Dwight David Eisenhower. Man he will kick Stevenson's ass in '56." The comment was not a question. Bauer, a World War II veteran, read the daily newspapers and loved to talk politics, especially about Ike Eisenhower.

"Dutch, you like the president because he's of Pennsylvania Dutch heritage, just like you." A few were surprised that Jimmy Contino, the local bookie, was even aware of the president's name.

"Nothing wrong with that, Jimmy. The main thing is the man does what's good for the country. Not too many of those guys in Washington."

There were a few more memories spoken of TJ—most good, some not so good—and the night ended early.

Chapter Fifteen

I got it

The predicted hot summer of 1955 arrived with a vengeance. The usual activities were ongoing in the Bruce Street schoolyard. The one-basket basketball court was usually a three-on-three affair. As more white families migrated to the suburbs to take advantage of the better schools and extra space for the kids, black families moved to the city in record amounts. Ronald, a new addition to the neighborhood, showed his aggressiveness under the boards. He was big, black, and a welcomed player to the accelerated competition that seemed improved each day.

Harold Lee and company engaged in stickball and a game of "asses up."

Across the street, in the Morris Avenue "lot," a hotly contested softball game was under way. The area was the size of half a football field, truly a vacant lot, all dirt and stone with some broken glass mixed in. When used for football, the broken glass and sharp stones accounted for ripped pants and shirts as well as bloodied bodies.

A slow pitch game, Barteck was the pitcher, Randinoli was the batter and Carmen Riccio was catching, without a mask of course. Newark's hot sticky weather contributed to the participants' foul moods. Randinoli was more pissed off than usual.

"What the hell are we doin' here? It's like an oven. We should be at Point Pleasant, in the ocean, on the beach with the ladies."

Randinoli hit a mile-high ball that headed down towards fair territory, directly in front of home plate, a two-inch thick piece of slab.

Riccio positioned to make the catch, smacked his catcher's mitt and yelled, "I got it, I got it."

Randinoli yelled, "Carmen, I'm gonna hit it again." He pulled the bat back in position to swing.

At first base, Deltucci yelled, "Oh shit!"

Riccio never took his eyes off the ball, tapped his glove readying to catch it just as Randinoli stepped forward, his eyes on the ball, and quickly took a mighty swing.

Later the crapshooters across the street in the schoolyard related that they heard the noise. The sound was terrifying. The bat struck Riccio dead center on his nose, which was already one of the largest in Newark. The blood was everywhere, on the ground, on Riccio and Randinoli. Even Barteck, who ran in towards home plate, acquired a few drops. No doubt that a bone or two in Riccio's face would require attention. Flat on his back, he moaned in pain and covered his bloody face with both hands. Someone handed the injured young man a towel to cover his face. The skin around both eyes immediately blackened. Barteck, never to be counted on for sympathy, said, "He's alive, I saw him move." Months later, whenever the incident surfaced, Barteck opined, "The people in Bayonne heard Carmen wailing."

Randinoli held on to the bat, visibly upset. "What the shit were you tryin' to do? I said I was gonna hit the stupid ball again. You Sieges ever listen?"

The last comment honed in on the fact that Riccio's Italian heritage originated from Sicily, while Randinoli's father was a Napolitano, from Naples, Italy. Years later, during Randinoli's New York career, he learned that owning a Sicilian ancestry aided one's chosen profession.

The moans got even louder, indicating he did not appreciate the interrogation. Riccio thought only of survival and was in no mood to get into an argument over where his father was born. He suffered real pain.

Randinoli attempted to hide his concern, showing a devil-may-care attitude. He showed a stupid smirk and asked, "Really Carmen, you okay?"

Riccio's even louder wailing was interrupted by his answer. "Die, you rat bastard."

It took three players to lift Riccio and carry him to Joe Deylan's truck. They gently placed him in the bed of the pickup, which held all sorts of rusty tools, a deflated truck tire and a few other worthless relics.

Mason jumped in the back of the truck, and he and the others held back while Randinoli explained why he refused to go to the hospital.

"I can't stand the stinkin' Newark City Hospital, it's a butcher shop. If I ever get hurt, shoot me before shippin' me to that dump." This commentary did little for the patient, whose complaints grew louder while positioning the bloody towel over his smashed nose.

Barteck recalled an incident from earlier in the year, and later he shared the story. "Brad and Gabe were looking at a side roofing job over on West Bigelow Street by Clinton Avenue. They no sooner got out of the car when some guys emptied out from a gin mill and jumped them. When they got back to the corner, Blackie and Tony drove them both to the emergency room at the Newark City Hospital. They ignored Randinoli's whining. He wanted to go to Saint Michaels, at the furthest end of the city. Brad said the doctors and nurses were great, real professionals. They were x-rayed, some ice packs placed on the bruises, a few stitches and out the door. They were in and out in a matter of a few hours. Not Gabe, though, who complained for weeks about how he was mistreated. Everyone ignored him."

Deylan said, "Right. Brad said that it would've been worse if a few of the black guys from the projects didn't jump in. One of them recognized Brad from the PAL where the two boxed a few times."

The NCH owned a long and proud history. In spite of the reputation the NCH enjoyed statewide, Randinoli criticized the hospital at every opportunity.

In September 1882, the Newark City Hospital was constructed with the underlying purpose to care for "the indigent poor of the city of Newark." The name changed in 1968 to the Martland Medical Center; soon students from the best medical universities in the country considered the hospital the number one teaching hospital on the planet. Randinoli possessed as much knowledge of the hospital as he did about many subjects—virtually none.

Mason's mother Ellen and grandmother Bridgit, known as "Bridgie," worked in the doctors' dining room on the fourth floor. A clear physical contrast existed between the two women. Mrs. Mason was a tall and slender beauty with soft blue eyes. Bridgie, a St. Joe's icon, was all of five-foot-five and did the work of most men. She would feign being angry at the young kids living in the neighborhood by the hospital, take her teeth out and make funny faces, causing them to laugh uncontrollably. She always had the undeniable twinkle in her blue eyes. On Sunday mornings, her hoard of grandchildren would visit, and after answering the mandatory questions about school, friends and church, she rewarded each with enough change to go to the movies. Some weeks, if she thought she could spare it, the kids received an extra dime for candy or popcorn.

Irish immigrants, Mason's mother and grandmother were more than in-laws. They were the closest of friends who loved the family and being with each other at the work place. Mason's step-grandfather Ed Ellis cooked all the doctors' meals at the huge kitchen located on the fifth floor. On some afternoons after school, Mason and Randinoli would visit the family in the hospital. Ellis would place the young boys on the hand-pulled dumb waiter and ride them up and down, from floor to floor. These became happy memories that would last a lifetime. Mason's father Philip, a roofer, was quiet and spent most of his time sitting in the kitchen, drinking from a pitcher of beer and smoking too many cigarettes. His right hand was covered with the brown stain of nicotine, proof of his smoking from an early age.

Later, in the emergency room, the pain medication kicked in and Riccio felt a little better. "I will get even with that guy. He gets away with a lot of stuff, but not this time."

Barteck tried to ease the situation. "Ya know, Carmen, I think Gabe really feels bad about this."

Riccio never did get even and the painful accident was forgotten like so many other neighborhood misunderstandings. However, the fact that Randinoli again made a bad decision and escaped responsibility for his actions did not go unnoticed.

On the drive back to Riccio's house, the radio played "Everything Happens to Me," a Frank Sinatra oldie now moving up on the charts. Riccio's head dropped as if he were going to cry. Deylan, always the compassionate one in the crew, benevolently switched stations.

While his friends took their wounded friend to the hospital, the one responsible for the accident did not take the trip. Since quitting high school, Randinoli found himself with much idle time. A year ago, he did some work for one of the crapshooters he met in the schoolyard. "Wrench," a so-called automobile mechanic, turned out to be someone dealing in stolen cars, operating a chop shop, and selling parts to several steady customers. After a few conversations with the small-time thug, Randinoli agreed to steal a car and damn near burned himself to death in the process.

Still, he remained sure of himself and decided to give the car theft business another shot. He worked for the thug on a few more jobs that involved less mechanical aptitude. Not yet twenty, Randinoli skipped shaving for a few days and looked older than his years. He collected a few debts for Wrench, using as much violence as necessary.

Brad is wrong about that bein' held accountable stuff. I'm not held accountable for some of the stuff I do.

Chapter Sixteen

Chick's Palace, Corner of 12th and Bruce

Chick's Palace, as it was known by the local inhabitants, was a typical *candy store* at the northeast corner of 12th Avenue and Bruce Street, located in the middle of St. Joe's Parish in Newark's Central Ward. The store, less than one thousand square feet, went straight back from the two-step concrete entrance to a small kitchen in the back where the owners sat for family meals. This local hang out was owned and operated by Chick and Rosa Rozella. The couple was blessed with two small daughters who relentlessly whined and seemed to be constantly underfoot. Some in the neighborhood refused to patronize the store if the two little darlings were present.

The building, constructed in the early forties, looked tired and worn. The Palace accepted many paint jobs and people walking in for the first time were surprised how clean the inside of the store appeared. There was a green, faded mirror measuring five-feet high by eight-feet long behind the counter. The aisle behind the counter stools led to the famous back room. Heated by a new oil heater, this is where the roulette wheel spun every Friday night in the winter. The room consisted of a wooden table and four chairs to the left, and on the right by the only window, the often-used juke box. The kitchen in the back provided a small area for Rosa to prepare daily homemade soups and sandwiches for sale.

To the right of the store's entrance were a small newspaper stand and penny gumball machine and to the left, a bright red Formica soda counter with six stools. The Bruce street side of the store featured a glass candy case, a stack of newspapers and daily racing forms, a few magazines, a well-used pinball machine, and an ancient Wurlitzer 1015 juke box. The old record player continually repeated Johnnie Ray's "Cry," Frankie Laine's "I Believe," and Tony Bennett's "I Left My Heart in San Francisco"—with a few other scratchy gems mixed in.

The six stools at the counter were a favorite subject for Chick's infamous homilies, especially following a few anisettes. He sounded much like Professor Hill in "The Music Man" hawking musical instruments to the parents. "The chrome base, red leather swing-around stools cost me a bundle of money. If anyone knew what I paid to have them installed, they would not believe it." He conveniently forgot that most of his customers were already in the neighborhood when he bought the place in 1950 from the Forrestal family. The entire store remained the exact replica of the day the Rozellas assumed ownership. Everyone listened and accepted his interpretation of people, places and things.

Quinn summed it up. "It makes Chick feel good, so let him shovel the shit."

The Rozella kids presented a problem during the winter months when the well-attended roulette game took place on Friday nights. Quinn and Capone gave the crap game a reprieve from the cold weather and ran the game. Chick's Palace became the site of the roulette game the year the Rozellas assumed ownership, and the game was held in the back room to the left, immediately in front of the kitchen.

Rozella always accepted his piece of the pie, but the Battiatos stayed away from the Friday night event and did not take their usual cut from the game. "Too risky," Louie Battiato would say. "And for what? A few dollars?" To Capone and Quinn, he said, "Remember, we will not be anywhere near 12th and Bruce on the Friday night of your game. This is strictly your thing. The cops show, it's on you. I wish you luck." The entrepreneurs already took steps to ensure the security of the game. The crime boss missed the boat on the estimated earnings as well.

The gamblers tried to be nice to the little Rozella sweethearts, but when somebody was stuck a few hundred the darlings became "dirty-faced, pestering brats." For the unlucky, it became very frustrating.

On a typical Friday night, the game pulled in more gamblers than could be accommodated. The game caught on immediately. It was an attraction. Regulars knew enough to park their cars down the street or around the corner on Cabinet Street. Quinn made it very clear. "The wheel spins at seven p.m. The early birds are in. The rest wait outside in your cars or just hang around. We'll let you know when a spot opens up." They usually squeezed in twenty-five players, causing a lot of closeness. Not unlike the crap game, Quinn and Capone ran the roulette like pros, controlled the crowd and did a masterful job of bribing the brats with goodies all night. The kids would be so full of sundry candies and bubble gum they would be tired early and in bed before eight. Music from the jukebox was continuous—there was even some new stuff. The Continentals' "I Only Have Eyes for You" stuck on the turntable. After listening to "Are the stars out tonight?" repeated over and over, someone gave the old recorder the appropriate shove and The Continentals took a much needed break. Quinn paid one of the roof climbers to stand outside the front door. He planned for the unexpected visitors. If the cops showed up, the lookout would bang on the glass and then actually faint on the front steps, blocking entrance to the Palace.

Gamblers with lots of money often showed up, including wise guys, politicians, local businessmen and attorneys. One Friday night a real problem surfaced. When the story circulated that Randinoli was in the middle of the incident, no one looked shocked. "Big Al" Fornio, a known gambler from Newark's First Ward, appeared that night with two of his friends. They arrived early enough to be present at the start of the game. As the big man with the big belly gambled, his two friends stayed close to him and observed.

It happened that a half-dozen neighborhood people were in queue outside the store, waiting for players to leave so they could replace them. A degenerate gambler, Fornio was a heavy bettor and on this particular night, the more scotch he drank the more money he lost. Rozella did well with the booze concession.

Randinoli, a solid specimen at age nineteen and now concentrating on speaking the King's English, took Capone aside and reminded him of the situation outside. Pointing to Big Al's friends, he said, "Two outsiders are taking space watching the action, not playing, while our people are outside in the cold and can't get in the game." In truth, the tough kid from the corner simply did not like outsiders and did not trust too many people from outside his neighborhood. He did not need a lot of time to make a decision. Randinoli would find an excuse to hurt someone.

"He'll be done soon. Leave it for now." Fornio was now close to busting out and Capone wanted to keep things peaceful.

Big Al was concentrating on his picks and heard part of what Randinoli said, but not who said it. The scotch contributed to his loud voice. "Screw anyone else. We were here early. I'm stuck a bundle and these guys are my partners—they stay!" His two friends were doing their best to look tough as nails. They never removed their hands from the pockets of their stylish overcoats.

Through the years, a few of the neighborhood regulars offered excuses for Randinoli's behavior, saying he was just being overly protective of 12ᵗʰ and Bruce natives. They believed that to him it was more than *just* a neighborhood. It was something he could touch, something he truly loved. Whatever the reason, and before Capone and Quinn could calm things down, Randinoli made a decision and was swiftly on his way toward Big Al and his two muscle guys.

Mason put his half-filled bottle of Pepsi on the counter and headed straight for his friend. It was too late to stop—Randinoli already was acting out his decision. Now within arm's length, he looked squarely at Big Al. He asked, "They stay?" He then answered his own question. "Wrong! They go—and you go with them."

Capone almost shouted, "Gabe, I told you to…"

The split second Big Al turned toward the voice was all the time required. "Who the…?" The question ended.

Randinoli grabbed the right sleeve of the big man's overcoat, placed his own left hand on the back of the collar and in one motion dragged Big Al across the store in the direction of the huge picture window facing Bruce Street. Big Al was attempting to stop his legs from moving so fast, but no luck. He was quickly on his way to the side window. "Are you too big to fly? Move, you piece of garbage." Randinoli's strength was too much to resist. The alcohol contributed to Fornio's speed toward the side window.

It happened fast. Big Al's two wannabes seemed to be in a trance, the noise level grew another octave, and everyone realized it would soon be over. Big Al was screaming obscenities and threats, some in Italian, trying to get himself upright but he could not stop his feet from moving in reverse, the direction his big body was headed. The more he attempted to gain his balance and disengage the grip on his wrist and shoulder, the more his own momentum carried him backward. Big Al's head ripped through the side window with a loud crash, followed by his shoulders, with Randinoli's grip strong and steady. The visitor screamed more curse words and as he attempted to protect his head, his right hand was ripped open by the jagged glass. The blood gushed out and immediately splattered his face and covered the collar of his light-colored cashmere overcoat. The bloodied man sat on the concrete and moaned in obvious pain. His hand now bleeding profusely, he mumbled, "You will pay, you will pay." Big Al suddenly appeared much smaller.

Randinoli stared down at his latest victim. His face without expression, the former tenor drummer did not speak.

Danny Sherman, waiting outside to join the game, hurried to look at Big Al. "Finally, a spot opens up for some new blood." He looked down at the wounded gambler. "Hey, nothing personal with the blood remark." On the corner, there was always room for a one-liner.

When Fornio's two partners came around and realized what was happening, they started toward Randinoli. As Mason and Coughlin stepped in front of them, Mason said, "Take your friend back to where he came from. You two need to leave while you still can."

The other players, who were mostly 12th and Bruce personnel, restrained both men. Tony Quinn was not about to let this turn into a small war. Pointing in their direction, he warned them, "You heard the man. You go now while you can still walk."

This was now definitely a 12th and Bruce issue. The visitors were wrong even if they appeared to be right. End of story! Blackie directed the removal. "Get the garbage out on the street." Someone from the corner had taken a position, and right or wrong it became a 12th and Bruce matter. The corner mantra took effect. "There is never a debate over right and wrong when it concerns one of your own." Now with their feet off the floor, the helpless bodyguards were quickly escorted through the length of the store and out the front door to the street.

In a manner of minutes, Big Al and his two friends settled in Big Al's shiny black Buick and quickly drove away. One of his friends drove as Big Al sat in the passenger seat nursing his wounds and his humiliation. The big car jerked and pulled away from the curb. Now outside on the sidewalk, Blackie and Tony feigned a half-ass apology but the visitors were not in a listening mood. They drove down 12th Ave. on their way back to safety.

Sherman waved as he yelled to the visitors, "Drive safe. See you in church."

No one was comfortable with the way things turned out. The incident would cast a dark shadow on the Friday night activity they all enjoyed. Inside the store, Fat Barteck was the first to speak. "Brad my man, you need to talk to him, he's getting worse every day." No one wanted to witness the displeasure of Blackie and Tony. This latest Randinoli episode would cost the game and the Palace money.

Mason went outside and approached Randinoli who was leaning on the pole supporting the "12th Avenue and Bruce Street" street sign, smoking a cigarette. A couple of their friends started in the same direction, one of them mumbled something, and the group stopped and walked slowly toward the schoolyard. They figured it best for Mason to speak in private. Randinoli appeared not to have a care in the world.

He smiled at Mason as he placed his forefinger to his lips in a *shiish* gesture. "Brad my man, there is no *mea culpa* for this one." Randinoli already decided on his position.

"You feel better now? All of that stuff was really necessary?" Mason asked.

Now the near-sinister smile. "You know me, kick ass first, then worry about who's right or wrong—and that big prick was wrong!"

That was that, the issue no longer a problem as far as Randinoli was concerned. No one could out-rationalize him. In his mind he considered the options and came to a quick decision and acted accordingly. Everything justified. There was no sense trying to discuss the incident with him. He felt vindicated; after all he acted on behalf of the neighborhood. In fact, he believed he provided a service for the neighborhood. For himself, he experienced a great rush when the big man crashed through the window.

Capone and Quinn expressed some concern that Big Al would be back with some of his people from the First Ward. This could develop into a major problem. Rozella lowered the Palace lights and benevolently turned off the jukebox. One more rendition of Elvis's "Blue Suede Shoes" could guarantee yet another incident.

By two a.m. everyone was bored with waiting around. The beer was in short supply. Someone spoke up and suggested that there would be no visitors returning.

"Quinn said, "Let's call it a night."

The group dispersed, ending another entertaining evening at 12th and Bruce.

Only one person was disappointed. "Man, how I wish he and his people would come back. That lump would need Doctor DeGregorius to order him a permanent hospital room." Randinoli was truly upset that he would not get another shot at Big Al, whom he considered small time. The regulars from the corner, well used to hearing Randinoli display his violent persona, knew he could back up his loud mouth. He was convinced that someday he would be big time—may as well start now.

Randinoli lamented, "Well, maybe I'll get another shot some other time. I may decide to kill the son of a bitch."

Chapter Seventeen

Gabe reaches out

Oftentimes, Randinoli would give one of his speeches to impress whomever was in hearing distance. This night was different. For some unknown reason, deep inside he did not feel good about what happened at Chick's Palace a few hours back. He disappointed Blackie and Tony and Brad for sure. Once again he had simply lost it and *it* ended before he could correct his actions. Now close to three a.m. he could not sleep. He telephoned his friend. "Hey, can I come over for a little while? I need to talk to you."

Mason said, "Sure, I'm trying to decide on possible courses for the night classes at either Rutgers or Seton Hall. I'm here."

Randinoli grabbed a few bottles of beer from the refrigerator, very quietly so as not to wake his father. He knew Mason's mother never kept alcohol in the house. Mason's dad and four brothers on occasion would drink too much of the sauce. The Mason clan sometimes created more than a little hell. The police knew the Mason boys and usually things quieted down without anyone getting pinched.

More than once, Mason's paternal grandmother Bridgie would patch her sons' wounds and give them each a good painful ear pulling. When speaking to a neighbor about one of her sons, she would proclaim, "He'll be fine if he doesn't take to the drop." Bridgie and Brad's mother, who worked at the hospital together, managed the doctors' dining room professionally but with a sense of humor. They kept the weary young doctors smiling after the long hours spent in the emergency room, the crowded wards, or around the surgery center. Often, Bridgie would scold a tired surgeon for arriving late for dinner. "Doctor DeGregorius, you know we serve at five fifteen, not ten minutes of six." The tired physician noted the twinkle in her eyes as she reprimanded him. He knew from past experience he would not go hungry.

Randinoli rehearsed in his mind what he would say to his friend. He would attempt to speak honestly.

Tara, the Masons' Maltese-Yorkshire Terrier, woke from a sleep and barked as soon she heard the front porch squeak. Always happy to greet her friend, Tara wanted to play immediately. Randinoli massaged her shiny black and white head. "You vicious animal. I'll report you to the authorities. Down, down, you crazy dog." The little dog got the message and returned to her nap. Randinoli walked to the living room and got right to business.

"Okay my man, before you say anything, I know I was a little whacko with Big Al. Maybe I went too far but I'm not sorry. The bum deserved a beating." He paused as if thinking about something serious. "I know the direction I'm heading, and it's okay because I know what I want. You know I'm not you and have to be myself and do my own thing." There—he said his piece and that's the end of it. He handed Mason a cold beer.

Again, Randinoli did not view himself as being responsible for his actions. Rather, he justified his conflict and sought support for what he did. Not a recent character defect, the behavior was present going back to the elementary grades. This repeated action of hit first, and then unnecessarily hurt your adversary became his modus operandi. Now he was counting on Mason to be understanding and overlook his friend's predictable violent behavior.

Mason placed the college pamphlets on the small table; his voice had a slight edge. "Maybe you went too far? You know you went excessively too far and we both know it wasn't the first time. He threw the *excessively* in to impress his friend he was serious. They both knew Mason attempted to learn a new word each day so that if accepted to college, he would sound a little more like college material, more educated.

Mason thought of the recent incident and could not hold back a smile. "Gabe, if the glass caught an artery the man could have died. So you punch him out. That would have been enough. You threw the guy through a plate of glass!"

"You're right. And it felt good." That was it. There's the justification. Randinoli added, "It felt good, so it was the right thing to do."

Mason found it difficult to listen to the explanation, even from Randinoli. "It felt good. It's always the same, all about how you feel. It may sound corny but the nuns were correct. I can hear Sister Francis now: 'Boys, we all have choices to make. Then we must live with those choices.'"

This was not at all what Randinoli wanted to hear. He took a long swallow of beer. A minute passed without any conversation. The radio was on low. Earlier the Yankees had played at home against their archenemies, Ted Williams and the Boston Red Sox. The night ended with the Yankees winning both ends of a double header behind great pitching of Whitey Ford and timely hitting of the young center fielder Mickey Mantle. Outside of Ted Williams's long home run, the Red Sox provided little offense in support of Tom Brewer.

"The Red Sox suck." Randinoli forced a smile and let in a little sarcasm. "So you think I should see a shrink or somebody. You're saying I was dead wrong, I should have done what the rest of them did—nothing! We ignore lumps like Big Al? Let them dictate the rules. Let them come into our space and control our game. Is that what you think?" Randinoli figured what the hell, nothing like trying a little offense. "I suppose when you become an FBI agent, I will have to really behave and tell you everything I do."

Mason laughed. "God forbid! I don't want to know what you do. I'll let my imagination run with that. Remember, lying to an FBI agent? That's a no-no." He held up five fingers. "That gets you five big ones in a federal gated community."

"Okay, enough of your legal advice. What about Big Al? Forgetting the glass window for a minute, don't tell me I was wrong." Randinoli was still holding out for some understanding from Mason.

Mason was tired. "If you came here to justify your actions or for a homily on how you should live your life, you know that's not going to happen. There's a seven a.m. Mass in a few hours and you can get your answers from Father Bradson. You'll get the straight scoop. But if you're asking me as a friend what I think, then here I am." Mason refused to enable Randinoli's repetitive negative behavior. He would not take it any further. It was now in Randinoli's court and they both knew it.

"Believe it or not, I've tried to control my temper on a couple of occasions but no deal." He thought for a moment. "I just lose it and once I start…well, you know. You've seen me go off plenty of times. Okay then, friend to friend, what would you do if you were me? Everybody knows that you fight harder than anyone on the corner does, and I'm not just talking about in the ring. But in the streets, you never go off like "King" Dowd or me. You go to work when it's necessary, but no more. How the hell do you stay in control?"

Mason never anticipated having this conversation. Maybe they were getting older or perhaps they were merely maturing, or a little of both. Randinoli would be twenty in a few months and Mason soon after; not that old, but they were no longer happy-go-lucky teenagers. Mason said a little prayer he would say the right thing and not vomit out meaningless words. Mason sincerely wanted to be of some help. He rightly sensed that his friend, now way out of character, hurt inside. Gabe Randinoli the tough guy was actually asking for help. He reached out to his boyhood friend, the only person he could or would go to.

A minute or so passed. In the background, the radio played Peter and Gordon's "Please Lock Me Away." Mason couldn't resist, "Hey, sounds like your theme song."

"What a pain in the ass. I come here for help and I get sarcasm. That's always been one of your problems. You make light of your elders. You need to show respect and take us seriously."

"Gabe, for what it's worth, there have been times I got so angry I really wanted to take things further and possibly hurt someone real bad." Now Mason took a deep breath and said, "I guess my prayers kick in and I take a step back."

Randinoli sat motionless without saying a word, watching and listening to his friend. He limply placed his bottle of beer on the floor and looked up.

Mason went on. "It may sound crazy. Sister Francis suggested something else to us a long time ago. Remember? Well, I've been following her advice. I get on my knees in the morning and ask God to help me do the right thing that day. I do the same drill at night before I go to sleep. On my knees, I thank Him for getting me through the day and for everything He's given me and my family and friends. I don't know, maybe other stuff from the nuns sunk in. Gabe, I don't have a clue if that's the key, but it works for me. Believe me when I say I actually look forward to each day, it's all good stuff."

Gabe half-heartedly said, "Maybe I'll give it a try."

"One more thing. You do not have to be me–God knows I've enough to do with one me. Be yourself." His friend leaned forward and started to stand. "Since you asked for my opinion, I also pray you stay away from the Big Apple. I just don't think you'll find any worthwhile answers hanging around with the wise guys." Mason did not expect his friend to pay attention to this last comment.

Randinoli smiled and said, "Get some sleep, you look like crap. And it's not all about me."

Mason thought of an old song. "Your new theme song is an old Ink Spot tune, 'My echo, my shadow and me.'"

"You're a riot. I'm outta here."

They both stood at the same time. Without a word, the two friends hugged each other for the first time.

Randinoli stopped at the door and turned. He smiled at his friend and kidded, "Hey, twenty-one coming up. We can drink legally in a year or so. We should celebrate; maybe have a few beers at the club with the old guys."

They both appreciated the humor. Although the legal drinking age in New Jersey was twenty-one, Mason and his friends began drinking beer at the club when they were in high school. "Good idea. Dutch will probably card us."

Randinoli left the living room, stopped to scratch the sleepy dog, got in his car and drove home. He felt good about his visit—always relaxed when he spent time alone with Mason. Tomorrow would be a good day. He had already made plans. He would drive to Brooklyn and meet up with some people.

Chapter Eighteen

Gabe's opportunity speech

One could never be completely sure how Randinoli accepted suggestions. Without doubt, the kid from the corner had a mind of his own. Mason grinned as he thought, "*I wonder if Gabe will say a prayer or two tonight? Not likely.*" After saying his prayers and before falling into a deep sleep, Mason smiled as he remembered yet another one of Randinoli's opportunity speeches.

From the beginning, the two friends held very different opinions when it came to right and wrong or earning a living by working or using other means. Randinoli argued that Newark's "City of Opportunity" label was for good reason. He shared his particular philosophy of opportunity with others more than once. Even though he knew Mason's position on the subject, he never tired of emptying out what he believed to be his business-like philosophy and his viewpoint of life.

Last spring, there were at least twenty observers on the corner watching the older guys pitch quarters and making side bets backing a favorite. Sleepy Chervak, the best of the pitchers, was cleaning up as usual. Randinoli finished perusing the racing form and, standing next to Mason, said to anyone who wanted to listen, "Damn right, City of Opportunity. If you are in the right business there's always plenty of opportunity—so long as you get there first." Everyone's ears perked up but no one responded. Everyone was now curious but unwilling to enter the guaranteed debate to follow.

Mason went along. "What the hell are you rambling about?"

Randinoli continued with his well thought-out theory. "Everyone is taking from you, am I right or am I wrong? The government, the banks, the businesses, the property owners, everybody. Am I right or am I wrong?"

Mason had never heard this argument from Randinoli. "Okay, I guess so. What's your point?"

"No, you do not guess so. You damn right know so." Now his audience observed the veins in the side of his head pulsating. The heat is showing. "So, you get to them bastards first." Now he became the college professor. "Understood?"

"No, not really." Mason wanted his friend to keep going with his homily.

"Geez, one time just pay close attention. For you I'll say it slow, very slow. You rob the other guy before he robs you. It's that simple. You got it now?"

Now Mason is fully aware that his friend is thoroughly frustrated. The lesson regarding recognizing an opportunity is going nowhere. "Oh yeah, right, steal his stuff before he steals yours and…"

Randinoli cut him short, saying, "Right, close enough. If you go in business, make sure it's the right one, with real opportunity."

"Like loan-sharking, right?" Mason attempted to look interested.

"You got it." This always led to a big laugh. "That's certainly one of the better ones. It works for the government. Ask Jimmy Carter. Brad, my slow friend, you always wear me out. Let's take a run to 8ᵗʰ Street. After dealin' with you I need about a dozen greasy White Castle's smothered with onions and peppers."

Shadow Deltucci whispered, "Anything to get him off the soap box." Five hungry young men piled into Randinoli's car headed for yet another gourmet meal.

These words of wisdom ended another life lesson from the annals of 12ᵗʰ and Bruce. The two friends definitely disagreed on right and wrong. Yet, they always found time to discuss life and its mysteries. Each day Randinoli involved himself in more and more of these discussions directed at his future employment.

Chapter Nineteen

The "club"

St. Joseph's T.A.B.S.—more commonly known as "the club"—was an old and weather-beaten, two-story redbrick building located in Newark's Central Ward, at the corner of Hartford and Hudson streets. It rest just one block west from the diminutive Saint Joseph's village, consisting of church, rectory and convent. The club was always a popular location for parishioners to relax and enjoy the company of their neighbors. Built in the 1930s as part of the parish-community recreational activities, the club looked every bit its age. The worn rubber mat at the top step of the building entry read T.A.B.S. The initials remained a mystery for years—their meaning finally revealed by a longtime parishioner.

Mrs. Donato, the self-proclaimed parish historian, spoke for many when she said, "Some interpretations should not be repeated." Never revealing her source of evidence, she proudly announced, "In the early days, an Irish Capuchin strove for temperance in drinking or total abstinence. The rubber mat was inaugurated when the original building, a wooden structure, sat on Warren Street. It became necessary to raze the old building and use the site to build the new school. When the parishioners voted to include a bar and offer alcohol in the new Hudson Street structure, the monk situated the mat for all to see." She waited for undivided attention from her audience. "T.A.B.S. stands for Total Abstinence Benevolent Society." She received a round of applause when the lesson concluded with, "Of course, few people pay attention to the intent."

After walking up the two steps at the front of the building and taking a turn to the left, visitors found themselves in a five hundred square-foot area containing a small bar, bumper pool table, two wooden tables and chairs. Eight wooden bar stools were permanently stationed in front of the old, well-used oak bar. The original jukebox sat to the left, between two frosted windows. The job of stacking the jukebox and updating it with current popular records fell on one of the locals, Wino Beasley, an indispensable part of the neighborhood. On certain Friday evenings, the room filled with couples dancing to the records from the jukebox. Beasley, a former drinker of cheap wine, enjoyed sobriety for ten years and worked as a master electrician. He kept the music as current as possible. "I'm here to serve. We offer only the latest and greatest from the music world." Some of this rang true, but there still remained records from years gone by.

If you turned right upon entering the building, directly opposite the bar area, you would pass through two twelve-foot-high doors that lead into a much larger space. Sitting on the right side, close to the windows, one could not miss seeing the ancient, thirty-foot-long shuffleboard. Its grooves were well-embedded from years of play. To the left of the large room were four bowling alleys, each with a manual foot pedal used to set up the pins. Now the alleys were seldom used. On a rare occasion a few people, after one too many drinks, would decide to roll a few games. For a right-handed bowler, a perfect score of three hundred was not unheard of. The years of use and lack of maintenance produced an incredible deep puncture in the lanes, from right to left and smack in the one-three pocket.

"You can bet on one sure thing. Either Hank "Dutch" Bauer or Mr. O'Brien will be behind the stick, but never at the same time," explained a regular visitor to the bar. The tale told was that the men experienced a minor disagreement many years ago that developed into a no-talk, no-tell situation. The various stories told about the falling-out all settled on one fact: Both men required medical treatment at the city hospital emergency room after the "disagreement." The clientele were well aware of the bad blood between the two men and the reason was never a topic for discussion.

Both men ran tight ships, monitored customer behavior and set the rules. No one seemed to know O'Brien's first name. On the nights Mr. O'Brien was on duty, he stored a sawed-off Louisville Slugger behind the bar. He wouldn't hesitate to use it should a customer act unruly. Randinoli remarked, "I've seen him use it more than once. Mr. O'B played some serious baseball in his day."

Bauer, quieter than his peer, enjoyed a well-deserved reputation as a former bare-knuckle prizefighter. He was a genuinely good person, which added to the respect given him by the regulars. Mason always received a harsh but friendly, "Bradie boy, how's it goin'?" Never Brad, always Bradie.

Dutch slept on an old, single bed in the small storage room in the rear of the building. Clifford, his fourteen-year-old black Labrador was usually with him. The customers loved the quiet, friendly dog. They could pet the dog at the edge of the bar, but he never came out from behind the bar. If Clifford even thought about it, one grumble from Dutch was all it took to dissuade the move.

The second floor served as a gymnasium equipped with a heavy bag, two speed bags, a few weights, jump ropes and a makeshift ring. Whenever Mason worked out in the second floor gym area, Dutch would watch him and offer pointers recalled from his bare-knuckle days. "Once you sense the other guy bein' cautious, go for the finish." He loved to smile and whisper, "up close and personal—that's where it happens. The other guy can run but he can't hide."

The club was not without its drama. One warm night in early August 1958, the two were working on strategy as Mason threw body punches into the heavy bag. The bullet crashed through the window closest to the stairway. Bauer grabbed Mason around the waist and yelled, "Hit the floor." Mason did not hesitate as both he and Bauer fell to the hardwood floor and waited. A car could be heard burning rubber in the direction of the church. The news of the incident stayed in the neighborhood, was never reported to the police and was soon forgotten. Bauer said, "We chalk it up to experience—and good defense."

Never a preacher, Dutch passed on solid and sound suggestions to the young boxers. Mason heard from more than one old-timer that Dutch was the real thing whenever he stepped in the ring. The young man listened closely and followed Dutch's counsel. The tips he received paid off in amateur bouts and in the Golden Gloves. At the fights Dutch could attend—limited due to his bartending duties—he was always in Mason's corner.

Jimmy Coughlin was another regular from the corner, a former Golden Gloves heavyweight champion. He managed Mason's corner whenever possible. Coughlin, a few years older, was an outstanding boxer who may have turned pro if the right opportunity had presented itself. He won the majority of his amateur bouts by knockout and now enjoyed assisting and working out with the younger fighters at the club. Later, when Coughlin became a Newark police officer, he continued his love of the sport and developed a highly successful boxing program in the Police Athletic League.

The second floor included a worn canvas mat used for boxing and, on occasion, wrestling. Most nights the upstairs was crowded, with usually two boxing matches taking place. Mason spent many hours working out and sparring with whomever showed up. Randinoli never did well in the ring due to rules governing the outcome. The streets suited his style—fast and dirty. Never without an excuse, he said, "You want me to work out? No way man, I read where too much sweat is not healthy. Hey, St. Joe's is the only place in the city where the youngsters can learn to drink responsibly at an early age. I'll be at the bar supporting my parish." He hung out on the first floor while Mason worked out. He drank a few beers and always hustled someone betting on a game of bumper pool.

On the back wall of the second floor, a small service bar saw much duty through the years. Bachelor parties, bridal showers, even wedding receptions took place upstairs. When one hundred guests filled the upstairs room, the place rocked. On one auspicious occasion, a visiting drummer spent a few uncomfortable minutes hanging by his feet out the second floor window. It seems one of the guests believed his hearing was being challenged by the loud drum beat.

First time visitors all received the same explanation. "Officially the building is the T.A.B.S., but it's known more commonly as the club." The building served so many uses— bar, gymnasium, bowling alley, party room and general good-time place where people forgot their troubles and discussed the world situation.

Sometimes the crap game in the Bruce Street schoolyard attracted social drinkers, but the club was the major local hangout. Drugs never became an issue at the club. Anyone attempting to introduce marijuana or some other substance would receive strong opposition. Only on a rare occasion would a couple of the Korean War veterans leave the building to smoke a few joints. Shots and beers were always plentiful.

It became a local joke when others spoke of their "clubs," usually referring to high-end, gated-community country clubs that offered restaurants, cabanas, swimming pools and spas, along with well-groomed golf courses, tennis courts, and perhaps bocce courts and many other amenities. St. Joe's Club did not fit the description of a country club. Father Bradson said, "The parishioners would not have it any other way."

When Johnny Zatz visited the club, he entertained the members with colorful accounts of prison life. "I resided in many gated communities. We had our own guards, barbed wire and prayer meetings. I have no intention of returning to those fun-filled days of yesteryear. This club suits me fine."

The club served as much more to a few of the young men. Mason and Randinoli and their friends spent many hours just listening to the adults and absorbing their wisdom and experience. These sessions helped form their lives and influence what they would become as adults. Although they heard the same dialogues, the two friends continued to travel very different paths.

Perhaps no two people digest information the same way. Whereas Mason heard talk of respect and following the law, his friend never wavered from his objective of becoming a mobster, albeit big-time—a real Mafioso.

Chapter Twenty

A short stay at Hartford Street

In 1956, the northeast corridor of the country experienced one of the coldest winters in history. Bad weather forced cessation of the schoolyard activities, and Capone and Quinn were forced to relocate the dice and card games to inside quarters. Mason, who had rainy day money set aside, discussed the need with Capone and Quinn and rented a small space a few blocks from the club on Hartford Street. Casey Fox was more than happy to run the game, and accepted beer and sandwiches as compensation. Fox, who either dropped out or was tossed out of the city's technical high school, showed up every morning at the iron workers local on Halsey Street. Many of the older ironworkers refused to work in bad weather, so each week Fox worked one or two days.

"Brad, it's no different than the roofers or any of the trades. It's who you know. There's a lazy jerk over there never misses a day. His uncle's the business agent. Go figure."

Fox showed up no matter what the weather conditions, and when he worked he received decent wages and benefits. When work slowed he enjoyed hanging around the corner, and on bad weather days he could be found at the Hartford Street location dealing poker. Mason expected him to cut out a small piece for himself and drink a few beers. Fox complied on both ends.

The big room on the street floor suited the needs of the action. The building previously accommodated a scissor factory, which left the space vacant when moved to a much larger building on Littleton Avenue in the Central Ward. The job market had slowly opened up since the government ceased burdening small businesses with tax increases—viewed as a win-win for both the factory owners and the employees.

The Hartford Street game attracted a few steady players and the cut from the games paid the rent, leaving a small profit for Mason and Fox. Word spread quickly whenever a new gambling site opened. Gamblers are curious when new action becomes available, and the game soon found fresh blood from outside the neighborhood. One cold wintry night, weeks after the roulette episode at Chick's, Big Al Fornio and a friend visited the Hartford Street location.

At first, it appeared to be real trouble. When Fornio knocked on the door, Fox turned to Mason, holding up two fingers. "It's two guys. I don't recognize either one of them—could be the law. You better take a look."

Mason said, "It's Fornio, the guy from the roulette game, the one Gabe helped through the big window. You missed that show. Let them in. We'll be okay."

The two men entered the room and a jovial Fornio introduced himself and his companion to everyone.

"Why would he come across town? There's plenty of action in the North Ward," Fox said to Mason.

Mason said, "Who knows? He's a degenerate. Maybe he wants a change of scenery, a change of luck. Foxy, you know these guys, they're very superstitious. Blackie says it all the time. 'If they follow the rules we don't care where they come from.' I hope Gabe doesn't show. This place will be colder than the North Pole if we lose the big window. They're not packin'—right?"

Fox answered, "No, I made sure of that. Please God, keep Gabe down at Atlantic City. Don't let him decide to drive back today."

Fornio closely looked over the players. He whispered something to his friend, smiled and appeared satisfied. He said, "Well, it looks like the action is right here. How's it goin' Brad?"

Mason thought about what Capone would always repeat at the school yard crap games. "Do not let the game get out of hand. Put out the fire before it gets going." Getting up from his chair, Mason walked over to the big guy from the First Ward and said, "It's good, Al. We stay dry in here, out of the weather."

"Great, that's what I'm here for, to stay dry and make some money." Fornio pulled a wad of bills—hundreds and twenties—from his pant pocket. Later, Fox would opine that the big man started with right around three thousand dollars. As things developed, Big Al proved once again that nothing had changed with him; he was just another perverted gambler. Fornio

smelled the action and showed up. He knew of the close relationship between the two friends from 12th and Bruce, but never spoke of the beating
he took at Chick's Palace. Fornio remembered Mason being present and
learned later that Mason escorted Fornio's bodyguards out the front door and
into the street.

At Hartford Street, Fornio and his buddy behaved as gentlemen. In fact,
the big man turned into a welcomed addition to the game. Each time he returned, everyone was delighted to gamble with someone who seldom left a
game holding more money than he started with. Fornio always seemed
happy just to be in the middle of the action and never caused a problem. It
was part of his character to complain out loud whenever he finished second
best at a hand of poker or blackjack.

In spite of Big Al's meaningless griping, the other gamblers enjoyed his
company. He had other addictions, one being strong coffee. Fox brewed
fresh coffee each morning so there was always a supply of the hot drink.
When Fornio arrived he would start with the same playful demand. "Hey,
where's Big Al's coffee at?" Then Fornio would sit down and drink the first
of a couple of hot cups. The others sat patiently knowing eventually he
would enter a game, usually ending with the same results.

Big Al's favorite card game was poker. He would lose a few hundred or
a few thousand, and leave mumbling something about having nothing but
bad luck. A terrible poker player, Fornio did not belong in the game in the
first place. Was he that stupid? Someone said he was a younger Wild Bill
Kennedy when it came to gambling, but Big Al's disposition differed
greatly. Fox said, "Wild Bill will go anywhere to help someone. Big Al
doesn't go any further than the racetrack."

Big Al returned several days before Hartford Street shut down.
Randinoli laughed after learning of the visits. "Good thing I've been a busy
man, he may have shot me." Lately, Gabe spent most of his time in New
York City, especially Brooklyn, impressing his new friends, all very important people.

The Hartford Street experiment ended abruptly after a narrow escape
featuring the outdated, oil-heated stove. It turned into a blessing that this
particular night the game included a Saint Joe's firefighter. Pete Bachezky's
quick response to the low-level explosion prevented a sure catastrophe.
Bachezky was not without a sense of humor. Speaking to Mason, he said,
"You guys always ran a hot game, but burning the place down…over the
top, man." The building escaped total destruction and the game ended without additional drama.

Big Al viewed the end of the Hartford Street game as an omen. "I think my bad luck had to do with the location. I don't do so good at first-floor card rooms. Maybe I'll look around for a second-story game."

Chapter Twenty-One

You disrespect my mother?

Shortly after the unexpected fire ended the Hartford Street game, Mickey Meade was a passenger in Randinoli's car as they returned from a losing day at the crap tables at a popular private club in Atlantic City. Tony Quinn, a friend of the owners, had vouched for the pair.

Everyone in Saint Joe's Parish and the neighborhood knew of the passing of Randinoli's mother a few years back, at the young age of thirty-seven. Mason was privy to the fact that Mrs. Randinoli preserved her only son's baby shoes and wrote on them, "Baby Gabriel." This was one of the few mementoes Randinoli had of his mother, whose untimely death had impacted him greatly. The shoes stayed in his car tied over the rear-window mirror.

Mason and Randinoli's closest friends never commented on the little booties. Mason shared his feelings with Deltucci. "If Gabe raises the subject, I listen to what he says. If not, then I respect his wishes and say nothing. He keeps a lot inside." The people on the corner listened if Randinoli chose to speak of the little shoes. Otherwise, they embraced one of the many 12ᵗʰ Avenue and Bruce Street mantras—it's nobody's business.

Only half-jokingly, Capone would always tell the younger 12ᵗʰ and Bruce people, "Remember, there's two kinds of business. My business and none of your fucking business." Some laughed, however it became another accepted standard for the neighborhood.

Meade never intended to upset Randinoli, but as they pulled onto the Garden State Parkway, North, Meade said, "I noticed the pretty little baby booties, what the hell are they doing in your car? If they're there for good luck they sure crapped out at the casino, right?"

Randinoli didn't reply as he turned into the nearest rest stop. "Get out Mick, I need to check the tires." They exited the vehicle, and both walked to the back. Meade reached down and felt the right rear tire.

Meade said, "They look okay to me, did you feel a shake or…?"

Without saying a word, Randinoli punched Meade in the side of the face, knocking him hard against the back door. Meade placed his hand to his head as he fell forward. Randinoli threw another hard punch to the back of the head. Meade's legs buckled and he landed on his side on the macadam surface. "You disrespect my mother? You mutt." Without another word or warning, Randinoli kicked Meade square in the solar plexus. The noise ugly, Meade struggled to breathe as his ribs cracked. His lips trembled as he gasped, "Are you crazy, what're you talking about?"

The traffic was unusually light on the Garden State Parkway. The drivers were seemingly unaware of the incident taking place on the shoulder of the road. If any of the speeding motorists observed the incident, none stopped to check out the obvious problem.

Without another word, Randinoli opened the driver-side door, slid behind the wheel, started the car and sped north on the parkway, leaving Meade in excruciating pain, dazed as to what happened. He was close to losing consciousness. A half hour passed before a New Jersey State Trooper spotted Meade and stopped to lend assistance. Following his 12th and Bruce training, Meade did not tell the officer what happened. He behaved like a hitchhiker who was assaulted and asked to call a friend.

Randinoli pulled up to Chick's Palace in record time. He lit a Lucky Strike before walking into the Palace. When Chick saw him, he asked, "Well where's the dough? I know you guys broke the bank at AC."

"No, the dice were cold. I got bored with the joint." Randinoli prepared for the next inquiry.

It did not take long. Chick asked, "Where's Mickey? I've got his favorite strawberry milk shake ready."

"I don't know. I came back by myself." Before any more questions, Randinoli walked back towards the pinball machine.

Meade placed a call to the Palace and spoke with Fat Barteck. The two were back on the corner in a few hours. When he arrived, his assailant left the store without acknowledging Meade, giving a lame excuse to explain his departure. The injured Meade never told what happened. He drove himself to the city hospital and checked in at the emergency room. Later, especially in cold weather, he would be reminded of that day on the parkway.

Barteck heard the story from a friend with the state police. Meade told the trooper that his friend had an emergency to attend to and had to leave Meade on the GS Parkway to get a ride back himself. Meade told the officer, "It's no big deal." The trained officer recognized that Meade was in pain and covering for someone, but decided to let the matter go without filing a report of the incident. Meade treated the event as yet another unexplainable Randinoli decision to act violently without cause. He thought *"the guy is sick. Still I hope he gets his."*

Again, Randinoli followed up on another decision, someone suffered, and he escaped being held accountable for his actions.

Chapter Twenty-Two

Finally—Creedon indicted

The Newark FBI Office paid attention to but never caught the mayor with his hand in the cookie jar. In spite of a steady diet of bad press, Mayor Marshall P. Creedon looked forward to a first-time ever third term.

The Star-Ledger's Martin Hatlas never held back with his salvo of reporting political corruption. He wrote, "Quid pro quo criminal activity sometimes goes unpunished, particularly when the activity concerns Newark politics and the Creedon family."

The mayor, desperate for votes, completed an egregious political error when he publicly disparaged the Central Ward and specifically the neighborhood and corner of 12th Avenue and Bruce Street. The newspapers quoted him verbatim. "Our city is plagued with five ghettos. 12th Avenue and Bruce Street is the center of Newark's worst ghetto area." Covering the story, Hatlas hinted that alcohol was involved when the mayor voiced the misguided remarks. Creedon's experienced handlers told him in no uncertain terms that he needed to make things right. If he failed to win at least fifty percent of the Central Ward turnout, his re-election was hopeless.

In past elections, the mayor ignored the Central Ward vote. It wasn't necessary for him to do well there, since his victory was assured from other loyal precincts throughout the city. Now left with no alternative and no connections, Creedon didn't hesitate. His daughter's innocent disclosure would be the answer to his problem. When he ascertained that Mason lived his entire life in the Central Ward, the mayor jumped at an opportunity. Creedon ordered his brother Leo to conduct a covert investigation and discovered the

Mason family was both well-known and respected. They were longtime parishioners of St. Joseph's Parish and had connections at the hospital.

The mayor telephoned Mason, and sounded like the two were longtime buddies. "Brad, I think you will be interested in what I have to say." Creedon asked him to come to his office. He sounded upbeat.

Mason, now very curious, accepted the invitation. He said to his friend, "What the hell is on his mind?"

Randinoli sensed an opening. "I'll go with you. While you talk to him, I'll send him to the emergency room." His friend was serious.

Quinn, the more rational of the corner group, said, "Gabe, we don't know what he wants to discuss. Brad, go and listen. It can't hurt."

Mason had already made up his mind. He would listen. He thought of calling the FBI. Maybe he would wear a wire. *"That's crazy,"* he thought, *"This guy doesn't even know me. He's not going to incriminate himself."*

Mason arrived on time. The office at city hall reminded Mason of something one would find in a low-budget Hollywood movie. The tapestry needed a cleaning and a little mending. The withered carpet, speckled with burn marks from cigarette and cigar ashes, showed where most of the office traffic took place; from the door leading to the office straight back to the two well-worn, solid hardwood chairs in front of the mayor's desk. The chairs' burgundy-colored seats and backs each showed small tears in the thick pads. The lighting was non-existent; the only light in the entire space came from a single desk lamp. Mason learned later that the décor was the mastermind of His Honor. Creedon intended the public to think he was a simple man with simple tastes, who would never spend taxpayer money on extravagant office furnishings.

Sitting in a high-back, oxblood leather chair, Creedon appeared to be a busy man and not one to waste time. He had experience giving orders and getting results. The mayor pointed to one of the chairs. "My daughter says you are a friend and a nice person. Now Brad, I know of your long affiliation with the Hilltoppers, your work at the shelter and your success in the Golden Gloves. I require your assistance. I expect to be re-elected without a doubt. In order to insure a victory it may be necessary for me to do well in the Central Ward. You help me, I help you my friend, and it's that simple. As payment for your help, you and a few of your friends will be given employment on the city payroll." He attempted a sincere smile. "*You* will work at city hall of course. Your friends will be placed wherever I decide." Mason noticed the mayor's obvious sneer when he said *work.*

Mason showed for the meeting to listen and learn so he too smiled as he reminisced about the corner and the lesson learned concerning strangers who call you "friend."

Creedon recognized the reality of his political situation. The FBI was not the only challenge confronting him. Recently Hatlas reported that "The Central Ward is an integral part of the incumbent's badly-needed victory. His campaign organizers told the mayor that without a win in the Central Ward, victory was not possible."

Mason decided to end the meeting quickly. Before he left the office, Mason wanted to be sure Creedon was aware that the kid from the corner fully understood the mayor's position. "Mr. Mayor, you say that 'it may be necessary' for you to carry my ward..." He was interrupted.

Creedon's warped mind reasoned that the young, inexperienced man in front of him was initiating negotiations. He believed that Mason wanted more for his cooperation. The crooked mayor understood this kind of language. He beamed and said, "Now there are jobs and there are jobs. You and your friends will be well satisfied, I guarantee it. You will find time to roof, go to school full time, or whatever you please. You will not miss a payday. I only..."

Now it was Mason's turn to finish his thought. "Sir, you misunderstand. I must refuse the offer. I have other plans for employment." He thought it might be overkill to mention the possibility of a position with the FBI, which was a long way off. Mason stood and left the dingy office without saying a word. He did not want to be in city hall any longer than necessary. The mayor was too stunned to react.

His friends were anxious to hear the results of the meeting. Mason never shared the short conversation but told his friends, "I wouldn't be comfortable having a beer with that guy." It wasn't the last time Mason would refuse to cooperate with a powerful person.

The mayor was frantic yet remained relentless. He was determined to find a way to win over the ward. Not wasting time, the next afternoon Leo Creedon, the mayor's brother and bagman, appeared unannounced at the corner of 12th and Bruce. He exited the back seat of a huge, city-owned black limo. A political hack, looking more like a leg breaker and acting as a chauffeur, exited the vehicle and looked threatening at the people standing on the corner.

Randinoli said, "I'm not bored anymore. Blackie, can I go over and kill the driver?"

Everyone laughed nervously. Capone said, "Try and behave. Brad will be discussing very important business."

Leo Creedon recognized Mason from the description given him by his brother. He showed a big grin and motioned for Mason to come to the other side of Bruce Street. Mason accepted the inviting wave more as a, "*c'mere, you and me can make everything right. You can trust me.*" The mayor's brother displayed a smile that any decent crapshooter could detect as phony.

Mason said to the group, "I think the mayor wants me as his number one assistant." He got up from the steps and walked across to the parked limo.

The bagman got right to business as if the two were the best of friends. "Listen Brad, sometimes my big-shot politician brother doesn't know how to talk to people. Believe me, this is a great opportunity for you," he motioned to the corner, "and for your friends. There's no heavy lifting. All you do is talk with your neighbors. I give you enough dough to have a few get-togethers, you know, barbeque ribs, beer, the whole enchilada. No licking envelopes, stuffing and mailing out shit. It's all about bullshitting. Tell them anything. You just talk and get them to vote the right way." It was now obvious the Creedons needed a lock on the neighborhood and necessary backing from the 12th and Bruce corner. Leo Creedon represented the muscle of the machine. He travelled this road before, the words flowed, and Creedon believed he held the controls. He added, "And whatever my brother offered you, just double it, no problem." This nobody-kid could not refuse the offer. The discussion drew the attention of the corner.

"I hope Brad does not buy a used car from this mutt," Zatz said, sitting on the schoolyard steps with a group of corner regulars.

Randinoli had another thought. "Man, if only the bodyguard dude would make some kind of move—anything. A visit to our handy emergency room would do them both good."

This comment a cause for concern, Zatz said, "Whoa big fella, it looks like it's over. Stay calm for a few more minutes." They heard Mason speaking.

Mason did not need time to think things over. He recognized he needed to be clear with his response. "No deal, Mr. Creedon. My friends and I aren't interested in low-level employment for a low-level administration."

Creedon's voice raised. "You just hold on…" Now every word could be heard across the street.

"I was respectful when I spoke with your brother. I will end with this and you can pass it on if you wish. I don't like him or his politics. As for you, we're not stamp lickers or ass kissers or anything else you have in mind. Bullshit my neighbors? Tell them anything?" Now visibly upset, "We don't bullshit or lie to each other. We take care of each other. Finally, your attempt at intimidation was lame at best." He pointed to his friends on the corner.

"Around here we deal with professional intimidators. Have a safe trip down town." Mason walked across to a smiling group of friends.

Leo Creedon did not respond. He immediately recognized the attempt as a waste of time. Speechless, he turned away and walked to the limo, opened the back door, got inside and gave orders to his driver. "Move it Peter. I told my smart-ass brother these people are not the type you push around. Back to city hall with the bad news."

Randinoli bent at the waist and smiled as he waved and mouthed "bye-bye" to the chauffer. Mason returned to the steps and Randinoli did not miss a beat. "I guess the dating game with the lovely Miss Creedon is out of the question. Good riddance, I don't think I liked that broad anyway."

Joey Coughlin said, "We're happy to know how you feel about things."

In 1954, after Creedon's close defeat at the polls, Newark welcomed its first black mayor, His Honor Robert Q. Blango, a lifetime Central Ward resident. Over the years, Blango was a regular in the schoolyard and participated in all the sporting events as well as an occasional roll of the dice. The corner people worked hard on Blango's behalf and showed up at the polls in droves. Hatlas covered the results in the Star-Ledger. "Central Ward Picks Winner." Over seventy-five percent of eligible voters in the ward cast ballots for the newly-elected mayor.

The new mayor offered Mason a position on the city payroll. Blango said, "You know Brad, I will have none of that no-show crap. The city will get a good day's work from every employee."

"Your Honor, I would have it no other way." Mason thought he would give it a shot.

Randinoli said to his friend, "Pay attention, a job with the city would look good on a resume." Mason's reward was a position as an account clerk at city hall. Officially, he was to be a "probationary" account clerk with the city treasurer's office at a near-poverty salary.

Mason lasted a week at the city job.

He told Randinoli, "Maybe you were right, but the position sucked and I couldn't stomach some of the crap that goes on at city hall. I met several well-paid, political hack no-shows from prior corrupt administrations." Mason thought long and hard about the city hall job before resigning. "I feel real good about my decision. Blackie was right when he said 'you don't have to carry a gun to be a crook.'"

Randinoli said, "My man you are absolutely correct. The pricks would try to own you. We still bet on the winnin' horse. One of our own, Bobby Q will do a good job. I think he's gonna offer me a job in the cash collections department."

"No doubt." Mason concluded the conversation.

The people from 12th Avenue and Bruce Street played a major part in electing the first black mayor in the city of Newark. Creedon would be the last white mayor to hold the position.

Mason's experience with politicians, political hacks, and all the bullshit that went with it set some of the groundwork for later FBI investigations and hands-on encounters with both elected and appointed, corrupt public officials. Mason, as an FBI agent and supervisor, would become involved in successful investigations and indictments targeting very powerful political figures in Chicago, Florida and the New England states.

The elections were followed by more bad news for the former mayor. The Newark FBI exerted pressure on major land developers who prospered to the tune of millions in crooked dealings with city leaders, especially the former mayor and his brother. The FBI developed a cooperating witness who agreed to wear a wire. The results were several self-incriminating statements generated by Creedon and his bagman and other ranking members of his political machine.

The trial held in Federal District Court in Newark lasted three weeks. After heated closing arguments by both sides, the jury returned guilty verdicts on all counts against the Creedon brothers and several co-conspirators. The judge sentenced the ex-mayor to serve twelve years in a federal penitentiary and pay several hundred thousand dollars in restitution. His brother the bagman received a lesser sentence of three years to serve. Both Creedons went to prison right after the New Year. Five of the mayor's hacks and the developers who cooperated with the investigation received lighter sentences and a few skated with periods of probation. In total, the defendants paid over two million dollars in fines.

The media in frenzy covered the demise of Creedon with interviews of many citizens, politicians, homemakers and anyone they believed could contribute to the juicy story. Hatlas, the St. Joe's alumnus and now a hard-nosed investigative reporter for the Newark Star-Ledger, authored colorful stories throughout the arrest, indictment, prosecution, jury verdict and now sentencing of the disgraced former mayor. Hatlas's earlier coverage of the indictment followed his editor's idea for a headline, "Finally—Creedon Indicted." As the trial progressed, The Newark Star-Ledger sold more newspapers than in any period of its existence.

Blango replaced the jailed former mayor, and for a few short years his administration enjoyed a somewhat quiet existence. Then city politics and race relations turned topsy-turvy. Riots broke out throughout the city in July 1967. The citizens of Newark experienced bedlam for five full days. One wild man in Vailsburg organized a group of mostly white people who served as vigilantes. Many of this group included local wise guys. Their objective was to keep the blockbusters from encroaching any further north into the Vailsburg section, now, along with the Ironbound section, the only remaining white sectors of the city.

Each night Cy Villani, now an aging WWII veteran, sat in his big rocker on the front porch holding a twelve-gauge shotgun across his lap smoking a big Cuban cigar. The media ate it up. He promised the black leaders that if the rioters crossed the line into Vailsburg, the leader, a black representative by the name of Bobby Langley, "would be the first to get it." Ironically, Langley and Villani were high school friends and named to the All-City football team together.

Hatlas continued to be uncompromising towards any sign of public corruption. He enjoyed the work and never missed an opportunity to sell more Star-Ledger newspapers. The Sunday headlines screamed, "Villani tells Langley: "BOBBY YOU WILL GET IT—GOT IT?"

Langley was too smart to get into a pushing match with Villani. He used common sense and kept his followers free of the Vailsburg area. In the next mayoral election, Langley threw his hat in the ring and won a landslide election. Langley proceeded to serve an unprecedented fourth term as Newark's mayor.

Chapter Twenty-Three

Fame and fortune

12th and Bruce never ran short of characters. Two of many infamous Saint Joe's graduates were Charlie Widman and Billy Youleau. Both were real personalities and inseparable friends going back to the first grade. The two often threatened to go to Hollywood and become movie stars. No one paid much attention to the young boys, viewing the idea as a wild pipedream without a chance of ever happening. The Hollywood aspirants were a year behind Mason and Randinoli in school. Whenever he saw either of the would-be actors and the topic of stardom came up, Mason would offer words of encouragement. "Hey, why not, nothing's impossible."

"That's the ticket," Youleau said. "We go to Hollywood, get discovered and become famous. Others have done it. It happens every day." Actually, they did resemble two famous screen personalities. Their confidence rose each time the subject appeared and the surer they became it would happen. It posed no problem to the two West Market Street residents, possibly without an ounce of talent or training between them.

The focal point always the same, Widman said, "Man, if I don't look and sound like Marlon Brando, then no one does. And you Billy, you could be Alan Ladd's twin brother. We'll settle for stand-ins if necessary, but only if not immediately discovered for ourselves." Widman was passionate about the scenario.

Widman, tall with dark, slick-black hair and dark eyes, liked to flex his muscles, proud of his powerful physique. Youleau, about five-foot-eight, was slim with light blond hair and baby-blue eyes. With each passing day, both were now convinced they were perfect replicas of the two famous movie stars. Widman even rode a motorcycle and owned a black leather jacket. Without a doubt, here stood "The Wild One." A new haircut now parted to one side, Youleau, with his new white cowboy hat, unquestionably resembled Alan Ladd, the famous movie star of "Shane." The more the subject emerged, the two friends convinced each other that it all made sense. It became a no-brainer. They were indeed the perfect look-a-likes soon on their way to California. After they were discovered it would be all up hill, on to motion picture greatness and fame and fortune.

The word spread like wild fire. Soon after the Blango mayoral victory, the historical journey would begin. It was nine a.m. and Bruce Street was packed with curious onlookers. Now near age twenty, the excited friends hopped on Widman's Harley-Davidson and soaked in the cheers of all the well-wishers of the Bruce Street schoolyard, after gratefully accepting small amounts of money from all their friends in the neighborhood. Widman sped easterly down West Market Street beginning their journey to beautiful and sunny California—where fame and fortune awaited them. Randinoli was heard above the other cheering mob. "Remember what I told you two, trust no one, admit nothin,' and take no prisoners."

The dream was short lived. Six months later they returned and told well-rehearsed stories of the Hollywood scene. No one ever discovered the entire truth connected with the journey, but most guessed correctly. The fantasy remained a dream. It wasn't to be.

"We saw movie stars all over the place!" Widman did his best to appear unshaken by the huge disappointment. The boys from New Jersey quickly learned of the huge expense living in California. In a few short months, the money ran out. They were grateful that some work was readily available. The Newarkers took jobs as bus boys, gas station attendants, and Widman worked a few weeks as a bouncer in a sleazy nightspot. In spite of real ambition and positive attitudes, the entertainment business never materialized for the two adventure seekers.

The neighborhood residents felt badly for their friends. As time passed, the accounts of the trip changed quite a bit, depending on who related the story. Widman seemed more honest and told it like it was. Youleau gave the impression he experienced a deep disappointment saying they never received a fair shake. "I'm tellin' you the truth man. We never got the opportunity to display our talents man. The one chance we needed never materialized, man." He never explained just what he believed those talents to be. He covered up a lot of the disillusionment with his self-serving account of the movie industry. Youleau said, "The amount of talent doesn't matter. Forget it if you don't have a rabbi."

People often spoke of the two adventurers but at no time made fun of their struggle. The two young men actually gained the respect of the neighborhood for their effort. Capone spoke for all, again his pronouncement equated to the crap game. "And at least they rolled the dice. Sometime we make our number, but all too often we seven out."

Mason and Randinoli were on a roofing job in east Newark when they heard the news, the return of the two wannabe Hollywood stars.

Not surprised, Mason said, "The competition out there must be too much, even for people with a lot of talent. I hope they got something from the trip. Who knows, maybe someday one of them will write a book of their adventures."

Randinoli did not like the results of the trip. "Book my ass. Someday I'll deal with those people. If I have anything to say about it, those Hollywood punks will put a lot of our friends on the payroll or go out of business."

Mason ignored this latest comment, pulled the hot, tar-filled mop out of the bucket and spread the hot stuff up and down the next row of roof. He lifted the mop back into the bucket and watched his friend daydreaming. "So what do you think? Are you saving the paper for something special?" Randinoli's part of the job was to place the roofing paper on the hot tar and roll it out, keeping it in the *ply* line.

Randinoli recovered from thinking óf how he would handle labor matters when he was in charge. "I'm on it, quicker than lightning. Let's go man, get some more hot down so I can set another roofing speed record."

Chapter Twenty-Four

Damn right—to opportunity

Randinoli and the younger guys were more than curious. They often heard Capone and Quinn talk of how the racket crapshooters would "launder" money at the racetrack. The language sounded foreign, what the hell did it mean, "launder" money?"

There were days the Battiato brothers left Newark in the morning and drove to Aqueduct race track in South Ozone Park, Queens. Louie Battiato preferred the *flats* over the harness tracks. After conducting business in the morning and afternoon the mobsters continued their journey, finishing up at Yonkers Raceway located off exit two of the New York State Thruway. These jaunts required at least an entire day, sometimes two.

One day Quinn said, "They get rid of all the big bills, the C notes, in exchange for smaller ones—twenties, tens, fives, even a pile of singles." He did not explain the details. The younger guys never quite understood just how the wise guys unloaded so much cash.

Zebep Fabrizio, a short, stocky man in his early sixties, came to the United States on a boat from Italy right after World War II. His waxed moustache above the upper lip invited many comments throughout the crapshooting community. Fabrizio was proud of the black, well-trimmed walrus moustache that curled up at either end.

He was the guru "don't bettor" of crapshooters in Newark, financed from two sources, Battiato mob money and Hank Berkowitz, his wealthy Jewish partner. Everyone knew Zebep throughout the crapshooting community in Newark and surrounding areas. A degenerate gambler, Zebep also played the horses and supported his wife's taste for gambling jaunts to casinos around the world. His cry was always the same. "That woman couldn't win a bet if the fix was in. She's slowly sending me to the poor house." He always ended with a few more observations, spoken in Italian. Those who understood what Zebep was saying laughed aloud. The non-Italian speakers just smiled. He rarely excluded the f-word from any conversation.

Besides being Zebep's personal financial backer and partner, the fifty-year-old Berkowitz was a best friend to the renowned crapshooter. The Berkowitz family owned many lucrative businesses throughout Newark's Jewish Weequahic section. Berkowitz appeared to be two feet taller than his partner and was always well dressed. The two men were the recipients of many comments regarding the height difference. "Hey, where's Mutt and Jeff today?"

Berkowitz and Zebep were inseparable, regular attendees at all the crap games in the city. Zebep said, "Hey, I taught my Jewish friend how to shoot craps ten years ago. Now I can't get rid of him." They were professional gamblers, both addicted to the action. Berkowitz drove the biggest, dark green Chrysler product ever produced. Well educated and wealthy after making a ton of money in the stock market, he never looked back. Berkowitz was easy-going and a favorite of the Bruce Street game. Having close friends in the Jewish mob in Newark did not hurt his reputation.

"Hank, thanks again for the coffee and bagels." Capone loved to eat and the fresh warm bagels from the Jewish bakery were a favorite breakfast before opening up for business. Berkowitz always brought enough for everyone to enjoy. He and Zebep were also favorites of the Battiatos because they made money and paid the syndicate on time. They had good reason to pay promptly.

It was not always the case. When the Battiatos first visited 12th and Bruce, the game included mostly local players. Neither Quinn and Capone nor Zebep and Berkowitz paid anything to anyone except the usual contributions to the detectives. Quinn and Capone started to kick back to the Battiatos when the game became highly profitable and the police assigned it more attention. They never argued with the Battiatos, they simply paid them—it was good business. Capone reasoned, "Let them deal with the cops, one less headache for us."

Not so with Zebep and Berkowitz. Zebep told his partner, "Fuck those guys, I know people too. We pay the usual percentage to Blackie and Tony, it's their game. But that's it! We don't pay anything to anybody except when we pay off a winning bet."

Louis Battiato, the boss and eldest brother, became very upset when informed of the position of the two "don't" bettors. He visited the 12th and Bruce game unannounced on a chilly Friday night. He wanted to be sure the game remained well attended and continued as a moneymaker. With two of his brothers and two other unknown guns, the Battiato boss walked into the middle of the game, smiled and said, "Zebep, you look like you are doing well. You and the Jew take a short break and come over here where we can talk."

"Louie, can it wait? I…" The dice were cold and Zebep was on a streak. Gamblers tend to be superstitious. Never upset the crapshooting gods. Zebep concentrated on the next number and called out the odds. "Okay, we're laying two hundred on the ten."

Philip, the youngest and biggest of the Battiato brothers, moved in and roughly shoved Berkowitz to one side. He quickly grabbed Zebep by the back of the neck, herding him from the game and toward his eldest brother.

Berkowitz recovered and said, "What the hell are you doing?"

Zebep sensed the situation and walked toward the Battiato boss. "Shut up, Hank. We'll talk with Louie."

Louie Battiato, his brother Rico, Zebep and Berkowitz walked out of earshot of the game and stopped near the wall close to the empty basketball court. The boss got right to it. "We come here to have a nice, friendly talk and right away you disrespect me in front of people."

Zebep attempted to speak, "Louie I meant no…" Battiato said sternly, "You or your friend say one more word without permission, it will be your last." He waited, but no one spoke. Rico Battiato watched, his eyes never wandering from both men, his right hand out of sight inside his overcoat.

The Battiato boss continued. "You two may think you are connected with someone, the Jews in the Ironbound or somebody else. I don't give a fuck who it is or who it is not." He now had the undivided attention of both men. "We are not here to negotiate with you. This is Bruce Street, Blackie and Tony's game, with our permission and protection." His voice grew louder. "You have been here engaged in business for over five years. Five years without paying a nickel. You were told the business tax would be five percent each week." Zebep and Baum gave the impression of being relieved. They could afford this and they were going to live. "That was before you acted disrespectful. The cost of doing business at this location has gone up. It's now ten percent per week. One of my people will be here at noon every Saturday." Without waiting for a response, he nodded to his brother and the four mobsters walked from the schoolyard to a late model Buick sedan parked nearby, and drove toward 12th Avenue.

That concluded the first and last business meeting between Zebep, Berkowitz and the Battiatos. From that day on, the two gamblers paid on time and never again questioned the arrangement—at least not in public.

One night at Aqueduct, Randinoli said to his friends, "We have to keep an eye on Zebep. I heard him and Hank talkin.' They brought a ton of Battiato money with them."

After the fourth race, Zebep sauntered up to the pari-mutuel window marked "IRS Window Only," to the same teller he always bets with, gave him a bag stuffed with one hundred dollar bills and whispered something. The teller nodded his understanding. After the fifth race, Berkowitz went to the same window, to the same teller, where he accepted a package of tens and twenties. Neither spoke a word. Unnoticed by anyone, Berkowitz stuffed his inside coat pockets with the bread, ending the transaction.

Now the younger guys, especially Randinoli, were curious about what went down. Later, discussing the matter on the corner, Mason and Randinoli learned from Capone and Quinn that the teller receives a small percentage for "laundering" Zebep's smaller denominations in exchange for larger bills. Quinn explained the operation in more detail. "It's simple. The employee needs a heads-up as to when the wise guys will show at the track. The friendly teller insures there's an ample inventory of tens, twenties and hundreds. If for some reason he can't come up with the amount needed, he makes a phone call and he and Zebep, or whoever is doing the deal, agree on a different night."

Leave it to the wise guys. There is always a new wrinkle to learn about betting on horses or dogs. On yet another visit to Yonkers Raceway, Randinoli observed an additional scam from a personal perspective. This little exercise excludes the IRS from seizing the government's share of the winnings. On this particular night, number three, a long shot, won the second race by a nose and paid thirty-eight dollars to win. Randinoli held a winning fifty-dollar ticket so rightly figured his return to be nine hundred and fifty dollars. Wrong!

Zebep explained any winning ticket paying over six hundred dollars is immediately taxed by the feds, twenty percent off the top. Mason made inquiries and confirmed the teller at the IRS mutuel window deducts the twenty percent. The winning ticket holder is required to present personal identification, a social security card and date of birth, all of which is shared with the IRS. The bettor must also relinquish the winning ticket and sign a tax form detailing the entire transaction.

Zebep continued with Randinoli's education. He said, "I can save you ten percent by shipping the winning ticket to one of my friendly tellers. The guy takes ten percent for his cooperation, the feds get zip. It's simple. You and the teller cut up the feds' twenty percent." Zebep explained that the teller fills in the IRS form, inserting phony social security numbers usually belonging to degenerate gamblers who never submit tax returns.

Randinoli said, "Okay, just get me the money."

Zebep spoke with the teller who agreed to cash Randinoli's ticket, and the crooked teller set up shop at one of the IRS windows. Following Zebep's instruction, Randinoli went to the same window and tendered the winning ticket. The experienced teller acted quickly. He wrote in a phony name and social security number, paid Randinoli for the winning ticket, minus the ten percent he pocketed for his trouble.

Randinoli never accepted this procedure. "I spend my valuable time and expertise to handicap the race like a pro. I pick the long shot, not the government, not those asshole tellers, and they get ten percent of my dough." Always the same conversation, Mason would say, "The law says…..."

Randinoli interrupts, "Screw what the law says. We pay tax on all our income, now they want a piece of a winning ticket."

Mason heard enough. "What, pay tax? You have yet to file a tax return. You lowlife, you and your friend the teller just beat Uncle out of twenty percent and you still complain. What kind of a citizen are you? Do everyone a big favor, move to another country." They stopped at a bar on the way home and had some laughs over a few drinks using Randinoli's windfall.

Randinoli knew he was on the short end of the discussion but that never stopped him. "Let's drink to the IRS. This is a great country, and Brad, my man, I am not moving anywhere. Let's throw back one to Newark, "The City of Opportunity." Now he was on a roll and could not stop laughing. He always showed a sense of humor when things went as he wanted them to. Still, his personality was gradually changing and, most agreed, for the worse.

There were very few occasions when Randinoli did not find something to complain about. When he lost, someone screwed him. When he won, it was never enough; someone held him back from an even bigger payday.

During the ride back, the radio played the big hit in jukeboxes around the country, the Crew Cuts' "Sh-Boom," so popular because of the funny sound and beat, nothing complex, just a happy rhythm with harmless lyrics. People needed some fun stuff. Not so for Randinoli. Although he could not sing a note, he ridiculed the lyrics. After chugging down a road beer, he crooned his version, "Spittoons, Spittoons," and some other garbage lyrics. He laughed hysterically, the only one to appreciate his rendition.

Chapter Twenty-Five

Another sure thing

From first grade forward, Mason always earned money doing chores, helping his grandparents and some of the elderly people in the neighborhood. As he grew older, his "clients" would dispatch him to the banks and stores. On occasion he accompanied Bridgie on bus rides to Atlantic City, where she and her Rosary Sodality pals played the slots at Resorts International Casino for a few hours, grabbed a bite to eat and returned home before dark. His grandmother always gave her grandson a few dollars to spend on the boardwalk.

Bridgie would say, "Why, it pays to go to Atlantic City. We seniors pay ten dollars for the nice round-trip bus ride, and they give us vouchers for lunch at Roy Rogers. Brad, now how can you beat that?"

He would tell his friends, "Bridgie never counts the change she pushes into the slot machines. However, we hear about it when she comes home a winner. I guess she enjoys herself and that's what matters." The more he thought about it the more questions he had. "Shooting crap in the schoolyard is illegal. Why? The money stays local. But for the elderly, going to church to play bingo once a week or busing them to the slot machines is okay. I don't know if that makes any sense." Mason always had a problem with how the politicians-in-charge defined gambling.

Quinn chimed in. "Since I can remember, the adults in my family have bought tickets on the Irish Sweepstakes. They mail their numbers in with the cash, their personal 'nom de plume' over the pond to the auld sod. No problem, everything is kosher."

One night after an Atlantic City excursion, Mason was very tired and in bed before ten p.m. He looked forward to a sound sleep before work early in the morning. The phone startled him—it was a voice he did not relish hearing at this late hour.

"Hey, you're in luck. Tomorrow night we go to Yonkers. Money in the bank, I have the surest of the sure." Randinoli was not at all sleepy; he was into one of his moneymaking sure things. He had money coming in from the service station business. Why save any? Break the bank, any bank.

Mason grumbled, "I am now in a deep sleep. If this phone rings again, I will search for you, and when I find you I will hurt you."

Before he could place the phone in the cradle, he heard Randinoli say very softly, "That's great, so tomorrow is a yes?"

"Yes, you…" Mason ended the call and immediately found sleep.

Randinoli believed he understood all the angles. The next evening Mason and Randinoli, along with Randinoli's brother-in-law Vic Roberts, Danny Stillin and Richie "Hot Dog" Nori, drove over to Yonkers Raceway.

It turned out that Roberts was the real brains behind this latest master plan. The way it worked, Roberts knew a driver from United Cab Company, who knew a guy, who dated the sister of one of the horse trainers. Roberts was so convincing when he talked about the horse, a pacer named Cottonwood Queen. "The Queen is a lock, and against this field of cripples, she can't lose."

Past history provided the evidence. When the sure thing was touted, word of the guaranteed windfall spread throughout Bruce Street and beyond. The money came in from everywhere, including a few women from the RS. Chick Rozella and many of his Palace customers got in on the action as well. He kicked in with his same old saying, "You can't win the prize if you don't have a ticket." He smiled and added, "Besides, how can it miss? Robert knows a guy, who knows a guy, who knows…"

Even the Central Ward cops and the St. Joe's firefighters all participated right along with all the other "investors." No one dared being left at the starting line—it became yet one more neighborhood near-spiritual phenomenon. Wild Bill Kennedy's Native Dancer's single *faux pas* was now an elapsed memory. *Be part of the multitude of winners or suffer the consequences.*

The five financial couriers collected the wagers and were well prepared to dump everything on Roberts's, and now Randinoli's, guaranteed investment.

Randinoli said, "We wait until a minute before post time, we keep the odds up, then we dump it all." That is exactly what they do.

One of the most painful experiences a horse bettor can endure at a trotter track is helplessly watching a horse that "breaks" during a race. It is much worse if your money is wagered on the breaking horse. This infrequent occurrence is a sad sight, the horse simply breaks stride, and the driver sits defenseless in the two-wheeled sulky waiting for the pacer or trotter to get back in stride. The hapless horse is powerless as it attempts to close the distance lost to the rest of the field.

At the start of the race, the pacers lined up across the track side-by-side in a straight line. The starting car, now with its gates opened, led the horses to the starting line. The car moved at a slow rate of speed, gradually getting faster as the horses followed. On this night, the gate opened smoothly on either side of the lead car and the horses were in perfect stride. The crowd roared as the race got underway. The starting limo continued straight down the track and veered off at the first turn. "And they're off!" To some of the nightly attendees, the start of each race is actually poetry in motion.

As the entire field of eight horses raced for the first turn, something was obviously wrong. The crowd, sensing the trouble, moaned in unison.

Roberts screamed, "Which one? Who broke?"

Nori focused his new binoculars on the horse in obvious trouble. "No! No! Get back in stride you rat mudda..." His voice disappeared under the now bedlam in the stadium.

The number eight horse, Cottonwood Queen, the sure winner guaranteed to bestow untold wealth to 12th and Bruce and beyond, had broken stride. The driver, Willie Keeley, one of Yonkers best, is unable to calm the big, tan-colored horse. His efforts are fruitless. By the time the poor horse recovers and resumes a normal stride, the event is half over. The pain continues as the five wise men from the corner view the race to its excruciating finish.

The public address announcer could not have struck a crueler blow as he bellowed out the results, "… and finishing eighth, number eight, Cottonwood Queen."

The investment forever lost.

Always the one to see a little ray of sunshine, Lamento remarked, "We can't blame the weather, right? It was a gorgeous night." This did get smiles from most of the passengers.

Randinoli looked puzzled. "What the hell is wrong with you? A gorgeous night?" Now an octave higher, he said, "Danny Dimwit, the son of a bitch broke. When you break you have no chance of winning. Our money is gone. Do you have any idea why? I'll tell you why. The fucking horse broke."

Lamento immediately ceased delivering his weather report.

For weeks after the disappointing race results, a few of the schoolyard crapshooters could not resist taking a few shots at the sure-thing bettors. No one admitted to the actual money lost. Barteck fibbed, saying, "Man I'm so happy I was not in on that one. As my man Fats Waller says, 'One never knows, do one?'"

Whenever any of the "Cottonwood Queen Boys" appeared in the schoolyard, someone would favor them with a raucous rendition of Nicely singing a "Guys and Dolls" favorite:

"I got the horse right here, his name is Paul Revere,
And here's a guy who says if the weather's clear, can do, can do.
This guy says the horse can do."

The singing was a little off tune, albeit always loud. Zebep wet his pants during one of the performances. "I'm sure my old lady had a few shekels on that dog."

Randinoli never appreciated the humor. "You should all drown in the Riviera," he said, referring to a city public swimming pool, Hayes Park East, more commonly known as the "Irish Riviera."

Before making his exit, he always added a pleasant farewell. "Die! All you rat bas…" Then without completing the sentence, Randinoli lit up a Lucky Strike and sauntered out of sight. He thought, "*Someone needs to visit that driver.*"

Chapter Twenty-Six

The entrepreneur

Randinoli had just turned twenty-one when he reached another well thought-out decision. "Pop, I'm lookin' to buy the station at the Five Corners. The owner's up in years, he's retiring. I know he wants out in a hurry."

Cuban Pete Randinoli said, "That sounds like it might be a good idea. You sure you ain't gonna do anything else with the property. No gambling, or selling anything other than gas?" His father had reason to suspect his son. Since quitting high school, Gabe spent most of the past five years hanging around and getting into trouble. "Gabe, I don't want any more nights of phone calls from the precinct that I need to post bail and all the crap that goes with it. I'm getting too old for that stuff." The elder Randinoli was mercifully spared the details of Gabe's many trips to New York.

He laughed at his father. Randinoli loved when Cuban Pete spoke. His English was getting better because he took advantage of the night classes at the Central Avenue adult program. "Pop, you always think I'm up to some-thin'. This is the break I need, a great opportunity. It's a gas station in a great location. I sell gas, cars come in and the owners buy my gas. I make a profit. That's it, end of story." He sounded so truthful, Randinoli almost believed his own words.

He explained to his father that this could be the chance of a lifetime. Randinoli had no intention of limiting the business to only the sale of gasoline and small mechanical jobs. The business, a small three-pump Tydol station, was located at Newark's Five Corners section, the intersection of 6th Street, Central Avenue, West Market and Orange Street. At the points sat a small savings and loan, a two-tree, two-bench, oval-shaped park, Phil's' Five

Corner Tavern and a paint store. He knew there were safer areas to open a business in the city, but this location was suitable for what Randinoli had in mind. The address was not important. Randinoli thought, "*A crap game and poker and gin rummy games will bring in serious bread. A touch of a shylocking operation will add to the profit.*"

Mr. Lewis, the owner of the gas station now looking forward to retirement, wanted to get the hell out of Newark and retire to the sunny shores of Florida. The sixty-five-year-old gent ran the business for twenty-five long hard years. "The kids are all on their own now. Me and the missus have had enough of the northeast and the cold weather."

Randinoli visited the station and told the owner that if the price were right, Randinoli would buy the old guy out. The price talks started and the bullshit back and forth would have been the envy of the most skilled negotiators. The owner was firm at "ten thousand dollars cash." Mr. Lewis recognized the kid as a wannabe businessman with big ideas. He dealt with many during his years at Five Corners. Lewis told his wife, "They never have an inkling of the amount of time and effort that goes into a business like ours. This kid figures he opens up and the money pours in."

Randinoli countered with seven, although having just gone through a hurtful period shooting crap at Bruce Street and elsewhere, he did not have two nickels to rub together. *No problem.*

Randinoli thought through his business plan. He'd hire some peon for the actual heavy lifting part of the business. He personally would handle the real money-making end of things. He always held different ideas when the subject was acquiring money, certain he found a place that would allow him to put his ideas into practice. He let a few of his friends from the corner know what he was thinking. He never mentioned that he had in mind bookmaking and excluded the part about lending money at shylock rates.

Randinoli was counting on his father and his ex-brother-in-law, Vic Roberts, to lend him the money or sign for a loan. More than once he exaggerated the venture to Mason. "The place is in a busy location and could be a gold mine if run properly. I can undercut the Shell up on Eighth Street. I sell at fifty-five a gallon, three cents lower than everyone else. There's plenty of room for a car wash in the summer months." Again, he neglected to mention the gambling and shylock operation included in his plan. This was Randinoli, the businessman whose only experience emanated from the Bruce Street schoolyard crap game. It was not open to discussion. He concluded that he somehow would own the station. The money required to close the deal was of no concern. It would appear somehow. He craved the action, and this move would enhance his resume. *The operation will impress my friends in New York.*

The two parties finally settled on a price of eight thousand five hundred dollars—still a lot of scratch for someone dead broke. The owner insisted that the cash deal close no later than two weeks' time. The Lewises were scheduled to close on a new, two-bedroom condominium in Florida. Randinoli now schemed. He needed to come up with real cash. His unemployment benefits expired. Roofing was not an option, not nearly enough time to get the needed money. The roofing jobs were more than slow. The older union guys utilized seniority and took whatever work came in the hall, leaving the younger guys dry for work. He and Mason and the other young guys were lucky to get in three days a week. Between his father and his brother-in-law, he put together four thousand five hundred dollars, leaving him four thousand short—a big number.

Mr. Randinoli recently sold a small piece of property he owned in Wildwood at the Jersey Shore. He would have the remaining money for his son in another month. Randinoli told Mason, "I may have to go to the stinkin' Battiato shylocks. It'll cost an arm and a leg but I need the scratch." They both were well aware that the *shys* would not put that kind of money on the street without charging at least four points. This meant he would be paying one hundred and sixty dollars a week "vig," the interest paid, none of which would reduce the principal. The *shys* doing business in Newark were no different than the rest of the country; a mean group who did not think twice about breaking a variety of bones to send a message to the slower payers and potential borrowers.

There were numerous examples of just how the interest was arrived at. But it was all the same when it came to deadbeats. If a borrower fell behind in his payments, he would receive a visit. One of the repeated deadbeats, a driver with United Cab Company on Hudson Street, walked around with his right arm in a sling for many months. There were always wise cracks when someone was injured. "Gino must have slipped coming out of the confessional."

Mason, friends with Randinoli since the fifth grade at Saint Joe's, knew Randinoli's father to be an honest, hard-working tailor. Mr. Randinoli was respected around 12th and Bruce and enjoyed a reputation for keeping his word. "Cuban Pete," a daily communicant at St. Joseph's, never uttered a negative word toward anyone. He would tell the two boys, "If you can't say nice things about a person, don't say anything."

Mason thought, *"It must be a God thing."* Unbeknownst to Randinoli, his friend had put away a little over four thousand dollars, saved from his junior crapshooting syndicate, roofing and labor construction jobs. It was a small fortune—ironically the exact amount needed to buy the station. Mason called his old friend and arranged to meet with the elder Randinoli. Mason asked Randinoli's father for strict confidentiality. No surprise, the promise given and his word kept.

Mason asked Mr. Randinoli if he was indeed going to finance his son with the obligatory four grand in about a month. The senior Randinoli assured him, "I will have much more than that by the fifteenth of the month, and will give Gabe the four thousand." Mason told him that he had the money and would give it to Randinoli because he did not want his friend reaching out to the shylocks while waiting until the fifteenth. "Even if he pays on time, the wise guys will find a way to own a piece of the business."

The tailor agreed. "I don't want him anywhere near those bastards. They bleed and bleed and then they own you. It was the same in the old country." He smiled at his "other" son. "Brad, I cannot believe you have that kind of money, but not really surprised. It's none of my business. I would consider it a favor if you give him the money now. You have my word of honor I will pay you personally on the fifteenth of the month." They hugged, shook hands and the conversation ended.

Mason drove around the neighborhood, found Randinoli pitching quarters in the schoolyard, and motioned for him to come to the steps where the crap game was in full stride. He handed Randinoli four thousand dollars in a manila envelope—forty crisp, hundred-dollar bills.

Randinoli, who rarely demonstrated surprise, quickly forgot his promise to the nuns on the use of the "f" word. "Where the fuck did you get this kind of scratch? Did you rob a fucking bank?" His hand pressed against his lips, recalling his promise.

Mason smiled. "No more f-words, Gabriel." He did sound a little like Sister Francis.

Still shocked, Randinoli said, "What about the bank, which one did you rob?"

"Already you forget Mr. Capone's philosophy: 'There are two kinds of business.' Just take it, work your ass off pumping gas, make a lot of money, and pay it back. Ann doesn't know anything about this." He left before Randinoli realized the import of what happened.

Randinoli figured correctly. The money came from working as a roofer, bartending and, of course, healthy returns from the crap games. Last year Mason, Billy Schulze and Knocko Riccardi had formed a partnership, which became known as the Junior Syndicate. Louie Battiato gave the name to the young gamblers and never interfered with their play. He liked Mason and viewed it as a win-win situation. The young "don't bettors" would attract newer players to the games in the city. The Junior Syndicate would be a short-lived operation, not a career. When gone, enough of the newer gamblers would relish the action and continue to play and contribute to the mob. It was a business decision that would benefit the Battiatos long-term.

Whenever both "syndicates" participated in the same game, it was understood the more established Zebep and his partner Hank Berkowitz covered the larger bets. The three entrepreneurs from 12th and Bruce were solidly invested in crap games throughout Newark and did very well as "don't bettors," the players who always bet against the dice. They did have a few rules, strictly enforced and suggested by Louis Battiato, reinforced by Capone and Quinn. "One, do not shoot the dice, we bet the wrong way. Two, never lend money to a player. And three, always give carfare to the losers." They stuck to these simple guidelines and never experienced any problems they couldn't handle.

At a Monday night game on Bergen Street, the participants were mostly the black guys from the neighborhood. Another degenerate loser made noise when the "Juniors" refused him a loan. Mason told him, "Not today Shake, you're too lucky, one long shoot and you wind up with our entire bankroll. And you do it with us backing your action? Not good business."

The Junior Syndicate handled whatever action came their way. Added to this, the players believed the Juniors enjoyed the official backing of the Battiatos. Schulze said it clearly. "Let people think whatever they like." Mason, Schulze and Riccardi now accumulated approximately four grand each. They could handle a lot of action.

There was the occasional issue that needed to be resolved. The Juniors on more than one occasion found themselves competing for business. One night at a crowded game at a Seventeenth Avenue warehouse, a group of rival don't bettors from Jersey City took exception when the three younger guys arrived on the scene and picked up much of the action. It was obvious that the Juniors were known to many of the regular participants, and they enjoyed a solid reputation for playing fair and never holding back any money. During the banter back and forth, it became apparent that the young upstarts were 12th Ave. and Bruce St. residents.

The older Jersey City crapshooters were familiar with the reputation of the Central Ward, but these guys were barely in their twenties. One of them said, "This game sucks, costing us money." They were unhappy. Schulze took a break from the action and observed as the other two conducted business. He bought a beer provided for the players and rested on an old couch. The jukebox was playing, who else, Sinatra singing a Cole Porter number,

"Anything Goes." One of the Jersey City crew, also an observer, walked over and sat down on the couch next to Schulze. "Hey, I need to talk with you. You guys are from 12th and Bruce?"

"That's right. What was your name again?" Schulze knew that the stranger was not making small talk and being friendly.

Ignoring the query, the Jersey City guy said, "Are you workin' for the Battiatos?"

Mason and Riccardi watched their partner being approached by the stranger but could not hear what was being said. They quickly agreed that the guy appeared to be too strong and excessively big for Schulze to deal with if things went sideways. "Knocko, you should be okay here. I'll check things out."

As he approached his partner, Mason heard Schulze ask, "Are you a cop?"

The big guy grinned as he stuck out his hand in a friendly gesture. "Hey, they call me Rocky. I'm only wonderin' who you work for."

Schulze shook the hand. "Right, but I don't know you. Are you a cop?"

"No way. Listen kid, you and your friends seem to know what you're doin'. If you're workin' for the Battiatos there's no problem." Mason had given his cash to Riccardi and drew closer to his partner and his new friend.

Schulze saw Mason out of the corner of his eye. "It really is nobody's business, but we work for us."

The smile quickly disappeared. Rocky had enough of this kid. He got up from his seat and said, "Suppose I kick your wise ass, then who will you work for?"

Schulze quickly stood up. Mason heard enough. He ambled next to the couch while keeping his eyes on Rocky. He said, "We're shooting a little craps, that's all you need to know. There's no problem."

Rocky heard enough. He reached out and grabbed Mason's shirt. Twisting the shirt, he said, "You and your two friends need to go back to 12th and Bruce right now. Or you won't walk out of here on your own."

The players were now aware of the disturbance. The entire game stopped. The experienced group running the game was equipped to handle problems. The steady players never caused any disruption but now the strangers needed to be dealt with in a hurry. The promotors already picked a favorite in this race. This was not the first time the 12th and Bruce people showed in this game and always behaved as gentlemen. In fact, they added class to the surroundings.

One of the game's promoters considered the Jersey City crew as troublemakers and decided to ask them to leave. He waited a second too long.

"I think you may have ruined my shirt. Bridgie bought this for me. That's going to cost you." Mason was in a good mood. "Imagine that, they're playing your song." Now it was Fats Dominos "I'm Walkin" filling the big room.

Rocky squeezed the shirt with his left hand and reached back with his right arm, clenching a closed fist. "Another smart ass…"

Mason's powerful, straight left caught the Jersey City crapshooter square on the chin. Rocky's grip on the shirt disappeared and he slumped forward toward Mason, who held him up as the two Juniors placed the big guy gently on a nearby cushioned chair.

The people running the game immediately escorted the Jersey City crew off the premises and to their vehicle before any more discussion, and in a matter of minutes it was back to business as one of Riccardi's friends from Bergen Street rolled the dice. "Come on dice…do your stuff for the man who truly loves you."

On the fifteenth of the month, Randinoli bought the station and, without delay, Mr. and Mrs. Lewis were on their way to the quiet fishing village of Bonita Springs, Florida, located on the west coast of the Sunshine State, squeezed between Fort Myers and Naples.

The new owner told an audience, "You may call me Mr. Gabriel Randinoli, now the new, young and very handsome entrepreneur of the Sixth Street Tydol gasoline service station. Remember our motto, 'service with a smile.'"

That evening, Willy Erickson, a successful plumbing contractor from the corner, stopped at Mason's house. "Brad, I just filled up at Gabe's place. He wanted me to stop by and ask you to come to the station."

"Right Willy, I'll stop by tonight. Thanks." Mason was not sure why Randinoli did not call and ask himself. Big shot energy tycoons always have subordinates at the ready.

When Mason arrived at the station, one of young kids from the corner was wiping the windshield of an elderly woman's super-spotless 1954 Chevrolet Bel Air. Mason thought *the place looks like a real business; maybe the owner will stay here where he belongs.*

Randinoli and his father were in the back office passing time, both smiling.

The tailor beamed. "Brad my man, it is the fifteenth of the month, and here is your money." Mr. Randinoli handed him a closed white envelope. "You are a real friend."

Cuban Pete Randinoli had heard his only son use the "Brad my man" expression many times.

Randinoli was surprised. "Hey Pop, you're getting so cool." Mr. Randinoli believed it to be an expression of love and respect. He hugged Mason and kissed him on both cheeks, a custom he brought with him from Naples. The tailor and his only son were both smiling from ear to ear. After they enjoyed each other's company, shared a few laughs and a few beers, Mr. Randinoli excused himself, said his goodbyes and left the station.

The two friends sat in silence for a few minutes. Finally, Randinoli said, "You know it hasn't been easy for him since my mother died. I really love that guy." The words were hard coming out. It was a rare occasion when Randinoli let his guard down and allowed true feelings to pour out. He was only seventeen when the beautiful young wife and mother passed away, and he genuinely missed her.

He immediately got back to business, quickly changing the subject. "Here, this is for you, a little interest." Randinoli handed Mason two crisp one-hundred dollar bills.

"No way, this was not our agreement. The four large was the agreement. Thanks, but no thanks." Mason pushed the money toward Randinoli.

"What, do I have to do kick your ass? This is business. Call it vig. The business people call it interest. You still do not know shit about business. I have to teach you everything. The old man and I talked about it and this is what we decided, case closed."

Mason started to shove the money back at Randinoli, who persisted. "Do you want to make a great guy like my old man upset, eh? Take it and take a shot at Bruce Street. With your arm you'll parley the hundred into a thou'. I will not tell the Juniors that you were a "do' bettor." They both laughed and the subject quickly changed.

A few months back at a late evening crap game, the candles glowed brightly for Mason. The "don't" action was dead. He decided to take a turn at shooting the dice.

Tony Quinn, as surprised as any, made a big deal of it. As he handed him the dice, Quinn announced, "And returning to the 'do bet' team after a very successful run with the 'don'ts, I give you Brad Mason." After receiving a few good-natured cheers, he proceeded to roll a ton of numbers and won just south of a thousand dollars from Zebep. Louie Battiato crowned Mason "the man with the golden arm." He plagiarized this title from a Frank Sinatra film in which "Old Blue Eyes" portrayed a hopelessly strung-out drug addict from the North Side of Chicago. The film had nothing to do with a neighborhood dice game.

Mason headed for the office door and remembered the messenger. "Why did you send Willy to get me, your phone broken?"

The smile, and then he said, "Hey, it's about time some of these guys learn to take orders and follow simple directions, you know what I mean?" Randinoli's ego was on the rise. He now believed that he was important and people should respect him and do his bidding. Randinoli's more-frequent sojourns to the Big Apple were beginning to influence his outlook on his old friends.

"Yes, I think I do know what you mean Mr. Big Shot. Willy Erickson would do most anything for someone from the corner. You know he was just being a friend, doing a friend a favor. You need to stop the bullshit, stop using people, especially friends."

Randinoli needed the last word. "What am I gonna do with you?"

Mason, not ready to end the conversation, said, "And now with the responsibility of running what could be a very lucrative business, there's no need to go to the Apple, right?"

"Please excuse me, a client needs pumping. I am a very busy man," Gabe said.

Chapter Twenty-Seven

The wedding—the funeral

Unbeknownst to most of the people living in the neighborhood, one individual was using illegal drugs for a couple of years.

It was 1957. There were often slow nights on the corner. One Saturday evening Mason, Jack "King" Dowd, Joey Coughlin and Michael Donato did something crazy—at least when compared to normal behavior. Dowd learned of an afternoon wedding to be held at one of the nearby churches with a reception to follow at a downtown hotel. He knew something of the families of the bride and groom, and reasoned the reception would be a huge gathering. With upwards of a few hundred people, a few extra guests would go unnoticed. Dowd developed the bright idea of crashing the reception. He elaborated on the plan. "It'll be simple, the place will be packed and there are always no-shows. We find us a table and join the party. We dress up, look cool and fit right in." He was about five-foot-eleven, two hundred and thirty-five pounds, possessing God-given brute strength. Not unlike Randinoli, Dowd loved to mix it up, and the dirtier the better.

Of all people, Randinoli said it best. "King is one dude you don't turn your back on."

The other three did not think it through and saw no problem with the idea. They agreed to go along with the simple plan. Coughlin agreed immediately. "Hey, it beats hanging around the club all night, it's something to do."

The Military Park Hotel on Broad Street was in the heart of downtown Newark. The four partygoers slowly walked through the huge, green and white canvas-covered arch at the main entrance, lost themselves in the crowd of two hundred plus guests, and proceeded to eat, drink, and behave like gentlemen. All but one. No one noticed Dowd acting unusual, crazier than usual. "King, calm down, we've got people staring at us." Donato never searched for attention, he was uncomfortable being noticed in a crowd. Built like a fire plug, he stood about five-foot-five and weighed in at two hundred pounds, which perhaps accounted for his uneasiness in a crowd.

Dowd and Donato were close friends. Whenever he spoke to Donato, Dowd never said Anthony or Tony. "Antny, they are impressed, when will they again have the opportunity to see such bad asses?"

The four intruders together went to use the restrooms. Dowd now showed a goofy smirk on his face. He smelled of marijuana, took a joint from his inside jacket pocket and lit it. His three accomplices were speechless.

"What the hell are you doing? You want us all locked up, you crazy bastard." Donato, the quiet one, let it all hang out.

A few of the wedding guests came in to use the facilities. Each young man combed his hair to make sure it was in perfect place, and then checked out their Windsor tie knots, assuring they still looked cool. The party crashers tried to look busy—washing hands and combing hair. No one said a word. The other crew took a long hard look at the boys from 12th and Bruce before leaving. They rightly figured that the aroma they smelled was not emanating from the soap dispensers.

When the others left, Dowd said, "Hey, don't knock it until you try it." He held out the joint offering it to his friends. There were no takers. His three friends were not happy. Mason said, "Get rid of the joints or you'll have a long walk back to Bruce Street."

They now understood why his behavior changed from bad to worse. Donato said, "If we get challenged for showing up uninvited, there will be a small war in this place."

Coughlin agreed and reinforced their position. "No one wants any of that shit, now get rid of it before someone else shows up here. The guys that just left smelled the stuff. If they let the manager know, we'll be dealing with the cops."

Dowd was not a happy camper. "Okay, you guys go back to the table, I'll get rid of it and be right out." As they were leaving, he was taking a big hit on the joint. Between all the beers he drank all night, the effect of the drug made him even wackier.

His friends hoped Dowd got the message and would calm down. As the night went on, no one noticed that Dowd made a move on one of the bridesmaids—who happened to be the bride's sister. She acted friendly and he took it as an opportunity to score. The bridesmaid's boyfriend took notice, alerted his friends of the ugly situation brewing, and primed them for the anticipated trouble. The angry boyfriend, a former football standout at Central High, was bigger than Dowd. He and his friends came to the Bruce Street table and he inquired to no one in particular, "Where is your jerk-off friend?" Dowd had been among the missing for a long stretch. His friends never knew what to expect. Earlier they surmised he may have headed back to the corner, or he could be back in the restroom sucking on another joint.

Mason stood up, paying close attention to big Stan, the boyfriend. "You must be at the wrong table pal. The entire contingent of jerk-offs are sitting in that direction." He pointed toward the area of Stan's table. Now on their feet, Coughlin and Donato were sure it was starting and selected their targets.

The angry boyfriend got louder and suggested the people from Bruce Street did not belong, had crashed the party, and "need to be taught a lesson." Everyone was on his feet looking for a bottle, plate, or whatever was available. The smart and sober people looked for cover. The dance floor was now packed with all the cool people, none of them paying attention to the fireworks about to start. The slow dancers were quite content. Of all the popular tunes available, the band chose "The Party's Over." The female singer looked and sounded very much like the artist who made the recording, the beautiful and talented Doris Day.

The Military Park Hotel, a several-storied building, included large office and meeting rooms above the main function room. The entire second floor featured a solid mahogany railing, used for guests to lean on and watch the festivities below. The second story settled approximately twenty-five feet above the dining area. Dowd, now completely stoned, giggled like a little kid as he observed the "discussion" below between Mason and Stan.

Having heard enough, Dowd climbed to the top of the mahogany-built railing, squatted down and with arms widespread leaped outward, feet first, onto the opposition's table. Now high on the weed, the big guy crashed through the thick tabletop and landed on his butt, unscathed. Coughlin could not believe what he saw. "Where the hell did he come from? It must be true that God takes care of children and drunks."

Now the real show began.

Stan, now totally enraged, ran at full speed and leaped on Dowd's back. The boyfriend had no effect on his target and before he had a grip, Dowd tossed him free with one quick jerk of his shoulders. Dowd was strong without drug use, but now appeared to be a superman. His face held a weird looking smirk during the entire fracas.

He was much like Randinoli in that he truly enjoyed beating on people. The place erupted. Mason, Coughlin and Donato banged a few of Vito's pals and all three pressured their way to the lobby and exited the front of the building. Dowd wanted no part of vamoosing just yet; for him the party was not over by a long shot. He knocked the big boyfriend to the floor and proceeded to boot him in the ribs and backbone. It was not the first time he kicked someone who was temporarily disabled. He and Randinoli relished kicking someone and both mastered the technique.

That same summer, in the middle of a schoolyard game, Dowd did the same thing to one of the basketball players. Once the other guy went down, it was over except for the pain inflicted by the kicking. It never mattered to Dowd who the opponent was. Tony Quinn opined, "He and Gabe have the kicking part mastered. If King knocked his own father to the ground, he would kick him. I don't want to see him and Gabe get into it. It would become a brutal dance contest."

The grand ballroom of the Military Park Hotel was in shambles. Broken glass, chairs and tables flew and the wedding reception turned into an out-of-control riot. Other fights broke out among friends and relatives. The alcohol kicked in and people who would never lift a finger against one another became world champions.

The three other wedding party crashers headed for the parking lot on Broad Street. Surprisingly the police had not yet arrived. Since the Bruce Street people never shared their correct names with anyone, they luckily escaped without being charged or, more than likely, incarcerated. By hook or by crook, Dowd escaped arrest and somehow made it back to the corner.

Dowd appeared as sober as a judge. "Man was I right or what? Those people know how to party, heh?" He went in to his spinning dance routine, and yelled, "Nostrovia, cheers, slantè, let's drink. Yay!" The others tried to hold back the smiles.

As an aftermath to the affair, the friends always spoke of their gratitude that Randinoli accompanied his father to a relative's house and could not attend the wedding reception.

A year after the Military Park occurrence, Dowd spent two months in the Essex County House of Correction. After being charged, he followed the advice of Edward Bloom and entered a plea of guilty to the use and distribution of heroin. He soon strayed from the corner and merged with people who were deep into the drug scene. A hopeless and very sad addict, Dowd spent several more months behind bars.

In the summer of 1959, Mason and a few others were outside Duffy's Tavern when a known neighborhood cop pulled up in his black and white.

His news: "Your friend is dead." The police officer came right to the point, no beating around the bush. King's dead body lay under the DL&W railroad trestle on Broad Street in East Newark. Only a few days had passed since his latest release from jail. The cause of death identified as the result of an overdose of heroin.

Sometimes news traveled fast in the Central Ward. Certainly, a plan to take action against a believed rat was an event hard to keep secret, even in the Central Ward. Everyone knew of the wedding episode. Whenever Dowd's name would come up in conversation, one of the women of the Rosary Sodality would say, "Thank God the other three were fortunate to avoid the temptation at the Military Park."

The cop had his theory. Dowd made it clear to certain individuals that he covered for the suppliers earlier and did time without opening his mouth. Since he never ratted out the pushers, he believed they owed him big time. He now demanded the drugs free of charge, whenever he needed a fix. By this time, Dowd required a great deal of heroin to keep going. The young police officer seemed truly sympathetic and after telling what he knew about the cause of death, he delivered a short homily on the dark results of using drugs. No one heard much of his message. The cop opined, probably correctly, that someone else probably injected the heroin, and afterwards transported and dumped the body. He claimed the city was now flooded with illegal drugs. Hearing enough, they thanked the police officer for his commentary on the source of the drugs. As King's friends departed, Duffy summed it up. "That is no way to go, the city is changing too fast—and not for the better."

The funeral Mass was celebrated at St. Joseph's, with the pastor officiating. Mason and five friends served as pallbearers. Mason, a few years younger, would not have been in the funeral party but substituted for one of King's classmates. Donato made it known that he would not attend the wake, the funeral Mass or burial. Donato admitted that seeing his friend in a coffin was too much for him. A tough street guy himself, Donato was hurt over the loss of his lifelong friend, and elected to mourn alone in his own quiet way.

St. Joseph's, always a beautiful church, seemed even more so for the funeral Mass. Mike Moss, the caretaker of many years and now in his seventies said, "We always have the church ready for one of our kids." Dowd had served as an altar boy when he attended St. Joe's School. The red carpet started at the freshly waxed mahogany communion rail, and ran up the three steps to the all-white altar. Immediately behind the crucifix at the top of the altar, sun shone brightly through the stained-glass windows depicting the Holy Family. Professor Jack Murphy, the St. Joe's organist and the choir consisting of thirty voices, added "Ave Maria" to the program. The nuns seated in the front pews on the left side of church remembered Dowd from his days in the school.

A friend of the Dowd family attended the funeral. He was a pulmonary specialist now teaching at the Martland Medical Center, formerly Newark City Hospital. The doctor was obviously upset at the cause of death. Speaking to the parents and a few others, he was heart-broken that such a young life ended. "I tell young people all the time, if ever someone attempts to convince you that smoking marijuana is harmless, you walk away. We see the evidence all the time. Marijuana leads to other stronger drugs and young people suffer greatly before dying at early ages, way before their time. It can be equated to an alcoholic taking the first drink."

Dowd, supposedly now the only member of the parish, the corner, or the drum corps to be caught up in the drug scourge, was dead at the age of twenty-one. The three people with him at the Military Park fiasco often spoke of how fortunate they were to refuse his offer that night. At the wake, Coughlin smiled and said, "There but for the grace of God go us."

It's not over until it's over. A few weeks after the funeral, the name Jimmy Zack was often spoken. The theory embraced that Zack introduced Dowd to drugs at the drum rehearsals. He once told a few of the drum line, "Real drummers need to be high."

Someone has got to pay, why not Zack? He came from New York as a hotshot drummer. He used drugs, albeit never around the neighborhood or within the confines of the rehearsals. Someone claimed to be present when Zack disrespected Dowd's parents. The theory escalated and the conversations elevated to a high pitch.

Without any meaningful or sensible discussion, a posse formed. The more the talk, the more people wanted to believe that Zack caused the death of a neighborhood friend. They sounded like vigilantes, demanding that someone pay for Dowd's death. Now it became gospel: Zack got the King, their friend, hooked on the shit. Absolutely! Randinoli wanted to pay Zack a surprise visit at his Mott Street residence in Brooklyn.

Ultimately, the neighborhood elder statesmen prevailed and the idea was shelved for the time being, but it certainly wasn't a dead issue. Johnny Zatz said, "Make sure of your facts. Why waste gas money and manpower on a wild goose chase." Coming from a character that set more bones than a chiropractor did, the consensus held that the group would wait before traveling to Brooklyn.

Randinoli confided to Mason, "Someday when I'm going to the city I will make inquiries and find the prick. He will pay. The King was one of us."

Mason listened, knowing that in the past Randinoli had indeed followed through with most of his threats. He hoped this one would pass with time.

Soon after the Military Park incident, Mason met with an old friend. "Blackie, I think you were right. Enough is enough. The city is changing. The thing with Dowd and the rest at the hotel put everything in perspective. I could be in the can if things went in a different direction. You know I've been dating Ann for a few years now. We'll be getting married and I'll stay with the night school stuff. My days on the corner are over. What say you, my friend?"

Blackie Capone was someone Mason admired since he and Randinoli were kids and started to spend time in the schoolyard. He knew of Capone's background as a decorated war hero and knew first hand that Capone and his partner Tony Quinn ran the Bruce Street dice game for many years. Capone liked the youngster from Cabinet Street from the first time he saw him. Through the years he offered advice and never steered Mason in the wrong direction. Capone had earlier predicted the downfall of the city and advised that Mason set his sights on his career in law enforcement. His reputation included never beating around the bush. Capone sensed that his younger friend sought an honest appraisal of his plan. The crapshooter entrepreneur would not disappoint.

"Brad, you never took the easy way out since you were a kid. You've obviously given your next moves a lot of thought. I say get out now while you can. School, marriage, a family, and a career in law enforcement are all the right stuff. But don't forget your promise. Never lock up a crapshooter."

They both enjoyed a hearty laugh. "Without question. I'll always remember your teachings—that a good crap game keeps the kids off the street and out of trouble."

Randinoli still admired the wise guys. When his time came to be one, he just might have the opportunity to square things with Zack in Brooklyn. The former tenor drummer thought, "*I never liked those snare drummers.*"

Chapter Twenty-Eight

The Continental

Mason knew Ann Murphy since the fifth grade at St. Joe's. Their families lived close by and they would often study together. A beautiful, petite brunette, Mason bragged to his mother that "she's been a straight A student all through school."

His mother told him, "You found a real keeper. You take care of her and you'll both be very happy." Mrs. Mason liked "the Murphy girl" from the first time her son brought her home. Watching the couple together, Mrs. Mason felt sure that her son would someday marry Ann.

After graduation from elementary school, Ann attended the prestigious St. Charles Academy on a full academic scholarship while Mason went to the public high school. They began formal dating in high school—going to the movies and high school dances. Even Randinoli recognized the inevitable. "When Brad looks at that broad he's all gah gah. Sometimes he forgets where he is—disgusting!"

The next few years were a time of change for Mason, Randinoli and their friends from 12th Avenue and Bruce Street. True to the predictions, the couple married at St. Joseph's in April 1958.

Randinoli served as best man and Ann's sister Mary was maid of honor. Reception, where else? The get-together was held at the Military Park hotel—without incident. While making arrangements at the hotel, Ann asked Brad, "Have you ever been at a reception here?"

Mason recalled the only wedding reception he attended at the hotel, the one he and his friends crashed and had to fight their way out of the building.

He left the King Dowd details out of his answer. "Yeah, a few of us were here a couple of years ago. The food was great. It's a lively place."

The wedding reception turned into an extra special event. The food, music and service exceeded expectations. No one drank too much, and there were no arguments or fights. Even the neighborhood uninvited behaved. They knew that Mason and his friends were aware of their presence and would not hesitate to remove them from the building.

Coughlin, one of the ushers, joked, "It's too bad the King is not here. Things would liven up; broken bottles, blood, cops and all the rest of it."

The groom smiled and said, "Yeah, he went too early for sure. By now he may have quieted down. Maybe not."

Randinoli's toast was brief yet classic. "I taught this guy all he knows." He lifted his glass of champagne and smiled at the bride. "Now it's up to Ann to keep him out of trouble." He choked as he finished, looking at his friend. "I hope you both will live long and happy lives together. Okay let's move on with this stuff. I am a very busy man." Randinoli seemed to realize that his days with his friend were coming to a close. He rubbed his eyes and lit a Lucky Strike. Mason realized that his friend had made up his mind a long time ago. Randinoli would be big time. He would reach the top of the mob world, one way or another.

The wedding guests were generous to the newlyweds. With two hundred and fifty family, friends and the mandatory gate crashers, the couple received a healthy amount of cash. Randinoli paid close attention to the envelopes stuffed with cash and checks. After an hour of socializing, the neighborhood rock and roll singing quartet the Fairmounts became the major part of the evening's entertainment. They always contributed to making a special occasion more exceptional. The group consisted of Gerald Border, Shadow Deltucci, Bebba Kaskie and Harold Lee. The group name was pilfered from a well-known street in the Central Ward. This was not their first performance; three of the four sang *a capella* on the corner when they were teenagers in elementary school. Lee, a fantastic alto voice, joined the group when he moved to New Jersey from the South.

Tonight the group sounded better than ever, the harmony pure. After two more numbers the guests applauded noisily, showing appreciation for the talented entertainers. Yet they were not finished by a long shot.

Mason earlier requested that they do something perhaps unorthodox for a wedding, but still he believed it would be something Ann would enjoy.

Harold Lee was a choir member of the First Baptist Church AME of Newark. He possessed a beautiful voice and sang gospel music since a small child. Mason had told him that Ann loved to listen to church music and she had a favorite gospel hymn. The week prior to the wedding, the Fairmounts acquired permission to practice in Lee's church on Newton Street, a few hundred feet from Randinoli's house. The church choir director helped the boys settle on a beautiful rendition. They rehearsed the number every night until Lee announced, "I think Brad's new bride will enjoy our gift."

The hall grew quiet as Lee stepped to the microphone and announced, "Ladies and gentlemen, we would like to dedicate this next offering to the special bride of our friend Brad, Mrs. Ann Murphy Mason. If you know the chorus, please feel free to join in." He looked out at the audience and then smiled, directing his gaze to Sister Francis and the several nuns at her table. He knew they would surely join in the chorus.

The quartet took their places as Lee nodded to Professor Murphy sitting at the Baldwin piano, said to have been used by Dave Brubeck, the jazz pianist. Murphy gently sounded a chord and the Fairmounts began singing an old gospel favorite, "How Great Thou Art."

O Lord my God, when I'm in awesome wonder…

The new bride wept as Mason smiled and squeezed her hand. The crowded hall went silent.

The four young men raised their arms in unison inviting the guests to join in the chorus. The room erupted in song. Everyone was on their feet. The quartet never sounded as they did on this night. The nuns were as happy as they could be. Even the crapshooters and those who hadn't a clue of the words sang out. Everyone seemed to be familiar with the melody:

Then sings my soul, my Savior Good, to Thee,
How great Thou art! How great Thou art!

As the Fairmounts left the stage, the applause and shouting escalated. During the rest of the evening, much of the conversation centered on the unusual selection and the classy way it was presented. Not everyone shared in the joy of the occasion.

After he threw back a few Jack Daniels, the conversation headed south. Randinoli offered Ann his unsolicited suggestion. "Take my advice. Before you go to Pennsylvania, make a stop at the schoolyard. With your brains and with that bankroll you two can take the heavy action from the do-bettors. You turn that in to a small fortune."

Ann laughed. "Gabe? Bankroll, schoolyard, heavy action, do-bettors? English now, what are you saying?"

Mason loved it. "It's okay. My friend the energy tycoon is always planning ahead. He has a way of seeing into the future. Tell Ann your Cottonwood Queen story."

Without hesitation Coughlin and Donato broke into song, "We have a horse right here. His name is Paul Revere…"

Randinoli laughed with the rest and said, "Enough, you people will never understand. Handicapping is an art form."

Ann said, "Really Gabe, thanks for your suggestion. We'll probably let it sit in a bank for a while before deciding where to invest it. It may go toward some wild purchase, like a down payment on a house."

Before the banter went any further, Randinoli said, "That's fine. Take the bankroll and go to the Poconos. Come back and buy a house. I will break the crap game by myself."

Mason added, "And as always, the game will survive."

Always the last word, Randinoli said, "Better yet, give me the bundle and I will personally invest it in other crap games in the city. And since it is you, I will only take a small piece for my work. I'd say twenty percent would be more than fair."

Before the new Mrs. Mason responded, Mason got up from his chair and said, "Don't even try. We don't want him making a decision. Care to dance?"

The reception turned into a wonderful time spent with family and friends. The couple would often speak of the fun-filled gathering. They drove out of downtown Newark to the cheers of friends and relatives. Mason headed north to Pennsylvania to spend their honeymoon in the colorful Pocono Mountains, driving the 1953 Chevrolet Bel Air, aqua blue with white trim. Mason stopped for gas in Lake Hopatcong and removed the standard "Just Married" white wash from the back window.

The week flew by. Ann, relaxed during the drive home, said, "I guess it's time to get back to reality including work and school."

Brad agreed. "Right, we're lucky to have all this good stuff to look forward to."

The newlyweds rented a second floor, two-bedroom apartment in Belleville. Ann attended Seton Hall college full time and Mason attended night classes at Rutgers. He was still thinking of a future with the FBI and aware of the requirement that an applicant must be a lawyer or an accountant. Mason loaded up with accounting courses and minored in psychology. A few weeks before the wedding he received an entry-level position in the accounting department of a GM supplier in Harrison. Mason said, "It helped during the interview that I'm now matriculating toward a college degree. The guy told me that the accounting department personnel are all grads with a few taking night classes. I'm not so sure I would have landed the job. The night classes turned into a real plus.

Mason always supplemented his income, working an extra job. In 1956 he went to work as a bartender at the *world famous* Continental Cocktail Lounge in the northeast section of Newark. His usual shifts were Friday and Saturday nights and occasional Sunday afternoons to cover the packed jazz sessions. After the wedding, Ann did not look forward to Mason working Sundays, but they agreed that the extra money was needed. When owner Max Baum spoke to Mason, he was very positive. "I'd love to have you come in during the jazz sessions. Brad, the place is packed because I'm bringing in well-known jazz artists from Greenwich Village. Between us, I will double the usual hourly rate and you can count on a huge tip night." Baum told the truth; tips more than doubled the weekend gratuities.

After finishing his full-time job on Friday nights, he left the GM plant and walked across the Graver Bridge connecting Harrison to the downtown section of Newark. It was not a safe area to be taking a nightly stroll, and he was stopped more than once. On one occasion Mason was confronted by two young thugs. He was tired from working all day and not in a good mood. He spotted them when they were about fifty feet away. One of them pointed at Mason.

"Yo, just your wallet and you walk away in one piece."

Mason picked up a loose railroad spike, *what would Gabe say now?* Mason spoke quietly, "Guys, I'm a little tired. So let's get this over with. You're not getting any money. And, you will not walk away in one piece. What you *will* get is a trip to Harrison General Hospital. Make up your minds."

The second would-be robber did not need time to think over the choice. "Hey man you prob'ly ain't got any bread anyway. We lettin' you go. Next time your ass is grass. Now get goin."

"Thank you very much, I appreciate your kindness." Mason smiled and continued his walk to his next job.

The Continental was a hot spot during World War II, with plenty of service personnel, women and booze. Its popular reputation held up through the years and military people who served in Korea filled the dance floor on weekends. During the fifties, the Continental was still one of the best-known joints in the area. There was booze, live entertainment and dancing. If young people wanted to meet new people, this was the place. Many of the wise guys from Newark, Elizabeth, and across the river places like Lyndhurst, would stop in and look cool. The place resembled a miniature gold mine when those characters popped in. The neck chains and Rolex watches would blind the other customers. Of course, the sixty-four dollar question was, "who wore the biggest pinky ring?"

Baum was one tough individual, a shrewd businessman and one of the most decent people Mason ever knew. The two met when Baum's son Howie introduced Mason to his father. Howie, a city hall hack, worked at some innocuous position obtained because of Baum's contributions to whatever city hall political machine held power at the time.

Baum, a survivor of the Nazi death camps, wore an amateurish numbered tattoo on his left forearm, a reminder of the time spent at the horrendous camp at Auschwitz. He was a very devout Jew. The entire Baum family attended temple every week. Mason saw firsthand that beneath the wise businessman persona, Baum was a caring and kind human being. He was more than generous with his wedding gift to Brad and Ann. At times, he displayed his emotional side. He once told Mason, "Brad, I have been in this business for so many years, and everyone takes. You have never stolen a nickel from me and I want you to know how much I appreciate it." Baum's eyes swelled up with tears. They experienced more than an employer-employee relationship, and even more than close friends. It was as close to a father-son relationship as one could get.

When he set a rule, that was the end of it. Baum prohibited Randinoli's presence in the Continental. It mattered not to Baum that Mason and Randinoli were close friends. "You were not here the night Gabe beat a steady customer so bad, I had to call an ambulance and the guy wound up in the hospital operating room." The vicious kicks to the abdomen did serious damage. The customer recovered but never returned to the Continental.

"Brad, this is business. The guy he hurt and his friends are history; a great deal of business went with them. Tell him that if he ever shows his face around here again, he will deal with me." Baum was serious and, even at age seventy-one, his reputation was that of a fair and honest businessman but one tough son of a bitch that you did not want to upset. He spoke another thought. "I sense your friend has some serious issues controlling his temper. He's a tough guy alright, but they're a dime a dozen. If he stays on the path he's following it will not end well for him. I came up against a lot of mean bastards when we lived in Europe. Sometimes it takes a little longer, but in the end they got what was coming to them."

The day after his conversation with his boss, Mason located his friend at Jimmy Buffs on Fifteenth Avenue. "No conversation, nothing, stay away from the Continental." That ended it. Randinoli understood the situation and never went back to the club, not even to visit with his friend.

Capacity at the Continental was about two hundred and fifty patrons by law, but did not matter when Baum dropped a few twenties with the captain of the local precinct. The bar seated approximately seventy-five with another one hundred and twenty-five at tables and booths. The solid mahogany bar had a strange contour, not quite piano-shaped, that went straight across the north side, then took a sharp turn to the east and a screwy twist for ten seats, winding up with the longest section of forty-five stools three feet in from the south wall. The entire area was about two thousand square feet, including a two hundred square-foot dance floor. The dance floor was located between the black and red leather booths and the weird-shaped bar. It stayed crowded on all weekends from seven p.m. until closing. The dancers packed in like sardines. Over the dance floor there hung a five-foot spinning aluminum ball, illuminated and powered with low-voltage lighting. The walls throughout the space were covered with shiny beveled, blue-tinted mirrors. Sitting on his high-back black leather chair, Max enjoyed a good vantage point of the entire space. Baum was feeling good when he told his favorite bartender, "Brad, from this seat I can see every inch of the place."

Capone and Quinn often visited with a few players from the crap game. Tony Quinn loved the music. "The entertainment is the best rock and roll in the area, and mandatorily loud." The two observed how well Baum took care of Mason so they too became friends with the owner. "Max, if you ever need a professional crap game in here, the dance floor would be perfect. Just let us know." Capone was only half serious.

Max laughed. "Thank you, Mister Blackie. I will consider your offer." Baum never got used to saying Blackie, but always Mister Blackie.

Most Friday and Saturday nights the entertainment was Don Scully and the Jumpin' Jacks, a popular group from Jersey City. Scully sang with solid background support, a keyboard, saxophone and guitar and, of course, the steady drum beats. The Jumpin' Jacks' theme song screamed, "Stick out your can, cause here comes the garbage man."

On occasion, a few neighbors complained of the noise. Baum resolved the problem. "I drop a few extras to the precinct captain and give the police discounted beer. We never have to answer any formal complaints. The neighbors get free beer as well."

When Mason finished a six p.m. to two a.m. shift, cleaned up, reconciled his cash register and opened a bottle of beer, his head still pounded from the music, especially the loud traps. There were usually three bartenders, which sometimes included Baum's son Howie. Mason figured Baum let Howie work so he could keep an eye on him. Baum knew for certain that his only son was stealing money from the business.

Baum kept a bundle of bills under a loose board in the very back end of the bandstand. You did not have to be Sherlock Holmes to observe "the Howie" as he sneakily raised the board and filled his pockets with a handful of bills. Baum confided in Mason, and called it like it was. "He is my only son and I love him" The old man smiled, "I know there are a few rungs missing from the ladder."

Baum liked Mason for more than his honesty. On occasion, a customer would misbehave. Not hired as a bouncer, Mason still reacted a few times to inappropriate behavior of some clientele. One early Friday evening, before the music started at eight, there were somewhere between twenty-five and thirty early customers. Ralph, a small-time hoodlum and one of the steadies who usually drank too much, became obnoxious and threatening with Baum about his line of credit and current outstanding balance. Baum was trying to calm Ralph down, even telling the young thug to forget all about the debt, suggesting he go home and get some sleep. Before anyone saw it coming, Ralph was on Baum and started to punch the elderly man. Mason leaped over the bar, grabbed Ralph by the neck, and, when Ralph tried to swing, hit him hard—flush in the rib cage. Mason then dragged Ralph through the swinging doors leading out to a huge oak door that opened to Clay Street. Scully saw the problem and did not miss a beat. He kept going with the Jacks' rendition of "Blueberry Hill," one of Fats Dominos big hits. The interruption ended quickly, before the customers realized what happened.

Outside on the street, Mason looked directly at Ralph. "You'll regret this in the morning. Go home and think about it. Tomorrow's another day." For the time being, Ralph did not have a choice. His options were to go home or wherever he was going, but he was not to return to the Continental until he apologized to Max and received the owner's blessing.

A few days later Ralph did make his amends, which Max accepted. The hood behaved himself and never caused any problems again, at least when Mason was working the stick. Baum expressed his gratitude.

Often, after a long night of noise and hard work, Mason would accompany his boss to Baum's big four-door, dark green 1948 Olds Series 60 sedan. On occasion they would stop, smoke a Cuban cigar, drink a cold bottle of Schlitz, and just talk. Baum always offered good, sound advice. Mason never forgot the wisdom of those private conversations. "Brad, keep working hard, love your family, find something you can be passionate about and allow God to do the rest."

Baum, with no formal schooling—a self-educated man—had read much about the FBI and respected what the bureau stood for: Fidelity, Bravery and Integrity. He loved reading about how the bureau removed another law-breaker from society. He supported everything the FBI represented. Whenever he read about an agent killed in the line of duty, Baum felt sincere sadness.

He often encouraged his young friend, telling Mason he would be a real asset to the FBI. "Would that be something? FBI Special Agent Brad Mason, formerly of Maxie Baum's world-famous Continental." The two friends enjoyed a warm laugh.

Chapter Twenty-Nine

We want change

At the recent wedding reception at the Military Park Hotel, Shadow Deltucci accurately opined about Mason and Randinoli's discussions. "I will miss those two going at it. The truth is the two friends are slowly parting company."

The following year, in September 1959, the new husband and brand-new father continued attending evening classes at Rutgers University's Newark campus and worked at his full-time accounting position at the General Motors plant in Harrison. During the first two semesters, he took two courses and attended classes one night a week. This schedule would later increase to three and then four nights weekly. On occasion, Mason and a friend and work associate at GM, Larry Fitzsimmons, stopped for a beer at one of the Newark joints downtown or near Fitzsimmons house in Kearny. Those stops usually ended up with Fitzsimmons, a decorated U.S. Army veteran, arguing with the bartender about the Yankees or, with more vigor, the New York Giants. A football standout at East Side High in the Newark Ironbound section, Fitzsimmons mirrored a sports information and trivia encyclopedia.

"You find me a better football player than Frank Gifford and I'll eat his helmet." If a dispute arose, Fitzsimmons would drown his opponent with every statistic known to man. If needed, he'd manufacture a few.

From time to time, Mason spoke of the possibility of joining the Newark Police Department and possibly the FBI after graduation. Like Blackie Capone from 12th and Bruce, Fitzsimmons did not like the Newark idea. "You could not pay me enough to take the Newark job. Things have been too uneasy and getting crazier." Fitzsimmons echoed the feelings of Capone when the crap game operator predicted that "Newark was in big trouble."

Both men turned out to be correct. A few years later, in July 1967, the street rioting in Newark resulted in twenty-six people dead and several hundred injured. The city was falling apart. The reality helped convince Mason that the Newark PD job was no longer an option.

Ann said, "We struggled to get out of the city and now we would have to again reside within the city limits for you to qualify as a cop." Things were out of control, caused by the criminal conduct of a few bad apples. It now became compulsory for Newark residents to enroll children in Newark public schools. This latest ruling meant that more children would now attend below-standard schools in an unsafe environment.

The cause or causes of the riots depend on whom one asked. There were more than enough opinions to go around. Most of the killings and violence occurred in the city's Central Ward, where Mason and Randinoli grew up. In spite of the increasing danger, the police and fire personnel showed up for work each day and risked their lives.

The race numbers had changed dramatically. In the early sixties, the black population in Newark increased at a rapid pace. As far as sheer numbers, they held the majority in the Central Ward but still were not in total control of city hall and the accompanying political structure. What caused the riots, injuries, looting, deaths, and all the rest? Unfounded media coverage festered rumors that the police killed a black man, a cab driver. The already-heated atmosphere worsened and the once peaceful neighborhoods became war zones. Violence and law breaking followed throughout the city. Later investigations, including numerous interviews, dismissed the rumor as false. The facts showed that the local NAACP, which was heavily involved in block-busting, was responsible for the allegation. Local newspaper interviews of several citizens, mostly blacks living in the Central Ward, confirmed the NAACP's instigation. A few years prior, the same group initiated a block-busting maneuver in the South Ward, forcing white, Latino, and Asian families to flee the city in lieu of the threats and ensuing violence.

Mae Johnson, a black woman from Morris Avenue and the mother of six children, all college graduates, lamented over what had been done to her city. She and her family were close friends with the Masons and a few other white families living on Cabinet Street. They all attended Saint Joseph's Catholic Church and the children were all classmates at the parish elementary school.

"Why, why?" She was asking the question of a newspaper reporter. "We all lived in the same neighborhood, blacks, whites, Hispanics, and others. Our children attended school and played together." She had read one of the biased and inaccurate newspaper accounts, an editorial opinion that stated the riots were the results of a government that overlooked the blacks, as well as alleged police brutality. "That just is not true. Our many white friends were living under the same government, the same laws and police department. You cannot make excuses for burning buildings, for the senseless brutality and acts of violence against our police and firefighters. Those brave men and women were doing their jobs trying to help people. That is not the behavior of Christian folk. The troublemakers masquerading as promotors of civil rights for blacks have forced my white friends, who I have known for over twenty years, out of their homes."

Many people shared her feelings. Unfortunately, Johnson's views were heard too late.

The most publicized *tragedy* centered round a Bergen Street landmark.

During the height of the riots, several buildings were set afire resulting in firefighters and policemen risking their lives to extinguish each blaze. Many of the arsons could have been controlled in time to save many of the structures, if not for the interference of the cowards with rifles. One such building was a mosque considered a historic landmark in the city.

The law-abiding black population was as surprised as the rest of the residents when information released described the raging fire and the alleged trapped victims. One of the fatalities was Said Ali al-Sikar, wanted by federal, state and local authorities for his planning of and participation in several terrorist acts. Sikar and his outlaw followers used the mosque, which filled an entire block, to ostensibly worship. In reality, the mosque served as a weapons warehouse and a hideout from the FBI and Newark PD.

The three-story building caught fire around noon when a strong wind thrust the flames coming from a burning factory located approximately two hundred feet down-wind of the mosque. The firefighters, responding in an NFD rescue vehicle, were met with a barrage of gunfire coming from the mosque. As the fire raged, Sikar and his gang moved up and occupied the third floor of the mosque. The terrorist had given orders. "We will not be taken. We will stay and kill as many infidels as we can." With the fire burning out of control, Chief Ed Fitzpatrick issued remarks later that evening: "The building was salvageable when our first ladders arrived. The mosque could have survived. Sikar and the other cowards shooting at my people prevented us from doing our job and accomplishing our objective."

The Star-Ledger's Hatlas was all over the story. Explaining the situation in great detail, the journalist wrote: "It was a miracle that the brave firefighters survived the salvo of rifle fire without losing any of their brothers. When the smoke from the extinguished mosque cleared, many interesting artifacts lay amid the rubble, religious articles not included. Fifty automatic weapons, most Russian-made AKM assault and U.S.-made Remington bolt-action rifles, burned beyond repair in a metal cabinet. Thirty-six revolvers to include Italian-made Beretta semi-automatic pistols and Glock and S&W 38 revolvers were burned but identifiable."

The Hatlas coverage was picked up by the AP and circulated throughout the country. "Sikar, a known terrorist responsible for the deaths of several Americans, lay dead in the middle of the cache of weapons. The FBI foreign counter intelligence agents and the Newark Police special ops team had maintained constant surveillance on the group and watched as the building burned to ashes. The investigators at the scene stated that they will be able to identify and account for each corpse. There were fifteen alleged worshipers. However, an early rifle shot from an adjoining rooftop intentionally or unintentionally found its mark. The bullet struck Sikar squarely in the forehead and he died instantaneously." In his account of the incident, Hatlas wisely excluded the fact that law enforcement at the scene, all familiar with Sikar's lengthy rap sheet, did not comment publicly or feign sorrow for the loss.

A veteran of the Newark PD, speaking with a bit of an Irish brogue, lilted, "Ah, bless her heart, as my dear saintly grandmother would say, 'We must not delight in anyone's death; but we can enjoy reading the obituary.'" The department was now ready to close several hitherto unsolved felony cases.

Mason and his friends recognized that the city's black population was concentrated in the Central Ward. They always believed, as they were taught in their homes and at St. Joseph's, that the color of a person's skin didn't matter. Still the reality of the situation was obvious. Existence in the neighborhood changed drastically and now life-influencing choices needed attention.

Everyone—white, black, Hispanic—living in these neighborhoods pre-1967 were far removed from the predominantly white governmental establishment. Most were low-income families, disenfranchised and alienated from city hall. The bottom line was during this time period Newark was governed by a primarily white, well-established political machine. Corruption and an unresponsive municipal government was a pattern of doing the city's business. Now many of the population began to abandon the city and the remaining, predominantly-black community now looked to deal with the enormous task of reconstruction. They now had the power that their so-called leaders had insistently demanded. People confused about the turmoil finally succumbed to the few agitators who adopted "We want change" as the battle cry. The majority, who sided with Mae Johnson and her friends, soon silenced completely.

The new political leaders soon exhibited complete power over the destiny of Newark's future. They were now in control to either make the city a great place to live—or allow it to deteriorate with time.

Chapter Thirty

Early days in New York—career time

From the middle of 1959 through 1960, Randinoli increased his trips from New Jersey to Brooklyn and Manhattan. Now he was driving from Newark three or four times a week. He found an affordable apartment in Brooklyn, not far from the store, that housed one of the crews of the La Cosa Nostra Bonanno crime family.

Quinn asked, "Gabe, what's the big attraction to New York?"

He never wavered, his answer always consistent. "I visit an old friend of the family from the old country; it keeps the old man happy. I take the guy to see a Dodger game once in a while." This lie kept the inquisition to a minimum. In addition to visiting his new mob friends, Gabe's frequent trips to the Big Apple were for an entirely different reason.

Mason didn't like it when Randinoli lied about his reason for the New York trips. Mason recognized that the purpose for the trips was two-fold, but did not discuss them with any of their friends. From the start of the New York trips, he knew that once Randinoli decided to do something he followed through. Sadly, Mason could never talk his friend out of his ambition to be a real wise guy. As to the second reason, he hoped that Randinoli was thinking only of a warning for Zack, at most a good beating.

"You don't have to lie to Tony or any of our friends. You put the wise guys in front of your old neighborhood friends and that's the way it is. Tell the truth. It will stop all the questions." Mason was frustrated. "You like whatever the hell it is you like. Period."

"Okay, I'll straighten that out." More words only—he had no intention of telling anyone anything about his new life.

The New York excursions did in fact have two purposes. Mason always thought that maybe this one time Randinoli would be too busy to think of their friend King and forget about taking revenge, which Randinoli viewed as his duty. Although years had passed by, he never forgot what happened. When King died of a heroin overdose, Randinoli decided that one person was responsible for the untimely death of the neighborhood icon. And he would square things with Jimmy Zack. No one could change his mind. It didn't matter what the others thought, they weren't like him. Gabe considered it loyalty and whatever else sounded righteous to him. He was going to handle the matter in his own way. It took time, but Randinoli definitely reached the dark side. *Zack gets what's comin' to him.*

Mason hoped that his friend would not find Zack in Brooklyn or anywhere else. Perhaps enough time had passed and the matter was no longer an issue. He thought, *"If Gabe locates the snare drummer then all bets are off. He will hurt Zack."*

Whenever Capone and Quinn took some time off from running the crap game at Bruce Street, they were comfortable assigning the responsibility to a more than eager Randinoli to substitute in their absence. In spite of his temper, Randinoli understood the game and the players, and was persuasive enough to keep the business flowing without interruption.

Quinn said, "Gabe is no longer a kid. He can turn on the charm when he has to. Maybe the rough stuff will wear off with age."

Capone said, "I wouldn't lay the odds on it."

Capone always filled Mason in on their itinerary. "Brad, I know you're busy enough yourself, but when you visit the neighborhood try to keep an eye on him. We don't want to come back to find our best customer in traction at the city hospital."

Before the Newark riots, the Bruce Street game enjoyed a solid reputation throughout the New York-New Jersey metropolitan area. The game lasted for over ten years. During this time, some of the people from New York visited the Bruce Street game several times a month. Occasionally, they filled a day by shooting crap in the morning, then stopping to eat at their favorite Italian restaurant in Belleville before finishing with the two-hour drive to the Atlantic City racetrack and a complimentary overnight stay at one of the new casinos.

James "Jimmy" Palmeri, a soldier in the Brooklyn-based Bonanno family, showed up at the game at least twice a month since the late fifties. A "don't" bettor, the gangster won more than he lost. He understood how the world worked and never questioned the percentage taken by the Battiatos.

He would laugh, "New York, New Jersey, South Dakota, hey business is business."

Palmeri, a bona fide wise guy, often displayed a unique sense of humor. "Blackie, is this a great country or what? A big breakfast before we leave the city, a nice relaxing ride across the historic Hudson, shoot a little craps, eat at Racanelli's Italian Bistro, drive to AC to watch the beautiful ponies, and finish with a freebie room at Resorts. *Paisan*, I ask you, is this a great country, or what?"

Capone heard these comments in the past. He loved the dialogue. "And Jimmy, you are a wonderful citizen who appreciates his many blessings."

"Do ya think?" Palmeri loved the attention.

Randinoli enjoyed listening to the hood from New York. The gangster was six years older than the kid from the corner. *Would the time come when Palmeri turned his back on the kid from the corner?*

Capone quickly changed the topic. "By now you must have tenure in your job." He said this more for Randinoli's benefit than to gather information for himself.

Palmeri said, "Ten what? Tenure, what the hell is tenure?"

Quinn jumped in to assist. "You know Jimmy. That's when your position is secure until you retire."

Palmeri thought hard on this piece of news. He smiled and said, "Right, I'm secure all right, really lookin' forward to a long and happy retirement. I may have been more secure when I was in the reform school." He stopped smiling, the subject dropped. "I'll lay forty—no ten."

Quinn said, "Right, I heard you mention that one time. What was it, Lincoln Hall or something like that?"

"Tony, you have a good memory. Right, all the wayward youths from Brownsville Brooklyn and Rockaway Queens were residents. I guess I was lucky to have a place to go. Things were rough on the street."

Quinn thought it better to drop the topic of conversation.

Whenever Randinoli managed the game, he paid special attention to Palmeri and the other New Yorkers. This is what he wanted in life, what he yearned for, to be someone special—a big-shot gangster. He told his friend, "They always seem the same, plenty of dough, women, the best cars and clothes. They have to be doin' somethin' right. Everyone knows who they are. People respect them. What say you, my man?"

Mason answered, "Maybe for right now. But they all wind up in the joint or dead. I don't think you want any of that crap. You can own and operate a number of businesses right here in the ward. You'll make a nice living and still be able to do the things you like to do. The crap game may move to another location. So you drive a few miles. No big deal."

"I guess you're right." The smile on his face assured Mason that nothing changed because of his little speech. *Gabe had solidified his decision. He will be a wise guy. Of this there was no doubt.*

For his part, Randinoli respected anyone connected to the rackets. When he learned that Palmeri and his friends were connected with the Bonanno crime family, he intended to stay close to his new friend.

Randinoli, not bashful, sensed an opportunity. "Jimmy, I need to visit the city next week. I'll be in your area, maybe I can stop by and grab a cappuccino with you."

"Gabe, anytime at all, I will be at the store every day. If I have to leave, someone will know when I'll be back. Tell 'em who you are. I'll leave word that you might show up. I'll find you." Palmeri sounded gracious to anyone listening to the conversation. He told one of his companions, "Gabe is a tough kid, I saw him in action. He also knows how to run a big game and make money at it. I can see why he wants to come to the city. Good, maybe we all benefit." Palmeri had the authority to bring "associates" into his crew. They report to him and earn money for the family.

Randinoli had little trouble finding the address given him by Palmeri. "Gabe, you run a very professional game, the players are treated with respect and always come back for more action. I like the way you handle the troublemakers before they get out of control, not to mention the necessary pay offs to the locals."

Randinoli accepted the compliment. "Jimmy, I learned from the best at an early age. I paid attention and it's payin' off. I'll be gettin' out of the neighborhood for good sometime soon."

"Let's take a ride." They were soon in the Bedford-Stuyvesant area of Brooklyn. "Here's where I grew up, Gates Avenue, look familiar?"

"Look at the playground, could be Bruce Street." Randinoli stared at the entire area.

Palmeri smiled. "I know, that's what I thought the first time I went to the crap game. And of course my reform school on Highlawn Avenue in Bensonhurst is not far from here."

Randinoli liked the way Palmeri said "the crap game." He didn't have to describe the exact location of the game; they both knew he spoke of "the game"—Bruce Street schoolyard in Newark. He was proud of the game and of his personal association with it.

As they looked around their surroundings, Palmeri said, "I can think of a lot of stuff that I went through here. I knew I had to get out and I did." He looked at the visitor. "Gabe, you have a chance to come with us. You can do what I do as far as 12th and Bruce is concerned—pay a visit once in a while. But with us you spend your time here in the city and you work for the family. I would do what I can to get you a spot."

Randinoli felt goose bumps up and down his arms. He didn't want to show his excitement. "Jimmy, let me think on it and get back to you. I think you know what my answer will be."

The following week the new guy spoke the expected answer. "I would be happy to work with…I mean for you."

Randinoli's visits to New York increased dramatically. Palmeri came across as a very likable, easy-going guy. The two became fast friends. He viewed the new member of his crew as someone who could bring in much-needed cash. Palmeri earlier convinced the boss that Randinoli impressed him with the business-like fashion in which the Bruce Street game operated and credited Randinoli for his managing expertise.

Randinoli, his dream of becoming a real Mafiosi constantly on his mind, was not the only one to leave the neighborhood. The reality was that the schoolyard, as the 12th Avenue and Bruce Street bunch knew it, was history. He now drove to the Big Apple on a daily basis.

Like so many others, Mason, too, moved from the corner and took the memories with him. Now a husband and father to Sam, Mason's firstborn, he was a few years away from completing his college requirements and anticipated leaving GM and beginning a career in law enforcement. Becoming an FBI agent was still his priority objective.

In a one-year period it completely disappeared—the community once acknowledged as the Saint Joseph Parish neighborhood. Soon after the rioting, a few families tried to hold on and save their homes as well as the church and school. The new residents made it unbearable to attend classes. Stones were thrown, shattering the beautiful stained glass windows, but the church survived. The following year Saint Joseph's school was a memory. The school closed completely and later housed offices and a soul-food restaurant. An elevator was placed in the back of the auditorium where the stage was originally located. When the ladies from the Rosary Sodality returned to visit their once beautiful church, they were shocked at what it had become.

Mrs. Donato could not hold back the tears. "My God, it's amazing how God spared our church, a place where the sacred liturgy took place for one hundred years."

Mrs. Washington was breathing heavily. "All of this because a few mean folks wanted to bring trouble to our city. Now they have a restaurant replacing the school where the nuns taught our kids for so many years."

Still business must continue. Capone and Quinn did not miss a beat. After weeks of searching for the right real estate, Hillside became an ideal location for the game. They bought an abandoned building on Bank Street, one block away from the main thoroughfare.

"A few grand sprucing the place up and we're on to bigger and better things." Capone sounded more optimistic than he actually was. He and Quinn truly missed showing up at the schoolyard in Newark and operating "the game." Slowly at first but before the first year ended, the new game embraced the old players. Louie Battiato turned out to be a prophet. When he allowed the Juniors to operate with his blessing, he predicted they would draw new blood into the dice-shooting community. Now many of the new gamblers showed up in Hillside to take their turn at rolling the dice.

Quinn said, "The place is comfortable. We have a kitchen, a bar, an oakwood craps table, and business is better than Bruce Street. I do miss the night games with the candles, though."

Capone joked, "For sure it's not the same without the Latin church music."

The operators had none of the business expenses they endured in Newark. They called the building the Roscommon Social Club. They even had legal papers showing the club was a private organization for the benefit of its members. No one ever questioned the "benefit" part. The legal stuff was all drawn up by none other than the law firm of Anthony Washington, LLC. Washington, from St. Joe's, now played an influential role in the New Jersey political system. He smiled broadly, saying, "I will always have a soft spot in my heart for the Bruce Street game of chance."

The Hillside police never looked for a piece of the pie. The chief showed up once in a while and enjoyed his favorite dish of pasta and hot Italian sausage. On their days off, a few of the officers stopped in to try their luck with the dice. No one ever asked to see the license to serve alcohol to the members.

In 1962, another business expense came to an end. Louie Battiato and his brothers were sentenced to serve long prison sentences for multiple murders in connection with the attempts of a non-mafia criminal group to take over the Newark territory. They left fourteen dead bodies on the streets of the Central Ward before being arrested, indicted and found guilty by a twelve-person jury. After the verdict, the Battiato boss screamed to the press, "Jury of our peers my ass. There were two white women on the jury, ten to two. Go figure."

In the Big Apple, Randinoli came to observe many mob figures. He admired these real gangsters. He could not help himself, his infatuation with the so-called wise guy world heightened. Randinoli believed that the Bruce Street crap game was a good minor league experience. It prepared him for the big time. Someday he would direct the big show.

The new guy from Newark met a few of Palmeri's crew. He shot crap and played poker with them. Palmeri, now a capo, liked the Newarker and was happy he brought the kid from Jersey into his crew. Randinoli, now a welcomed addition to the 4th Street crew, was considered a bona fide "associate" of the Bonanno crime family. He became a regular resident at the 4th Street Cafe headquarters, and each day he absorbed more of an insight into the life he desired since his early days at 12th and Bruce. He moved in with a woman, a hairdresser he met in a Brooklyn bar.

His capo loved to speak of the family history. One day over a cappuccino, Palmeri offered some La Cosa Nostra historical insight to his new student. He trusted Randinoli and shared a great deal with the new man. Not his first time explaining the story, his diction changed. Palmeri sounded like a college professor.

"Gabe, Joseph Bonanno, Sr., now dead, was the original boss of one of New York City's five original families. The senior Bonanno took control in 1931 from the Maranzano family. Following in his tradition today, the family continues to feed off prostitution, gambling, protection, and of course, the required contracts." He let that sink in. "He lost control in the 1960s. Today, Salvatore Cassando is head of the family." The captain smiled. "Cassando, in spite of his frequent incarceration, still runs the family from prison." Palmeri removed a piece of paper from his wallet and, reading from it, said, "A newspaper reporter once wrote, 'The message system to and from the gated communities mirrors that of the U.S. Postal Service.'" Palmeri appeared proud of his obvious authentic data.

Each year that passed found Randinoli more involved in the day-to-day business of being a gangster. Now a trusted member of the crew, he took part in operating a nightly crap game in the Bronx and, on occasion, would join his new friends as they made collections from slow payers. His brutality stood out immediately. He never settled for promises of payment. The new gangster persisted until the money came in. Word of his work ethic spread to the boss, Salvatore Cassando, himself a violent individual. It took only a few years. Gradually the people who mattered to Randinoli recognized him as an up-and-coming associate of the Bonanno crime family. They quickly recognized his potential.

His actions spoke louder than words. He was obsessed with the thought of becoming a "made" man and was ready to fill the requirement. Each day Randinoli's reputation increased and he became known as someone who was smart, tough and willing to do whatever it took to be a real Mafiosi. His goal never changed. Gambling, loan sharking, international money laundering, assault, battery and strong-arming were all now part of his life.

He convinced himself of the major requirement. He was willing to kill to become a soldier in La Cosa Nostra. Would he ever get the opportunity? Would he get the chance to murder someone to prove his worthiness?

Randinoli always touched base with Mason, still a few years away from his Bachelor of Science degree at Rutgers. The calls were good for both of them. They still enjoyed each other's one liners. "Two boys and a girl? Slow down, my man."

Mason was prepared. "It's all that stuff we learned in St. Joe's. Something about 'propasomething' the faith. How are things with you?" Mason would be greatly troubled if he knew what the future had in store for his friend.

"Really great. No fooling, I'm moving along with this and that. You notice my English is improving. It helps as I deal with real smart people. No kidding, everything is great." Randinoli was serious. He truly felt like he was on top of the world. It never left his mind. *My day will come.* He would be acknowledged as a man of honor. "So the good stuff now— how's the family?"

"Couldn't be better. We tried skiing last weekend. It's not my thing but the kids had a ball." Mason heard from a reliable source that Randinoli lost the Five Corners gas station and now lived full time in New York. His friend did not mention anything about it so Mason avoided the details.

Like other telephone conversations, the two friends kept the conversation light and said their goodbyes.

Randinoli was no longer the newest member of the crew. New people soon accepted him as someone demanding respect. In spite of his non-Sicilian background and the fact that he did not speak Italian—although he did understand most conversations—he secured a reputation as an earner and someone who spoke the language of the streets. When Gabe was very young, both of his parents spoke Italian in the Randinoli household and, like many youngsters with parents who emigrated from European countries, he and his older sister were at times embarrassed to hear the foreign dialect. Some of the conversations sunk in via osmosis and now, although not fluent, he understood more than he revealed. He used this skill to make judgments of a few of the crew who said things in Italian believing their words were safe from "the Napolitano."

Randinoli reflected regularly on his well thought-out decision. He would be a made member of LCN. It was now only a matter of time before he became a fully accepted man of honor. He knew very well of the requirement of "doing the right work." Not satisfied with merely being an associate, Randinoli fantasized of becoming the ultimate, the Don, the boss of the family. As to the language, he intended to create and install a rule for all Bonanno family members. His head filled constantly with ways to make the mob a more up-to-date operation.

He became friendly with Specs Buchanan, a family associate and more ruthless than Randinoli. He would later learn of Spec's specialty. Over a few drinks, Gabe told Buchanan, "Between us, of course, when I take over the family English is the language of choice." He reasoned, "If you want to speak Italian, go to Italy. In this country we make money in English." The 12ᵗʰ and Bruce graduate did not trust too many people and believed it important for him to know precisely what his associates were saying at all times.

Buchanan smiled. "I like that Gabe. You can even let a few Irishman in once in a while. Of course, they will have to talk English, right? None of that Gaelic shit."

"Absolutely and you, Specs my man, will be at the top of the list." Randinoli raised his glass and toasted, "Sláinte!" He paid attention at the club when some of his Irish friends offered a toast to good health.

Buchanan was surprised. With his best brogue, he said, "I knew ye had some of the old sod in ye. Sláinte back at ye."

For now, Randinoli and the other members of the crew received the word that the bosses were not satisfied with the revenue being generated. Palmeri's crew earned more than any two of the other crews put together, but still the bosses cried poor mouse.

Stevie Lombardi spoke up. "The greedy bosses are never satisfied, the crew gets the crumbs, with barely enough dough to live on, and we get no thanks from the big boys." Lombardi overlooked the fact that he and the others drove big cars, dressed well, and never seemed to encounter difficulty getting their hands on plenty of money with which to gamble. The crime business mirrored other businesses as far as some things were concerned. It was par for the course to complain, and a component of the mafia as well.

The discussion along these lines never ended and Randinoli tired of listening to the whining and the complaints. His theory very simple: Keep the big guys happy. He told Palmeri, "So we bring in more money. It would mean more for everyone." Randinoli acquired a few lessons from 12th and Bruce. When he ran the crap game and took sports book at the gas station at the Five Corners, it was common sense to solicit new customers.

At the crap game, Quinn often told Randinoli, "Keep it simple. You want a new player to come back. He will bring someone with him who will bring someone and so on and so on. The idea is to make as much scratch as you can, keep the customers happy and, of course, never declare income to the government. The game thrives on new business."

Besides, when he eventually became boss he would use his power to change things. Plans for increasing revenue would come from the top and filter down to the street peons. Under Randinoli's leadership, the family would run more like a successful business and not rely on lower echelon mutts to develop the business plan.

After more than enough time as an associate, Randinoli decided to do something about the constant shortage of money issue. There was never enough to keep everyone happy. He gave the money situation a lot of thought. "Jimmy, the gambling revenue would grow if we open additional crap games in the joints we already own and operate. We have the space. We reach out for new blood to bring to the crap games and high stakes poker rooms. We kick more up to the bosses, we all get more and everybody's happy."

Palmeri said, "Go for it. See what you can do."

Now Randinoli was actively involved in the loansharking end of business, making collections, encouraging customers, by force if necessary, to pay on time. His methods accounted for the steady flow of money coming in. He was a workaholic by mob standards. The vigorish, or "the vig, the juice, the take," increased when he believed it to be a reasonable business decision. He liked to tell the crew that all borrowers in the city had paid excessive rates of interest since 1935, so a little rate increase now and then was justified.

Randinoli, who saw himself as a natural leader, reasoned, "Besides our rates are still lower than Uncle Sammy. What's he grabbing now twenty, twenty-five percent? Yeah, and all legal. Right!" This, another tidbit of information learned in the schoolyard.

Randinoli always attempted to be present at the new crap games opening in Brooklyn and Manhattan as well as the bookmaking parlors. He stayed ready to lend money to some degenerate gambler with, of course, the right points and vig coming back to him and the organization. Palmeri allowed him to do his thing his way. More than once the capo witnessed his subordinate in action. In truth, the head of the crew did not want Randinoli as an enemy. Besides, the results were what counted and the cash continued to pour in.

The bosses notice everything. Randinoli's reputation grew as a business-man, solicitor and collector. He always believed that the gas station at the Five Corners in Newark was a good place to get educated. He joked to his now subordinates, without mentioning names, of Mason's loan. "My good friend spearheaded a great business career." He never revealed this good friend would now spend energy putting away people in Randinoli's line of work.

Randinoli's physical toughness was never an issue, particularly after some of the collection discussions led to actual altercations among the crew. On one occasion at the 4ᵗʰ Street headquarters, Randinoli dropped Mike Masucci with one punch, walked away without saying a word and casually returned to enjoy his plate of linguini with white clam sauce, with a glass of Chianti. Since Masucci enjoyed a genuine tough-guy reputation, Randinoli thereafter accepted the respect he believed he earned. One of the crew later described the punch. "Mike went down like a poisoned flea." Randinoli thought, "*I should call Brad. I didn't kick once. Not even a little dance step. I better be careful, I must be getting soft.*"

Randinoli always dressed a little sharper than the rest of his associates. Even the big boys recognized his style. The first time John Gotti met Randinoli, he half joked, "I better be careful, that guy looks almost as good as me."

He stayed occupied with a personal matter as well. Years ago, Randinoli made a decision to settle a score. When his friend King Dowd turned up dead of a heroin overdose, the 12ᵗʰ and Bruce residents believed that Zack was at least partly responsible. That was good enough for Randinoli to complete the deal.

Now intending to follow through with his decision, he had been conducting surveillance of Jimmy Zack for two weeks. Each day for Zack was a repeat of the day before. The former drummer would leave his apartment on Mott Street and go three blocks to a second floor dump he used for selling drugs to crackheads.

Late on a Saturday evening, Randinoli waited in the hallway leading to the Mott Street apartment.

"Hey Jimmy, how the hell are ya?" He sounded jovial.

There was not enough time to think. Surprised but not suspicious, Zack responded, "Gabe, what the hell are you d…?

The six-inch blade went straight in the heart of the drug dealer. Randinoli twisted the blade. "You remember King, you piece of shit. This is for him." He slowly pulled the blade out, and wiped the blood using Zack's shirt. The body slumped forward and lay face down in the hallway, the blood beginning to ooze out. The first-time killer placed the knife in his jacket pocket as he headed down the hallway. Randinoli stopped and smiled and then walked back to where Zack lay dead. He looked down and kicked the already lifeless figure in the hip, as violently as he could. "You were a lousy drummer, you worthless bastard."

Chapter Thirty-One

Sandusky, Ohio

The Mason family moved to Sandusky, Ohio, in 1965 after Mason accepted a position in the accounting department at the General Motors plant in Sandusky. It made financial sense for the company to move from New Jersey to the Midwest at the time. The move guaranteed overall lower costs, not the least of which was the proximity for shipping parts around the world. People out of work now found good paying jobs at the new plant. The politicians and the business leaders envisioned the city thriving, especially the downtown waterfront area of Sandusky.

The Mason children adjusted to their new surroundings with youthful enthusiasm. Ann was kept busy with the family—Sam eleven, Michael nine and Kate, the baby, six—as well as church and other ancillary activities, such as art and yoga classes. The family joined a summer pool club that featured championship swimming and diving teams. The three Mason children took advantage of the facility and spent many happy hours at the pool. Fortunately, they enjoyed their schools and the exceptional nuns and teachers. Mason gave Ann the credit for the academic success the kids enjoyed.

Depending on the time of year, on Thursday nights Mason either bowled with a company league or golfed in a nine-hole league in nearby Huron. During these times, there was always conversation concerning GM and all the company politics that goes along with it. Mason truly enjoyed the people he worked with but his mind was never far from a career in law enforcement and the FBI.

Larry Fitzsimmons, Mason's close friend, knew well that Mason's employment at GM was short lived. "Both our families transferred to Ohio at the same time. It's hard to believe that we've been here near two years already. In a short time, you will have the degree in your hands. Soon you will be history. I know our family will miss you guys when you leave GM. But I know this is not for you."

"That goes both ways for sure," Mason said. "I hope it's not a mistake, but Ann and I talk about it a lot and it seems like the right path to follow. If she hesitated I wouldn't make the move." He shared his intentions with a few other friends who also transferred from New Jersey to Ohio. They each understood his wish to change careers.

In 1970, right after Christmas, Mason decided to get the ball rolling. He was aware of the FBI satellite offices all around the country. There was one such Resident Agency (RA) in Sandusky with two special agents on assignment. After discussing it with Ann, Mason decided to call the RA.

"FBI, Agent Mike Provost." The voice answering the call showed a distinct southern accent.

"My name is Brad Mason. I would like to speak with someone about possible employment with the FBI."

Provost said, "Sure thing. Give me some idea of what position you're considering and we'll go from there." Mason wasn't sure what he expected at the other end. This was the first time Mason spoke with a real FBI agent. He was impressed with both the professionalism as well as the friendliness of the agent.

Mason told Provost a little about himself—where he worked, his transfer from New Jersey, and his status as to his college requirements. "I should have my Bachelor of Science degree soon, two more semesters at Bowling Green. I drive to school two nights a week to finish up a few minor requirements."

"Good, right now the accounting major is a big thing with the bureau. A lot of international money laundering, bank fraud, mail fraud, that sort of stuff." He named a few more acronyms Mason didn't understand. During the conversation, Provost learned that Mason played on the GM softball team.

Provost said, "My partner and I will stop by one of the games and we can talk. We will give you all the information we can about the job." Mason thanked him.

The following Friday, Special Agents Mike Provost and Hank Fannin visited Battery Park where an Industrial League softball tournament progressed under the lights. Mason played a respectable third base and knocked out a couple of hits. The agents were aware that he needed a few credits to satisfy his degree requirements before submitting an application to the FBI.

Rutgers had granted permission for Mason to complete the compulsory courses at Bowling Green University. His accounting requirements complete, Mason was still a few credits short of fulfilling the necessary prerequisites leading to a Bachelor of Science degree from Rutgers.

The agents appeared impressed that Mason drove sixty-five miles each way, two nights a week, to the "Falcon's" campus to complete his college studies.

The family joined him on two of the Bowling Green trips, expecting a little different look of the Ohio landscape. The kids were disappointed. "It's all pretty flat, just like Sandusky." Sam expressed the feelings of the rest of the family. On the nights they went with him, Mason reported to and was marked present at class, but he'd quickly cut out to join Ann and the kids. On both trips the family stopped at a recommended barbeque restaurant at the east end of town.

Michael loved to eat. "Maybe we can take some home for tomorrow night." Kate liked the idea. "Mom, can we take the French fries home too?" The kids loved the ribs with a special sweet dressing.

When the softball game ended, Provost walked over and introduced himself to Mason. The team members were aware of the strangers and their purpose in being there. Mason and the agents sat on a bench and enjoyed a quiet conversation along with a few beers. The beers were mandatory after a game and the GM manager always made sure that there was enough to go around. As they spoke of Mason's interest in the bureau, he filled them in on his current education status. Mason was correct in assuming that the agents obtained a truckload of information from his friend Fitzsimmons. The agents were aware of where he grew up, the time he spent with the Hilltoppers, and the Golden Gloves experience. They were complimentary and sounded as though Mason would be a welcomed addition. He liked the way they spoke to him. There were no war stories, just conversation about how they viewed their jobs. Both agents shared that they were lawyers and would retire within a few years. The maximum entrance age was thirty-five, and it was mandatory that agents retire by age fifty-five.

Mason commented that he thought that "fifty-five seems young to retire."

Fannin half-jokingly said, "It is, especially when you look at your situation. If you're accepted what will you be, thirty-three, thirty-four?

Mason said, "Thirty-five in a few months. Just under the wire."

Provost jumped in and said, "If the truth be known, the firearms instructors have a lot to say on this subject. They would like the official reason to be that we don't want *older* agents going through the front door in a bad situation. There are varying opinions. If you stay in condition and qualify at the range, then you should be able to handle most situations. Right now, the weight of the argument lies with the gun people."

"Anyway, in a couple of years I won't argue. I will head out the door and not look back. I'll turn in my guns, vest, handcuffs and all the other fun stuff belonging to the government. There is life after the bureau." Provost sounded like he had given the subject a lot of thought. He left no doubt of his position.

Thus began Mason's voyage into the FBI.

When he returned home, Mason excitedly shared details of the meeting with Ann. He was enthusiastic about the thought of joining what many considered to be the pinnacle of law enforcement. He told Ann what guys from the corner would say when the FBI topic came up. "Tony Quinn quoted from a New York Times article, that the FBI owned a reputation as a world premier law enforcement organization." He added that Hank Berkowitz, the well-to-do crapshooter, often joked, saying, "I do not want the fibbies looking for me, no way."

Ann said, "See, I was right. They've been waiting all these years for a Brad Mason to come along."

The resident SAs liked this part of their jobs, talking with prospective candidates. They agreed that Mason was honest, intelligent and sincere about his desire to become an FBI agent. Fannin said, "I see him as the real deal. Let's do what we can to move it along once he finishes his degree requirements."

Provost agreed. "We have the applications in the RA. He can begin to compile all the necessary names, dates and places. It will save time with the background investigation when he's ready to make the move."

"Good idea. At his age, places you lived, schools you attended, teachers, and friends through the years, it becomes a lot of soul searching. I don't see him having any problem with the reference requirements." The SAs were pleased that Mason wanted to join the FBI.

About this time, the FBI became the lead investigative agency dealing with major stock fraud investigations on the East Coast. The sophisticated white-collar criminals utilizing the scarce computer software gained national media attention. A few in the press apparently were not happy with the deluge of positive coverage, so they reverted to the unfounded reports concerning Director J. Edgar Hoover. They ignored the evidence regarding Hoover's past. He worked in the administrations of eight U.S. presidents and as a patriot served his country well by advancing the FBI. Bureau people praised the Director's character and ignored the mean-spirited, non-factual innuendoes. Some accounts portrayed him as "not macho enough for the position." Half of the stories depicted him as a woman chaser, dating many of Hollywood's starlets. One such version claimed that Hoover "dated more women than even President Kennedy."

Mason resolved that the topic was none of his business and he was committed to keep out of any such discussions. This mindset resulted from his Central Ward background. During his career with the FBI, Mason would always answer such *Hoover* queries directly, smile and revert to his 12th and Bruce training. "I know nothing, never ran with the man, may he rest in peace."

After the initial meeting at the softball game, Mason visited the RA on two occasions. He got to know both agents better each time he met with them. The two Sandusky SAs were outspoken and opined freely about the organizational structure of the bureau. They believed that most of the people assigned to the FBI Headquarters hierarchy in Washington D.C. were overrated.

SA Fannin remarked, "The success of the FBI can be attributed to the work of the street agents assigned to the various divisions." Both served in several offices before their transfers to Ohio, and now, a few years away from retirement, were less concerned with any consequence resulting from their comments.

One night at home, Mason said, "They both are good people, but the closer to retirement it seems the more they whine. If they spent more time addressing the crime problems in the RA territory, they would find less time to complain. I asked about the two recent bank robberies in Port Clinton. Provost shook it off as not a big deal. Maybe after all these years they are just burned out. I need to cut them some slack. As a famous crapshooter often said, none of my business, right?"

Without hesitation, Ann said, "Correct, soon-to-be Special Agent Brad Mason. It's none of your business. Now to *your* business. The garbage is waiting to be taken out."

In the coming years, Mason would learn first-hand that many of the Sandusky SAs observations held merit. Supervisory special agents and the special agents on each squad carried the brunt of the investigative load. True also, certain headquarter personnel contributed to the success of the very complex bureau cases, which incorporated over two hundred and fifty violations of federal law. He would later be convinced that when both headquarters and the field worked in harmony, they were an unbeatable team.

On a cool day in April Mason was mowing the lawn when Ann called, "Brad, a call for you." She never told him when calls came from the northeast. She enjoyed it when he picked up the phone and smiled.

"Hey, do they really grow corn in Ohio?" Randinoli enjoyed opening his calls with a question for his friend.

Ignoring the inquiry, Mason said, "What's up with you? Still leading a life of serenity?"

As expected, Randinoli never missed a beat, "Absolutely, I am thinking of joining this monastery I read about, in the hills of Kill-the-man-Jarro, or some such place. Everything is so quiet. On some days, I even miss TJ's screaming."

"That's funny. I think about those times as well." Mason did in fact recall the corner during infrequent quiet times.

Randinoli said, "I thought you would be running the war on crime by this time. Still with GM?"

Mason said, "I am, but things are moving along. Between us, I may be making the move, waiting to hear from some people."

"Okay, just remember the Big Apple is off limits, right? Let me know when it happens. I have to go now. The evening prayer bells are ringing." Short and sweet, no news was good news. Randinoli ended the conversation.

After such calls, Ann would open the same inquiry. "You two grew up together. You stay in touch. And you still don't know what kind of work Gabe does? What does he live on? Where do all the fancy cars and clothes come from? Aren't you even curious?"

Mason smiled as he answered, "At present, he's in sales. He's concentrating on guarding his investments. I ask you, does this lawn look great or what?"

Gabe is still a very busy man.

Chapter Thirty-Two

The offer

In February 1972, Mason received an expected call from the Cleveland office of the FBI. Assistant Special Agent in Charge (ASAC) Dennis Moore sounded friendly but came right to the point. "Brad, I wanted to give you a head's up. We'd like you to come in for the testing and interview phases. The background investigation is complete so we're at the final stage. I will follow this conversation with a letter showing the date and time you'll be expected. You will have it in a day or so. The sessions take the better part of three days. We'll get you a reasonable rate at a nearby hotel or you can commute back and forth, it's up to you."

"Yes sir, I'll make the drive home each night. That's no problem." He and Ann had discussed it. Mason hated to think about being away from the family. Mason knew the training at the FBI Academy was a four-month duration, so if accepted, he would be away from the family for a long time—the first time ever. A few hours' drive back and forth was not a big deal.

Mason thought he recognized Moore's name from a recent story in the *Cleveland Plain Dealer*. His memory was correct. He later learned Moore headed a Special Weapons Attack Team (SWAT) team involved in a shootout with a longtime fugitive named Barry Reid, wanted for a brutal homicide in Wyoming. Moore fired a shot wounding Reid, and the incident drew a lot of national attention. As it turned out, Reid had outstanding warrants in other places. Added to the homicide, law enforcement in the state of Wyoming would be charging the fugitive with multiple felonies, to include aggravated rape of three young women and several white-collar violations.

Mason liked ASAC Moore the first time the two met. They were close in age. Neither realized that the two would work closely together as FBI agents and become intimate friends. Moore was professional yet friendly. "Welcome Brad, I know you'll do well here and I wish you the very best in your new career."

"Thank you, sir. I hope I get through the tests and the interviews in good shape." Mason was still edgy about the whole process.

"I'm sure you will." The ASAC left the new man and returned to his office.

After traveling from Sandusky to Cleveland for three days of testing and interviewing, things happened quickly. Mason received a letter via airmail, signed by Director Hoover and dated April 27, 1972, offering a "probationary appointment in the Federal Bureau of Investigation, United States Department of Justice" as a special agent with the FBI.

Ann read the first paragraph aloud, sounding very official. As she read she ragged that the bureau pay would be less than they were receiving at General Motors.

"Dear Mr. Mason:

You are offered a probationary appointment in the Federal Bureau of Investigation, United States Department of Justice, as a Special Agent, Grade GS 10, and $12,151 per annum less 7% deduction for retirement purposes. Following assignment to a field office, additional compensation in the amount of $3036 per year may be earned for overtime performance in connection with official duties provided certain necessary requirements are met."

The offer continued with discussion of mandatory employment: *"for a minimum period of three years; to proceed on orders to any part of the United States or its possessions; not to expect an assignment to an office of your own preference; and, be available to accept any assignment wherever the exigencies of the service may require."*

The final paragraph concluded with specificity: *Should you accept, you are directed to report for oath of office and assignment to Room 625, Old Post Office Building, 12th Street and Pennsylvania Avenue, Northwest, Washington, D.C., at 9 A.M. on May 22, 1972.*

Sincerely yours,
John Edgar Hoover
Director

Mason and others disregarded the customary part included in the letter about giving the letter no publicity. He shared it with family and a few friends.

Hoover died five days later, May 2, 1972. Ann joked that the letter was "J. Edgar's last official act before he passed away." Larry Fitzsimmons expressed it best when he said, "The Director is at peace knowing that the country will be in the capable hands of Special Agent Brad Mason, former third baseman of the GM Never Sweats."

The family voted to speak further about the offer over a couple of large pizzas at their favorite Cameo Pizza restaurant in Sandusky. The steady customers still perused the walls, filled with hand-painted sketches of many of the antique homes of the area. As for the pizza, the tradition continued; one would be extra mozzarella cheese and the second mushroom and pepperoni. The Masons finished the feast in record time and the more they spoke, the more evident it was that everyone anticipated the relocation, wherever it may be. Ann was proud of her husband, and the kids were unanimously on board with the decision and looked forward to the new adventure. Tara, the family dog, had a vote as well and at home the Yorkshire-Maltese barked her affirmative opinion.

Now that things were moving quickly, in private the parents struggled over the whole deal. It required packing and moving again, with a likely guarantee that there would be a subsequent move soon after Brad left Quantico, en route to his first assignment. The bureau policy during this time insured that a special agent completed only a minimal amount of time in a first office assignment before a transfer to another division. New agents never received early assignments to their home states; only after a substantial amount of time served were transfers to home states a possibility.

Brad alerted Ann to a well-known bureau fact. "The RA guys said that regarding office of assignment, nothing is sketched in stone. Sometimes transfers make no sense; 'for the good of the bureau,' overrules any disagreements."

Sam, the eldest boy, would be thirteen in July and enrolling as a high school freshman in September. Michael, the second boy, would be eleven in a few weeks and wherever the family transferred he would be in the eighth grade. Kate, no longer the baby, was approaching "eight going on thirteen" and fourth grade was now around the corner.

Ann and Brad discussed the matter openly. She understood how much her husband aspired to become an FBI agent, but he insisted it wasn't a big deal and perhaps staying in Sandusky might be the best choice for the family. He needed assurance that she held no reservations concerning the big move.

Their parents, other relatives and friends, although excited, expressed concern about the FBI, speaking specifically of the potential danger for Mason, and what they perceived as the constant travel for the family. The Masons' parents, aunts, uncles, and cousins telephoned Sandusky with their thoughts.

Recently, many news reports seemed to include coverage of FBI and police shootouts with bad guys.

A week before a reply to the bureau was required, Brad, Ann and her parents sat at the kitchen table. His jovial father-in-law cracked opened a beer, and went right for the jugular. Ann's dad opined, "Hey Brad, those bank robbers are mean, and they shoot first. Remember John Dillinger and Baby Face Nelson and all those guys. You never know what to expect with those kinds of people."

"Murph, you're right," Mason said, "but if I come up against one of them desperados I'll them one of your stories. They will laugh so hard they'll drop their pieces and surrender."

The four laughed, yet by now they all were certain what the reply would be to the Hoover letter. The FBI Academy would have a new resident and the Mason family would be minus a husband and father for four long months.

Ann said, "I have already started to pack some things. The next focus of everyone's attention is to get the house ready for sale."

Ann was always the daring one and, as it turned out, the three children apparently inherited her rare sense of adventure and travel. The family would miss people, places and things they were comfortable with, but the thought of a change and new challenges and experiences made the difference. The vote was unanimous, four to zip, with dad abstaining. After sixteen weeks at Quantico for Brad, the Masons in October or November would be relocating—only God knew where. Mom smiled and said, "No big deal. A different state, a different house, and the same five people together."

"Don't forget Tara," Kate yelled. The dog barked her approval.

The family's many friends in Ohio learned that the Masons planned to move—destination unknown—before Christmas. They agreed to surprise the family with a going-away bash before Brad left for Quantico and the FBI Academy. It was heart-warming and emotional to say goodbye to close friends whom the family shared so many good times with for seven years.

The call came late Saturday night. "Hey, the word is out, finally made it eh? *L'Ufficio federale di investigazione?*"

Mason kept in touch with others from 12th Avenue and Bruce Street, so he had an idea of the business dealings Randinoli was involved with. It made him sad, but he still welcomed the sound of the familiar voice. "I am impressed," Mason said. "You never quite got the hang of English, and now you're fluent in Italian."

"Maybe not fluent, but I have picked up a lot. I guess if I paid attention at home when my mom was alive I would be fairly proficient." Gabe's tempo slowed. "I don't have to tell you. After she died the old man never spoke Italian again—at least not in the house." Mason's friend was obviously thinking back to what might have been.

"Well, as usual, the rumor mill is correct. I leave soon for the FBI Academy. It sits on the Marine Corps Base in Quantico, Virginia. After that, no one knows."

Randinoli was encouraging. "From what we hear in God's country, you are one lucky dude to have a family willing to take such a big step. *Paisan*, please don't tell me I will have to address you as Special Agent Mason."

"No, never, that will be for the law-abiding, tax-paying citizens. For you it will be Very Special Agent Mason."

Randinoli was never one to engage in lengthy telephone conversations. "Duty calls. Seriously, you take good care of yourself. I will catch up when you get settled in."

"Gabe, they only allow emergency family calls into the system." He did not want his friend calling whenever the notion struck him.

"Am I not with the family?" Randinoli laughed at what he believed to be a very witty remark.

Mason sounded firm. "Listen up. Don't make any attempts at getting…"

His friend interrupted. "A man's work is never done, and I am a very busy man. Hi to the clan. Ciao." The connection went dead.

Busy I'm sure, but doing what?

Chapter Thirty-Three

Three point two beer

His recent conversation with Mason left Randinoli with a strange feeling, one that he could not grasp. It was innocent enough what Brad said, "*I may be making the move.*" His mind raced. He wondered whether the two friends would see each other again. Randinoli believed he, himself, was indestructible. But suppose something crazy happened to the FBI agent? There was a lot of crazy stuff going on in the world. They both chose careers that could lead to unexpected results. His friend will soon be in Quantico at the FBI Academy. Randinoli believed that soon he would be given an assignment. This work would change his life. He was confused. His friend could be killed. *Stop it… he'll be fine, I'll be fine. Case closed.*

Still, he arrived at one of his decisions. Breaking away from a gin rummy game in the Fourth Street headquarters, the gangster picked up the phone. He decided to get in touch before Mason left for the FBI Academy.

"Yo my man, today's your lucky day. It so happens I will be in your area tomorrow. Where can we meet? And I don't have a lot of time so we'll make it short."

"My area? Do you have any idea where Ohio is? It's not across the Hudson." Mason wanted to be sure that Randinoli knew that the drive would take more than a few hours.

Randinoli said, "Just tell me where to meet you. I look forward to a nice, quiet, eight-hour drive all by myself. I jump on I-80 and I'm there."

In Sandusky, the small diner across the street from the GM plant was not crowded. They found a booth in the rear and sat down.

Three years had passed since they met face to face. Randinoli, a bona fide wise guy, held his dream to be a made man in the LCN. He was recently released from an upstate New York correctional institution, having served eight months of a two-year sentence for bookmaking and committing bodily harm in connection with collecting an illegal debt. As an associate in the Bonanno crime family, he broke many laws as well as bones. His friend knew of the stretch in prison.

"Look at you. All married, three beautiful kids and the career in high gear." Randinoli was truly happy for his friend.

Mason said, "I've been blessed. You wouldn't take any calls inside. What was that about?" The waiter brought them a menu and asked to take their drink orders.

He frowned at the menu. "That's the best I can do here, three point two beer? Where the hell am I, Ohio or someplace? Where's Toto?" Randinoli was only half joking.

Randinoli left no doubt he was not a local. The young man, somewhat flustered, smiled and said, "Yessir, this is Ohio. In this place three point two is as strong as it gets. You need to go to a bar with a full license for something stronger."

Mason offered some help. "Ignore my friend. Anything stronger and he gets wild. He becomes someone else. He believes he's a gangster or some crazy thing."

The confused waiter took the orders and left them alone.

Randinoli said, "I thought it was better not taking any calls. To be honest, I didn't want to talk with some of my so-called friends. I took the rap by myself. I deserved what I got but…"

Mason interrupted. "Remember our deal. No business, right?"

"You know it's been so long I almost forgot. Okay, down to the good stuff. Tell me about *your* family."

The friends spent the next two hours mostly reminiscing about the days on the corner of 12th and Bruce; the schoolyard, the shelter and, of course, the crap game. Each reminded the other of incidents that were near forgotten. Randinoli recalled several stories of how Shadow Deltucci managed to put on a show whenever he got caught by the police.

Mason remembered as well. "That's right, Shadow could shed real tears when the cops were about to snap the cuffs on. But as usual, he always got away without a scratch. He told stories that had the cops crying."

As agreed to years ago, the conversation purposely avoided speaking of the undertakings of the FBI or the LCN. Mason updated the visitor from

New York on Ann and her busy schedule as well as the ages, schools and activities of his three "super" children.

"I know you will not stay the night but you have to stop by for a few minutes and see them." Mason did not expect an acceptance but put the invitation out as best he could.

"I already told you how busy I am. I will make it a point to stay the next time I see you. I hope it will be a more civilized place. Maybe even with a crap game and real booze. I definitely will get back here. I know I'll have a craving for this smooth tasting, three two brew. Anyway, it will be dark when I get back to the city. You know how I avoid going out at night."

Randinoli always respected the *deal* they had both agreed to. He tried to avoid bringing up his business, yet something bothered him. He figured that he may not be given another opportunity to get it out. Randinoli leaned forward as he spoke. "This is not business. So just listen okay? Somehow some people know that we go back, that we're friends. It may have come out when the feds did your background stuff."

Mason started to say something, but Randinoli raised his hand and continued. "Just listen, okay?" Not really a question, he went on. "I never mention names but you know Jimmy Palmeri and a few other people know we're both from the neighborhood, the crap game, and that sort of stuff. It's never been a problem and it's not one now. I just want you to know that word gets around and now a lot more of these guys know that I grew up with a fed. It's not a big deal. Palmeri or someone may have mentioned your name but no one said anything. If anyone does I will handle it. Period."

Mason answered, "Right. From my end, I don't see a problem either. The extensive background investigation included a lot of people. I know some of the neighborhood people were interviewed. No questions came my way and I received the offer. People know each other, not a crime. Don't sweat it. Remember what Blackie said." In unison, they near yelled, "There's two kind of business. There's my business and none of your fucking business." The two laughed so hard tears came to each of them. The waiter came over to check on his customers. They waved him away and got up from the table.

Mason picked up the check from the table and stood. "No, you keep your hands in your pockets. I'll get this one. I don't want you to break your streak. You cheap…"

Randinoli raised both hands in front of him. "You can't expect a man of my standing to pay for three two beer. I will leave a generous tip. I have a reputation to uphold. Man, that is the worst tasting stuff I ever drank. They would not allow that stuff in the joint."

Randinoli was happy he spent time with his friend from the corner. He always felt better about things when given a chance to see the soon-to-be federal agent. They walked out to the parking lot and both found it difficult to say goodbye. "You deal with Ann and the kids. Tell them next time for sure, I'll visit for a day or two and we can catch up. We can have a few beers. We'll have it shipped in from Ohio. Maybe not. Later."

"You take care. Think through those decisions, right?" Mason waved as his friend pulled the big Buick out of the lot and headed toward the Big Apple—where the action was. There may be a surprise waiting for the ex-con.

Chapter Thirty-Four

May 1972: Old Post Office, Washington, D.C.

Brad Mason and Gabe Randinoli, lifelong friends and graduates of a Newark, New Jersey, ghetto, pledged very different lifestyles.

Where would this divide in the road take both men?

Mason left Ohio en route to the nation's capital, en route to Quantico, Virginia, and the FBI Academy. Now the first time away from his home, Mason would be separated from his family for the next four months. Mason resigned from General Motors after thirteen years of service in New Jersey and Ohio. Seven of those years he spent attending night school as a student at Rutgers and Bowling Green. Now, at the ripe old age of thirty-four, he fulfilled a dream of becoming an FBI agent. "They need old people like you." Ann's sense of humor aided her husband's preparation for the big move.

Mason recalled a night at home years ago, the two of them alone, when his wife said, "If you attend evening classes, you will have a degree in no time." Actually, it took seven years, but with family, full-time work at General Motors, part-time tending bar at the Continental, and three or four classes a night for five nights a week, the time did pass. When they said their goodbyes on the front steps, she smiled and said, "The dream continues. Now please do not shoot yourself in the foot or anyone else your first week at Quantico."

He picked up the heavy bag and waved goodbye to the family. "I'll be careful." It was difficult saying goodbye to the kids. "I love you" to each of them was about all he could get out.

The children laughed when their mother added, "And you play nice with the other children—no rough stuff."

He had prayed that this was the right decision for the family. Mason often said, "None of it possible without Ann and the kids."

Mason's closest friend at GM, Larry Fitzsimmons, drove Mason from Sandusky to the Cleveland Hopkins International Airport. This was the preferred approach when compared to another teary separation with the family. The Masons had talked constantly about the move after the Hoover letter arrived. The youngest heard the name Hoover now more than one time. She asked, "Dad, does Mr. Hoover own the company?" They were now prepared, although it did not sink in yet, that they were without a husband and father for a lengthy time period. Sam had assured his father, saying, "Don't worry Dad, I'll watch out for everyone while you're in Quantico." Michael smiled and chimed in, saying, "I'll write and let you know what's happening in Sandusky." Their father missed them already.

When he arrived in D.C., Mason registered at the near-falling-down but least expensive hotel, the Harrington Hotel located on 11th Street NW. The good news was that the Harrington was located just one block from the metro subway if he decided to go sightseeing—which he did not. Mason did not get much sleep the first night. Early to rise, he stopped at a coffee shop and ordered a quick coffee-to-go that helped get the system working. He hailed a cab and reported on time to the Old Post Office Building.

At 9 a.m. on May 22, 1972, Brad Mason, wearing the new, conservative dark-blue suit given to him by Nana, the name used by his kids for his mother, stood with forty-eight new-agent trainees. More than a little anxious, he wondered what was in store for each of them. He earlier confessed to the taxi driver, "I'm away from the gang for one day and already homesick." Raydel, the Cuban driver, understood well, as he was married and the father of three very young children. The driver proudly held up a picture of the children. Mason said, "This is actually the first time we'll be separated. I get to spend sixteen glorious weeks at the marine base in beautiful Quantico, Virginia."

Raydel never asked the purpose of his passenger's trip. A taxi driver in the District learns from experience that people tell you what they want you to know. Raydel shook Mason's hand and smiled. "I wish you well, and I am sure your family will be fine."

Joe O'Dea, a classmate from New York, announced to the interested candidates, "Construction of the Old Post Office Building, at the southwest corner of Pennsylvania Avenue and 12th Street, was completed in 1899." He read from one of the many Washington, D.C., information pamphlets in his possession. "It certainly looks its age."

One of the two class counselors assigned to the new group directed them into a large auditorium. "Sit in the first three rows." The roll was called, to which each candidate responded the usual "Here." When everyone settled in, the counselor introduced the Assistant Director.

Assistant Director Maxwell Blaney, a black man who was well over six feet and appeared to be in solid physical condition, stood before the group. "Welcome to the FBI," he said, and got right to business. "Please stand, and raise your right hands." The class heard the first of many orders they would respond to while in training. In unison with the rest of the class, Mason repeated the AD's words, mandatory before becoming a special agent of the Federal Bureau of Investigation.

"I, Brad Mason do solemnly swear that I will support and defend the Constitution of the United States against all enemies, foreign and domestic; that I will bear true faith and allegiance to the same; that I take this obligation freely, without any mental reservation or purpose of evasion; and that I will well and faithfully discharge the duties of the office on which I am about to enter. So help me God."

There are times when an impression is made and one person accurately reads another person. Mason liked Blaney the minute he first watched and listened to the AD. He thought *"this man is the real deal. I would love to work the streets with him."*

"Okay people, outside now. We board the black and gold bus parked on the east side of the building, which is that way." One of two class counselors, Mr. Conboy pointed in an easterly direction. His lame attempt at humor went nowhere. The new men, tired after a full day of travel, looked forward to a bed and a good night's sleep.

The long day not over; a downside was close by. It occurred when someone from the Director's office entered the bus and announced, "Now listen up, my name is Todd Price. My assignment is FBI Headquarters. I represent the office of the Director. I welcome each of you and assure you I will be available to answer any questions you might have while at the academy. I might add that I report directly to the Director." Price looked to be six feet, brown eyes, brown hair parted neatly, and more than a little overweight. He came across to the new agents as a pompous ass with too much time on his hands. They later learned that Price invited himself as a greeter whenever new agents arrived. Later, they would discover much more about Price. In truth, he had little concern for the new arrivals; his interest was solely on his own career and his aim at becoming the next Director of the FBI.

O'Dea remarked, "Everything out of that guy's mouth is I, I, I. Let's hope we don't have to listen to his story anymore."

When Price stepped off the bus, O'Dea continued with his assessment. "Right Mr. Price, you'll be the first person we'll call in the morning." Now he sounded like an army drill instructor. "Men, after you check in, let me know if you are happy with your accommodations. I will promptly report my findings to Herr Price and have all difficulties handled immediately." The New Yorker blew a breath of fresh air for the fatigued class.

A few weeks later the class discovered that Price, an attorney, did in fact work in the Director's office. The new agents decided to stay as far away from him as possible.

After Labor Day, at the conclusion of the arduous training, most of the same new agents will again raise their right hands, and repeat the same oath. A few classmates will be lost along the way. This time the oath was administered by Director Hoover's interim replacement, the new Acting Director of the FBI, L. Patrick Gray. The graduation ceremony concludes with the trainees given credentials, badges, firearms, handcuffs and transfer orders to their first office of assignment. They are once again sworn in as special agents of the Federal Bureau of Investigation.

Price held negative opinions of most people. AD Blaney knew of Price's inappropriate comments regarding people at the academy. He was present in the cafeteria when Price expressed a sick opinion. Price believed that because of his status of assignment to the Director's office, he could expound on any subject, free to say anything he wanted to.

The subject of the commentary centered on the Interim Director's appointment of the first females in the FBI. Price said, "L. Patrick Gray should've stayed in the military. We need women and minorities in the FBI like we need another pecker." Soon after his appointment, Gray hired the first two female FBI agents, an ex-marine and a former nun.

Blaney hesitated and decided to not get into a confrontation. He thought, "*His time will come.*" In spite of the ever-present microscopic surroundings, Blaney believed that both women would serve with integrity. He understood what it was like, the feeling that you were constantly being observed. He believed that nothing but your very best was acceptable. Blaney enjoyed a well-deserved reputation as a perceptive street agent, a fair and qualified supervisor who moved upward in the FBI, worthy of every promotion. He remarked to a friend, "I think Price misuses his power. Some of his actions are intolerable." The AD paused and said, "No, I'm being too nice. Price is a scumbag and I look forward to the day when he answers for his inexcusable behavior."

The new class was now officially the "First Office Agents A28" class. The new agents were now curious about their future at Quantico. The majority of the class looked forward to the upcoming training. They would be one of the first classes to train at the newly built FBI Academy situated on the U.S. Marine Corps base. The qualifiers lasting from the middle of May to early September would graduate together as a class.

The lowly first office agents, now officially known as FOAs, had no clue where their first field assignment would be. Every telephone conversation Mason had with Ann was the same, with Ann asking, "When will you know where we'll be living?"

"As soon as I get the word, you and the kids will be the first to know." Mason and the other trainees would get the word sometime in the tenth week of residence at the academy.

Immediately after the ceremony at the appropriately named Old Post Office Building, the new agents boarded the black and gold government bus that transported the fresh meat to the Quantico Marine Base, where they would move into the spanking new FBI dormitory. Mason thought of the bus ride as non-eventful, recalling the Mighty St. Joe's days traveling cross-country in a hot and humid, not-very-comfortable bus. Being one of the first classes in the new building meant that the new arrivals' first assignment was to lug mattresses, dressers, desks and other necessities up several flights of stairs. The elevators were non-operational. Staring at the pile of new mattresses, O'Dea thought aloud, "Not a problem, the elevators are not in elevating order so we carry those babies up seven stories. Maybe I should call and complain to AD Price—maybe not."

Each segment of space encompassed two bedrooms, each comprised of two single beds and two small desks. The rooms were assigned alphabetically. Mason met his roommate, Barry Mazalewski, and the two other SAs who shared the shower-toilet accommodations set between the two bedrooms; Joe O'Dea, a vocal, six-foot-six brute from the Bronx, and Ray Mendez, a native of San Diego, California. One third of the class comprised men recently discharged from the service, most military-intelligence types. A military-intelligence background now qualified an individual for consideration into the FBI, along with the attorney and accountant requirements.

When the roommates discovered that Mazalewski was recently discharged from a military intelligence unit, Mendez jumped right in. "Maz, military-intelligence? Is that not an oxymoron?"

Mazalewski said, "I can see you'll require many hours of work. No, it's an accurate portrayal of military know-how. A fair description of an oxymoron would be a teachable-Californian. Sweet dreams, trainees."

There are no coincidences. Mazalewski was born and raised in the Iron-bound Section of Newark. He could become the perfect roommate. The roomies understood each other from the start, they spoke the same language. While at Quantico, Mazalewski would get married to his high-school sweetheart. After a beautiful ceremony at the Marine Corps chapel, Mason hosted a bachelor party at the Globe and Laurel Bar and Restaurant in Dumphries, Virginia. The place was a well-known hang out for marines and FBI agents since a retired marine major opened up in 1951. The two NAC A28 agents often confided in each other and remained close friends throughout their careers with the FBI, as well post-bureau.

During many of their late-night confabs, the roommates covered a myriad of subjects. One night Mason spoke of 12ᵗʰ and Bruce and casually mentioned his friend from the early days. "Barry, this guy could have made it in any walk of life. It looks like his love of the wise guy element won out and now as they say, it is what it is."

Years later, after a few stops along the way, Mazalewski was happy to accept an office of preference transfer to New York, where he became aware of Randinoli's important contribution pertaining to the Bonanno crime family's total integration in the rackets in northern New Jersey. Mazalewski discreetly followed the mobster's career path, but never spoke of him with Mason. The roommates would remain current on each other's jobs and personal family matters.

During one of their private conversations, Mazalewski brought up Price's name. "I hoped the FBI didn't have any like him in the ranks. He turned the class off as soon as he stepped on the bus. I hope we never have to deal with the shithead."

Mason knew the feeling. "He did come on strong. We all come across people like Price, a guy who fakes it, not too sure of himself. Price reminds me of Blackie Capone's description of a blowhard crapshooter. Blackie would say, 'The guy's a legend in his own mind.' Anyway, if we have to deal with him, I suppose we will."

The lugging of mattresses continued for another week, and the manual labor didn't sit well with some of the new trainees. Mason, himself a little weary, tired of the complaining and decided on a little light-hearted, good-natured question. He picked one of the real big people and loudest whiner, Gordon Mineo from Minnesota. "Have you ever worked as a roofer, climbing up a ladder three stories while carrying roofing material weighing ninety pounds on your shoulder?"

Mineo was not impressed. He somehow heard of Mason's night school education and decided to impress the other classmates. "When I graduated from Yale I had no intention of becoming a roofer or any other manual labor peon." The big man's tone emphasized how serious he was. The conversation captured an audience.

Mason smelled trouble, probably picked the wrong guy—no sense of humor. "There's no problem. It was a question." Mason figured his apology would end it. Evident his attempt at being a calming influence failed, humor was certainly not the big guy's strong suit. At 12ᵗʰ and Bruce the matter would end in a confrontation. Mason was not in the best of moods and thought, "*if it goes any further so be it.*"

He figured wrong—the apology: "I think it was a dumb question." Mineo who was twenty-seven years old and recently discharged from the military, appeared to be in great physical condition. He objected to the assignment requiring physical labor on his part, believing it was beneath his status. The Ivy Leaguer would take his displeasure out on the elder statesman, the Jersey jerk with a tint of gray in his hair. Many of the classmates did not appreciate Mineo's thin skin.

"Lighten up man, no one is happy about the mission. Let's get going and finish the job." Mazalewski's suggestion did not go over well.

Mineo, never hesitating, said, "You mind your own business." He pointed a finger at Mason. "He wants to ask stupid questions, let him ask someone as stupid as himself."

"This is my business, I..." Mazalewski did not finish his thought.

Mason's mind now raced. *This is the first day, should I just walk away or pull a Randinoli on this moron. I think I will end it gracefully.* "Listen, I meant no harm. You call it dumb and stupid. Okay, drop it and we can move on." He smiled as his friend came to mind. Randinoli would have added, "*You drop it or I drop you.*" Mason tried to contain the smile. He reminded himself that this was the FBI Academy, not the streets of Newark. And neither the twain shall meet. Don't screw up an opportunity to become part of the top law enforcement organization in the world.

Mineo however, intended to further his FBI career in any way possible. He would draw on his Ivy League boxing championship while at Yale and develop his reputation early. He would embarrass Mason and force him to step in the ring.

"Now he's telling me what to do." Mineo's tone of voice sounded edgy as he spoke, ignoring Mason and addressing whomever cared to listen. He misread Mason's comments as someone who avoids confrontation, and spoke louder. "We can go to the gym and continue with this discussion." He was now determined to enhance his reputation as a no-nonsense tough guy and leader.

Jack Otis, the other class counselor, was within earshot of the entire encounter. The responsibilities of counselors at the academy were many. Their most important assignment—keep the peace. They insured each class followed direction in the classrooms, the firearms ranges, during the physical fitness classes, and generally were "babysitters" for the good of the bureau. An interim assignment given to personnel with extensive field experience, the class counselor position usually led to promotion as an assistant special agent in charge (ASAC) of a field division, or to a higher-level position at FBI Headquarters. Otis, a genuine representative of the bureau, tired quickly of Mineo's bullying behavior. He didn't need a division in the ranks at the outset of a four-month training period. Besides, chaos of any nature could blemish his personal record and hinder any opportunity for upward mobility.

Before a new class arrived at Quantico, the counselor's duty included studying and becoming well acquainted with the backgrounds of his half of the class. Mason and Mineo were now Otis's responsibility, as he was assigned the FOAs with last names beginning with A through M. The two personnel files bore similar facts, each more than interesting. Both men shared a boxing background. Mineo won a title at Yale and Mason's background in the ring included victories in the New Jersey Golden Gloves. Thus far, neither Mason nor Mineo mentioned their respective successes in the ring.

For Mason's part, he saw no reason to divulge his boxing history. It came back to Blackie Capone's theory concerning two kinds of business.

Looking at Mineo's physique, the counselor held no doubt the bigger man could hurt people. Mineo was seven years younger, an inch or so taller and perhaps five to ten pounds heavier than his opponent, but Otis had a gut feeling. He believed Mason's background would be a match for the big blowhard. Mason, too, appeared physically fit. Before Mason could respond, the counselor spoke, "Not tonight men, it's been an eventful day and after dinner and a shower, it will be time to turn in. Tomorrow will be a long day. You will find the schedule in your rooms before you turn in tonight." He walked over to where Mineo was standing. "Special Agent Mineo, what is it in the gymnasium that interests you?"

Mineo smiled and never hesitated. "Maybe the roofer and myself could go a few rounds, assuming he can climb the ladder into the ring?" The others observed that Mineo omitted the mandatory "sir" when addressing the supervisory special agent. The perceptive counselor made a mental note of the omission. For the time being, he elected to ignore the affront from the former member of the military. At the appropriate time, Otis would indeed discuss the matter with Mineo.

Otis whispered to his co-counselor, "Does this guy really believe that we do not go through each file with a fine-tooth comb? We do not know of his boxing history?"

Mason considered Mineo's comment about the roofer and the ladder climbing. He decided that his new classmate attacked both his age and former occupation. This was not the time to express his displeasure. Instead, he would apply the wisdom learned listening to a decorated hero of the Korean War. Tony Quinn often told the young schoolyard residents, "Never give your position to your enemy. Never show your feelings. Act normal, even quiet, wait for the right time." The crapshooter would then smile as he inhaled the huge cigar. "Then hurt him very much."

Again the counselor jumped in, looking at Mason. "Mr. Mason, if gloves work for you, I will arrange it. If not, no big deal." He appeared to give Mason an out. Otis appreciated that Mineo's choice of boxing gloves suited Mason quite well. Now the counselor enjoyed the apparently well thought-out response.

Mason appeared nervous as he looked around to the others as though he was unsure of the situation, a little 12th and Bruce theatrical presentation. Mineo enjoyed every moment, sure that Mason would gracefully refuse the challenge. Some of the classmates were concerned for Mason, mistakenly thinking the poor guy didn't want any part of the instigator. Still deep in thought, he feigned uneasiness with the ultimatum before him.

Finally, after the appropriate time passed, Mason looked at Otis and spoke softly. "Sir, if you will alert me to the day and time, I'll be there."

Mineo's face showed the expression of winning the lottery.

A typical day at the academy meant early rise, shower, shave, dress and breakfast. Mason found all the meals exceptional, but still a few, including Mineo, complained at every meal. "Is this supposed to be soup?" The Marriott people held the contract and offered great food. FBI agents from around the country attending seminars and police personnel from all over the world used the facilities, so the providers met and surpassed the very high standards.

The door to their quarters closed, the four roommates discussed the "Mineo problem." When Mason asked Mazalewski if he would be in his corner, his roommates were surprised. O'Dea said, "You're really going in with that guy? The word is he was a champion in college. You have to be pretty damn good to get through the college challenge."

Mendez looked serious. "Have you watched him in the weight room, the guy's a gorilla?"

"He is strong, no doubt about it." Mason asked again, "Barry, will you be in my corner? No pressure. If not, I'll ask someone else."

Mazalewski saw that his new roomie was dead serious. "You bet your ass I will. And I may add that I will be happy to count the moron out when he hits the canvas." Mason's friends did not know what to expect but figured it better to put on a positive front.

O'Dea added, "If things go south on us, I can always jump in and hit him with the stool." The other three believed that he meant it. The closer the friends got, the more they understood each other.

Mendez laughed and asked, "Joe, New York rules? They are non-applicable at the FBI Academy in the state of Virginia." The four new special agents said their good nights.

At the PT class on Wednesday afternoon, Otis posted an announcement; the fight was set for Friday afternoon immediately after the Hogan's Alley firearms training.

The morning at Hogan's was stressful, the trainees attempting to shoot and kill the bad guys while protecting life and limb of innocent citizens. It was lightning fast and embarrassing when an innocent bystander took a round in the K-5 area of the chest.

Otis passed word to the academy staff and the other residents quickly became aware of the match. There was a National Academy class in session, consisting of over one hundred police officers from around the country. The upcoming bout became the main topic of conversation throughout the space. Grudge matches were infrequent but when scheduled they always filled the gymnasium. A police lieutenant from Omaha, Nebraska, asked, "I know where we are, but is a small wager allowed on the outcome?"

He wasn't the only one thinking this way. A motorcycle cop from Baton Rouge, Louisiana, answered, "Absolutely. Personally, I like the blue corner for twenty bucks."

Every academy resident showed up in the gymnasium. Somehow, even the exterior security guards showed up. "Who the hell is watching the store?" Mendez sounded truly concerned.

The gym had been used for previous bouts; the ring was set up in the middle of the basketball floor. The dimensions came close to standard size; twenty-three feet by twenty-three feet, and the inside twenty feet by twenty feet. The expected red, white and blue covered the ropes and three-foot-high platform. Mason felt very much at home as he entered the "red corner." He purposely stumbled on the bottom rope as he made his entrance, causing the Mineo supporters to smile.

Mineo grinned and said, "This is going to be over even faster than I anticipated."

The supervisory physical training supervisor assigned himself as referee. Gibby Bruneau cupped his hands to his mouth and yelled, "As agreed by the participants, this will be four rounds, each a three-minute round. Two judges and the referee, that is me, will judge the outcome."

Mason's counselor got close enough to ringside so that Mason could hear. "Okay SA Mason, make believe this is Jersey." Mason recognized Otis's voice, nodded and smiled. The supervisor could become a friend.

Bruneau pointed to both participants and got down to business. "Over here in the blue corner is SA Mineo and in the red is SA Mason." A smiling Mineo raised both arms over his head and gave a little spin for the crowd. His opponent stood and nodded. Bruneau continued, not wasting time. "The sound of the bell indicates the start and end of each round." He looked at the timer, who acknowledged he was ready.

Mason reflected on his Golden Glove bouts. He heard Jimmy Coughlin in his ear, *"Pick your spot, shoot a couple of jabs; look to take this guy out early."* There were a few occasions when Randinoli would pitch hit as a "manager" when Coughlin, a Newark police officer, worked a night shift. The man who did not grasp the sport of boxing offered great instruction, "Remember pal, when you drop this guy, don't let 'em up." Mason smiled to himself. He would heed the memorable advice of the infamous "kick first, talk later" advocate.

Mason knew something of Mineo. He boxed in college and looked big and strong. During a summer vacation, Mason and a few others from the corner went to see a college fight program. He remembered the impressive styles and the fact the boxers knew how to punch and hit hard. He thought about what his strategy would be with Mineo. He would stay focused and not take any chances. The longer he stayed in with the bigger man, brute strength would dominate and overwhelm him. The 12th and Bruce graduate intended to follow instructions. He had no intention of playing cute, of feeling out his opponent or giving Mineo the opportunity to land the big one. Mason wouldn't attempt to punish him with jabs and body shots. He concocted one game plan—end it as soon as possible. The planning stage ended, Mason had his game face on, and he was ready. The bell rang.

The crowd of law enforcement personnel sat stunned. It ended that quickly. At the sound of the bell, the bigger and stronger fighter came charging out of his corner like a raging bull. Mineo let go with a straight left, which Mason sidestepped, followed by the big right intended to end the fight. Actually, it did lead to the end. As he crouched to his left avoiding

Mineo's right, Mason landed a crushing left hook to Mineo's rib section, and moving forward quickly followed with a straight hard right to the face. It took a few seconds for the crowd to grasp what happened. Then the police officers and agents stood and cheered. Bruneau could have counted for another minute. It took a while for the Ivy Leaguer to regain consciousness.

Mason could hear Randinoli shouting, *"now the cha, cha, cha."*

Mazalewski went crazy, leaped in the air and screamed, "I love the way this guy follows instructions."

The entertaining but short fight was one of the highlights of the sixteen weeks at Quantico. The roommates and a few of their classmates finished off a few pitchers of beer before heading back to the dormitories.

Before going to sleep, Mazalewski muttered, "I bet the SOB never played box ball."

He never heard a word, the boxer snored loudly.

The remainder of the time at the academy was filled with mandatory law and administrative classes, daily firearms training, and the rest with PT and meals. Before he left Ohio, Ann and Brad decided to save the airfare they would have used for back and forth weekend trips. Instead, they'd use the money to buy something for their new house. Each night he and the family spent long periods on the telephone. They spoke of the neighbors, church, school and the Saturday excursions to the local swimming pool. He told Maz, "I hear the three kids growing up each time we talk."

It wasn't all hard work and concentration at the academy. The trainees soon learned that they could count on one of the law instructors to ease the daily routine. A former agent and Harvard Law School graduate, Newell Scully nonchalantly demonstrated a sense of humor in the middle of a complex legal question. His one-liners, quoted throughout the academy, released the pressure of the curriculum. During one of his lectures, a young man from Wisconsin struggled with the "mindset of the common criminal."

Scully orated with a strong Boston accent. "Tis true, the majority of criminals are not gifted with exceptional intelligence, yet a few might be considered Mensa material." Suddenly his voice lowered a few decimals as he began an impersonation of Humphrey Bogart, including the side of the mouth delivery. "Listen up you mugs, mosta deez bums ain't smaht, yiz got dat? Dey don't sit around and discuss space exploration or Macbeth, yiz got dat?" The laughter erupted as the period ended. "Yiz got dat?" became the mantra throughout the academy.

Randinoli missed his friend and tried to stay connected. He called the academy a few times and engaged in small talk, reminiscing of the 12ᵗʰ and Bruce days. During one of his calls, Randinoli said, "Hey I got a look at the salary they pay you. You know I make more than that in a week. You sure y…" The phone went dead.

One evening during week number seven, Mason heard the PA announcement: "Special Agent Mason, NAC A28 report to the FOA administration office." The message repeated again.

Mazalewski recognized that his roommate looked worried. "It's probably the Director looking for some highly sensitive advice." The first thought is never warm and fuzzy. Is it bad news? It took some time to ride the elevator from the seventh floor of the west dormitory and hustle through the maze of hallways to the office located in the middle of the "admin" building. There was indeed a telephone call for him. The young "New Agents" clerk did not hide her displeasure. She looked pissed. She perceived personal phone calls as a nuisance, an inconvenience, and not included in her job description.

The husband and father thought of the family, perhaps news from home about Ann or one of the kids or some other family member. The young clerk checked his credentials, offered a forced smile and handed Mason the phone. "Sounds like your personal attorney."

Out of breath, Mason blurted, "Hello."

"Hello my ass, you think I have time to wait around for you to get to the phone." Randinoli was laughing, enjoying the moment. Sitting at a local hangout in Brooklyn, he threw back another belt from his tall Jack Daniels. Mason relished the fact that his family was fine, but was not too joyful to have his balls broke after an extra grueling day and night in the classrooms, firearms range, gymnasium, and outdoor running qualifiers at the marine base. He was in the best physical condition of his life, now spending weekends running the hilly trails throughout the marine base with a couple of the marines he met the first week at the academy.

Mason said, "You will pay." The clerk looked up and smiled. She answered previous calls and Randinoli likely won her over with his bullshit.

Randinoli just wanted to pass some time, perhaps talk about their younger days and tell some lies about 12th and Bruce. "I am probably the busiest man in the city. I'm tired, man."

Mason cut it short. "Yet you have time to scare the crap out of me with your calls. Now you're tired. You know how I despise a whiner." In all the years, despite the circumstance, he never got really angry with his friend.

"You sound very tired. Maybe you should stop all that sweaty physical stuff and use my method." Mason wouldn't bite. "Stay out of the gym. I covered about ten miles already and I'm not finished. And you know the gas mileage on the monster is not that good, it gets expensive." He laughed and imagined his friend smiling a little, so not a total loss.

"Okay, I'll think about it. Everything else is good?" Mason did not have to feign fatigue with the mobster, his voice told the story.

Randinoli got the message. "At the top of my game. Okay, hi to Ann and the kids. I'll be in touch. Now it's back to the grind."

Mason said, "Okay, I get the picture, catch you later." The conversation ended.

He would have loved to tell the new SA that the hottest rumor circulating in wise guy world is that one Gabriel Randinoli would be given an opportunity. Perhaps he would tell his friend when he reached the pinnacle, a real Mafiosi. He decided against mentioning any of these thoughts to his friend. Besides, the feds could have all the lines bugged.

NAC A28 guessed out loud about the next week. The fantasies were nonstop. "I just know Honolulu will be my first office." The class anticipated the tenth week at the academy as the time when the new agents receive notice of first office assignments. They speculated where their families would spend the next few years of their lives. It was an anxious time for everyone. Mason tried to remain optimistic, telling the family after New Jersey and Ohio they would more than likely relocate to part of the country with a year-round warm climate.

Both class counselors called everyone to one of the empty law classrooms. The excitement of learning their first office was always a big deal for every class going through the academy. The FOAs believed that process was legitimate, on the up and up. They remembered the first week at Quantico when each new SA filled out a "dream sheet." The counselors instructed them: "Select the top three field offices for where you and your family would prefer to spend the next five years after the academy." Mason and Ann discussed it very seriously and methodically. The northeast was a great part of the country, however, cold is cold. The family had never lived in a warm climate, so Florida became the pick. Miami, Tampa and Jacksonville became the Masons' top three selections.

The "dream sheet" turned into a fraud, a big joke. The two class counselors laughed for days. The raw meat agents eventually appreciated the attempt at character building. One SA out of the class did receive his chosen office. It may have been because his prior job was as clerk at FBI Headquarters, in the office of the Director himself. More importantly, he was a known ass-kisser and informant of Todd Price, the egomaniac AD. In any case, the rest of the class received transfers all over the country, far removed from their "dream sheet" picks.

Mr. Conboy, the counselor with the more morbid sense of humor, announced the first office assignments one by one. He enjoyed the suspense. Finally, he got to M. "And Mr. Mason, from the mostly cold yet great states of New Jersey and Ohio, and requesting the tepid great state of Florida, the Sunshine State, will indeed be going south." Mason is thinking this guy is breaking balls, but it could be true, what a break, and warm weather. The counselor continued, saying, "The South Side of beautiful Chicago, located in another great state, Illinois." When he handed over the envelope containing the official transfer there was an eruption, congratulations, condolences—all in good fun. It was now official; Mason's first assignment was to be the very cold climate of the Chicago Field Office as a first office agent.

Later on in private, Counselor Otis told Mason, "I'm not blowing smoke. Our Chicago office needs people with street savvy. They're overwhelmed with fugitive cases, public corruption and bank robbery investigations. The criminal informant program is not up to par. I think there are too many cigar smokers in the office who believe they need not give it their best shot. Anyway, I know your family will be okay and you will do the job. Nothing else matters." He smiled as he shook the hand of the Chicago-bound FOA, "and keep that left up."

A classmate, Mike Vance, was born and raised in Chicago. Vance spent the remaining weeks at the academy tutoring Mason about the Windy City and his beloved White Sox. Vance was from the South Side and often reminded Mason that the Cubs were verboten. The two friends also spent time working on Mason's much-needed Chicago-ese. "C'mon man, it's not 'Shehcawgo.' You'll be killed." The last tidbit reminded the soon-to-be Windy City agent that pronunciation determined a real citizen or an outsider. "And one more very important fact to remember is that there are more Cub fans because they can pick up the games on WGN. But as far as intensity goes, the real people are my people, the Sox fans."

The family was happy to finally know the destination. They welcomed the news with enthusiasm. The eldest said, "Great, the Bears are expected to have a good offense this year." The middle boy said, "We will be there in time for the holidays. Christmas in Chicago sounds cool." And the youngest asked, "Do they have snow, like New Jersey and Ohio?"

Ann had already started on the sale of the house. "Hopefully it will go fast. If not, we will camp out at, what is it, Comiskey Park?" The family would indeed get to see a game or two at the W. 35th Street landmark and to keep things even they would also visit Wrigley Field in the North Side, at the corner of Clark and Addison.

During the last week at Quantico, things got hectic. Ann ably handled the important stuff, and spent days with the realtor pushing to get the Sandusky house sold. It happened that an interested buyer tendered a reasonable offer and the house sold the week before Mason reported to his first office of assignment. The closing took place two days before he walked into his new surroundings.

The last day at the academy ended with Acting Director L. Patrick Gray presenting a long and very tiring pep talk to the new and very anxious-to-leave FBI agents. He filled the Director's position a few weeks before the break-in at the Democratic National Committee headquarters in June 1972. A graduate of the United States Naval Academy and holder of an impeccable war record resulting from his several combat missions as a navy submarine commander during WWII and Korea, Gray became an unfortunate leading figure in the Watergate scandal. As the new Director, he placed his trust in Richard Nixon and the staff that surrounded him in the White House. This trust proved misguided.

Gray received Senate confirmation as Director in early 1973. One of his comments to the outgoing class did receive a laugh when he described himself as "the ugliest Director ever to head the FBI." True, J. Edgar was no Paul Newman but Director Gray had a mug that could actually scare people. The attempt at humor was not enough. The very exhausted audience heard a few noisy snores.

Months later, a few reporters fairly and accurately gave credit to Gray for the FBI's comprehensive, evidence-gathering investigation leading to indictments of several of Nixon's aides.

When the new agents returned to the dormitory, one of the young clerks came to the NAC A28 floor, and went directly to Mason's room. "Call for you, a guy who sounds important, gave the name Mr. Bruce."

Mason did not have a clue who was calling him at the FBI Academy, missing the Mr. Bruce clue.

Mason spoke, "Hello."

He recognized the familiar voice. "So have you been named Director yet, or will they wait a few weeks to make the announcement?" Randinoli sounded as though everything was just ducky, not aware that he was calling at a most inopportune time. Nor would he care.

Mason, somewhat relieved, said, "Since when are night calls to the outside world allowed from the joint. You must be taking good care of the guards." A ball broke is a ball broke.

Randinoli was actually calling from one of his New Jersey hangouts, an Italian hot dog joint on 15th Avenue in Newark, a favorite the Bruce Street boys visited many times in the past. "This gorgeous body will never again see the inside of any of your federal gated communities. How much more time do you have to serve in that joint?"

"It will be over soon. What's new in your action-packed life?" If he told Randinoli about the assignment to Chicago, it would be ammunition for further inquiry by the wise guy.

The conversation continued for another half hour. They both pondered the small stuff and poured over more serious matters. Randinoli mistakenly believed Mason stayed current with the wise guy's career. Randinoli was now an up and comer in his chosen profession—an exceptional earner for the family. Randinoli said, "Brad my man, I hope you come to the Big Apple after your release. I'll show you the city; introduce you to some very important people."

"If I do, you should consider relocating." The two insured the conversation remained on the light side. On occasion, Randinoli queried his friend about what Mason actually did at the academy. He was more than curious and received the oft-repeated response about "physical fitness, lots of law, some other classroom stuff and not a whole lot more."

Mason noted the longer they talked, the more Randinoli's voice changed. Now he did not sound like his confident self. Something was different. Mason tried to convince himself perhaps his friend understood his chosen career path was not what he anticipated. Alternatively, perhaps Randinoli was trying to figure a way out and was unsure how to make it happen.

"Okay, gotta go. I'll stay in touch. Call me when you get to your next stop. Hi to the crew."

Mason answered, "Will do. You take care of yourself." The call ended.

When Mason returned to the room, Mazalewski inquired, "Everything okay?" He was checking that things were all right with Ann and the kids.

"Thanks, just a call from a friend from way back when." He had mentioned Randinoli to Maz before. Mason could not get to sleep right away, thinking of his friend who had entered a very dark place, now perhaps unable to free himself from his chosen line of work. Like Mason, Randinoli might someday take an oath, a serious and powerful promise to his new family of once in, never out.

After each conversation, Mason sensed his friend sank deeper into the dark hole.

During one of their talks, he asked, "If you wind up in the northeast, would you arrest me?" Randinoli thought that scenario could not and would not happen.

Mason never hesitated, "My friend, I hope we never get to that point. If the job called for me to cuff you and bring you in, I think you know the answer." The truth, even Mason did not know the answer.

"I absolutely do know the answer and I would not have it any other way. Later, Eliot." Randinoli hung up the phone. His parting shot was an attempt at humor, a reference to Eliot Ness, an alleged crime fighter who worked for the Bureau of Prohibition in Chicago in the early thirties. The two friends became experts on Ness when the name came up on the corner. Ness received undeserved credit for the prosecution of the notorious Al Capone when in fact the IRS constructed the solid case charging Capone with tax evasion violations. Ness, known for exaggerating his accomplishments, would brag in bar rooms until his early death at the age of fifty-four.

Lying in bed staring at the ceiling, Mason mulled over all the subjects discussed. There was never a doubt that Randinoli always longed for the life of a wise guy with all the trimmings. *God, I pray our paths never cross.*

Chapter Thirty-Five

Your turn at bat

In January 1973, while incarcerated, family Boss Sal Cassando ordered the death of Bonanno captain Cesare Alizzio. He considered Alizzio to be a "threat to the well-being of the family."

On Cassando's orders, underboss Giuseppe "Joe" Nittoli visited the head of the family at the Beaumont Federal Prison in Beaumont, Texas.

The boss issued specific instructions to Nittoli. "Joe, pass the word to Anthony Spero his capo that the work will be done by Gabe Randinoli. Gabe will take people from Spero's crew and you make sure he has all the required back up." Cassando made it clear why he wanted Randinoli to do the work. "Anthony is pushing for Gabe to get work. Gabe stays busy, and he has shown much patience. He's our best worker. No one earns more money for the family than Gabe does. And he's tough when it becomes necessary, keeps deadbeats in line while never complaining about his end. He deserves this chance."

The underboss assured Don Cassando that he understood the order. "I will explain everything to Gabe and Anthony. The work will be done right. Sal, you know how I feel about Gabe. He does what's required. The crew respects him and will follow his lead. Gabe does deserve the work, but remember," he added, "he is not Sicilian." The number two man in the family believed it his duty to remind Don Cassando that Randinoli's family was from Naples. For centuries, only men whose blood traced to Sicily were eligible to be full-fledged "made" members of La Cosa Nostra.

"I appreciate the reminder," Cassando said, smiling. "Your college training is paying off." Nittoli, who furthered his education attending night classes, was now the most educated man in the family—perhaps in all five of the families. "I'm well aware of our history and I realize his roots are not Sicilian," Cassando said. "It does not matter. We are in a new period and things change. I don't care about the past. It is final. One, the work must be done. Two, Gabe deserves his chance to move up in the family. This is my final decision. I want him to do the work."

Nittoli quickly responded. "That is why you are the boss. You see things that others do not. I will get things moving."

Nittoli did not waste time. He met with Spero at Bonanno headquarters in Brooklyn and filled the capo in on Don Cassando's order. Spero telephoned Randinoli at a girlfriend's apartment and, since specifics were never spoken over the phone, spoke in shorthand, in a staccato tempo. "Gabe, it's your turn at bat. He chose the place in Queens. Just the two of you."

Randinoli immediately recognized the purpose of the meeting with the underboss. It could mean only one thing. "Okay, what time's good for him?" Randinoli understood it was not necessary for his capo to be at the meeting. This way only he would receive instructions and only he would be responsible for carrying out the order.

"The restaurant is busy from six until closing. Make it seven. I will arrange that you have the booth in the back by the big picture of Kennedy. It is more private and enough noise so you will be able to discuss your business."

Delbuono's restaurant, known for its Italian seafood cuisine, featured huge dishes of mussels Fra Diavlo that literally flew out of the kitchen. When Randinoli walked in, hungry diners already packed the restaurant and bar and a waiting line ran from the end of the bar to the front door. Randinoli spotted Nittoli sitting under the huge portrait of a smiling JFK. He greeted the number two man with a big smile. "Joe, you are always the first to show for any meeting."

Nittoli accepted the compliment. "I should let you guys show first so you can talk about me? I remembered how much you raved about the mussels in this place."

"Absolutely the best in the city. You could not have picked a better place. I remember the last time we were here, soon after your promotion. That was a great night." Randinoli was serious and the underboss recognized the sincerity. The underboss liked the young man from the first time the two met in Brooklyn.

After a feast of mussels and garlic-flavored, roasted asparagus, the two men enjoyed a Chianti selected by Nittoli. Beginning the business discussion, Nittoli said, "I have work for you. It comes direct from Sal with his blessing."

"You know I appreciate the opportunity. I've waited and I'm ready to do what needs to be done." He did well camouflaging his excitement, a lesson learned on the corner. Blackie had often said, "You give your hand away you may as well surrender."

Nittoli looked around the crowded restaurant before he spoke. "The newest member of the hit list is Cesare Alizzio. You know the rat."

"We collected a few overdue debts together," Randinoli answered.

"I know. Things have not gone well for Cesare." Nittoli raised his hand in a wave. "But things happen and mistakes are made. Anyway, that is not why you and I are here. The reality is he made the hit parade and it is his problem."

Randinoli wanted more information. "He must've really screwed up. He gives the impression that everything's great, and he's doing the right thing."

Nittoli sipped at his Chianti, smiled and quietly responded, "Gabe, the family does not forget. We have a long memory." Nittoli quietly relayed the story behind the decision to kill the captain at this time. "For many years Alizzio acted as Don Cassando's trusted bodyguard. He obviously did not perform his duties in an acceptable manner. The boss has waited for the right time. He says the time is now. Alizzio handled deliveries of large chunks of money. We know the money went missing on more than one occasion. That's more than you need to know and it stays with you." They agreed that Randinoli would choose his own crew. "Of course, you let me know who you take with you." Nittoli, who disliked the intended victim, then added, "If you like, I will be happy to join you."

This offer took Randinoli by surprise. "Certainly Joe, I would be honored."

"No, I know you will be effectual without me." Nittoli, giving yet another example of his higher education, injected a seldom-heard word or phrase into his business dealings whenever possible. He took hold of Randinoli's forearms with his strong hands. "Sal is counting on your success. We all are. You will earn your place in the family with this work."

Randinoli hesitated. "To be honest with you, I thought the Napolitano thing was holding up my chance to…"

Nittoli waved a hand. "Do not concern yourself with such things. Sal and I came to this decision based on your performance. Where your family lived in the old country does not matter. The only thing that counts is that you plan well and fulfill the contract. One last very important item Sal reminds you of—no body."

Randinoli spoke firmly. "I will not disappoint either of you."

Anyone within earshot of the casual conversation would never believe the two men were calmly plotting the murder of another human being. Everything now said, the meeting ended.

Randinoli shivered with excitement. Finally recognized as someone trusted to accomplish a major assignment, Randinoli's new-found energy kept him from sleep. This was huge—his first real test, an opportunity to show he had the right stuff. Cassando and Nittoli trusted him to carry out an important mission for the family. The task to take out a captain, a "made" guy, was an important job. Randinoli had worked on a few things with Alizzio in the past, the most memorable occurring when a successful butcher shop owner fell delinquent on his loan payments and succeeded in avoiding the lenders for one month. Alizzio and Randinoli caught up with the deadbeat in Queens and the two beat the businessman to near death. The following week the outstanding debt plus interest appeared on the books as paid in full.

Randinoli always thought of Alizzio as someone on the way up. He thought it ironic that he would now be responsible for sending Alizzio to an early grave.

For the next two days, Randinoli couldn't think of anything but how he would accomplish the mission. If only he could call his friend and share the news. The soon-to-be contract killer smiled and thought, "*No, not a good idea. 'Special Agent Mason, what's up? Next week I get to whack a guy.'*"

Randinoli thought a great deal of the people he wanted with him and finally arrived at one of his decisions—the plan now finalized in his mind. It would require the right labor force to get the job done and dispose of the body.

His decision was made. With him would be Charlie Sassano, whose reputation included being the most accurate shooter in the city. Sassano once said to a few friends, "It's hard to believe that some guys survive after bein' clipped at close range. I have never had a problem, it's so simple, three in the head. End of story. Then you check him over. Is there a heartbeat, a pulse? Is the son of a bitch breathin'?" Randinoli next chose an old friend, Jimmy Palmieri, a capo and a pain in the ass but well known for his brute strength. Acknowledged for his love of cars and driving expertise, associate Eddy Rizzo would drive the vehicle containing the corpse to the disposal area. Finally, Louis Calabrese, a veteran of many similar executions, would complete the crew.

Randinoli contacted each of them and on Tuesday evening visited with the prospective team members one at a time. He kept it simple. "I have the contract and I want you on the team." He never revealed the identity of the rest of the team nor the target. He explained only their part in the assignment. Each understood that the contract required a well thought-out plan and agreed to wait for word of the final meeting before the job. No one asked the identity of the unfortunate citizen—considering it none of their business. Prior to a hit, it was policy and acceptable procedure to reveal only limited details. The reasoning behind this thinking was no one could slip and disclose pertinent information regarding the intended victim or the people doing the work. No one stopped from speculating on their own.

On Friday night, Randinoli and the four chosen members of his team met at a small pizzeria on the east side. He did not waste small talk. "We won't be here long. The latest member of the hit parade is Cesare Alizzio." Aware of the relationship between the two, he noted the look on the face of Calabrese.

Calabrese spoke, "Wow, I never would have guessed it. He was tight with Sal Cassando for years. He was his personal driver. What the hell happened"?

Randinoli had no intention of discussing the reasons behind the boss's orders. "Not our concern Louis, right? This comes directly from Sal. The boss made it clear, no body. Everyone will help with the cutting."

The plan Randinoli devised was simple. Calabrese, the friendliest to the target, would summons Alizzio from his Friday evening crap game in the Bronx. "You and Cesare get in your car. Eddy, you're waiting outside, you walk to the car and put your piece in his face. Jimmy will be in the backseat of Louie's car." He looked at Palmeri. "When Alizzio gets in, you rap him on the head. That's as simple as it gets. I know you have more experience than me so speak up if you see a problem. Any questions or suggestions?" There were none.

The Friday crap game drew a big crowd.

"Cesare, can you take an hour off, I need a hand with a thing." Calabrese sounded like business as usual.

The dice were not going his way. "Sure Louie, maybe a break is just what I need. The rotten dice are ice cold." Gamblers never admitted their own faults; it was always bad luck, the dice, weather, the company, or anything except their actions.

Calabrese said, "My car's outside, I'll wait for you." He quickly headed for the front door so he wouldn't be seen leaving the club with Alizzio.

The unsuspecting Alizzio followed and the two friends got into Cala-brese's shiny new, light blue Caddy Deville. "What's up, you havin' a prob-lem with…" Alizzio never finished the sentence. Rizzo quickly approached the car, pushed his gun through the open window on the passenger side while pointing it at the captain's face.

"What the f..." From the back seat, Palmeri walloped the back of Aliz-zio's head with a rusty tire iron. The blow to the head may have been all that was necessary to finish the job. His head bled profusely, covered immedi-ately with heavy towels that Calabrese had at the ready.

Calabrese shouted, "Shit! Don't let the blood stain this baby. Wrap him up good."

Randinoli entered the back seat. "Okay, time to go." He leaned forward and took a close look at the victim. "It looks like he won't wake up for some time, if at all." Rizzo took over as driver and Callabrese maneuvered the limp body to the floor before sitting in the passenger seat. Palmeri and Sas-sano walked to the second Caddy parked a few yards away.

Both vehicles drove in medium traffic for nearly an hour and arrived at the previously agreed-on destination. The Bonanno crew carried their victim to the second floor of an abandoned scissor factory in Clark, New Jersey. The only sign of life in the desolate space was a scattering of cigarette stubs, a few nasty looking hypodermic needles, and broken glass from empty wine and beer bottles. Alizzio seemed to be coming around, moaning in great pain and uttering unrecognized gibberish.

Calabrese and Rizzo dragged the limp body from the car and turned Alizzio face down on his stomach. He continued to moan, the volume grow-ing louder. He now lay motionless on his stomach. The mobster's face rested next to a jagged piece of metal. Randinoli killed before when he ended Zack's life by stabbing him with a knife. This would be different, something he thought about but never did before. The others watched him and waited. Was he ready to pull the trigger?"

Randinoli held the weapon a few feet from the limp body and fired three rounds from his five-shot revolver, a thirty-eight caliber special S&W Model 36, into the back of Alizzio's head. He then looked at Sassano, who had been assigned the close-up work. "Let's be sure on this, your turn at bat. Do it, Charlie." Without hesitation, Sassano fired three more rounds into the life-less victim with his Glock revolver, leaving no doubt the captain's life ceased to exist.

The work wasn't complete. After the execution, the specific order in-cluded getting rid of the body. Earlier, Randinoli gave strict instructions to the crew: "No identification, and no body."

Rizzo opened the trunk of his car and he and Palmeri removed two never-used, 24-inch heavy-duty, gas-powered chain saws. The plan called for Randinoli, Palmeri and Calabrese to dispose of Alizzio's remains. If by some miracle Alizzio still lived, the next operation would remove all doubts. Donning hospital dressing gowns and powering up the chainsaws, the three Bonanno family members severed the entire body. They emptied the body parts into previously stored 55-gallon steel drums and covered them with the hospital gowns splattered with blood and bone chips. As planned, they rolled the drums to the edge of the second-floor roof and pushed them over into the industrial dumpster below. Randinoli forced himself to keep from vomiting.

Before they left the building Randinoli managed to say, "Thanks, good job."

The entire next week, Randinoli could not keep anything in his belly. The FBI New York organized crime squad, assigned to investigate the Bonanno family, learned via a reliable asset that those responsible for the murder were members of the family, but specific identification was absent. A rumor circulated that Randinoli stayed sick for a week. One of the agents said, "Apparently, the clean-up work did not agree with him."

An unnamed member of the hit team coined a new alias for Randinoli, the "Exterminator." The term would never be said in his presence.

Randinoli's problems escalated when, a few weeks after the brutal murder, the remains were discovered by a sanitation worker. The FBI now had ample body parts and dental work to make a positive identification of Alizzio.

Cassando and Nittoli went crazy when they learned of the discovery, knowing the public would figure correctly that the mob killed one of their own and desecrated the body. "What is the world coming to?" screamed Cassando. "They will think we are animals."

The FBI and NYPD added the Alizzio murder to their already unsolved open files on the Bonanno family. Law enforcement held little hope that the responsible parties would be identified, or ever prosecuted, yet unsubstantiated bits of information were recorded and placed in open files. Mob hits were a guarantee that worthless informant *assistance* would follow. There were always several low-level hoods furnishing insignificant malarkey when a wise guy "bought the farm."

James Wells, the OC supervisor, said it best: "This guy heard this, that guy heard that. Every lowlife in the city wants to ingratiate himself with the law. Some of them even name names just to show they know the players."

Two names that came up more than once were Gabriel Randinoli and Jimmy Palmeri. This scant information caught the attention of the young prosecutors familiar with the LCN family. They decided to take a shot and contacted the mob lawyers, feigning to have more evidence than they actually had. They claimed that Randinoli and Palmeri would be indicted, but they would charge them with lesser violations if both copped to the murder, named their accomplices and fingered the person who gave the order. The lead lawyer for the Bonanno family laughed. "Good luck with that. You have nothing because my clients are innocent of any and all charges."

The legalese went back and forth. The so-called case against the family members alleged to be responsible for the brutal slaying of Alizzio was never strong enough to bring charges. The prosecutors knew that they had nothing. The mob lawyers challenged the prosecutors at every step. "Show us some solid evidence." The investigation hit a blank wall. The last people to see Alizzio alive had no memory of where or when they saw him, what he was wearing, or if he was with someone. No one saw the four suspects traveling from New York to New Jersey. No one was aware of any ill feelings between the suspects and the deceased gangster. The lead lawyer for the crime syndicate put it bluntly. "My clients are mourning over the loss of their friend. You either charge these innocent citizens or stop harassing them." There was not any reliable asset information pointing to the identities of the members present for the hit. The investigation was put on hold.

Randinoli eventually recovered from the dry heaves and assumed everything was fine. "Cesare is gone, over, finished, what's the problem?" Historically, he always skated away from what he considered to be inconsequential, the small stuff. Now he was not willing to accept the fact that an identified body makes a murder prosecution more feasible. He swept it aside, thinking, *"Maybe it's time to get another game going and bring in more scratch. Money always solves any problem with these people."*

Chapter Thirty-Six

An oath for an oath

FBI Special Agent Brad Mason was now looking forward to the challenge of the "Windy City," Chicago, Illinois, his first office of assignment. In 1972, two weeks after Labor Day, the Mason family settled into their new home in Park Forest. Randinoli was experiencing changes in his career as well.

Randinoli's ceremony would take place in the summer of 1973. Becoming a made man required two qualifications. Randinoli had demonstrated his exceptional earning competence, but even more noteworthy was the work he put in with the Alizzio killing in early January. True, body remains were found and positive identification followed. Randinoli gave it little thought; dead is dead, no problem. Soon he would be a full-fledged member of La Cosa Nostra. A boyhood dream began to take form. What would old friends from the corner think of him now?

On July 28, 1973, the tradition continued; the induction ritual would emphasize "omertà," the rule of silence. The gathering is both a serious and joyous event. The ceremony occurred in Brooklyn at an apartment used by the mob for such Bonanno family business. Through the years, law enforcement obtained sparse information from mob sources about what actually took place at these gatherings. No member of law enforcement actually witnessed a ceremony and could give only second-hand testimony as to the proceedings.

Following the death a decade earlier of New Jersey capo regime Anthony "Jersey Tony" Zale, the bosses searched for someone who could fill the void and secure a prominent presence in northern New Jersey. Zale performed well for the family and a suitable replacement never materialized. The petty infighting blocked all attempts to operate efficiently. Years passed and the New Jersey mob consistently failed in their attempt to operate the territory properly, and great deals of money were lost because of their incompetence. The Bonannos were well aware of Randinoli's background in New Jersey, his history as a top earner for the family, his reputation for being dependable, and his ability to be tough when necessary. It was no secret; he could be ruthless when necessary. They were more than pleased with the manner in which Randinoli controlled his end of the gambling network in New York. Randinoli showed initiative; he organized and operated lucrative crap games, and he and his crew collected money without any serious problems. The mobster's background at running the biggest crap game in Newark contributed to his resume. What he had learned growing up at the 12th Avenue and Bruce Street schoolyard put him a step ahead of his peers.

Randinoli had the endorsements of the family underboss Giuseppe "Joe" Nittoli and a caporegime Carmine Cuccio. Although Randinoli was not a favorite of Cuccio's, the underboss knew that the Don would expect him to sponsor the new man. Consent of the commission was required. Responding to the request of Don Cassando, the five-family commission, made up of the heads of the five New York families, wasted little time granting the mandatory permission. They voted unanimously to accept the new man.

Randinoli had never experienced this sort of excitement in his lifetime. When he got the news, he couldn't wait to tell his friend Specs Buchanan. "The word came down from the top. The commission opened the books." Cassando was still serving time in federal prison, having been convicted of several counts of racketeering. The don happily passed down the announcement. "We have a great opportunity here, and we make Gabe Randinoli, the man who will give our family a presence in Jersey."

The ambitious mobster from Newark thought of little else. He will be a faithful member of La Cosa Nostra. He will be a "made" man, a person of rank deserving respect and feared. He believed this the start to reaching his goal; someday, he will rule the family. He wanted to shout the news to everyone he met. For some crazy reason, Randinoli thought of the corner of 12th Avenue and Bruce Street, of the roulette and crap games, of the fun and fights in the Hilltoppers, and most of all, of Mason and all their adventures. He smiled to himself, thinking, "*probably not a good idea to call an FBI agent and inform him that I will be starring in an upcoming mafia ceremony.*" In earlier times, tradition dictated that only men of Southern Italian decent, most from Sicily, were eligible for induction into La Cosa Nostra.

Neither former police officers nor law enforcement personnel were eligible for membership. Not totally unlike other enterprises, there were exceptions. The very well-known John Gotti, the Don of the feared Gambino family, is a descendant of a Russian mother. The current boss of the Bonanno family, Salvatore Cassando, broke a rule and insured the acceptance of his brother-in-law Peter Farrugia, a former corrections officer for the city of New York. Now, having an Italian surname and a father with Italian blood sufficed for membership. Cassando and the members of the commission were aware that Randinoli's father, Cuban Pete, was born in Naples, Italy.

The boss charged his underboss with the details. Nittoli handled all necessary arrangements, including the celebratory meal following the ceremony. He ordered Cuccio to obtain one of the old time native Sicilians, Gino Villenti, to act as master of ceremonies.

Randinoli earlier received approval to drive to the apartment alone. He wanted to remain focused on what was about to take place and having someone with him would be a distraction. He planned to arrive at the apartment ten minutes before six. His crew all wished him well as he left the 4th St. store headquarters.

Buchanan said, "What a way to spend a weekend, eh Gabe? Don't forget, 'up the rebels.'"

"Damn right Specs, the first thing I do today is making sure the Irish get in on this deal. And it won't matter if their family comes from Belfast in the north or County Roscommon in the Republic of Ireland." They both laughed as they waved. It was a private joke. Buchanan, not Italian, would never be a made man. The two friends often joked that Randinoli would change the rules when he became the boss. He would say, "I want my Irish friends in so I can get real soda bread on Saint Patrick's Day."

The radio in the big car was tuned to his favorite station. He relaxed listening to the mellow sound of Ruby and the Romantics, singing "Our Day Will Come." He thought, *It's here baby, it's finally here!*

Randinoli always looked the part; a six-hundred-dollar suit, power-red silk tie, the latest black Gucci shoes shined to a luster. Following a leisurely drive through Manhattan, the new inductee arrived at the Brooklyn apartment right on time. He exited his Caddy and smiled as he glimpsed at the two cars parked directly across the street. Each car contained two guns on duty as security lookouts. He recognized from the crap games one of the menacing soldiers serving as a lookout. He reached out and shook the hand of the security guard at the front door. Randinoli went down four concrete stairs and entered the old brownstone building.

Palmeri represented Don Nittoli and earlier gave the notice to spread the word. "No game this Saturday night. There will be other business conducted at six p.m. Pass the word. We will conduct our business as usual next week." On Saturday evenings, the basement apartment usually housed one of Brooklyn's biggest and most lucrative crap games. No one needed to ask why the game was postponed.

All made men, a dozen Bonanno family members wearing suits and ties attended the important ceremony. It spite of the sweltering heat, the men dressed appropriately; witnessing such an occasion was considered an honor among their peers. They were special. The apartment was air-conditioned and large enough to accommodate the group seated around the huge, age-old mahogany table dating back to the roaring twenties. The black leather chairs were new and quite comfortable. Randinoli half-smiled at the tabletop that bore years of cigarette burns and scratches. The room quickly filled with smoke emanating from the cigars and cigarettes. The ashtrays would fill by the time the ritual concluded.

One of the Arthur Avenue attendees from the Bronx murmured, "Thank God for the air conditioning, the humidity would kill us. The weather forecast was right. Ninety-eight degrees, the hottest day of the year."

Cuccio stood and spoke. "I wish to welcome everyone." The murmuring ceased. "We are here to welcome a new man into our organization." He spent a few minutes discussing loyalty and togetherness. Cuccio enjoyed listening to himself.

The Don was seated at the head of the table. In his early fifties, six-foot-four, with a full head of wavy, blackish grey hair and just south of two hundred and thirty pounds, he was an imposing figure. The underboss looked at Cuccio who immediately sat down.

Cuccio nodded to the older man. The room found instant quiet, and, as he folded his hands together as in a holy place, Villenti began to speak slowly, recounting the ancient words voiced through centuries.

The first half of the ritual was the required oath known by the mobsters as "La mia famiglia."

Villenti spoke slowly, the words in Italian:

"Voglio entrare in questa organizzazione per proteggere la mia famiglia e i miei amici. Prometto di non rivelare questo segreto o e obbedire con amore e omertà."

Gabe Randinoli, still an associate, read his response from an index card. *"I want to enter this organization to protect my family and my friends. I promise not to reveal this secret and obey with love and silence."*

Randinoli had asked Anthony Spero to be his sponsor. The first part of the oath concluded, the inductee and his godfather faced each other and held out their right hands. The master of ceremonies pinpricked the index finger of each man, drawing blood. Randinoli and Spero squeezed their index fingers together, meshing the blood of both men.

Villenti placed a holy card in the palm of Randinoli's right hand, ignited a match, burned the card, and continued speaking in Italian. Randinoli accepted the card depicting a picture of St. Francis of Assisi and looked at Villenti as the aging Sicilian spoke:

"Come questa carta brucia cosi anche brucerà la mia anima. Inserisco questa organizzazione viva e lascio in morte."

Then Randinoli repeated the words that so many others had spoken before him.

"As this card burns so also will my soul burn. I enter this organization alive and I leave in death." As Randinoli spoke these words, he struggled to prevent himself from experiencing an orgasm. The kid from 12th Avenue and Bruce Street was now a fully initiated *soldato,* a soldier of La Cosa Nostra, *"uomo d'onore,"* a man of honor. The initiate had achieved a lifelong obsession. He allowed his mind to wander as he scattered the burnt card on the table. He knew the history. The ashes symbolized the annihilation of traitors to "this thing of ours." A thought flashed through his mind. "W*hat would Cuban Pete think of his only son? He already knew what Brad thought."*

Villenti, speaking broken English, then delivered a customary history lesson to the new man as well as the other attendees. "They call us many names: Mob, Mafia and La Cosa Nostra. This is just our thing—what we are. It is different in Sicily, but we are all the same."

Continuing in English, looking at the inductee, he explained various rules, guidelines to live by. "Your wife, your child, your family members come second. You obey your capo. You do not dishonor this thing of ours." Villenti paused and looking directly at Randinoli, simply said, "Congratulations." The attendees gently applauded as Villenti was the first to hug and kiss both cheeks of the new man of honor. Shouts of *"uomo d'onore"* followed. Villenti, looking sleepy, smiled at Randinoli as he clasped both hands. *"Ti auguro ogni bene."* Translated, the elderly wise guy said, *"I wish you well."*

The attendees gently applauded as Nittoli moved to the end of the room and embraced Randinoli, kissing both cheeks of the new man of honor. "You and I will speak later."

Each attendee kissed and hugged the celebrant. They appeared truly happy for his good fortune.

The celebration that followed took place at a popular restaurant owned by the Bonannos. It turned into a festive evening. The plates of Italian dishes were plentiful and the Chianti came from one of the best wineries in Italy. The cigars burned and the off-color jokes flourished. There was never any mention of family business or the reason for the dinner celebration.

As was customary, Nittoli chose the wine. On this count there was never a debate; the underboss considered himself the wine connoisseur of the family and perhaps the entire universe. "As you know it comes from my private source on Mulberry Street in Little Italy," he said.

After a few drinks, he expounded on his expertise. "This red Chianti, Castello di Brolio, is a truly great wine." Each man raised his glass in a toast. "Saluda, Saluda." The boss smiled proudly and exclaimed, "Prosit!"

Gabe basked in the attention he received; he loved what he had become. The soldier looked forward to the future.

Cuccio leaned over to Randinoli and said, "Gabe my friend, I am so happy for you."

"Thank you, Carmine. I will not disappoint you." He remembered the crapshooter from Bruce Street who lived by that expression. Whenever he called you "my friend," you knew from that point on that whatever came out of his mouth was bullshit. It was common knowledge that Cuccio would someday be Nittoli's underboss when the family leadership changed. Cuccio was not Randinoli's favorite person, but for now the newest soldier would show respect and say the right words to the underboss. Randinoli would not allow anything to spoil the happiest day of his life.

"Now you and I will talk in private," Nittoli said as he escorted the new man of honor to a private table. "Before you came to New York, we really didn't know much about you. Now I believe I know much more." He waved his hand and smiled. Randinoli understood that his boss was referring to the business conducted on behalf of the family, to include the Alizzio murder.

"You know I started in Jersey, my father came here from Italy—he was born in Naples. What is it you want to know about me?" Gabe had made a decision, underboss or not, get to the point. Besides, *someday this guy will work for me.*

Nittoli appreciated this direct approach. "To be honest, when you first came to New York, I and others were suspicious. There is work to be found in New Jersey as you know better than anyone, why come here?"

Gabe looked directly in the boss's eyes and spoke so only Nittoli could hear. "I was fourteen when my mother died, and my father and I were alone. He did his best to watch out for me and keep me in line, but he worked in the tailor shop many long hours. I had lots of time by myself and with my friends. My neighborhood in Newark was similar to those right here in the city. We had black and white. The Irish, Italians, Polish, Germans and a whole bunch of other nationalities lived in a community and everyone looked out for the neighborhood and, for the most part, everybody got along." He paused to take a breath.

"Go on." Nittoli was truly interested.

"One of my close friends died very young, an overdose of heroin." Randinoli remembered King's funeral. "We knew how he started with beer, marijuana and graduated to heroin, and we knew the person responsible for his death. When we buried him, I made a promise to myself that someday I would even the score for my friend. The others just wanted to forget the whole thing. I realized I had been different my whole life. Anyway, I needed to get familiar with the streets here and learn about the neighborhoods. I took my time doing the research. The responsible party lived in Brooklyn. It took a long time but…" Gabe now waved his hand and looked at his boss.

Nittoli did not hide his delight with the new member's candor. "I understand Gabe, there is no need for you to go any further. You needed to take care of some personal business, which you did. You became acquainted with Jimmy Palmeri when he visited the game in Newark. You met some of our people and decided that you wanted to be part of the family. It's that simple. Most important, you made things right for your friend." They both sipped the Chianti. The underboss smiled and gently waved a finger. "Remember Gabe, what you did for your friend did not count for the honor given you today." Gabe smiled and nodded his understanding.

Randinoli fully comprehended the rule; Zack was personal, a 12th and Bruce matter. The right work related only to family matters, contracts authorized by the boss. Any other business and you are on your own. Killing for personal reasons does not count.

Randinoli continued, "I always knew who I was, what I wanted to do, and who I wanted to be. It was a matter of time. Joe, I love this life." Randinoli believed a little smooching could not hurt.

"I know you will do well. You should be happy to know you will be spending much time in your home state conducting the family business." Nittoli heard what he needed to hear and was now more than satisfied. He would personally report on the day's activities to Cassando. The don would be happy to hear that the ceremony and the celebration concluded favorably—as well as the inquisition.

In law enforcement circles, the ceremony is recognized as a serious gathering. Although when mobsters rat on each other and divulge information to save their own skins, the oath of silence is often scoffed at by outsiders. One veteran New York detective remarked, "The ceremony is an Italian wedding. Each party says 'I do.' Then when the shit hits the fan, divorce is imminent. You can't count the number of wise guys who became made men via the infamous code of silence, the omertà ceremony, and later sang like a flock of whippoorwills."

Chapter Thirty-Seven

Chicago—Okay, Cubs or White Sox?

As a first office agent (FOA), Mason learned you do exactly what is required, work any type of investigative matter assigned, and be prepared to grind out irregular hours and long shifts. The remainder of 1972 and 1973, and half of 1974, were filled with all the challenges and excitement an FOA could ask for.

The first few months, the new SA labored on a White Collar Crime (WCC) squad that was responsible for investigating the national vote fraud case receiving tremendous media attention. Some believed the corrupt political machine controlling the city of Chicago was responsible for the election of a presidential candidate. The issue sold lots of newspapers.

On one cold January morning in 1974, the entire squad, consisting of a dozen agents, left Chicago Headquarters at five a.m. and proceeded to arrest fifty-four "precinct captains" on the south and west sides of the city. This type of investigation did not suit Mason's psyche. He had witnessed similar election procedures in Newark and understood you either worked for the political machine in office or you did not work at all. If mandated to investigate vote fraud for his entire career, he pictured a very short career with the FBI. The thought did not do much for Mason's personality. He shared his concern with one of the squad members, asking, "I wonder if this will turn into a short career?"

No secret, the Daley machine ran Chicago. The crux of the investigation dealt with false votes cast by unregistered residents, deceased citizens, folks voting multiple times, and numerous other schemes to boost the vote count

of the party candidate. The precinct captains, comprised mostly of city employees, followed orders from city hall and did what it took to expand the
vote. "Vote often and early" was the cry. This mantra mirrored an earlier
Boston slogan, "Vote often and early for James Michael Curley," referring
to the infamous four-term mayor of Boston.

Conducting monotonous interviews, pouring over voting records and
perusing death certificates were all part of the investigatory process and became too much for Mason.

Office of preference transfer requests to the Big Apple was a rarity, but
Mason thought he might request a transfer to the New York Office. Mason
told his partner, "At least in New York or Newark I have an inkling where
some serious shit is going down." Mason's brain raced, he laughed to himself. He wanted to call his friend the mobster and tell him that the FBI was
hot on his trail. *I have the task of going to the Big Apple. Your sorry ass is
grass.* The monotonous work was now playing tricks with his mind.

He did enjoy a few lighter moments in the Chicago office. Everyone
now prepared for the office to undergo its annual inspection. The office examination, considered a time-consuming ritual by the agents, necessitated a
team of suits from Washington Headquarters spending three weeks in the
division reviewing cases, interviewing all personnel and generally becoming
unpopular. This procedure repeated throughout the year in each bureau division. The inspection staff, usually agents on the way up the ladder, received the brunt of office cheap shots. Some of the staff considered the three-
week interruption of casework nothing more than bureaucratic bullshit. It
was compared to the federal government telling the states how to address
local issues.

A Chicago office icon Judy Nassan, Mason's squad secretary, took the
annual interruption in stride. She appeared very serious instructing the FOA
on how to deal with the inspectors. "Now remember Brad, admit nothing,
deny everything and make counter allegations." She let her words sink in
then added, "When they ask you about the squad supervisor, you say, 'Sir,
he is fair but firm.'" Mason could hardly stop laughing. She reminded him
of a woman from the neighborhood who had a problem with alcohol and
would frequent the club. He welcomed Nassan's sense of humor. The squad
secretary truly enjoyed sharing her years in the Windy City and her
knowledge and experience with the FOAs. Neither realized that the two
would remain friends and working associates long after their days ended at
the bureau.

If not for the YMCA, eight city blocks from the office, Mason may have
gone off the deep end. A steady, forty-five minute strenuous workout

brought the mind back to the real world. Back at the club, Dutch always said, "Brad my boy, ain't nothin' in the world compared to hittin' the heavy bag." Mason thought Dutch could not be more correct. While a few rounds on the big bag made some people feel invincible, it exercised Mason's mind as well.

It paid off in spades, the advice given at the academy by Mike Vance. Finally, away from the vote fraud stuff, he tackled an old-dog fugitive case. The second week of duty he drove to the Gresham District on the South Side, hoping to pick up some local information on the wanted fugitive possibly living in Chi-town. There, Mason received his first Chicago Major League Baseball loyalty test. Luckily, Vance prepared him well for the big day. Vance had warned him about the White Sox-Cubs historical "friendly rivalry." His classmate said, "The Hatfield and McCoy feud is a love fest compared to the Chicago North Side and South Side baseball fans. Thank God for the Bears."

The cops relished going after fresh meat from another part of the country. Sergeant Vito Bianco and Mason hit it off from the beginning, and Bianco even offered to accompany Mason on the arrest when he located the perp. The two developed a friendship that lasted throughout both careers. But for now, it was test time for the new fed in town.

Bianco bypassed the foreplay. "So Brad, what are your thoughts on next season, will the Cubbies or Sox even have a chance?" The detectives in the squad room didn't acknowledge their presence and feigned reading reports, writing reports—anything a busy detective does. Mason remembered that Vance had warned the police were the worst when it came to the feud. His exact words: "Do not commit unless you're positive what side the interrogator supports. Geographically, if you're on the South Side, you should be safe with the White Sox. The North Side is the Cubs."

Mason paid close attention now. This rivaled the Yankee–Red Sox wars at the Club or the roofers' union hall for the Friday night fights. At the academy, he pressed Vance. "What if the guy lives on the North Side but works on the South Side? What then?" Emphatically, Vance said, "Do not guess. Do not give an answer if you are not sure. You can always feign a heart attack."

He needed to be positive of his position. Over the entrance reception area hung a huge poster of the highest paid player on the White Sox—number fifteen, second baseman Dick Allen. Mason rightly concluded if there were cops in the precinct who were Cubs fans, the second baseman would be on the permanent disabled list, not to mention the bullet holes plastering the poster. "I cannot see the Sox losing this year, can you?" Good answer, the agent was off the hook for now. A relaxed Bianco expounded for the next ten minutes on how the season would progress and how the White Sox without a doubt would take "the whole nine yards."

Shortly after his acceptance as an "okay guy," Mason took a shot. Five detectives occupied the squad room looking over files, discussing current cases when the FBI agent asked, "Do any of you have family members or friends that root for the Cubs?" Luckily, he smiled as though he already had the answer.

"No!" The five officers responded as one.

"That's what I thought. Good for them." The discussion ended.

After the first few weeks in the Chicago office, Mason collaborated with one of his 28A classmates at the academy, Tim Norman, the only other classmate to receive Chicago as a first office assignment. Later they learned that it was because of their backgrounds and so-called "street smarts" that they were so blessed. Norman was born and raised in Detroit, the eldest son of a former FBI agent, a bureau icon of the Hoover era.

During their Chicago assignment, Mason and Norman volunteered for the "special" at Wounded Knee, and were advised FOAs were not taking part in that operation. Two agents ended up getting killed during that confrontation. After the Wounded Knee massacre, fewer complaints came from the firearm ranges as this was a reminder of the importance of mandatory firearms training. During this time, the bad people always seemed to be better equipped than some law enforcement agencies. Indian sympathizers paid for the murder weapons found at Wounded Knee. A few Hollywood people, including actor Marlon Brando, outwardly supported the actions of the fugitives while condemning law enforcement personnel charged with investigating violations of laws of the United States.

The real world of law enforcement on the streets opened up quickly. Very early on a hot and humid day in June, Mason and Norman were waiting outside a residence on Ada Street on the South Side. They earlier ascertained that a fugitive had arrived at the single-family house late the previous night. A few minutes before seven, the agents prepared to execute the bust before the fugitive was out of bed. Mason heard a commotion at the north end of the street and called to his partner, "It's time to wake up Rip Van Winkle." The two FOAs proceeded in the direction of the noise at the end of the street. A lone Chicago police officer was attempting to apprehend and arrest four individuals fleeing the CPD.

The four bad guys abandoned the stolen car they were driving and were now on foot. They intended to escape by exiting the south end of the street.

The four were armed and moving in and out of sight as they exchanged gun fire with the officer. Mason thought, *"There goes our fugitive."*

Norman yelled, "FBI, put down your weapons!" The Chicago police officer stopped shooting when he saw Mason and Norman. The perps started shooting at the agents. Bullets were bouncing off the ground, buildings, cars and a few were embedded in trees. The FOAs had completed over three months of intensive daily firearms training and heard gunfire each day, but this was different. The agents knew this was not another day of firearms practice at the range at Quantico. All the shots aimed directly at them were real bullets. Mason, kneeling behind a huge oak tree and Norman, shielded behind the bureau vehicle, returned the fire. They both hoped that there would be no need to reload. They remembered a crusty firearms instructor at Quantico shouting, *"make the six shots count gentlemen—may not have time to reload."*

Mason yelled, "Tim, make sure the officer is not in the line of fire." Norman gave a thumbs up.

Bullets crashed through windows of a first-floor apartment directly behind the agents. One of the bad guys moving between parked cars took two rounds to his right shoulder.

Norman yelled the good news. "The cavalry has arrived." The Chicago police officer had called in and the help arrived. He wisely let them know of the agents' presence. Several SWAT team officers emptied their units at both end of the street. A few positioned on a first-floor porch fired at the three remaining shooters.

"That's it man, that's it," called one of the three gunmen. They threw their weapons out to the middle of the street and showed their empty hands. They were immediately searched and relieved of loaded weapons on their person, handcuffed and escorted in CPD units to the Cook County Jail for booking. An ambulance arrived and transported the wounded thug to the local hospital. The wounds turned out to be far from life threatening.

This would not be the last time the partners would use their weapons. The arresting officer called Mason later. "They each had lengthy rap sheets including B&Es, Assault & Battery, and Indecent Exposure. There are outstanding warrants from other states on two of them, all state violations. Those four were good ones to get off our streets. I'm glad you showed up. Our people will remember the help."

Mason followed the case, and Chicago Police Detective Bill Jeffries called in periodically as the four young men travelled through the Illinois justice system. The gunmen followed the advice of the lawyers and pled out to one count each of carrying a concealed weapon and attempted assault on law enforcement officers. The judge, not at all lenient at the sentencing procedure, ordered they each spend two years in one of the gated communities operated by the state of Illinois.

The two SAs received recognition from the CPD as well as a commendation from the FBI Director. They learned from some of the older agents that it was unusual for a FOA to receive FBI Headquarters' recognition for good work. Mason thought this was more like it, and maybe he would postpone his request for a transfer to the northeast. The new SAs were surprised at the recognition received for the arrests, but heeded the advice of more experienced SAs and just kept quiet about the whole deal. The worthless squad supervisor qualified it by saying, "The bureau could not overlook something initiated by the City of Chicago." During their time in Chicago, the partners made many friends on the CPD.

Back at the office, the squad secretary called, "Brad, for you."

He recognized the voice. It was his friend from the CPD, Sergeant Vito Bianco. "Good job, the cop you helped is a close friend of mine. The word is out, anything you need from us, do not hesitate. You may even be in line for a few tickets to Comiskey Park, and keep rooting for the real Chicago team. See you Friday." Bianco ended the connection.

Mason told Norman about the call. "Really great stuff. One cop reaching out to another and saying thanks. He invited us to Towey's bar Friday night."

Always a smile on his face, Norman, a bachelor, replied, "I will have to check my busy schedule."

Dick Vogt, a former CIA agent and the most experienced and street-smart agent on Mason's squad, worked with several quality informants. Mason desired to develop a worthwhile informant, someone to furnish much-needed information on the on-going bank robbery epidemic in the city. First office agents were not required to develop informants. The rationale behind this mindset was that FOAs needed more experience, more time on the street. Mason and others did not agree with this philosophy.

Vogt, easily recognized wearing a grungy *Colombo* raincoat, shared an unusual idea. "When you have an opportunity to visit Cook County, ask to look at the list giving the names and records of the inmates soon to be released."

The following week, Mason transferred a prisoner from Chicago Heights to Chicago's infamous Cook County Jail. At Cook County, the new agent perused the "soon-to-be-released" sheet. It was a novel idea to develop criminal sources.

One of the inmates, from the West Side, possessed an interesting rap sheet. Mason wanted to meet the inmate so he created a story. "I think this

guy knows something about an outstanding case we've been working on."
Cook County administrators allowed Mason to meet with Cass Mitchell.

Mason and Mitchell developed an instant rapport, and Mitchell agreed to meet with the FBI agent after his release from jail. Mitchell, in his late thirties, loved boxing and kept current on the entire fight industry. At one covert meeting on Rush Street, Mitchell gave his new handler his entire collection of Ring magazines. Mitchell, a black man, six-feet tall and 175 pounds, stayed in great physical shape, a result of daily workouts. Another interest was robbing banks; he was a member of an active, West Side bank-robber gang. He spoke to Mason about getting out of the crime business, but expressed fear of retaliation by the other members of the gang. He once joked, "Hell man, we are just like the Correlones—once in, never out."

"Right, I did hear something about how that works," Mason responded.

In late July, Mitchell told Mason that his people recently cased a job and planned to pull it off very soon. The target was one of the busiest banks in the city, the Chase Bank on LaSalle. Most of the money taken in during any given week was stored in a secure vault. The gang was satisfied with their preparation for the heist. Surveillance showed little police presence in the area, and neither the female tellers nor the elderly bank guard would offer heavy resistance.

"Man, I had enough of this life. I'm ready to get out for good. I tell ya I'm a little scared of what the brothers will do if I refuse to go on this one. I got a place to go to. I got some folks in South Carolina my boys don't know nothin' about." The two agreed that after Mitchell furnished the time and date of the planned robbery, the bank robbery squads of both the FBI and CPD would arrest him and his three armed accomplices as they entered the bank. Later, Mitchell would be released, and if necessary, would testify against the gang. Mitchell's plan was to then "boogie out of this city once and for all." He added, "Hell, I never said any that omertà shit, right?" He loved to use the word.

When the two first met, Mitchell made it clear he would not furnish any information that would harm his friends. Things changed as the other three members became more violent and heavily involved in buying and selling drugs. "Agent Mason, I know it's only a matter of time before the entire gang ends up in the morgue or incarcerated for life—I want out now." He justified his giving up the others. "Hell, that Italyen omertà shit don't work in this town. It's always a race to see who gets to the precinct first. My black ass will be first in line."

Mason was skeptical of the plan so he went to his mentor. Vogt liked the deal. "I only wish we could use our squad to run with it but the BR cigar smokers have the manpower and the jurisdiction," he said, referring to the so-called heavy weights on the bank robbery squad. They believed smoking cigars increased their persona. "It will be their job to coordinate it with the Chicago PD and we can work the details out concerning Mitchell with the United States Attorney's Office."

In late August, a lifeless body appeared in the trunk of an abandoned car on the West Side of the city. A black male wrapped in heavy, clear plastic and covered with an old tattered blanket laid face down in the trunk. Cass Mitchell had taken three rounds at close range in the back of the head, the back of his scull blown free of the rest of his cranium. Maggots infested the decaying body. The stinking odor finally forced neighbors to report the strange stench.

Sergeant Vito Bianco called his new friend immediately following the fingerprint ID of the coroner's office. "Brad, it looks to be an acquaintance of yours, Cass Mitchell. He set three days in the back of a trunk. An agent from your BR squad told our detectives the black group from West 51st Street was responsible. He also said that they expect the group to pull a BR job on Saturday."

Mason was straining to keep cool. "That's true Vito, and Cass is a…was a pretty good guy. We talked boxing quite a bit. We even went a few rounds at the Flood Gymnasium over on Racine."

Bianco said, "I don't know how the brothers learned of this. Anyway, it looks like they figured Mitchell talked too much and whacked him. I'll check further and get back to you."

"Thanks Vito, yeah, call me back."

"One more thing," Bianco continued, "Mitchell doesn't have any known family. None of the neighbors will make the ID, they're afraid of his friends and want nothing to do with the police. Would you be willing to identify the body? I can meet you there."

"Right, I know of no relatives. I'll bring Dick Vogt along and we'll meet you at the morgue in twenty minutes." He thought it better not to mention what Mitchell said about having someone in South Carolina.

Mason smelled it immediately. The distinct smell of formaldehyde permeated the morgue located on West Harrison Street. It did not take long; the body was pulled out of the cooler and Mason identified Cass Mitchell's remains. He signed the necessary forms and then he and Vogt quickly left the building. The experience reminded Mason once more of 12th and Bruce, and how dreadful things happen to people. His thoughts drifted to his old friend. *"If Gabe stuck to gambling in the schoolyard maybe he could escape some of this shit."*

Mason recalled the information he and Vogt shared with the cigar smokers on the BR squad. They spoke just two weeks ago, a late Friday afternoon. They provided the BR supervisor with valuable information outlining a job that would take place on Saturday morning at the Chase Bank on LaSalle Street. Vogt explained in detail: "The four, armed bank robbers are to be arrested before entering the bank, case closed. One of the robbers, SA Mason's informant will take a pass and be released immediately. Only the names of the other three perps will be included in the required press release."

"Right, got it." Supervisor Charles Rivers looked attentive as he penciled in the information.

After Mason and Vogt left the BR squad room, apparently the big shots decided to consider the information as bogus. One of the old timers said, "After all, it comes from a first office agent who obtained it from a mug trying to make points with the bureau." The fact that Vogt produced quality results for years did not enter the discussion. "The guy is a CIA hand-me-down, forget him!" Besides, the veteran agent had plans for the weekend with no intention of disrupting them. The supervisor made a decision. Rivers told his squad, "Mason is listening to Vogt, that screwball CIA jerk. Neither one would recognize a bank job if he fell over one."

Rivers had been around from the long-gone Hoover days. His reputation would suffer if he caused his BR heavies to sit on a bank on a Saturday. The weather forecast pointed to a hot and humid weekend. He decided to alert their peers at the CPD bank robbery detail, and ordered one of his agents to call with the information and let them decide what they wanted to do. "Pass the intel to the next pew. I doubt if they sit on LaSalle Street on Saturday. Make sure they understand we will not be in attendance."

The BR agent given the task of making the call to the PD made sure his ass was covered. The official story was that the informant's information lacked substantive facts or support of prior successful investigations.

When the call reached the CPD detective on the complaint duty desk, the bank robbery agent identified the West Side group allegedly with plans to rob the Chase Bank on LaSalle Street. He added, "We have had no prior dealings with this *new* informant so we cannot support the validity of the information—simply insufficient intel."

This move satisfied supervisor Rivers. "We passed it on to the appropriate office," he said. "It was the bureau's official investigative decision not to pursue the matter."

The Chicago Bank Robbery Squad wasted little time, executing a loud entry into the seedy West Side apartment where three members of the gang spent most of their time snorting cocaine. It was a crude entry to say the least. They were there for one reason—to send a message. The officers screamed at the three gang members, saying they knew of the plans for the Chase Bank. The sergeant in charge of the operation threatened them. "Every cop in the District will be waiting for you," he said. The police did not have to mention who the snitch was; only one gang member was not present.

The young thugs interpreted the interruption as the cops doing them a favor. They cancelled the robbery and avoided getting pinched and a long stretch in prison. More importantly, they knew they needed to quiet someone. The cops left the building believing the gang would smack Mitchell around then he would hit back and the matter would be forgotten. It turned out Mitchell did get a beating and a whole lot more. What the hell, the main objective was achieved; no one was required to work the weekend.

Sergeant Bianco worked tirelessly attempting to obtain an ID on the people responsible for the execution. Mason and Norman spoke with many folks in the West Side neighborhood. Most were young black men around the same age as Mitchell. The majority of them were drug addicts with prison records. Mason recognized the neighborhood as a tough place to survive. It brought back memories of growing up in Newark. He wished he could offer the young men some semblance of hope, but he fully understood the doctrine. *Do not trust a cop, particularly a white one.* The undisputed evidence supported the reality that black-on-black crime in Chicago was epidemic. Most young black men died as the result of gunshots received from other blacks. Whenever a young black man died a violent death, a few so-called black leaders could be counted on to fan the flame of racial violence. The self-named neighborhood leaders and organizers did nothing to get at the root of the problem. Mitchell had little regard for these phonies. "They take care of themselves, period. Chicago neighborhoods would be a whole lot better without them."

Mitchell trusted the FBI agent, but he died because law enforcement failed to do its job. What made it so profane is that no one seemed to give a shit. Mason told his partner, "We need to give this our best shot. Someone has information, and we need to get it."

The day and night attempts to identify Mitchell's assailants turned futile. No surprise—no one saw, heard or suspected anything. Many of Mitchell's friends denied even knowing him. The three-monkey street scene played out. See no evil, hear no evil and speak no evil. The new agents would get this response many times during their careers. Norman, from the streets of Detroit, also appreciated the lack of assistance. "I suppose we might as well get used to it," he said. "This neighborhood has no reason to regard the fuzz as allies."

The Chicago newspapers did not waste space reporting the killing. Hidden on page twenty-four of the Sun-Times appeared the headline, "Man Found Dead in Car Trunk." Cass Mitchell remained another statistic, an unsolved case of a brutal gangland murder. Who told the killers that he was working with law enforcement? It was clear that someone in law enforcement put out the word that Cass was an informant. It was either very poor judgment or the cop or agent figured one less mutt to worry about. The street will deal with Cass Mitchell—and it did.

Each twenty-four hours ended on the same note. Both agents tired, with little to show for their efforts. Mason was disappointed but still prepared to get some satisfaction. Norman drove down LaSalle Street toward the office when the dispatcher signaled Mason to call SA Vogt immediately.

"I called in a chit with an informant. He explained the whole deal." Vogt told Mason of the CPD visit to the West Side apartment and relayed an almost verbatim conversation that took place.

Lost in thought, Mason murmured, "Tim, I need to see someone when we get back." His partner had a good idea who Mason was talking about, but said nothing. Maybe the senior Vogt could talk him out of doing anything crazy.

Mason was on his way to have a talk with Supervisor Rivers.

Vogt stopped him. "Look Brad, the guy's not worth it. He's a heavyweight in the office and nobody's gonna take him down."

Norman added, "Dick's right on, the guy has pull. Let's live to fight another day."

They both followed as Mason headed in the direction of the BR squad. They were close behind as he stepped inside River's office and closed the door. The BR agents scattered around the squad area, now alerted to the three agents' presence, started to walk toward River's office.

Blocking their way, Vogt said, "They're having a little talk, one on one." Norman stood in front of the supervisor's office door and motioned for the heavies to stay back. The cigar smokers sensed both agents were ready to do whatever it took to give their friend some privacy. The squad room got very quiet. The BR agents expected the visit. They were now more familiar with the background of the FOA. They knew for certain that the BR supervisor did a bad thing and he gets what he gets.

They could not hear voices, only the music from a radio in River's office. Six minutes later Mason opened the door, walked out of the office and headed in the direction of his own squad area. Norman snuck a peek in the office and saw Rivers sitting behind his desk appearing very ashen, his mouth slightly opened and his lips quivering. Norman and Vogt followed their friend back across the office and sat at their respective desks. It was back to business as usual, with no discussion concerning the visit.

No one ever learned the exact details of the discussion, but River's application for early retirement led to some educated opinions.

Mason learned another valuable lesson, one he would remember throughout his career. Protect your valuable sources as necessary and irreplaceable assets. Keep them in your hip pocket.

After only two years in Chicago, it was already time to move on. Historically the recipient of news before it happened, Judy Nassan stood by Mason's desk. "Good news, bad news," she said.

"Uh oh, just give it to me. I'm being transferred to the bank robbery squad, right?"

She smiled, "That would be good news—at least for me, and you would still be here in Chi-town."

She had Mason's attention. "Already, another office? Okay Judy, lay the good news on me. Which beautiful southern city?"

Nassan truly felt bad for her friend. "I wish it was," she said. "No more suspense, your next stop is Boston. You will get the official word this afternoon. Remember to act surprised."

Mason begged, "Judy, you're killing me, what's the good news?"

She spoke softly and looked very concerned. "Brad, I did some research when I got the news. Yes, we know Boston is cold but you, Ann and the kids can handle that. The schools, culture, hospitals, sports—all good. And do not forget beautiful Cape Cod." She purposely evaded mentioning the high cost of living and the reality that a young family would have trouble acquiring an affordable home.

Nassan said, "You report right after the New Year, so you and the family can spend the Christmas holidays in Jersey before the move to Boston."

Vogt, Norman and Bianco organized a party at Towey's Irish Pub, about two blocks south of the office. They invited the squad, other agents, friends from the CPD, the USA's office and many support personnel. After a few choruses of "The Irish Soldier Boy," the group enjoyed a night of stories and more stories.

Ann was already making plans for the move to Boston. The Chicago experience was ending almost too quickly, and the family would miss the many friends acquired in Chicago.

At the party Nassan cornered the guest of honor and said, "Remember that little piece of trivia I taught you."

Mason said, "Right, that will come in handy, I'm sure. Let's see if I have it right. Chicago's "Windy City" nickname has nothing to do with the weather. Around 1890, Chicago was being considered to host a world's fair of 1893. Her leading citizens boasted that Chicago would be the best choice for several reasons."

"Very good, Special Agent Mason. Please continue." Nassan was truly enjoying her pupil's recall.

"So it wasn't the persistent southwesterly breeze that brought the nickname, but rather the big talk."

"And who came up with the nickname?"

"He was a New York editor," Mason explained. "Charles Anderson Dana first wrote of the Windy City.'" Mason surprised himself with this bit of information.

Nassan laughed. "A-plus," she said. "The Bostonians will be impressed with your knowledge of this historic city."

Mason smiled. "Judy if I had the juice, you would be transferred to Boston tomorrow. I don't know what I'll do without you." He meant it.

"Brad, my mother always says, 'God never gives us more than we can handle.' We never know what's around the corner. Who knows? We may be working together some time in the future. You take good care of yourself and Ann and the kids. Where did the past two years go? I can't believe we'll be saying goodbye to 1974 in a month or so. We'll stay in close touch. Tell Ann I already miss her great pot roast." Nassan was sad to see her friend leave but confident that the future would take care of itself.

She had one more thought to pass on. "And don't forget what I taught you, admit nothing, deny everything and…"

Mason laughed as he added, "Right, and make counter accusations."

With the goodbyes finished and all the necessary paper work completed, the Masons were on their way to the "Hub of the Universe" and a new adventure.

Chapter Thirty-Eight

The party's over

In the winter of 1974, Salvatore Cassando died in prison. The boss of the Bonnano family, known by his subordinates as Don Cassando, spent the last two-and-a-half years of his life behind bars, the result of an FBI sting operation targeting the mob's lucrative loan sharking and money laundering operations. Cassando's bad luck happened as the result of court-approved wire taps installed by the New York FBI office at the Bonnano family headquarters in Brooklyn.

No surprise to anyone, before his death Cassando named his underboss to be the new Don. The chosen man, Giuseppe "Joe" Nittoli, took over as head of the powerful crime family. The new Don's first official act was to name his replacement as the family underboss. As expected, his close friend and confidante Carmine Cuccio stepped up to the number two position of the Bonanno family syndicate.

In the summer of the following year, Cuccio accepted his first important assignment at the behest of Don Nittoli who gave the order: "Manzi goes." Francis "Frank" Manzi would join many other unfortunates on the hit list. The new boss acted swiftly and proclaimed that Manzi "needs to go immediately." The contract would be given to one of his favorites. "Gabe managed the Alizzio thing with a minor problem. The work after the thing—not so good. He deserves another shot."

Cuccio said, smiling. "Although with this guy it will take more than one. Don Nittoli, remember that Gabe…"

The underboss held back his thought as the well-educated Don continued. "I know at least two elderly capos are still upset about how Gabe

Randinoli handled Alizzio. I respect the opinions of others and I accept the fact that our business is similar to many others. There is jealousy, second guessing and all the rest of human frailties. I don't care, you give it to Gabe. With Manzi, I want the body left on the street. We begin the New Year by delivering a clear message. It's no secret. Everyone knows Manzi is heavy into the drug scene. We were laughed at, of course behind our back, when he made the papers for the heroin raid in Manhattan. The cops will be happy to see him gone. More important, he owes a lot of money to the Cabronas." The Don spoke of a major Columbian drug cartel. "They know he is self-employed with the drugs, it does not affect us. We will not be considered suspects when the law looks for the shooters. As for our own people, you get the word out that Manzi was freelancing and in over his head. Most important, we will not tolerate independent contracting. If someone decides to go into his own business, he will pay the price."

For years, the family regarded the drug business as evil. Freelancing was worse, a mortal sin. Don Nittoli spoke emphatically to Cuccio. "Carmine, everyone must know why I am angry with Manzi." He pounded on the table. "There is to be no misunderstanding, in particular with those members who may be considering the drug stuff already. What other families do is there business. We stay away from the drug business! I want them to think of Manzi if they disobey my order. Carmine, make it your priority to get my message to everyone in the family. You deal in drugs, you pay. I am reminded of the words of Don Cassando, a very intelligent man, who said, 'let us make money, not headlines.'"

Nittoli liked the way Randinoli, a proven earner, handled himself. He was confident he would complete the contract without complications. He ordered Cuccio to "meet with Gabe, just the two of you and insure that Gabe fully understands the importance of the work. We cannot afford any mistakes with this. A screw up could mean the end of more than his career. Carmine you tell him from me, word for word." The new Don was well aware of the bad blood between his underboss and Randinoli. He spoke the last words to impress on Cuccio the fact that the boss would not play favorites. "I cannot make it simpler. If the work is done right two things are accomplished—the cops pin it on the Columbians and, even more important, our people receive a strong message."

The word would soon be out. Francis "Frank" Manzi, an ambitious soldier, worked his own independent operation in the illegal drug business. Manzi acted carelessly and often after a few drinks opened his big mouth and openly displayed a chunk of extra cash. When asked about the expensive automobile he purchased, Manzi sluffed it off. "I always liked my rich Uncle

Julio." This was the first time anyone heard of any rich relatives. His extra-curricular activities could not be overlooked. Added to his stupidity, Manzi neglected one most important detail. "Where is ours?" cried the Don. Not only did Manzi break the rules by acting independently, he never offered to push some of the scratch upstairs to the bosses. If Manzi had asked for-giveness from Nittoli and shared his profits, perhaps he would have gotten away with a stern warning. The fact remained that he broke the rules and added insult to injury by not going up with the boss's cut. Don Nittoli, left without options, decided to end the soldier's life.

Cuccio did not waste time. Nittoli correctly assessed the relationship between his underboss and soldier. Cuccio did not like the soldier but would follow orders and not alter the specific instructions from Don Nittoli. He sent a messenger to Randinoli and arranged a meeting for the next morning.

The underboss spoke plainly: "Joe wants to be very clear. Frank Manzi, the rat, goes. You leave him dead on the street. This will send a message to our people thinking of going into drugs as a sideline business. And listen very carefully. The boss reminds you that a screw up could mean more than the end of your career."

"I understand, Carmine. The work will be complete." Randinoli thought, *"This moron is supposed to be scaring me. Joe never said any of that shit. Someday me and Mr. Underboss will discuss the matter."*

After assuring Cuccio he fully understood the situation, Randinoli came to one of his decisions; he would limit the amount of assistance on this one. His best friend once said, "We are responsible for our own actions." So why complicate the matter, include more people, create more room for error? Ninety percent of the Alizzio job went well because of his planning. If he botches Mr. Manzi, there will be one person to take the heat. On a more positive note, if the contract completes as expected, then only one person will deserve the credit. He already picked out his helper for this one. His decision completed an important first step.

Gabe elected to keep it simple. He would do the work and bring one other back-up shooter in case his piece misfired or something went wrong. One person came to mind, someone with a well-earned reputation for bru-tality. Randinoli liked working with family associate Dinny "Specs" Bu-chanan. Since early childhood, Buchanan wore eyeglasses as thick as the bottom of Pepsi bottles. Randinoli used him many times and the *gun* proved his value in previously tight situations. Palmeri accurately remarked, "Specs lives to hurt people." He specialized in strangulation.

Randinoli contacted Buchanan and the two met in the rear parking lot of a mob-friendly service station on 3ʳᵈ Street.

After a thorough explanation of the necessary details, Randinoli said, "Specs, the street is usually quiet. After the work we move out fast."

"Gabe, I can go quiet with this guy. You get him in the car and in a few minutes Manzi is not with us. No shots, no noise, no Manzi." He truly wanted to do the work himself. He wanted the opportunity to try out the new silk scarf.

Randinoli stared directly at his helper. "I appreciate the offer, Specs. But I've given it a lot of thought. We can't have any witnesses. You check the perimeter before and after I get the work done. You got all that?"

"Let the show begin, chief." Buchanan always viewed Randinoli as a leader and realized this could be Randinoli's opportunity to move further up in the ranks, which would help Buchanan's status with the family. The associate stayed focused; they needed to complete this work without any mishaps. *No big deal. So, I don't get to use the new scarf.*

The target lived with his girlfriend in a two-bedroom apartment in the middle of the block. 159th Street in Brooklyn was an easy place to conduct surveillance. After one full week, Randinoli felt comfortable believing that Manzi always traveled alone when he returned home each night between 11:30 and midnight. The two hitmen became familiar with the neighborhood, especially the Tauriello Italian Social Club where Manzi spent most of his time. The weather was approaching a forecasted heat wave. He decided to do the work on Friday evening.

On Friday, Manzi stayed away from the already-crowded crap game. He played in a cash poker game, five-dollar ante, ten and twenty dollar stakes. Two hours later, he realized it wasn't his night. After a few stiff drinks at the bar, he said his goodbyes, left the club alone and headed his big black Buick toward home, arriving at exactly 11:05 p.m. The surveillance proved accurate. Except for a single pickup truck parked on the other side at the corner of 159th street and 4th Avenue, the street seemed empty. Manzi exited his vehicle, closed and locked the door. He heard the steps coming towards him and turned his head. "What…?"

"Yo Francis, my man, how're they hanging?" Randinoli was now three feet from the unsuspecting target.

Manzi turned to see only the flash of the weapon. The S&W Model 37 now pointed, released three successive rounds at Manzi's head. The first round completely removed Manzi's left ear, and as his head turned to face his attacker, the next two were direct shots into the right temple area. The five-shot weapon held two more bullets. The body cradled backward against the car's front fender, slid down a few inches and turned to slam face first, at rest on the sidewalk. Randinoli then leaned over and pulled the trigger twice more. Carefully, he pressed two fingers against the carotid artery and concluded his victim was beyond help. There would be no reason for anyone to question this operation.

The gunshots resulted in people yelling from inside the house. As the front door opened, before anyone came outside, Buchanan waved his revolver at the middle-aged woman in the entrance and screamed in his deep voice, "Inside or die." He looked and sounded like the whacko he was and the front door instantly pulled closed and loudly bolted shut.

It ended in lightning fashion. Randinoli and Buchanan casually walked to the car, got in and drove away. A few blocks away the capo looked over at his accomplice. "Specs, 'inside or die?' You don't mince words, my man."

Buchanan sat back and smiled. "Gabe, I know you could have taken one or two of the other guys. I really appreciate that you picked me." He idolized the made man. The radio broadcast a fifty's tune from 12th and Bruce, Willie Nelson's version of "The Party's Over." Manzi would go along with that.

"Hey Gabe, listen to that, 'the party's over turn out the lights.' I like that cowboy singer. The party's over when you make the hit parade, right?"

Gabe said, "Yeah Specs, that's Willie Nelson. He wrote that one too."

Chapter Thirty-Nine

FBI Boston

For many decades, the Boston FBI Office occupied the ninth and tenth floors of the John Fitzgerald Kennedy Building in the heart of Government Center. From the ninth floor of the old landmark, one could look across the mall to Boston City Hall and beyond Congress Street to the bustling Faneuil Hall marketplace. A few of the supervisors' offices became popular when the Tall Ships from all over the world sailed into Boston Harbor. Apart from the view, the office space itself was a drab collection of ancient government-gray desks, chairs and telephones, but the lackluster interior did not prevent the very active agents and support personnel from obtaining exceptional results.

The SAs assigned to the division investigated all matters within the jurisdiction of the Department of Justice for the states of Massachusetts, Rhode Island, New Hampshire and Maine. Smaller satellite offices identified as resident agencies (RAs) were strategically located throughout New England. Traditionally, two or three agents operated the territories within these locations. Places like Worcester and Springfield housed more personnel because of the population of the area and the corresponding investigations required. Mason was familiar with the RA concept since he was introduced to the FBI by the two Cleveland SAs assigned to the Sandusky, Ohio, RA.

In 1975 when Mason arrived at his new assignment, the head of the Boston office was SAC Gene Gallagher. The SAC, familiar with Mason's reputation in Chicago as an innovative investigator, enthusiastically greeted the new addition to the office. "Welcome Mister Mason, I promise we'll keep you busy."

Gallagher's immediate subordinates were two assistant special agents in charge (ASAC): Elbridge Fetchcock, the person responsible for the criminal investigations, and Marshall Jones, who handled the foreign counter intelligence side of the office. The SAC and each ASAC occupied medium-sized offices and each man was assigned a personal secretary. The ninth floor housed all the criminal squads and a large conference room, while the foreign counterintelligence and bureau applicant squads utilized space on the floor above. Support personnel, including stenographers of the typing pool, photographers and computer analysts, occupied a large portion of the tenth floor.

An American flag and photographs of President Gerald Ford and newly appointed FBI Director William S. Sessions brightened the otherwise drab reception area. A tiny room in the middle of the ninth floor belonged to the overworked photographer, and separated by a single wooden door was the always-active vehicle radio dispatcher.

The space was cordoned off by squads. Depending on the caseload, some teams had as many as twenty-five SAs assigned, others as few as ten. The squads dealing with federal criminal violations—including bank robbery, drugs, organized crime, public corruption, violent crimes and major white collar crime—were on the ninth floor. Each squad supervisor occupied a small office, with a squad secretary and file clerk stationed immediately outside.

Mason felt at home from his first day in Boston. He learned New Englanders are hardworking, independent and patriotic in their love of the country. Bostonians go crazy for their sports teams—the "Celts, Red Sawx, Pats and Broons." Joe operated the coffee shop on the sixth floor of the JFK Building and was a diehard fan. He described to Mason a Red Sox victory from the 1974 baseball season, concluding his story with, "Boggs hit one out of the pahk, a monstah home run," and forgetting to mention that Boston finished the season in third place in the American League East. The season ended for the Sox when their superstar catcher Carlton Fisk underwent knee surgery in June and stayed out for the season. Joe's story of one positive thing he remembered from a single game was typical. Having been disappointed for so many seasons, the fans cherished the good moments. After visiting Fenway Park for the first time with Ann, Sam, Michael and Kate, Mason became hooked as a member of the Red Sox faithful.

Mason loved listening to the different New England accents. Through osmosis he acquired a bit of a Boston accent—helpful during interrogations, which accounted for eighty percent of an agent's time.

Three months after his arrival in Boston, Mason developed a partnership with an SA originally from the finger lake area of upstate New York. Bill Dermody, a certified public accountant, was smart, ruggedly big in stature, and known for being creative with his interview techniques. Dermody would occasionally use one of his trademark techniques when working with Mason. He would sit on the sidelines and without any apparent effort rip Yellow Page telephone books in half while Mason questioned an uncooperative suspect or witness. This show of strength and, even more so, the appearance of having "a few lights out," added apprehension and often encouraged the subject to cooperate. The two agents investigated bank fraud & embezzlement, fraud by wire, federal housing authority, veteran affairs, vote fraud, and a few other white collar crime priority matters. They were always two of the first SAs to be assigned to office specials, such as kidnapping, major takedowns of fugitives and full office interstate transport of stolen property (ITSP) investigations. The squad supervisor, a little guy "who would not say shit if he had a mouthful," gave the two agents a wide berth. He never micromanaged as long as they produced.

Dermody's career gained rapid momentum early when the SAC promoted him to the position of relief supervisor. It would be the first of several moves up the ladder, culminating with an appointment as an Assistant Director at headquarters. He turned out to be one of the best and most respected at headquarters.

Mason worked in an undercover agent (UCA) capacity in the mid- and late-seventies. He used the name "*Pat Rushe*" as an alias, supported with all the necessary identification and back up. One of the best-known wise guys in the New England criminal scene was a hood named Peter Amadi, who operated most of his illegal activities out of a sleazy bar and grill in Peabody, Massachusetts. Amadi paid tribute to the mob in Boston and was allowed to operate with their protection.

The ultimate con artist, Amadi already spent half of his life in prison. He once told Mason, "If I ever decide to walk the straight and narrow, I'll be one of the richest men on earth." Amadi often spoke of getting out of the rackets. Like most of his chatter, it was all fantasy. He sometimes pulled stunts that reminded Mason of his friend from the corner, pure brutality at times. One time a drug customer was caught stealing cocaine from Amadi's office in the rear of the pub. He surprised the druggie, hitting the addict with a baseball bat he kept at the ready, badly enough to send the surprised thief to the Massachusetts General Hospital emergency room. Amadi cautioned his victim, saying, "Next time no hospital for you maggot, straight to the coroner."

When Mason heard of the incident, he said, "Some people kick, some use baseball bats." The squad secretary didn't understand this statement, nor did she ask for an explanation.

Boston was a hotbed for high profile cases. Organized crime and political corruption matters ate up most of the office resources. The Boston Division became the sounding board for the entire FBI. The successful investigations and prosecutions reached an all-time high during this time period.

In the summer of 1975, the Boston Division SAC agreed to work with the Jacksonville, Florida, agents who were attempting to infiltrate an epidemic of corruption in the greater Jacksonville area. The prosecutors assigned to the United States Attorney's Office were seeking a major breakthrough. The investigation developed into a six-month undercover operation with the Abbott Restaurant and Lounge on Phillips Highway as the focal point. Numerous recorded audio and video tapes became important aspects submitted into evidence at the trials.

Mason and Dermody spent a month in Florida orchestrating a sting operation targeting several state politicos, building inspectors and other state and county representatives. Using aliases, Amadi portrayed the big-money restaurateur from New England and Mason played the part of the money person for the wealthy family enterprises. Amadi, perfect for the part, subscribed to the operation after the United States Attorney (USA) agreed to lend support with his on-going criminal charges in the District of Massachusetts.

Amadi faced a long prison sentence resulting from his involvement with a crooked Wall Street hedge fund owner. The fund, a huge Ponzi scheme, accounted for millions of dollars lost by pension funds and individual retirement accounts throughout the country. Amadi perfected his job of coaxing unsuspecting investors into the scheme promising super high returns. He took a healthy ten percent for his trouble. The USA, under pressure from the heavies at DOJ, required Amadi's cooperation to prosecute the well-known hedge fund operator. He and Amadi's attorney reached an agreement. In return for his testimony against the big dog and his participation in the Jacksonville sting, Amadi would make complete restitution and be sentenced to three years' probation—with no jail time. This was a no-brainer and Amadi joined the Jacksonville sting.

The newly renovated Abbott's nightclub became the center of the operation. The grand opening attracted politicians, entertainers and an assortment of music lovers. Entertainers such as the Platters, the popular fifties singing group, appeared on three successive weekends. The heavy cover charge and the booze sales brought in a huge cash business. The place stayed packed. The sharks moved in.

The sharks immediately smelled the blood. It started with a lowly, political-hack county food inspector who showed up looking for his piece of the pie. This was not his first rodeo; he went straight for the money. He threatened Mason, who was operating under the alias Pat Rushe, "I would hate to find health violations in the kitchen. You could be closed for weeks with all the red tape." Rushe, wearing a wire, paid off in large previously marked bills and the restaurant received a clean inspection report. In the first two months, a state senator, the mayor, three high-ranking police officials and sundry other public employees all were present, and receiving their just desserts from Rushe. Each transaction took place at Rushe's private table in open view, each the subject of audio and video recording. The individual cash payoffs ranged from two thousand to twenty thousand dollars.

After it closed down, the sting operation received a great deal of media attention. The investigation corralled several individuals. Three months later two trials were held and others were scheduled to follow. Mason periodically returned to Jacksonville to testify at jury trials that included politicians, lawyers, policemen and a few inspectors as defendants. After the jury returned guilty verdicts on each defendant, the judge issued sentencing dates. It turned out that the defendants miscalculated by not pleading out to the charges. The media screamed for justice. A popular daytime radio guru said, "They can't just walk away with a slap on the wrist." The overwhelming evidence caused the judge to be annoyed when the earlier cases went to trial. For each guilty verdict, she imposed the maximum time allowed under the guidelines and handed down harsh sentences. The remainder of the defendants took legal advice, entered pleas and received sentences of far lesser jail time.

On a Friday afternoon, the judge ended the week's activities announcing, "We will resume on Monday, at nine a.m." As Mason and one of the SAs from the Jacksonville office were leaving the courtroom, they were confronted by one of the defendants. The defendant insured they were out of hearing range of anyone who might be listening.

"You guys are pretty smart. Let me tell you both. If I get time, you two will not be so smart. You will be in the fucking hospital." The defendant was an associate of the DellaGiustina Florida crime family. As the business agent for the local carpenters' union, the thug faced charges of several counts of taking money from Rushe in return for allowing the Amadi "family" to continue with the Abbott construction overhaul without union interference to include work stoppage.

It had been a long week and a stressful day of testimony for Mason. He stepped closer to his assailant. "Louie my man," he said. That is not nice talking to the feds like that. You could be looking at more time to serve. Now move your ass…"

Before he finished, a mob attorney came between his client and Mason and roughly moved Louie down the hall. The lawyer could be heard saying, "Are you crazy? Do you know what threatening an…?" The agents could not hear the rest of the lawyer's reprimand.

The New England states were not alone in facing a variety of criminal activity. During one of the Abbott payoff stings, two of the targets, speaking by themselves, discussed matters concerning a large-scale, offshore sports-betting operation. Mason and the agent assigned to the kickback case turned this information over to the supervisor of the OC squad. Mason handed over the tape, saying, "You'll be interested in listening to this."

As a result of the incriminating discussion, an investigation by the Tampa and Jacksonville FBI offices and agents of the United States Secret Service got underway. This resulted in several arrests, indictments and trials leading to guilty verdicts and commensurate prison sentences. Most of the individuals caught up in the investigation were members of the Michael DellaGiustina LCN Florida crime family. Few could verify legitimate sources of income and all had prior gambling and bookmaking convictions. After the first day of a lengthy trial, the head of the family was seen on television as he left the court house. A chubby and jovial boss, Don Peter DellaGiustina asked the reporter, "What's this country coming to? A person can't make an honest living anymore."

The same Federal District Court judge from the Jacksonville sting case presided over the LCN matter. She showed her disdain for the defendants. "I am appalled at the exposed corruption in the state." She backed up her anger as she pronounced sentencing on each defendant. "Following the federal guidelines, I am handing down maximum prison sentences on all defendants. The sentencing is not harsh enough. If I had my way the guidelines would be set aside in this matter."

Boston SAC Gallagher later honored a request from FBI Headquarters. When the UC case concluded, he sent Mason and Dermody to the academy to introduce an accelerated program to assist other offices with public corruption undercover scenarios and operations.

Shortly after returning to Boston, Mason received a call from his old friend. Randinoli, too, had been busy during the summer of 1975—successfully completing the contract to take out a Bonanno family soldier, Frank Manzi.

Randinoli asked, "So what's up?"

"Not too much. Still keeping you safe," Mason replied, glad to hear his friend remained among the living. He had no idea of Randinoli's recent activities.

Randinoli remembered something. "I ran into one of our old friends, Tony Quinn. He's been meaning to call you but something always comes up. I can't believe other people are as busy as me."

"I'd love to hear from him. Where is he, what's he up too?" Mason had not heard the name in years.

"Believe it or not, no more craps, not even a poker game. He and Blackie bought a car dealership in Union. He said that they're knocking it out of the park. They're selling Caddies like crazy. I told him my next vehicle will come from him. Two of the guys from the corner, Kennedy and Deltucci, are on the payroll. I didn't ask what those two knuckleheads are doing and he didn't offer. Tony said that Blackie is the same—quiet and all business. Before we hung up he said something about getting everybody together, ya know, like a reunion of 12th and Bruce. He didn't get into it, sounded busy. Anyway, just bringing you up to date."

Mason said, "Sounds like a plan. You can provide the entertainment."

"Do ya think? A few cha-cha-chas. The crowd goes wild."

Chapter Forty

I'm clean, I'm innocent and I didn't do it

After he fulfilled the Manzi contract, Randinoli appeared to be in a good mood. A week before Christmas in 1975 his friend called from Boston. "I'll be visiting the Newark FBI office on Saturday and in Jersey for a few hours. I thought a stop at the hall would be a good change of pace. If your busy schedule allows it, I'll see you about five or so."

The two friends were gracious and truly happy to see each other. They hugged and the expected wise cracks followed immediately.

After taking the drink orders the shiny-headed Walt Giordano, the bartender at the roofers' hall for many decades, got it started. "You both are still in good health, a miracle in itself. No, really Gabe, I just have one question."

Randinoli appeared insulted. "Walt I'm clean, I'm innocent, I was nowhere near the joint, and I didn't do it."

Giordano continued. "The truth now. How many did you whack today? I know it's still early, but a ball park figure?" Now a small group listened closely. They had not heard this stuff for some time and looked forward to the show. Mason felt at home.

The gangster threw back a Jack Daniels. Walt my man, you forget today is Saturday. Union rules, remember. Time-and-a-half after three during the week, double on weekends. The cheap bastards want everything done during the week—in the daytime!"

Everyone laughed, some more nervous than others.

He looked at his friend. "You think I work for the federal government and hold a nice soft nine to five job like some people?"

Mason joined in. "Just keep paying your taxes. I'm looking forward to retiring someday with an adequate pension."

Randinoli chugged a beer chaser. "Right, taxes. Uncle and me are tight. He leaves me alone and I return the favor."

The spectators heard rumors but could only surmise what the kid from the corner had been doing. After a few more one liners, the group followed the bartender's lead. Now the two friends were isolated, without anyone within listening distance. Brad told Gabe that he looked well, that life was agreeing with him. However, he knew Gabe was not the same kid who had volunteered at the mission. He had aged considerably, but more than that, Gabe's eyes were the eyes of someone who had seen some cruel and despicable things. You cannot conceal debased behavior.

The union hall and bar owned many memories. They spoke of the shape-ups at daybreak hoping that Whitey Strycharz, the grouchy business agent, would scratch their names in chalk on the old blackboard. The closer your name got to the top of the list, the better chance you had to get work for the day. Some jobs would extend to a week or maybe even a month if you were lucky. Roofing was not an easy way to earn a living but the hourly wage surpassed most of the other construction jobs. They laughed out loud as they recalled some of the more humorous incidents and other harmless stuff. The two former roofers let it all go and got away from whatever they did now to earn a living.

As they reminisced, the crap game in progress in the back room continued without interruption. Everyone acknowledged the presence of the two former roofers from the old neighborhood. Still the crap game endured as the priority. The visitors could not deter Wild Bill Kennedy and others from rolling four the hard way.

"I heard about some of the work you did in New England. They must love having you around." Randinoli sounded sincerely proud speaking of his friend's accomplishments. Before Mason responded, the soldier added, "So, you must know what I've been up to, right?"

"Not a clue, should I open a case?" Mason said, refusing to travel that road.

Randinoli let go with a real laugh. "I should know better. No quid pro quo for Brad my man." His mind wandered and he said, "Maybe some days I have second thoughts. I think of ..." The words would not come out.

Mason looked at his friend and said, "You know Gabe, it's never too late for change." Smiling, he added, "Maybe going into something less noisy, like a quiet neighborhood crap game."

Randinoli answered, "Change? Even if I wanted to I..."

"That's cool, so you want to." Mason liked the direction the conversation was taking.

"You're always putting words in my mouth. I said *even* if I did, not that I wanted to change. It's not as easy as you think. Look, I'm doing what I always wanted to do. We leave it at that."

"Fair enough." Mason knew that particular topic of conversation was at an end. "I stopped in to see the old man, he looks great." He didn't mention that Cuban Pete was disappointed that he saw so little of his only son.

"That was nice. I need to give him a call. I've been busy and ..." Randinoli never finished the sentence.

Mason interrupted, "He would love to see you. Maybe you should stop by before heading back to the city." This sounded more like Gabe had no choice.

"Good idea, I'll do that." Randinoli looked deep in thought, and began laughing.

Mason said, "What's so funny?"

His friend answered, "I was thinking of the wine…"

"Oh no, don't go there." Mason laughed out loud.

As teenage altar boys, the two decided to try a little white altar wine. They were alone in the sacristy and, what the hell, no one would miss it. One taste led to another, then another, and in a short time the adolescents were "feeling it."

They filled the carafe with water from the faucet as a replacement for the wine and made their getaway. The two altar boys were in a good mood and laughing as they left the basement of the church and walked outside into the hot sun.

"Holy shit, I feel dizzy. What the hell was in that stuff?" Randinoli said, "I think…"

Mason laughed uncontrollably. They both held on to the wrought-iron fence bordering Saint Charles Academy as they made their way up the Cabinet Street hill.

Mr. Randinoli was sitting in a rocker on his front porch enjoying his pipe and newspaper as he noticed the two boys turn the corner and head toward the house. A former altar boy, Cuban Pete refrained from laughing as he rightly guessed that they had helped themselves to the church wine. They offered him their best looks of innocence.

Randinoli smiled and said, "Hi Pop, Brad and me were just…"

"You should go in the house, throw some cold water on your face and sit down for a while." The elder Randinoli recalled his days serving as an altar boy. Some things never change.

Now the two sat in silence for a few minutes. Gabe choked, "I only wish I was a better son, he deserved better. Maybe more like…"

Mason interrupted, "Whoa champ, you left the guy a boatload of fond memories. The drum corps, the shelter, the good work on the roofs, the gas station…and most of all how he laughed when we were on a roll."

Randinoli smiled. Cuban Pete loved the neighborhood and was happy his son knew many good friends and enjoyed such a close relationship with Mason. "I guess so, and he really knew nothing of anything…about anything else." Randinoli had many mixed emotions. As an only son was he expected to take over the tailor shop and carry on in his father's footsteps? That would never happen. His dreams of becoming successful always ended with being recognized as a big time bad guy. He felt guilty about being a disappointment to his father but was convinced that his career choice was the right one. He struggled when recalling the words of his smiling mother. "Gabriel you can be whatever you want to be. Keep God next to you and your life will turn out just fine."

For Randinoli, hearing wise counsel and adhering to its wisdom were two different things. He would do what he decided as a young boy.

They slammed back a couple of shots and the conversation drifted off to the less serious stuff. It was getting late and was time to end the visit.

An angry looking Jimmy Contino hurried in. "Dafuckizzy?" he asked, but no one answered. He looked around, waved an acknowledgment to the visitors, and stormed toward the back room and the crap game.

One of the young roofer apprentices at the bar questioned, "What the hell was that? What did he say?"

Attorney Edward Bloom, who made regular stops at the hall where he sometimes furnished legal advice pro bono, smiled as he sipped his gin and tonic. He sounded lawyer-like. "That sightseer, my young gentleman of the roofs, is identified as Mr. James Contino, an alleged bookmaker and party of the first part. He is inquiring as to the whereabouts of one Mr. William Kennedy, the party of the second part. It seems Mr. Contino searched far and wide for Mr. Kennedy who apparently owes Mr. Contino a sum of money. And Mr. Contino requires the debt be paid. As regards Mr. Contino's interrogatory? He questioned, 'Where the fuck is he?'"

Fortunately for Kennedy someone tipped him of the bookies presence when Contino exited his car. Kennedy could be heard scurrying up the stairs to the second floor where he gracefully jumped to the ground unscathed—another successful escape completed.

The interruption was just what was needed to bring a smile to the faces at the bar. Randinoli said, "There's the proof, some things never change.

Anyway, I'm glad the family is in good shape. I'll be in touch. I kind of miss bothering you at Quantico. You should thank me for keeping you focused, right?"

"Absolutely, I couldn't have made it out of the academy without your guidance. Listen, you be well, be careful and all the rest of it." Mason and his friend hugged and that ended it until the next time. They separated and continued on different paths.

Randinoli sat still in his shiny new car. For a moment the mob guy couldn't turn the key to the ignition. Not looking forward to the drive across the Hudson and back to his stomping grounds, the mobster looked back at the club and listened to the chatter coming from the bar and the crap game. On the drive back, his mind wandered to the past and he realized he owned a fear of the future. He sometimes struggled to accept the life he chose and wondered how things would have been had he stayed closer to his roots.

The FBI agent headed for the airport and a flight back to Boston. His mind did not wander. He could not stop thinking, "*Is Gabe aging? No, it's my imagination.*"

Chapter Forty-One

Lucrative New Jersey

The bosses increased the pressure for more money. They issued constant notices. "The family cannot function without revenue, where is the money?" In 1976, Randinoli made another decision. Seeing an opportunity to ease the family's revenue complaints, Randinoli received permission from his capo to speak with Don Nittoli. He intended to convince the boss to try out his idea to obtain a broader presence in New Jersey. Northern New Jersey was a potentially lucrative location but was currently operated by inexperienced members of New Jersey's Philip Tarantino family.

Randinoli articulated his well-thought out plan with confidence. "Joe, New Jersey is the answer." The Don insisted the members call him "Joe." "It sits waiting for someone with smarts and guts. If managed correctly, I believe New Jersey would bring to our family the money you're looking for." It pleased the highly-educated Don Nittoli to hear how Randinoli spoke and argued his position. Nittoli, too, thought the possibilities endless. What better choice than a native to represent the family and bring in some serious cash? Nittoli wanted a reason to promote Randinoli, make him a capo. Respected in New Jersey for his street smarts, connections and toughness, he believed Gabe would be the perfect selection to further the family's fortune. Randinoli always brought in the cash in New York, so why not New Jersey? The boss admired his ambition and as long as the family benefited, he agreed to discuss the idea further. Don Nittoli would put forth the guidelines. The last thing the Bonannos wanted was a war with the New Jersey family.

Randinoli met with Nittoli on several occasions in well-known restaurants in Manhattan. As a practice, Nittoli moved around, not wanting to make it easy for his enemies to learn his whereabouts at any given time. The possibility was real; given the opportunity, one of the other families would take a shot at the powerful head of the Bonanno family. Much like Michael Correlone in *The Godfather*, Nittoli made sure that the meeting places were mob-friendly. He often repeated a line from the film. "It has to be someplace where I feel comfortable." Randinoli always handled the preparation and stationed back-up close by. He never pushed Nittoli too hard with his theory. He knew the boss favored the idea and did not require any pressure.

Finally, the big boss agreed. "I like it. I cannot see a downside. We stand to lose nothing and perhaps gain a great deal." Nittoli, a fast learner, immediately initiated a plan to commence a series of meetings with the Jersey people. "I will reach out for Philip Tarantino, the New Jersey boss. The heads of the two families will agree to meet in Newark, a place you will select." Randinoli already had a meeting place in mind.

With the date of the first meeting set, Nittoli said, "Gabe will drive, I will be in front and you two in the back." He spoke to Jimmy Palmeri, a capo and the underboss Carmine Cuccio. "You will each carry appropriate protection."

Randinoli selected a familiar site, a small, one-story, red-stone building almost directly behind city hall in Newark. An old friend owned the property. Years ago, Randinoli and Mason were frequent patrons of Tony the barber and Mazalewski's bar, both located on the south side of Mulberry Street. Randinoli would have been surprised to learn that the Mazalewski's youngest son became Mason's roommate at the FBI Academy and was now a hard charging SA in New York.

Nittoli stressed the importance of his people being on the same page. In order for there to be no misunderstandings in the future, Nittoli would insist that several New York-New Jersey meetings take place. "They must know that this move is important and will benefit both families. I don't want Tarantino to feel pressured. He must feel every base is covered so he has no doubts when we reach a final agreement. We give it time so the two families get to know and trust one another." The occupants knew that Nittoli did not trust anyone outside of his own family.

Philip Tarantino was recently named the New Jersey boss, now supposedly Nittoli's equal. Nittoli did not see it that way. He viewed Tarantino as an interim leader at best with minute power of a weakening family.

At one time the New Jersey LCN family enjoyed more stability than any of the other families, but now they experienced difficult times. In existence since 1931, the original "Familio/Skiano" family was now riddled with members cooperating with the FBI. Attilio Familio had brought the family down since the brutal murder of his mentor Ralph Skiano in 1974.

The Tarantino family experienced problems from several directions. They felt the aggressive competition of other groups popping up in the Down Neck or Ironbound section of Newark and the southwest section of the state, especially from the city of Trenton. There were now some high level African-American gambling groups operating in the Jersey Shore-Philadelphia area. The New Jersey boss looked forward to the Newark meeting, wishing to reduce the stress of his family disorganization and simultaneously to bring in some compulsory money. Tarantino knew very well that because of the mistrust and discord within his family, business in the northern New Jersey territory suffered. He accepted this fact for the present, understanding that his family did not have the brains or the labor to work the area. This was an opportunity to bring the territory back to profitability. He perceived the arrangement with New York as a temporary arrangement. Tarantino, in due time, intended to regain control, but firstly he needed to look after more pressing priorities. The Don figured, *"Let someone else handle the stress and make us money at the same time. We take it all back in good time."*

The current bosses of both families were in obligatory attendance at the first meeting. They both agreed to be present at the final gathering to give their stamp of approval when the negotiations were final. Tarantino outwardly agreed with the New York boss. "Right," he said, "this is a get-together meeting. We eat, drink some wine and enjoy some good conversation." Three of Tarantino's guns accompanied their boss at this "get-together" gathering.

One soldier who attended each meeting was Lou Sparmo, known also as the numbers man for the New Jersey family. When he graduated from high school, Sparmo attended bookkeeping classes at the local community college. Although he had taken the bare minimum, Sparmo swayed others, including Tarantino, into thinking he equaled any accounting wizard. It did not go unnoticed; at every opportunity he sucked up to the bosses. He longed for the opportunity to become a soldier in the Tarantino family.

Subsequent meetings took place at the same location without the bosses being present. Both sides agreed on where the Bonanno people would operate, the size of the cut the Tarantinos would receive, and other incidentals required to insure a smooth operation. Randinoli led the Bonanno contingent during all of the negotiations.

Sounding like any powerful CEO, Nittoli told Randinoli prior to the meetings, "You are the architect of the merger, and most important, you know all the players from both families."

Everyone listened as he made his case. Randinoli methodically offered a strong argument and made clear he was knowledgeable about how things should and would work. The Tarantino delegates were impressed with how much he knew of the New Jersey gambling landscape.

As the month of March ended, the representatives of both families discussed plans for the required final meeting. As agreed, Nittoli and Tarantino would be present to furnish final approval. Randinoli spoke with his boss concerning a location for the final meeting. After a full explanation of the pre-agreement, Randinoli said, "I believe we should select the site." Randinoli reasoned that if the New Jersey people were having second thoughts they just might attempt something ugly. "I don't like and I don't trust Lou Sparmo." Nittoli agreed. "You pick the time and place. I'll let Tarantino know our choice and we go from there."

Randinoli called a friend in Belleville.

The final New York-New Jersey mob organizational meeting would take place in April on a Saturday afternoon at the Branch Brook Tavern, a Belleville, New Jersey, restaurant. Randinoli was at home at the BBT. The 12ᵗʰ and Bruce people still frequented the restaurant, the owner a throwback to the days in the Central Ward.

Billy Bambrick, who owned the BBT for over twenty-five years, ran a successful restaurant and sports book. Bambrick had a special fondness for Mason and Randinoli.

Years back, after a long day on a hot roof, the two friends were at the bar when a group from Jersey City started to raise hell and broke a few bar stools. Mason and Randinoli decided that Billy needed some assistance. The Jersey City guys left after four of them took a sound beating.

Randinoli told Bambrick all he needed to know about the *business* meeting. He said, "The guests do not have names and leave it at that." The owner gave his assurances that no one would interfere with the gathering, and "the food and drink will be quality." He gave Randinoli a tap on the shoulder and said, "the mussels are still the best in Jersey."

Don Nittoli looked forward to the trip; he was in a good mood. On this day, the Bonannos would accomplish two very important goals. First, the new operation would create work for the soldiers, and second, and most importantly, the *spondulex* would roll in.

As the four men entered the big car, the boss said to his capo, "*Paisan,* we are not going to Newark. Are you sure that you can find this Belleville place? New Jersey is a big state." This got a laugh from the others.

Randinoli smiled and ignored the fact that some of his friends believed that New Jersey was a tiny place compared to New York. True, the Garden

State paled in comparison to other states in actual space, but was still the most densely populated state in the country. "I think so boss. This time of day with the traffic, we are looking at forty, maybe forty-five minutes." The radio was set on low volume and a lively tune, Helen Reddy's "I Will Survive," played. Gabe, the musical aficionado thought, "*you got that right Helen.*"

Randinoli drove through the Borough of Manhattan, with Nittoli in the passenger seat, and two strong people, Sal Lupo and Jimmy Palmeri, in the back. All except the boss were carrying. Earlier the boss warned, "Who can know what the new Don is thinking? There is much at stake for both families. If Tarantino believes we anticipate taking over his entire operation, he may be ready for war. Stay focused. Be prepared for anything. You two stay awake and ready." Lupo and Palmeri understood their assignment. They would shoot first and worry about the consequences later. The ride continued on 34th Street into the Lincoln Tunnel, exiting into New Jersey. Gabe made note that the underboss Carmine Cuccio was not invited. It could have been because the boss wanted younger members present for the talks. Who knows? *Not my business.*

Nittoli reemphasized the family position; there would be no mistakes. "Remember you two, no matter what is said, you do not react. You say nothing, not one word from either of you. I do the talking." The two guns could never mistake their assignment. "When the time is right for us I turn things over to Gabe. Understood?"

As though they rehearsed the reply, in unison Lupo and Palmeri said, "Understood!"

Randinoli, perhaps now a rising star in the family, had much riding on the success of the meeting. The boss included him as the key participant. He prepared with detail and was confident he would handle any issues requiring an immediate solution. The kid from the corner thought, "*Wise guys throughout the country will talk about this. Imagine, one family taking over territory from another without bloodshed.* The name Gabe Randinoli, respected as the brains and CEO of the entire deal. He thought of his friend; what would he think of the decisions and choices now? He thought of his next move up the ladder. "*It's a lock. I will move up quickly. First capo, then the next underboss.*"

The light blue caddy exited the tunnel and Randinoli eased his way west toward north Newark and Belleville. "You are in for a treat." Randinoli smiled and cocked his head toward Nittoli." Now in the city's North Ward between Forest Hill and the Roseville section, the four Bonanno family members entered a beautiful park. The traffic slowed with people gazing at hundreds of colorful flowers. "No reason to rush, we can enjoy the scenery."

Nittoli looked all around and asked, "What is this place?"

"This is Branch Brook Park, the country's first county park and April is the month of the cherry blossom festival." Randinoli obviously proud to show off a place he, Mason and friends would come as kids. "We would steal row boats and row all around the lake." He continued doggedly behind the slow-moving cars. "Everyone knows about the blossoms in Washington, D.C., but not many people outside of New Jersey have seen this park. There are over three hundred acres with over four thousand cherry blossoms. The trees were a gift from Tokyo in the 1900s, and many more were contributed by the widow of a wealthy Newark department store owner." The others smiled, thinking he sounded like a tourist guide enjoying his work.

There is always one not appreciating the beauty of the blossoms. Palmeri mumbled, "Go figure, we give the Japs the big boom, they give us cherry blossoms." Ignored by the others, the boss frowned at this remark.

The leisurely drive ended. Randinoli parked in the rear of the restaurant parking lot. He nodded to Billy Bambrick who stood on the small loading dock, and the owner responded with a quick hand gesture that assured Randinoli backup support was at the ready, if necessary. Nittoli never missed a beat and, after observing Bambrick's acknowledgement, said, "It's good to know that we will do business in a friendly atmosphere."

Before exiting the car, the boss spoke: "One last thing, remember the get-acquainted bullshit is over. We trust no one. If one of them even reaches for a handkerchief, assume the worst. Be ready to shoot first, and then we sort things out."

The restaurant and bar looked very festive, with summer flowers including cherry blossoms, roses, and daffodils filling the ivory vases at each booth. "Please gentlemen, follow me right this way." Bambrick led the Bonanno entourage into a large, tastefully decorated room situated in the back of the building. Three young waitresses were already there, ready to accept drink orders. With Tarantino and Nittoli seated at either ends of the long oak table, it was time to drink, eat and relax with small talk.

After everyone settled in, without any warning Lou Sparmo became very vocal. It was immediately clear that his objective was to increase the Tarantino family percentage of the revenue, knowing that at earlier meetings everyone including Sparmo agreed to the percentage. While the agreement allowed the Bonannos to work the northern part of New Jersey, the percentage returned to New Jersey, in his mind, remained negotiable. Sparmo now pushed to add another five percent and appear the hero in front of the New

Jersey contingent. Sparmo miscalculated, believing that the New York people would be thrilled just to acquire the new territory. "I think we should get the percentage on the table and out of the way before we go any further."

Tarantino, visibly annoyed by Sparmo's impertinence, withheld his usual quick temper. The New Jersey boss forced a smile and quietly said, "Lou, we're all hungry. Let us first enjoy the great food that this establishment serves and then discuss our business. After all, we are the hosts and wish to have our friends from New York experience a relaxing meal after their long ride." He raised his glass of Chianti. "To our dear friends, to a mutually beneficial meeting, to all our health and prosperity for the new year."

Nittoli made eye contact with each of his people. His eyes said it all. Sparmo's short speech and Tarantino's smooth coating comments made the Bonannos nervous. Each man readied for the worse.

Tarantino toasted the visitors. "Salute!" In unison, the group raised glasses. Sparmo was obviously off to an auspicious start.

All business discussion ended for the time being and the luncheon progressed without incident. Everyone enjoyed the meal of antipasto, veal saltimbocca and oil and garlic-flavored spinach with roasted potatoes.

The hosts were aware of Nittoli's wine expertise. Tarantino said, "Don Nittoli, we thank you for the fine selection of wines. Now we can discuss our business. Lou, you have attended all the meetings. You seem to have something that needs to be made clear." Tarantino appeared to have his soldier's back. He thought, "*It cannot hurt. If he convinces the New York people to open their wallets a little, that's good for us. If not, we know what our take will be and we'll live with it—for now.*" He waved his hand toward the soldier. "Go ahead."

This was his moment. Sparmo needed to sound impressive, to show the guests he knew his stuff and was someone of importance. He avoided eye contact with Randinoli, who occupied the chair next to his boss, at Nittoli's right side. Rather, Sparmo got right to the significant part. He turned toward Nittoli and said, "Let us not forget Joe, this is still New Jersey, our territory. As we all know I have done the math, gone over all the numbers. Very simply stated, it is clear that our piece needs to be five points higher."

Sparmo's feigned familiarity with the New York boss was an apparent blunder. The Bonanno representatives recognized the obvious disrespect. Randinoli thought, "*Let us not forget Joe? Who does this moron think he is?*" His thoughts now focused.

At prior sit-down negotiations without the bosses present, both factions agreed the Bonannos would kick back fifteen percent of all shylock and gambling revenue to New Jersey. Sparmo's remark brought an uncomfortable silence to the private room. Randinoli had reminded the New Jersey attendees at the earlier meetings, "Remember, we will be doing all the work. You take fifteen percent without breaking a sweat."

All eyes were now on the New York boss. Nittoli raised his glass and slowly took a sip of his Dewar's scotch. He, too, was not happy with the New Jersey associate's manufactured familiarity. The Bonanno boss did not say a word. He slowly gestured to Randinoli. "Gabe, your thoughts?" While preparing for this gathering, Nittoli learned of the prior history between Randinoli and Sparmo. They did not like each other. The Bonanno boss knew of Sparmo's reputation as a mathematician. Some even referred to him as "Numbers." He understood from Randinoli the size of Sparmo's balls was in question. Mobsters follow standard procedure when they became familiar with the status of other mobsters. The New Jersey people were well aware of Randinoli's reputation on their side of the Hudson River, his temper and brutality well documented on the streets of New Jersey. They each respected this behavior as necessary to conduct business.

Earlier, Sal Lupo had observed, "They might not like what Gabe says but you can bet your ass they will listen."

Randinoli coolly waited what he figured to be the required amount of time, and without looking at Sparmo or anyone else in the room, kept his eyes riveted only on his boss. He had made a decision. Something he learned on the corner, brevity would reign. Almost whispering, he said, "My memory is the percentage has already been agreed on, at several prior meetings. We stand behind our word." He was not about to deliver an extensive homily. The quiet in the room spoke volumes.

When Sparmo recovered, he opened his mouth to speak. "Waddaya...hold on a...."

Randinoli ignored this and continued very deliberately, his eyes now focused directly on the New Jersey boss and the other Jersey members. "With all due respect, Don Tarantino, I believe you will agree if the territory received the proper attention in the first place we would not be having this meeting. During the several negotiations, our family has been more than fair." When he finished, his gaze went directly towards Sparmo, who was now perspiring in spite of the cool, comfortable air permeating the restaurant.

Quick to smell the advantage, Nittoli never hesitated. "Right, I agree, for the time being let the number remain in place as previously agreed." He smiled at his peer, and raised his glass. "Of course, Don Tarantino, should anything change, then we will discuss again like gentlemen. After all, we are reasonable businessmen."

Tarantino recognized that he would appear foolish to argue with someone holding all the cards. His representative put him in a bad position, with no room to negotiate. The New Jersey Don was actually satisfied with the contract. In truth, Tarantino never intended to live up to any deal. For him, it was not a permanent arrangement. When the time came that Tarantino's family regained its muscle, he would rid his territory of all intruders. He smiled as he rose from his chair and approached the New York leader. "Don Nittoli, of course we are in full agreement. Both families will prosper and live in harmony." Tarantino and Nittoli stood and, facing one another, shook hands and embraced, then, following tradition, kissed on both cheeks. Randinoli and the three Bonanno family members led the polite applause.

The meeting ended. The original business agreement remained intact.

One of his subordinates pulled back Tarantino's chair and the Don moved in the direction of the front exit. The New Jersey boss glanced in Sparmo's direction. The numbers man was grateful looks could not kill.

The Bonanno people later learned Sparmo received the riot act for embarrassing the New Jersey Don and his people in front of another family. Tarantino delivered a short yet emphatic message to the numbers guy. "You are no soldier. You are nothing. You disrespect my peer in front of the world. You act like a worthless worm. Never open your mouth without first understanding your adversary." His voiced raised, "And you do not attempt to bluff someone who holds the superior hand."

A week following the meeting at the Branch Brook Tavern, Sparmo, after more than enough alcohol, expressed to a friend that someday he would even the score with Randinoli. One of Tarantino's capos warned, "You better be riding in a heavy tank when you make that move, pal."

When they returned to New York, Palmeri commented on Sparmo's faux pas. "He apparently missed Sonny in "The Godfather." Everyone laughed in agreement. The reference was directed at James Caan's portrayal of Sonny Corrleone's shooting off his mouth in front of people outside of the family.

Enjoying a celebratory dinner, Cuccio toasted the boss and gave Randinoli well-deserved kudos. Don Nittoli praised Randinoli for the way he maneuvered the negotiations and arrived at the favorable settlement for the family. Randinoli felt great, his decision-making still keeping him at the top of his game. No one anticipated the next surprise.

The boss rose and looked at Randinoli. "This has been a historical day for our family. I congratulate you in earnest—my captain." The startled group raised their glasses and spoke as one. "Bravisimo!" The new caporegime raised his glass and beamed his acceptance. Nittoli summoned him as the boss walked toward the new capo. "Well done, well done." He hugged Randinoli and kissed him on both cheeks. Each man then came forward and offered congratulations. They understood the significance of the announcement. Gabe Randinoli would now run his own crew. It was known that a crew in the family averaged twenty to thirty men. Each member earns and reports to his caporegime, sometimes referred to as captain, capo or skipper. Randinoli would now have the power to develop his theories.

The underboss appeared to be the only one not enjoying the festivities. Cuccio believed that Don Nittoli should have shared the news of the promotion with him before publicly making the announcement.

Noticing the displeasure of Cuccio, Nittoli later said to his underboss, "Carmine, do not feel left out. The truth of the matter is that I surprised myself. You and I spoke of Gabe and you were aware he would move up. I got carried away by the long day and the great way things turned out for us. I decided not to wait. Do not give it another thought. We both know that Gabe will be an important part of the family for many years." He smiled, "Of course, you and I will benefit more than most."

Mason's friend Ian Murphy, a graduate of 12ᵗʰ and Bruce and now a highly-rated Belleville Police Detective, reached out. "For information, our friend met in Belleville with the Bonanno people and the heavy hitters from Jersey. It appears the New York mob is spreading out into Jersey." He provided a list of the attendees and pointed out that Randinoli appeared to be the New Yorkers' main spokesman. The police officer reported that the New York crew left the meeting in the best of spirits. "Our friend looked like he won the lottery."

Chapter Forty-Two

A rat festers

In the mid-1970s, underworld activity increased throughout the country. At FBIHQ, the organized crime bureau chiefs were feeling the pressure from the media reports, especially New York newspapers. The news accounts targeted the La Cosa Nostra as the group responsible for the "almost daily" disregard for law enforcement. Each crime syndicate experienced problems among its members and each handled the problems in the same manner. They eliminated the troublemakers, the people who had trouble following the rules. Headlines screamed the same message: "Mafia Killing Spree Continues." The body of each story complained of apparently blatant criminal activity. The public ate it up; the illusions produced eye-catching headlines and sold many newspapers. Dozens of unsolved murders, dating back to the early seventies, were cited in the coverage. One report cited Randinoli's visit to Cesare Alizzio as one of several unsolved brutal killings.

The little elderly woman playing bingo, the workers traveling the public transportation means—everyone loved reading and hearing about the Mafia. "They dismembered the body, how gruesome. Pick me up a paper when you go out."

Never allow the facts to get in the way of a good story. The media ignored the realities; the prosecutors assigned to the Brooklyn-based Bonanno crime family didn't possess any solid evidence for indictments. When the mob murders one of their own, it's rare that body shows up, unless someone talks. Periodically, body parts would be discovered in a Bronx garbage dump and vacant lot across the Hudson River in New Jersey. What would follow these discoveries is the common story for a contract killing. There are no witnesses to any foul play. No one comes forward with any worthwhile information. The United States Attorney in New York, a recent appointee, was anxious to produce a case or a number of cases worthy of going to trial, but she wasn't stupid. "There can be no arrests or indictments until the investigative aspect is complete and a successful prosecution feasible." It was always a legalese response. Put the ball in the investigator's court.

New assistant attorneys on occasion forget their jobs and decide to be investigators as well as prosecutors. Street agents would respond by flooding the USA's office with everything current, but keeping them in the dark when it came to promising leads they were following. This approach hindered the attorneys from getting involved with the actual investigative techniques, something foreign to their duties. The agents' position was clear: "We will not attempt to prosecute the case in court, you stay off the streets." Most AUSAs accepted this strategy. They did not cross the gray line and concentrated on the legal aspects of the mission. The experienced prosecutors realized that involvement in the actual investigation could lead to their presence as witnesses at trial. No lawyer desired such a problematic circumstance.

In late 1978, the recently named Assistant Director Todd Price called in a few chips. It happened quickly. In his new position, Price was expected to offer valuable insight and direction to the troops, while simultaneously managing the bureau's challenging organized crime investigations and fending off media assaults.

To the press, Price gave the impression of being articulate and friendly. At his spontaneous, personally-announced press conferences, he always provided them with enough material to fill a story. The AD never failed to include himself as the FBI representative who would save the day and bring the bad Mafia folks to justice. He refused to have a Q&A with the reporters, being smart enough to know that he was unable to answer their specific questions regarding particular crimes and individuals. If pressed, the AD could not even furnish names of the LCN players. Price never bothered himself with perusing bureau files of OC cases. He figured that he could lie and dazzle everyone with bullshit.

An attorney, Price was forty-eight years of age, six feet tall, a sharp dresser, and noticeably overweight. His family, ruled by his father Redley Price, ranked as one of the richest in the country. After graduating from a prestigious Ivy League university, the AD spent two years as a legal aide in the office of the bureau's first Director, J. Edgar Hoover, and entered the FBI as a Special Agent in 1971. Price was psychotic when it came to his ambition. It was Price's intention to become number one in the bureau, conceivably the top law enforcement official in the world. His ultra-wealthy family expected nothing less so what the hell, he'd acquire the job and move on. *No big deal*. The position would guarantee that he follow in his father's footsteps and head the vast Price financial empire.

SA Al Prazolami, a friend of Mason's from the academy now working bank robberies in Boston, told his classmate, "Brad I spent a year at headquarters. This guy Price is without question the most treacherous man in the bureau. To know him is to hate him. He deserves this reputation and contributes to his status every day. The other ADs are stand-up people and, unfortunately, too busy to pay attention to this bum. They give him a wide berth. The only way he could get what he deserves is if the Director catches his act early on. That will not happen."

Price hailed from upstate, suburban New York. It was a mystery how his father had accumulated his vast wealth. He sent his son to the most prestigious schools available. Price managed to avoid the Korean War and the one occupation displayed on his federal application was that of "assistant to the president" of a large international computer software company. The form did not require the name of the president of the firm, which in this case was Redley Price.

After obtaining a law degree, Price landed a position as a law clerk in the office of the Director. There he met and worked closely with an individual who would become Price's only close acquaintance in the FBI. A fellow law clerk, Melvin Mayhew was himself an Ivy League graduate. Mayhew became the only person to speak with Price on a daily basis. The difference between the two: Mayhew survived without the least amount of ambition, happy to slither along performing menial tasks and occasionally researching legal questions for the Director in preparation for a speech or testimony on the Hill. So often, Mayhew listened to Price's grandiose plans for becoming the next FBI Director. Mayhew thought, *"why should I be the antitheses, anything is possible. If it did happen, I would have a soft position with no heavy lifting for the rest of my career."*

Mayhew once confided in an old friend. "Like everyone else at the bureau, I despise the son of a bitch, but I will wait it out." Mayhew played the part of a good listener for Price. He didn't disclose he was also a proficient note taker.

Price's history of accomplishment in the bureau was without distinction. He pleased certain people, doing favors for agents, ASACs, SACs, and even congressional bigwigs and their staffers on the Hill. He never spent one minute on the street nor did he intend to do so. He was good at what he did— telling people what they wanted to hear and taking credit for anything good that resulted.

Price's first and only assignment transfer occurred in the District, from FBIHQ to the Washington Field Office (WFO). Co-workers found it difficult to overlook. Price never relocated and remained living in the same house in the same neighborhood his entire bureau career. Price gained a well-deserved reputation as a cold-hearted bureaucrat with zero experience as an investigator or a supervisor. His rocket-like ascent to the top was the dividend paid for ass kissing, lying, cheating and removing himself from the real work in the field. It happens in an organization where employees believe everyone else is performing as expected. Ninety nine percent of agents and support personnel believe in and practice the Fidelity, Bravery, and Integrity of the FBI.

Price was an excellent delegator of work and a champion of accepting praise earned by the efforts of others, or throwing someone under the bus when things went wrong. It was unavoidable, some opined, that every organization had at least one Price in its employ.

The fact that he rose to a lofty position in the FBI was troublesome, but his frightening ambitions were of much greater concern. Price exemplified the few who get by unchallenged. To term him as a survivor would be putting it mildly. The question often asked by support personnel, "How does he get away with it?" was answerable. The position of Director of the FBI is the result of a political appointment.

The Director stays busy with public perception, budget matters and spends much time in preparation and appearances before various congressional committees, usually justifying actions taken by the bureau. He seldom challenges his ADs unless something very drastic surfaces. The lone criminal or even gang of criminals raising hell in New York or Montana is unlikely to be the topic of some congressional committee's agenda. Congress does not call on the Director to account for a missing person investigation or to elaborate on a few indictments issued by a United States attorney's office. When the Director asked him for a clarification on a priority matter, Price designated a subordinate, most often Mayhew, to create a harmless boilerplate presentation. Then either Price would accept credit for a job well done or, when things turned sour, attribute the blame to someone else. He was the league leader with his unprincipled behavior. Mayhew said, "He never hesitates to throw someone under the bus. So long as he comes out without a scratch, then the other person suffers the consequence."

"Todd, you really believe that you could be the next Director of the FBI?" Mayhew stirred Price's ego once more. He never challenged his boss nor ever dared argued with him.

271

"Not only believe old chap, you may wager on it. The two years spent at the seat of government will pay dividends. Again, I will do whatever it takes." As he spoke the last sentence, his right eye blinked rapidly.

"Whatever happened to your theory of going with the Justice Department as an Assistant United States Attorney, and then using your contacts with a major law firm here in the District? As I recall, millions of dollars would soon follow the big shot lawyer." Mayhew added the "big shot," tired of hearing Price's smarter-than-everyone-else dialogue. He would go just so far with his minor stabs at the egotistic AD. *Why upset him?*

Before joining the Department of Justice, Price did not have a life. Ambition was never part of his vocabulary. It was not until the prospect of becoming the next Director of the FBI appeared did he come alive with the always-present obsession. Continuing with his superior style, Price countered with his condescending manner. "Melvin, Melvin, someday you will commence thinking big. Hoover was the man for close to fifty years, correct?" He did not wait for an answer. "The Interim Director was supposed to last a few months and then he would be gone. He lasted longer and then got another appointment. The current Director is now getting ready to leave because of ill health. The recent crime wave aids my position. The president will require someone current with the situation, someone with the necessary experience—from the inside. The next Director will possess more power than most on the Hill, maybe to exclude the president." He appeared to be in a trance. Slowly he continued. "Whatever it takes, that person will be me—I guarantee it!" Mayhew the exception, Price never went public with his grandiose plan. Price truly believed whatever he sought to accomplish would happen and no one could alter his plans. After all, there was no doubt he was smarter than most humans were. The financial trust allotted him by his father guaranteed his financial security, so he was not in it for the money. He sought the unfathomable power attached to the position.

When he first met Price, Mayhew recognized the apparent ego disorder. He remembered the words of a veteran prosecutor at the Justice Department, speaking of Price. "That guy's problem is not only that he is overly-sick with the wrong kind of ambition, Todd Price is dangerous. Everything he speaks of is calculated. Mix that in with his total lack of criminal experience, he is a stick of dynamite waiting to explode."

Mayhew attempted one last reasonable approach. "You have made many political contacts, I will grant you that. But, the Director is appointed by the President, who does not know Todd Price from a hole in the wall."

Never without an immediate response, his right eye twitching rapidly, he said, "Are you not saying anything new? I am well aware of that lame argument. The Director is a short timer. You have seen it. He is over-whelmed with the mountain of mandatory speeches as well as his testimony on the Hill. He's out of his element. He is not expected to last much longer, right?" Not waiting for a reply and clearly enjoying each syllable he spoke, Price continued. "As his number one aide and the primary source of information, I will have his support, coupled with my connections, already in place. Yes, I have had to promise favors to certain people. So be it. That's the cost of doing business." Price grinned passionately, "The president and his advisors will have no choice. I have constructed my position and game plan. I am dead sure of where I stand."

Mayhew looked at the man as he spoke, thinking, "*God help us, he is nuts but stranger things have occurred in the nation's capital.*"

Price had not yet concluded with his master plan. He continued, "A lateral transfer as an AD right here at FBI Headquarters, a mere matter of a signature here, a glad hand there, and it's done" Price stared and now spoke as if alone in the office. "Where is the action, the headlines? I will head the organized crime program for the entire bureau. The big metropolises, New York and Chicago, are in a shambles according to the media, and require drastic measures. Remember the days when J. Edgar, for reasons of his own, denied the very existence of the Mafia. I will not only scream of its existence but will be the one person recognizing the OC threat to the country. I will lead the war against organized criminals, commencing with the Mafia in New York."

Mayhew recognized that Price had a problem with alcohol. One night after work and more than a few drinks Price continued to spew his obsession, his master plan. Price rightly believed he could say anything to his subordinate. He viewed Mayhew as a lowly bureaucrat destined for mediocrity and never a threat to hinder Price's loftier plot. "Besides, I have a trump card to play. We have an employee assigned to the Boston Division who will be hearing from me. This individual will assure my rise to the top of the OC investigatory ladder."

Mayhew took a gamble. "What's that all about?"

"This particular gentleman spent his youth in New Jersey. One of his friends, perhaps his best friend, is now a big shot with the Bonanno organized crime family in New York. I have learned that the agent will soon be a supervisory special agent. I will wait until he is promoted. He has a bright future in front of him. Our agent does not know it yet but I will order him to visit with me at headquarters, at which time I will offer him the opportunity of a lifetime, a guarantee to further his career. He will proceed to exploit his relationship with the wise guy and construct a solid case against the Mafia.

It is that simple, nothing complex, he just does what he is paid to do—what I tell him to do."

"Suppose he refuses?" Mayhew could not believe what he just heard.

The smile appeared, the eye twitched. He finished gulping down another martini. "My good man, first he is given the opportunity. Next, I give him his instructions. There is no option here. He follows orders or he goes down in flames." Now beaming, he continued, "My friend, I have already set the stage. My visits to New York had real purpose, not the bullshit I outlined on my expense vouchers." Now too excited, he could not stop his motor mouth. "When I last visited the New York office I made it a point to meet with the boss of the Bonanno family, who incidentally is just another stupid lowlife. I introduced myself and I left it that I can call and meet again if necessary." Satisfied he convinced his subordinate of how clever he has been and how far the plan has developed, AD Price sat back and picked up his pipe.

Mayhew could not escape the words of another attorney acquaintance, a warrior of many court battles. "'*Todd Price is much more than dangerous.' He is a disgrace and a threat to the reputation of a great outfit. Yet what can be done?*"

Mayhew heard of an incident that took place in one of the downtown bars. A female bureau employee was observed in a quasi-drunken state as she celebrated a birthday with a few of her co-workers. The young woman apparently did not drink very often and the booze worked fast. She needed help negotiating her steps so her friends wisely removed her from the bar and transported her home. The story circulated the office in record time; most employees expressed amusement since the incident was out of character for the young secretary.

Price heard of it from Mayhew and decided to use the information for his benefit. He waited for the right time. The AD watched the secretary enter an elevator and quickly stepped in. He never hesitated. "Hello Katrina, my name is Todd Price." Before the surprised woman could respond, he continued, "I am aware of your public inappropriate drunken behavior. For now, I've decided to let it go. You will repay me at some future date if you want to stay employed here." He smiled and exited the next floor. Katrina found the nearest rest room where she vomited and sobbed for a long time.

The AD filled in Mayhew on his approach with the employee. "I may never need to use her but one never knows."

Meanwhile, Price's name came up in Boston. Over a few beers at Downey and Judges, a cop bar on Friend Street, Prazolami relayed a true story to Mason and a few others. "The piece of crap ordered a great guy, one of the experienced supervisors in Phoenix, to launch an attack at an unfamiliar location believed to be occupied by a gang of notorious drug smugglers connected with a major Mexican cartel. The supervisor, someone with solid military background, spoke up and disagreed with the idea. He pointed out the numerous drawbacks. Price said, "You do it my way or you better get busy updating your resume." The supervisor quit his opposition and followed orders to the letter. He figured the guy's an AD, just maybe he knows his stuff."

The others heard of the shootout but not the details Prazolami offered. Mason said, "I remember hearing that the druggies greatly out-gunned our people."

Prazolami continued. "The Phoenix agents asked to wait until more weapons and ammunition came to the site. From his home in Washington D.C., Price ordered that the raid take place immediately. One of the radio operators heard him say, "This is the FBI son, you can outshoot a few drug dealers, get on with it. He was slurring his words." Earlier Price tipped a reporter with the Washington Post, giving the details of the raid. He wanted the operation over so he could report his success to more of his so-called investigative reporter sources."

The Boston agent, now pissed, said, "That coming from a turd who never even served a subpoena."

Prazolami picked up the story. "Of course the operation went sour, and the agents took heavy fire. One of the younger guys, with two kids, is out of service permanently. The damage caused by a direct round he took in the left knee. The bad guys had more firepower, he took a round from a shotgun and his knee blew out completely. A lengthy complicated surgery saved the upper part of his leg."

Mason said, "I read an all-bureau report that said the group was arrested last week in Tempe, Arizona. It won't help the agent or get his leg back. The locals also had a legitimate beef. We never brought them in on the op. Al, there was an Office of Professional Responsibility investigation, right?"

"Brad, they can call it an investigation or whatever they want. We all know what an investigation is. This was not an investigation. Price issued specific orders to keep the raid in house. He didn't want anyone to minimize his thunder and the great planning that went into the job. The bureau did not disclose to the public that a pissing contest existed within the ranks. God forbid anyone embarrass the bureau. The supervisor told the story as it transpired. He outlined exactly what he wanted to do and what AD Price ordered him to do."

Mason looked at his friend. "That should have been enough. The supervisor has no reason to misinform OPR or anyone else."

"Right we all know that. Price of course covered his sorry fat ass and laid everything on the supervisor." Prazolami finished his narrative. "At the OPR hearing, Price never missed a beat. He said, and this almost verbatim, 'The supervisor was feeling the pressure and misunderstood me. Of course, I would have allowed our agents to wait until more back up and firepower came. It was his call and he just went with his gut feeling, he made a bad decision,' blah, blah, blah. At his press conference he said, 'Ladies and Gentlemen, I can assure you that I will be recommending every one of the agents, for not only letters of commendation from the Director but incentive awards as well.' Prazolami hesitated, pretending emotion, 'As for the brave agent who lost his leg, we will have a special day in his honor right here at FBI Headquarters. I will personally notify each of you of the date.'"

"The Office of Professional Responsibility settled with a slap on the wrist for both AD Price and the supervisor who followed orders. The report read like 'Cool Hand Luke' and said something about an obvious failure to communicate, blah, blah, blah." The veins protruded from his neck as he became angrier at each word he spoke. "We all know he is the exception to the rule. I still can't believe how a lowlife can not only survive but thrive on incompetence and ill-will." Prazolami called for another round of beers, his update complete. As far as he and others were concerned, the AD's irresponsible actions were covered up in connection with the incident. The case and the manner in which it was reconciled will remain in the memories of many people.

Gene Gallagher, the SAC of the Boston office, finished off a quick mug of beer. "On a happier note, in a few months our good friend Special Agent Brad Mason will officially be known as Supervisory Special Agent Brad Mason. I wonder how he would handle a similar situation." Gallagher and Mason were close friends, together on several difficult cases including a shootout in Yarmouth Port with a bank robbery gang headquartered on Cape Cod.

He smiled at the SAC. "Sir, I'm not one hundred percent certain." Mason scratched his head feigning an attempt to solve a challenging problem. "I believe before I took an unprepared group of agents to face a well-armed bunch of no-goods, I would respectfully request a sit-down with AD Price—a private discussion."

They all got his meaning. Gallagher said, "Remember lad, that ruthless prick holds all the cards."

"Yes sir, but as one of my mentors, Mr. Blackie Capone, once said, "Having the cards is one thing, can he play them is the question?" Mason saw no sense mentioning that he met Price the very first day of training. He recalled Price entering the new-agent bus and proceeded to expound on his importance. Mason took his own personal inventory of the egomaniac at that time, and concluded *he hasn't changed much, maybe gotten worse.*

Price realized that it would take political pull, which he actively pursued, and something big to happen in the bureau for him to achieve the position he craved all these years. He spent his waking hours creating scenarios wherein he would be a lock for the job. *What is always a guarantee to grab national headlines? Without any doubt, organized crime, the Mafia!*

He shouted to his secretary, "Get me the SAC handling OC matters in New York." The New York office, because of size and population of the city, required three SACs. Price planned a trip to the Big Apple; he would speak with the OC side of the office.

The official justification for the travel expense voucher would read, "Meetings with SAC, AUSA and others." Who would question an Assistant Director?" His true purpose for misusing government funds was to meet personally with Gabriel Randinoli.

Chapter Forty-Three

A comeback in Jersey

Last year, 1978, Don Nittoli ordered the promotion. The honored position offered many titles. Randinoli, now a capo, led a crew of soldiers and associates of the family. Randinoli's shrewd handling obtaining the lucrative territory was recognized by the boss and now he had spent an entire year running the family operation in the newly-created northern New Jersey territory. The gambling, loansharking and extortion resulted in more money coming in than even he expected. At age forty-two, he was one of the younger members to be elevated to such a position of authority.

At first the crew complained about their new territory and commute. They were unhappy with the early morning drive through Brooklyn to the Holland Tunnel and across the Hudson. Within three months the mood of the commuters improved. Stevie Lombardi prophesized correctly. "It's all about the scratch. My income more than doubled since the relocation. I'm happy."

The Bonanno New Jersey partners were ecstatic as well. Don Tarantino told his people, "Look at the money coming in. And we don't do a thing except count it. I am so happy I thought of this, but sorry it didn't happen earlier."

There are no secrets. A newspaperman, recognized as a Mafiosi historian, in a recent story referred to Randinoli as "the predominant Bonanno family member in northern New Jersey." The writer detailed the success Randinoli attained when in control of a gambling network in New York. This recent notoriety caused much *agita* with some people in New York. The underboss, Carmine Cuccio, became more jealous of Randinoli. Cuccio was always worried about his personal status in the family. He saw the young captain as a threat.

The story didn't bother everyone. Nittoli was elated; very few complaints from customers in the Garden State about the vig, and the additional revenue turned out to be even greater than anticipated. The Tarantino family never expected fifteen percent to equal so much money. Nittoli laughed and said, "If Don Tarantino knew of his own people borrowing money from Gabe, he would be very angry."

In some ways the new captain remained a creature of habit. One morning Randinoli, Mike Iovita, and Jimmy Brando were at breakfast in a local mom-and-pop coffee shop in Elizabeth. A huge breakfast became a ritual before making the collections. Randinoli maintained his sense of humor. He liked to preach. "One time I heard Louie Battiato tell his brothers, 'Never go to work on an empty stomach. Even more important, never threaten to beat people on an empty stomach.'" Business was booming in the new territory. Randinoli capitalized on his relationship with old associates and his knowledge of the territory to expand the business.

It's a small world. Also a product of New Jersey, Mike Iovita, a former leg-breaker from Newark's First Ward, became one of the most feared members of Randinoli's crew. He also provided the technical work for the family. When he was a young man, Iovita attended one of the well-regarded vocational-technical high schools in Essex County. Whenever the family needed a place bugged or required a recorder of some nature, Iovita got the job. The two met twenty years ago when the First Ward wise guys dispatched Iovita to a CYO basketball game at Barringer High School, a structure built in the early eighteen hundreds. Saint Joe's players found themselves in a bitter, highly contested quarterfinals game with a team from the First Ward. The Saint Joe's coach got into a screaming match with the two city employees assigned to open and close the gymnasium building. Both men were from the First Ward. They influenced who would referee the games held at the high school and took kickbacks from their selections. The employees, associates of the New Jersey mob, each received a percentage of each referee's paycheck. The two caretakers intimidated the young referees in favor of the First Ward neighborhood team. On this particular evening, Mason, Randinoli, Jimmy Coughlin, and Shadow Deltucci were at the game to support the younger guys from 12th and Bruce. The two custodians heard more than enough of Saint Joe's coach and sent word to the First Ward wise guys. "Send one of our people over to handle a situation."

The six-foot, five-inch Mike Iovita, the younger of the Iovita brothers, looked even bigger and wider wearing a blue cashmere winter overcoat. One of the stooges pointed to the Saint Joe's team and said, "That's him with the white sweatshirt, the loud mouth on the bench."

"This will be over quick. Just make sure you open the door and let me out when I finish." Iovita wasted no time, and headed toward the very frightened coach. Mason and Coughlin were in front of the big thug in a few seconds, but before they reacted, Randinoli picked up a heavy oak bench, quietly moved behind Iovita and, gripping its legs with both hands, brought the bench down square on the big man's head.

"You two try what you're thinking and you get the same." Mason stood in front of the custodians who had followed behind Iovita and now, armed with clubs, made moves toward Randinoli. Instead of mixing it up with four obvious nut jobs, the employees decided to aid Iovita who was lying flat on his back. The big man laid still, his eyes closed. Iovita would be out of commission for some time.

The young basketball players watched without saying a word. Deltucci walked toward the bench and said, "That's what neighborhood means. You're never alone."

Iovita finally regained his senses and agreed to go for a quick checkup at the nearby Graver hospital. He was still wobbly on his feet as he was escorted from the gymnasium. The referees resumed the game. The two employees didn't make any more phone calls while the game continued.

The St. Joe's players, aware of what happened, were now anxious to get back to business. The opponents, now hesitant to continue with the game, reluctantly lined up for the jump ball. The referees displayed a different view of the teams and the calls started to go in favor of the boys from Saint Joe's who won the game by three points. Previously, the Saint Joe's players had seen Mason and Randinoli in action in the schoolyard, but this was different. Petey Sherman, the team captain, summed it up. "They never hesitated. We were gettin' screwed and it became a 12th and Bruce thing." That accurately summed up the event. The episode became a certain favorite for future storytelling sessions. "Yeah, I was there, the team cleared the bench. Gabe picked it up and hit the huge dude on the head."

Iovita loved to tell the story of how he met his boss. "I was focused on my job. I never saw Gabe or his friend Brad or the other two. I didn't even know they were in the building. I was concentrating on the shithead of a coach. All of a sudden I see flashes of light." Now animated and raising his voice an octave, he said, "He didn't use what normal people use, a bat or a two-by-four. Gabe dropped me with a bench, can you imagine, who would a thought—a freakin' bench. I ask you, was that fair?"

Mike Iovita remembered something. "Hey, I almost forgot. Carmine called about next week, New Year's, right? We have reservations at the Copa. We bring in 1979 with a bang. Ya know, with noisemakers and whistles and that stuff. Not the bang bang you guys are thinkin."

Randinoli smiled at his old friend. He thought, "*Just what I need, a night of hugs and kisses with my favorite underboss. Be patient.*"

It was time to get to work. Clearing the dirty dishes from the table, the coffee shop waiter, a big Latino, accidentally spilled coffee on Randinoli's lap. It was hot and the mobster jumped up without saying a word. What concerned him was that his new girlfriend had recently purchased the khaki pants. Before the waiter could offer his apology, Randinoli picked him up at the apron straps and threw him toward the kitchen in the back of the restaurant. Perhaps that would be enough, but Randinoli had made a decision. He walked toward the kitchen, stopped and drove his foot into the Latino's ribs. Iovita and Brando held him back as the waiter moaned in pain on the floor. His friends asked how badly he burned. "Burned my ass, these new pants cost more than this entire dump." His subordinates thought it funny, but Randinoli never saw any humor in the whole deal.

The owner was grateful to see the three men leave the restaurant. The waiter mumbled something in Spanish. It was just as well that Randinoli and crew were out the door. He was still a busy man.

Chapter Forty-Four

My sick grandmother

Every business has its problems.

The following three years moved along without major setbacks. The Bonannos considered the New Jersey operation a huge success. But once in a while certain business problems had to be addressed or things could get out of hand. Randinoli stayed alert to such matters.

One of the collectors working for Randinoli, Jimmy "Brown Bag" Andalora, decided to keep a little extra for himself before turning in his collections. The theft may have gone unnoticed if not for the robust Andalora and his craving for the booze. He couldn't seem to get enough booze in his system. The big man frequented a wise guy hang out located on Broad Street in Hillside. During a night of drinking with a few friends, he once again consumed too much brown stuff. Andalora's shady reputation included his high level of tolerance for Seagram's VO Canadian whiskey. "He drinks the stuff like its water." His drinking sessions usually lasted anywhere from two to four hours. The booze always dictated the duration. The wise guy's behavior was easy to forecast. Andalora, hammered each time after he picked up the first drink, could never leave the bar until he could barely stand up straight. As usual, he went off at the mouth.

The bartender, one of Randinoli's steady bettors and borrowers, got the word back to his lender. "It sounds like Jimmy has been keeping a chunk for himself."

With Jimmy Falco and Mike Iovita, Randinoli visited Brown Bag at his condominium in Hoboken, New Jersey, birthplace of "old blue eyes."

Andalora gave it his best shot, as Iovita sat on his chest. "Gabe, honest to God, I needed the extra scratch for my sick grandmother." A humorous comment but business was business.

Before he supervised the beating Randinoli said, "Jimmy, maybe you need a part-time job. Oh, besides, we all went to your grandmother's funeral last year." Andalora gave up every nickel in the condo and still ended up with multiple fractures to the face and head. Before leaving the apartment, Andalora received a stern reminder to be at work early Friday morning. "You get going early and do not miss a stop. Maybe a visit to an AA meeting would help your career."

Before they left the apartment, Iovita went to the small refrigerator and removed the last can of cold Schlitz. "What the hell, Brown Bag won't be able to swallow."

When things slowed, there was more time for games. One day at the store in Brooklyn, Jimmy Falco decided to stir the pot. He brought up a question to his capo about New Jersey. "Hey Chief, how come you came to the city from New Jersey every day? Is it that much of a dump?"

"New Jersey?" Louie Calabrese chimed in, "I thought you was from freakin' Newark, Gabe?" Calabrese was a cold-blooded killer and possibly the dumbest gangster in the city, maybe the state. A Luca Brasi look-a-like, Calabrese could turn violent.

Randinoli really liked Calabrese. "I am Louie, and Newark is in New Jersey." There were a few minutes of silence, while Louie let this latest revelation sink in.

"Oh, I thought Newark was in Jersey City." No one laughed or said a word. Anthony Spero almost choked on his cappuccino but held his composure. No one dared have Calabrese think he was the brunt of a joke.

Randinoli quietly said, "No Louie, Jersey City is a city, like Newark, both located in the state of New Jersey." He sincerely wanted to have Calabrese understand the geography. "You know, like New York City and Albany are both cities in the state of New York."

With this, Falco took another shot at the target, ignoring his captain. "C'mon you guys, of course Louie knows that each state has a bunch of cities, right Louie?" The phone could be heard ringing in the front of the store.

Calabrese absorbed enough geography for one day. "I think that's for me." He hurried out to answer the phone.

Everyone smiled, a few laughed aloud, all except Randinoli. Once Randinoli had resentment, it stayed. He didn't appreciate Falco's comments;

it wasn't the first time he took cheap shots at Calabrese. Occasionally, someone had the task of driving to Queens late at night and checking the property. One of the past Dons was very careful in this regard. He often said, "You never know if the cops learn of the location and attempt to dig up one or more of our old friends."

The capo made a decision. He thought, *"Why wait? The comedian has too much free time. He needs some midnight shifts at the dump."*

Randinoli never looked up from the newspaper in his hands. "Jimmy, it's time to check out a few locations. You wait until dark and run over to Queens tonight and check out the area." Falco almost frowned. The capo took notice and continued. "We haven't been to the Jersey ditch in a while either. Tomorrow night run over to Jersey and make sure we're good there, too." Randinoli returned to reading the sports section. The others went quiet. They had no doubts; the capo was sending an unmistakable message to Falco. It would be some time before the soldier poked fun at another member of the crew.

Chapter Forty-Five

Mae Yong

"How many broads are you tied up with now, Gabe?" Mike Iovita, the family techie and an important member of the crew, was seriously curious. The capo and Iovita knew each other from their early days in Newark so Iovita could take liberties the others could not. The six-foot-five soldier loved to tell the story about how "Gabe dropped me with a bench" and now he wanted to know about Gabe's love life. It seemed to him like his capo dated a new woman every week.

Iovita was not the only one unaware of the capo's early marital fling. After five years of a tumultuous marriage, Randinoli deserted his wife and two young children. Too busy being a big shot in New York, there was no time to be a husband and a father in New Jersey. When she sued for divorce, his wife Diane obtained it without any complications. Few people from the corner or his New York friends were aware of his marriage and divorce. The goodbyes involved a lot of screaming and name calling. Diane ended the shouting with, "I hope we never see you again. You're a scumbag and I pray you get what you deserve." The young family man never looked back.

Randinoli looked at his friend. "Mike, I do my best to keep them all happy. Sister Francis taught us to be sociable." In fact, Randinoli was not a considerate companion to his female acquaintances. On more than one occasion, he displayed a vicious temper and became physical. As a young man, Randinoli never apologized for his deviant behavior and always offered a lame request for forgiveness. "Sorry babe, let's go out to that new restaurant and enjoy ourselves." He convinced himself that he took responsibility for his abhorrent actions if he bought an expensive gift, such as jewelry or a trendy outfit.

He gave himself the weekend off, leaving Palmeri to watch the New Jersey operation. Randinoli knew he would be busy. Three months prior the captain moved in with another new girlfriend. An Asian-American, Mae Yong was petite, good looking, intelligent and very quiet. He relished the quiet part. The two developed a very satisfactory arrangement. She always looked good when accompanying the big shot. In return, Mae enjoyed a life-style of expensive restaurants, big cars and more than adequate gifts. No one was aware that Yong had other close friends.

SA Terry Gordon of the New York FBI Office dialed the number of the Boston office.

The squad secretary called out, "Brad, it's the New York office, a guy named Gordon for you."

Mason grabbed the phone and pronounced his usual brief greeting, "Mason."

The caller said, "For information, a friend of a friend of yours just got arrested." Never one to give out too much detail at one time, he waited.

"Okay Terry, will I be given twenty questions before I get the answer?"

"Brad, you recognize my voice, cool, very cool. Okay, I pinched a young, very good-looking Asian female, name of Mae Yong." Gordon paused again for effect. "Ms. Yong being the latest live-in acquaintance of one Mr. Gabriel Randinoli of Mafiosi fame in the Big Apple."

Mason answered, "That is without doubt the longest sentence you have ever uttered. I'm listening."

Gordon gave his friend a fast synopsis of the basis for the arrest. "We have her on violation of bank fraud and embezzlement, Title 18; USC 1344. I let her know she's looking at potentially thirty years in federal prison."

Mason asked, "What's the damage?"

Gordon filled Mason in on everything he had on the young woman. "It looks like the bank is missing over one hundred thousand dollars. Yong is a...was a teller supervisor at Chase Manhattan downtown in charge of the vault. The bank employed a system so that whenever a teller's cash depleted to a certain level they were required to fill out cash request cards. The idea was simple. The teller presented the card with the amount of cash requested written in and delivered it to Yong, who refurbished the teller's drawer. Like so many banks, systems seemingly working remain unchecked and, even more dangerous, unaudited. Yong's responsibility included cash disbursements and allocation for all tellers, as well as the cash reconciliation of vault currency."

Gordon knew of Mason's history with Randinoli, and knew that his friend was a capo in the Bonanno crime family. When assigned to the Cleveland office, Gordon lived in Avon Lake, Ohio, and his family was familiar with the Sandusky area where the Masons lived. "My kids would live at Cedar Point forever, if we'd let them." The two agents became friends when both attended a gambling seminar a few years back at the FBI Academy. Mason was one of the speakers at the two-day meeting of agents and police departments from all over the country. Of course, Mason spoke about some of the intricacies of the crap table, black jack and poker. The games at Bruce Street and Hartford Street provided much knowledge of the gambling mentality. The casino industry invitees included security people who were happy to return to their businesses and share new knowledge with the pit bosses and dealers. He thought, *Blackie was right, one never knows when a good old American crap game will come in handy.*

When Gordon worked in the Boston division, he and Mason investigated a gambling/loansharking case a few years back, in the fall of 1980. As co-case agents on the investigation, they spent many nights running surveillances in the city and traveling to the Providence, Rhode Island, area on several occasions. The joint task force case ended successfully when twenty-eight members of the LCN from Providence and Boston received an unwelcome surprise. While attending a major fight at the Boston Garden, they found themselves handcuffed, arrested and transported to the JFK building at Scully Square in Boston. The occasion at the garden was the closed-circuit television coverage of the Middleweight Championship of the World bout between the champion, "Marvelous" Marvin Hagler, and Roberto Duran. The contest, one of the first closed-circuit live bouts, turned into one of the great matches of the decade. Hagler retained the title after fifteen grueling rounds of boxing.

Gordon later explained to Mason, "The bank procedure is not complicated, in fact, it is too simple. If Yong refurbished the vault cash with the amount given to tellers, the account would balance. Yong devised her own system. She inserted teller requests with fictitious amounts, took the cash overage for herself, and used the phony requests when reconciling the vault cash account. Yong simply put stacks of neatly-wrapped cash in her purse prior to leaving the bank at the end of a work day."

Mason had personal experience with victim banks. The FDIC-insured banks considered their employees to be honest and trustworthy. The pre-hire practice utilized throughout the banking industry included thorough background investigations. The victim bank in this case never considered searching Yong before leaving work at the end of the day. Most of Yong's individual thefts amounted to at least ten thousand dollars, always in large denomination bills allowing easy storage in her extra-large hand bag.

SA Gordon made quick time of the investigation with the help of the New York office accounting squad, scheduling dates and amounts of the bogus transactions. The total shortfall amounted to just north of one hundred thousand dollars. With only one suspect, the investigation moved in one direction. After several comprehensive interviews of bank employees, he said, "The other tellers agreed to testify concerning the withdrawal tickets. Yong forged the tellers' signatures on each ticket."

Yong copped out to her illegal operation; she called it her indiscretion. It turned out to be her first offense. SA Gordon sensed that Yong was smart and could be helpful in future bank cases. "You will need to explain the entire scheme to me so that I understand enough to go to the prosecuting attorneys with it."

Yong offered no resistance. She recognized a good deal when she saw one. Her boyfriend advised, "It's a first offense. You cooperate, no big deal, no one gets ratted out, no one gets indicted. We give back some of the cash, we keep the rest. I invest it." She agreed to cooperate and SA Gordon included Yong's valuable assistance in his reports. The Assistant United States Attorney (AUSA) assigned to prosecute convinced the judge of Yong's full cooperation with the FBI. The government recommended that Yong not serve time in jail but be given extensive probation and make full restitution. Yong did not serve time in jail, received three years' probation and made restitution of forty-six thousand dollars, swearing the rest of the money was history.

Gordon offered his opinion to the AUSA. "Who cares what she did with the dough. The bank paid for acquiring a valuable lesson. They've already incorporated new accounting procedures pertaining to available cash. Besides, she may be more valuable than we first thought. Her roommate is one interesting individual."

Gordon told his friend of a particular visit he had with Yong. She appreciated the attention received from the agent. She talked more than usual. Yong told the agent of an incident involving another wise guy and described how Randinoli reacted to the situation.

"She told me a story. I remembered hearing of a wise guy connected with the Lucchese family. One night he drank too much, went cuckoo and smacked an Asian girl around. Mae said she was the unfortunate victim. This guy tried to pick her up at a jazz club in Manhattan. She wanted nothing to do with him. The gangster became enraged and beat the hell out of her. She had just met your friend and, when he saw her after the beating, Gabe quickly made up his mind about what needed to be done."

Mason said, "Sounds about right, he made a decision. So he found the guy?"

"He sure did. He brought one of his goons along with him, Specs Buchanan. We know that Buchanan is a longtime associate of the family. He idolizes Randinoli. Your friend treats Buchanan with respect. The word is the capo takes Buchanan with him on difficult collections. They are a most successful team when it comes to keeping the accounts receivable in order. Buchanan is always about business. Anyway, once they located the Lucchese guy, Gabe made short work of beating the living crap out of him, sent the guy to the hospital. There was a near war after the word got out. Joe Nittoli met with the Lucchese boss, who wanted an apology from Gabe. Nittoli defended his capo and convinced the Lucchese Don an apology would not happen. The Luccheses did not push the issue. They viewed their member as the bad guy for hitting an innocent woman. It was finished."

"Gabe got an insignificant punishment, warned about going after another wise guy. His defense held up, he protected his girl and he'd do it again. Nittoli put out the word, 'It's over. No more to do. She views Gabe as her protector. An apology to a woman beater is not happening.'"

Mason smiled, "Good luck with an apology from Gabe."

Gordon told Mason, "She knows I went to bat for her with the prosecutor. I'll try to utilize Ms. Yong as an asset. If anything pops up re your friend, you will hear from me. And no need to say thanks." The phone went dead.

Special Agent Gordon officially opened Yong as a confidential informant. During the several meetings, he gained a valuable understanding regarding her association with the OC element, particularly her personal relationship with Randinoli.

The agent met with Yong at least every other week. She was intrigued with her new dual role, being Randinoli's steady girl, and she now perceived herself as an important person in the eyes of the FBI. She trusted the FBI agent, knowing she would be behind bars if not for his interceding with the courts. During a meeting with SA Gordon, Yong let it slip out that Randinoli had removed her of the remainder of the embezzled bank proceeds. He convinced her by saying, "We give back a piece, screw the bank. We keep the rest of the bread. You do the probation without a problem and you'll find another job."

"Gabe told me that he would invest it for me." Yong remembered him saying he would "put the money on the street. I don't know what he meant. He said you needed money to make money." Gordon correctly interpreted this statement. The mobster would loan out the money on the street and pick up extra cash for himself. The FBI agent viewed the stolen bank funds as history—no way would he confront Randinoli and put Yong's life in jeopardy.

SA Gordon passed this latest update to his brother agent in Boston. "Our Asian friend just told me what happened to the rest of the hundred grand. Your friend became richer thanks to some unreasonable procedures at a big New York bank." He brought Mason up-to-date, assuring him Randinoli did not know of Yong's connection to the FBI. Mason agreed, thanked him for the information, and chalked it up to more of Randinoli's decision-making.

Gordon added, "Big Joe Nittoli would not agree with Gabe's business philosophy if the capo did not include the family in the proceeds."

"Remember when I told you about the two kinds of business?" Mason wanted to make a point.

Gordon did recall and said, "Right. One, it's his business and two, it's none of our business. Gotcha. Life continues."

The relationship with Yong worked out well regarding intelligence gathering of a made mob guy. Yong confirmed some details regarding Randinoli that were previously considered hearsay. He was paranoid about law enforcement tails. She said, "Gabe sees the fed vehicles wherever he travels, even believes he recognizes particular agents whose only assignments are to watch him. When I try to calm him down, he becomes very angry with me and lashes out. He never hits me but punches and kicks whatever's available—a door, table, he once left a deep dent in the hood of his dark blue Buick Rivera. He kicks things."

Mason thought, "*If she only knew!*"

Chapter Forty-Six

Joe is watching very closely

Mae Yong, usually soft spoken, wanted some answers. Still on probation, she wondered where the forty thousand plus dollars disappeared to. Randinoli told her he would invest it, would "put it on the street." She expected to receive a comfortable income. The truth: her boyfriend invested alright, and suffered huge losses investing in high-stakes crap and poker games. "Gabe, where did it all go? On the street? What does that mean? When will we get it back?" The capo needed something to take his mind off such trivial shit. It happened.

Randinoli received an order from the top. "Take out Anthony Yandola."

Yandola, not considered a lightweight, was for years an associate of the Bonanno family and union delegate of the largest Teamsters Local in the city. When now deceased Salvatore Cassando served time for federal racketeering, he more than once shared his feelings with his underboss Joe Nittoli. "Anthony Yandola is a liability. When the time is right, he makes the list." Now the new boss felt certain Yandola deserved the ultimate punishment. Nittoli never dared issue an order for a hit or reached a major decision without Cassando's blessing. Now in total charge, the members expected him to generate the difficult choices.

Among the duties and responsibilities delegated to Yandola, he served as the conduit between the family and the International Brotherhood of Teamsters.

Nittoli recalled a conversation with his boss. "I remember what Sal said on the subject, he made it clear. He said, 'Mr. Yandola is playing cute. The last two payments were short and now he's meetin' with an attorney or a cop. My source is not sure who the guy is but knows he's some kind of law.'"

For two decades, Yandola survived as a crooked union delegate. The job did not require heavy lifting. His real job was to coordinate and deliver kickbacks received from union bosses. The most important part of his existence included the transfer of cash directly to Cassando. In return, the Bonanno family guaranteed that none of the dues-paying members disrupted the jobs or interfered with union business. The family enforcers kept the workers in line, prevented strikes and work stoppage. Unfortunately, Yandola's personal gambling debts increased and he withheld huge sums of money for himself. This turned out to be a bad decision when the boss noticed the obvious cash shortage. Nittoli pressured the local business agent and learned the exact amount the family should have received. He told his underboss, "The numbers do not come close to matching. Carmine, send someone for him now. I will speak with him about the discrepancies."

Yandola sat in a chair in front of Don Nittoli. "I am not happy with you. I have more important matters to attend to than to chastise you." The boss sounded almost friendly. He would not let Yandola guess his life could be in jeopardy. "Sal Cassando, may he rest in peace, gave you a pass. You took advantage of his kindness and disrespected him and the family. I offer you no such benevolence. Next week the entire amount, thirty-four thousand, right here. You give the envelope to him." The Don pointed to one of his bodyguards who stared at the frightened union delegate. "Then you begin again as a member in good standing." Nittoli waved and turned away.

The important matters referred to by Don Nittoli centered on the pressure coming from Sicilian-based heroin traffickers. For years, the Bonannos managed to stay free of the drug business but now they witnessed the financial bonanza of the other families. They could not ignore the potential for enormous wealth. Eventually, the Don would acquiesce and the Bonannos would become the main players in the drug business. The FBI utilized undercover operatives and made the connection between the Bonnano family in the U.S. and their counterparts in Italy. It became apparent to the investigators that the Bonnanos were already the biggest and most violent of the five families. If they became heavily involved in the lucrative drug business they would be the most powerful of any criminal organization in the world.

The boss did not convince Yandola that he would be off the hook. The union leader left his audience with Don Nittoli believing that he would be killed even if he paid back the missing funds. The pressure escalated when he made another decision. He sought out a close acquaintance, employed by the NYPD. Yandola asked questions pertaining to the witness protection program. Not at all discreet, these conversations took place in a public building in downtown Manhattan. A coffee shop employee named Manuel recognized the union delegate in what appeared to be deep conversation with the city worker and like any good mob snitch, made a call. "I don't know the guy's job except he's a suit and tie guy and works in the PD office in city hall. Yandola looked bad. I heard him clearly. He said that he wanted the guy to find out about the witness protection program. And this is a quote, he said, "'I need to know who I have to see. I need it now.'"

The members never learned the reason why Yandola had received a pass and was allowed to continue working and living. Now Nittoli knew that the former allegations were all true and that Yandola continued doing his own thing, filling his pockets with money rightly belonging to the family.

A week later, Yandola met again in the same building with the same man he spoke with the previous week. Nittoli knew for certain Yandola never intended to pay the money owed the family. The boss would not wait any longer.

Nittoli issued the command to the underboss Carmine Cuccio. Yandola's future now out of his hands, his future was decided for him. "Enough! No more discussion, give it to Gabe." Nittoli sucked in a long drag on the big Cuban cigar. "He proved himself and deserves additional work. Lately, with this drug business, the heat is getting closer. I would place this on hold for a while but we are through being nice guys. Carmine, be very clear with Gabe, another mistake will not be acceptable."

Cuccio smiled as he answered his boss, "Thy will be done."

Cuccio summoned Randinoli to the Knickerbocker Avenue headquarters in Brooklyn. When Randinoli arrived, the underboss sat alone at a table in the corner of the dark room. The members often held sensitive one-on-one meetings at this table. It remained private and well out of sight from the front of the store. Two of his bodyguards sat at the counter nearby. Randinoli nodded, recognized them both from the crap games and a few social occasions. Randinoli could not keep from thinking, "*Here it comes, the crying from the top for more money.*"

The capo sat across from the underboss who offered the cappuccino brewed earlier by one of the leg breakers. They exchanged a few pleasantries and sipped their drinks. Cuccio wasted little time in getting to business.

"I have work for you."

Surprised, yet always appearing confident, Randinoli quickly responded, "Here I am."

Randinoli knew that the contract came directly from the boss. "The unfortunate citizen is Anthony Yandola, the Teamster union guy. Do you know him?"

"I know the name, I may have seen him at a game but I never met the guy." Randinoli did not have any direct knowledge of Yandola's business with the family. "The word on the street is Yandola did some business with Sal Cassando. Then a rumor circulated that someday he would make the hit list but it all died out and he continued doing his thing." Randinoli continued to speak without sounding illiterate. He knew it annoyed the underboss, caused him to be uncomfortable. Randinoli worked hard at improving his English and was proud of his efforts.

The underboss spoke clearly. "It's no longer a rumor and he's finished doin' his thing. He goes! Two things and both unforgivable. He's stealin' from us. And second, he ignores strict orders to stay away from certain people."

Cuccio slowly shook his head, pretending sadness. "The man never listens. He heard the warnin' more than once. For all we know he's talkin' to the feds as we speak." The more he spoke of Yandola the angrier Cuccio became. "Just two weeks ago Joe sends for him and tells him in no uncertain terms, *'Mi stai facendo arrabiare.'* Almost immediately he does the same thing over again." He turned his head slightly. "He broke rules and he made it personal when he betrayed Sal and now he disrespects Joe. The scum ignores Joe's direct orders."

Randinoli understood barely enough of the Italian; the boss became angry with Yandola and told him so, and still the same thing happens.

Neither of them said anything. After a few sips of the cappuccinos a full minute passed and Cuccio stared directly into Randinoli's eyes. "Joe's exact words: 'Take out Anthony Yandola.' This is your most important assignment. He goes. You make sure of it."

Randinoli nodded. "Anything else?"

"Yes. Joe made it clear to me and I will do the same." His words slowed down considerably. "You cannot bungle this in any way. There is absolutely no room for error. One thing goes wrong and you answer. *'E si risponde.'* Understood?" Not giving the capo an opportunity to answer, he continued. "Joe is watching very closely. In particular, the ending. Ciao." The two men stood, Randinoli walked to the underboss and they embraced.

Cuccio had delivered the order, now he left the store without looking back. Unmistakably, this contract required finalization without the slightest bump in the road. Included with it was an unspoken warning to Randinoli.

"Screw up again and no matter how much scratch you bring in to the family—you pay dearly."

Randinoli sipped the rest of his drink, stepped away from the table and marched out of the store. He attempted to place the obvious threat out of his mind. He felt exhilarated, the excitement of the meeting remaining with him. He would not disappoint. The former altar boy from Saint Joe's convinced it was only a matter of time before he became the head of the family. *"I will enjoy moving Carmine out the door,"* he thought. He actually looked forward to his next murder.

Business thrived but the big boys were never satisfied. They constantly demanded more. LCN history is clear. For some reason, each time someone gets killed business picks up considerably. The assignment given him by Nittoli would be recognized by the members as more than a hit. The members were aware that the Yandola hit was imminent. Many questioned why the union delegate lived this long.

Randinoli believed this to be the most important contract assigned by Nittoli. His status would rise as a result of a successful hit. He admitted the Alizzio work turned into an unfortunate mistake, yet, he reasoned, the first time at bat is a little scary. He relied on people who did not stay focused on business. The Manzi matter more than made up for any mistakes and even more important to him was the fact that he still delivered the *casheroo*. Most importantly, he earned the confidence of the Don himself. He would not mess this one up. There would be no mistakes. He assured himself, *"Yandola is a dead man. And I am back in shape with Joe."*

For the next twenty-four hours, Randinoli stayed isolated. Now settled, his decision-making mode felt complete. He decided he would keep the assignment quiet until the right time, and then he would notify those who needed to know. He missed Specs Buchanan, now doing a stretch for illegal gambling and interstate transportation of stolen property. He knew it essential to select the right people for the job. His future, maybe his life, depended on the success of the contract.

He needed a diversion, and decided to call his friend. "Yo my man, I keep checking the papers. It can't be true. You are not the Director yet?"

"Gabe, I'm in the middle of something. I will reach out tomorrow or the next day."

"Got it. Be careful, there are some bad dudes out there." Randinoli hung up the phone. He knew when his friend immediately called him by his first name and omitted a little joking that Mason had business needing his attention.

Specs Buchanan would clearly be his first choice for the work. However, the psychopath remained behind bars and was not an option. After deep thought, Randinoli made one of his decisions. The capo would tell only one of the crew of the impending contract assignment. One person would be brought in now, a proven member, experienced in the detailed planning required for the hit. An easy decision, he chose his sponsor Anthony Spero. He called and they agreed to meet in a quiet, out-of-the-way Italian restaurant in Brooklyn. Randinoli made it clear from the beginning that he intended to do a first-class job with this contract. He emphasized: "No one can screw up the work." He laid out for Spero the meeting he attended with Cuccio, leaving out nothing. He made sure Spero grasped the importance of the work that lay ahead.

Over dinner and a few Jack Daniels, Randinoli relayed everything he knew of the target, Anthony Yandola. "You keep this to yourself until I tell you it's okay. Understand?"

Spero nodded. "No one knows anything until you give the word. You got anything worked out yet?" Spero recognized his fellow capo's ruthlessness and was more than uneasy with him on many occasions, yet he always respected Randinoli for his smarts and toughness. He favored a successful operation for Randinoli. It would help his standing in the family as well. After all, Spero served as his sponsor when Randinoli became a man of honor.

"No, I just got the thing, I will be in touch. When I decide who we use, I will let you know. We need to know a lot more of this guy's habits. He realizes he is in trouble because of the shortages. He is avoiding everyone since he disobeyed Joe's orders. Yandola will be on guard. Be ready to go on some research trips." Ending the conversation, Randinoli said, "In the meantime, keep your ears open." The two men parted company.

Randinoli did not want to use a rental vehicle for the job. The car would be disposed of after the work so it made more sense to stay away from paper work, pick up, drop off and just dealing with a rental agency. He visited an auto mechanic friend. "Eddy I need a car. Maybe a Chevy would work."

"You're in luck Gabe. There's a Bel-Air in back. It just came in. Clean as a whistle and for you the price is right." Eddy did more than work as a mechanic. He dealt in stolen vehicles and turned them over quickly. If the would-be assassins got stopped for any reason, Randinoli and his friend occupied a light-colored, Chevrolet Bel-Air purchased from some unknown person.

Two days later, at eight thirty p.m., Randinoli and Spero occupied the Chevy parked across the street from 400 Sheridan Road in Manhattan, the home of the International Brotherhood of Teamsters. Yandola, with three other Teamsters, left the building at nine fifteen that evening. The intelligence gathering revealed that Yandola held a special meeting of the officers every Friday night. The meeting usually started around seven and ended at nine.

Most nights Yandola drove by himself and usually went directly home. He very seldom stayed for drinks with other union members. He lived a few blocks east of the union hall.

Randinoli called a meeting. Wednesday evening at seven, Spero, Charlie Sassano, Louis Calabrese and Stephen Lombardi showed up at Club 82 at East Fourth Street, Manhattan. "Gabe, what's the occasion?" Charlie Sassano liked to know things.

"Let's eat. I like to see you guys get muscular. Louie, have a few plates of meatballs." That would relax the crew. Calabrese earned a reputation for possessing a voracious appetite. One helping of meatballs would never last long with him in the vicinity.

"Good idea Gabe, I don't mind if I do. The jogging is killing me," he said as he patted his enormous stomach. As always, he got a huge laugh.

Spero could not resist. "Marone, what a gut! I mean truthfully, Louie, when was the last time you saw your balls?"

Without a moment's hesitation, Calabrese said, "Truthfully Anthony? About the same time you picked up a check, you cheap bastard. You make Palmeri look like an out-of-control spendthrift." The others appreciated the comeback. Capo or not, Spero's frugality was legendary and well earned. Calabrese laughed hard and choked on the warm bread. Tears fell from his eyes.

Lombardi said, "He's crying. Louie, you look like Onion Mary." This reference brought uproar from the crew. He cited the infamous woman who was paid money to mourn the departed. She was featured at the most crowded wakes and funerals of major wise guys. Onion Mary cried loudly at the drop a hat. It didn't matter that she had never met the deceased: "Oh Vincenzo, what a beautiful man."

The ball breaking continued throughout the big meal and several carafes of Chianti. Randinoli decided it now time to get to business. "Okay, you probably are wondering why I invited you to such a great restaurant. You guys ate as though everyone is going to the electric chair in the morning. I should make it Dutch treat."

Calabrese said, "Gabe that's it, just the appetizer?"

Randinoli put on his game face. He placed his arms in front of him and folded his big fists on the table. He now had everyone's attention. "Not our last meal—but the night after tomorrow some unfortunate soul will have had his last meal." Except for Spero, the others never expected to be discussing a hit. He had their full attention.

The first to react, Calabrese asked, "Geez Gabe, who the hell made the hit parade?"

Randinoli always treated his crew with respect. He continuously insured that they felt needed and an important part of the business. They respected him for this. "Before that, I want you guys should know what I know. I filled Anthony in on most everything." He looked right at Spero. "You did good work to this point." He spoke to the others, "I asked Anthony to help me with some preparation work. He will learn the final plans now, same as you guys. When you hear the entire deal, we can discuss it and clean up any loose ends. There can't be any mistakes, we go like clockwork."

He waited for the right time. "I want you to know, this comes straight from Joe, through Carmine of course." Randinoli thought it a good idea to slow down, let the men hang on to each word. It emphasized the enormity of the assignment. Of course, he expected his importance and obvious recognition by the bosses would be noted. The men already were aware of Don Nittoli's regard for Randinoli's contribution to the family.

As usual, the popular restaurant started to fill. Earlier Randinoli requested a corner table, the perfect place to discuss business without interruption. After making sure of an ample supply of Chianti on the table, the waiters smartly became invisible.

"I'll go through it, just listen. Like I said earlier, we'll discuss the details later." He lit a cigarette, took a long pull. "The unlucky contestant is Anthony Yandola."

Sassano said, "The big-shot union guy. Whooda thought?"

The music from the stereo system played at just the right volume. The Beatles' "Yesterday" pleased Calabrese, who said, "I could listen to those foreign guys all day." His comment drew smiles from his friends.

Randinoli waited another minute until he was satisfied that he owned everyone's undivided attention. The crew appeared to be focused on the job ahead. He noted no visible reactions. Then, for some reason, Randinoli thought that Stevie Lombardi's attention was drifting. Maybe it was just his imagination, but Randinoli made a mental note; if need be, he would pursue the matter later.

For the next ten minutes, Randinoli went into detail—describing the Teamster union hall building, the width and parking problems of the street, as well as each adjoining side street and all parallel roads. "It's not heavily travelled after five p.m. We're looking at Friday night, after he leaves the union building. He drives himself home." He then turned the meeting over by simply saying, "Anthony."

Spero did not miss a beat. "A new, dark green Buick Riviera, always shiny." As an afterthought, he added, "The shit drives like a little old lady from Florida." After a quick look from Randinoli, he added, "But we never know, we can't depend on anything for certain. Friday night he could become a NASCAR driver."

Randinoli and Spero described Yandola's residence in detail. They detailed the distance from the union hall and the approximate driving time to cover the three-and-a-half blocks to where the work would take place. Spero emphasized, "He leaves his meeting like clockwork, between nine and nine thirty."

Randinoli picked up: "The weather forecast for Friday is more of the same, clear with no rain. We'll use two cars; Anthony drives with Louie shotgun and Charlie in the back. Stevie drives with me in the second. Stevie and me do the close-up work. You three guns are close by, in case something unexpected should happen like he makes us and tries an adios. I am considering having a truck parked north of his house halfway up the street. If we go that way, I will let everyone know beforehand who will be in the truck. No drawings, depend on your memory. Stevie will leave our car parked a block away from Yandola's street."

Randinoli spoke slowly and clearly. "Stevie and me will get to our car at 8:30 p.m. and wait for Yandola to pass. You three will be at the north end of the street and follow Yandola when he leaves the union hall. We believe he's nervous, he may figure he made the list. If he makes you he'll bolt like a rabbit."

The captain's plan stressed simplicity. When Yandola turns the corner and drives in the direction of his house, Randinoli and Lombardi "will exit our vehicle, leave the engine running and walk slowly to Yandola's house. We intercept him in his driveway as he exits his car. We will fire at close range." The capo looked at Sassano and Calabrese. "You two are out of your car, and you cover the house and the street in case someone decides to get involved." The crew felt good about the job and greatly impressed with the precise planning.

Randinoli looked directly at Lombardi and repeated an earlier order: "We will empty all our rounds to be certain he's finished."

Lombardi nodded in agreement. "Understood. Yandola will be history."

Everyone gave assurances that each understood his assignment. "Tonight, you individually take a drive by the area. Get together and decide so that you are not there at the same time. If you see anything that raises a question, call me and we will work it out. I think we're all set."

It seemed like Friday would never arrive. Randinoli earlier instructed the crew to stay away from the usual hangouts, not even to talk with anyone "until the work is complete." He rightly believed the least said about the job the better for everyone. Randinoli did not want the crew in a position of answering questions of the other family members.

Randinoli spent the day with his girlfriend at her apartment. Spero, Sassano and Lombardi visited the racetrack at Saratoga Springs in the afternoon and left just in time to make it to the city. Calabrese slept late and went to visit his mother in Brooklyn. He needed some home cooked food.

At 8:30, the streetlights shone brightly. Both cars and the backup truck were in place.

It ended abruptly. The surveillances proved accurate. Yandola, like clockwork, left the Teamsters hall at ten minutes after nine accompanied by two board members. They were jovial, said their goodbyes and walked to three separate cars. Yandola pulled out of the parking place, drove to the end of the block, turned right and in a matter of minutes slowly pulled into his narrow driveway.

Randinoli said, "Show time, we go now." Randinoli and Lombardi exited their vehicle, walked toward Yandola's house and moved directly to their mark as he opened his car door. The ambush began. Randinoli pointed directly at the target emptying all rounds from his favorite five-shot Smith and Wesson, and Lombardi's Magnum fired four rounds. Yandola clutched at his chest, fell face down and did not move as blood began oozing out of his body. Within seconds, the other three came to the driveway with their weapons out. Sassano reached down to check the carotid artery. Randinoli held out his arm and quietly said, "It's okay Charlie, he doesn't need a checkup. Let's go." No one fired any more shots. Yandola did not move. The crew left believing no one could survive the onslaught.

As the two cars left the neighborhood, the killers heard screams coming from the Yandola residence. Neighbors poured from their homes, hurrying toward the Yandola house.

After a few blocks of driving, Randinoli broke the silence.

"Stevie."

"Yeah, Gabe?"

"Did you know that guy?"

Lombardi was perplexed. "Personally? No, only that he was a big union guy. Why, is there a problem?"

"I hope not. I'm wondering why you did not empty your piece after I told you more than once. You still got some bullets left, right?"

"I'm positive I put four in his chest. He took enough. Guaranteed Gabe, the man is gonzo." Lombardi believed what he said.

"I hope you're right. You better be right." Randinoli raised his voice an octave. "More than once, more than twice, I said we would completely empty our pieces. You heard all that, right?"

"Yeah, but…" Lombardi was not able to complete his thought.

Why did he stop Sassano from making sure Yandola was dead? Randinoli now had an uneasy feeling, not convinced the hit was complete. "No more, for now it's forgotten, not another word. Understood?"

"Understood." Lombardi now appeared concerned.

The news report came in a little fuzzy. At the initial broadcast, the reporter stated the victim "apparently lived within a few yards of the attempted assassination." She added, "The victim, identified as Mr. James Yandola, a Teamster union official, is being treated at Saint Mark's for multiple, serious gunshot wounds. Hospital officials say Yandola's condition is listed as critical. We'll keep you up to date as reports of this shooting come in."

When Nittoli heard of the report, he could not believe his ears. Out of character, the Don screamed, his face red with rage. "Treated for wounds? Dead men are not treated for wounds. Dead men die when shot in the head. His condition, what condition? His condition should be dead! It's over. He's alive? He can talk—he will talk!"

Not good news for the shooters, the official medical report disclosed Yandola received nine rounds from close range. The papers bold headlines shouted, "UNION BOSS LIVES AFTER ATTEMPTED MURDER." The connected story discussed how "an apparent mob attempt went sour" and mentioned the "intended victim is closely associated with Giuseppe 'Joe' Nittoli, the alleged head of the Bonanno organized crime family."

"A freakin' miracle, the rat bastard survived nine rounds from up close and personal. The best laid plans…" Spero stopped short of recapping the entire event. The undeniable fact remained. Yandola received nine bullet wounds at close range and lived to tell about it.

Yandola knew he was lucky to be alive. "They will try again." He jumped at the opportunity and accepted an offer to enter the federal witness protection program, although he refused to give testimony against the attempted assassins. "I did not see or hear anything but the shots," he said. The federal prosecutors were satisfied when he later testified in a Rico case against Nittoli and Frank Zullo, a family capo.

By Mafia standards, Randinoli screwed up and stood solely responsible. The error found itself recorded in the "not-very-good" section of his personnel file.

Randinoli realized there could be repercussions. For two days, he sat alone in the apartment. Mae Yong worked during the day and made a point to return late to the apartment. It was standard practice for silence to be the rule after a hit or, in this case, a bungled try. There were no efforts to speak to any of the crew. He needed to make a call. His friend was not aware of Randinoli's recent activities. He made the call from a public telephone. "Can we talk somewhere?"

They agreed to meet at a joint known to them both, a quiet bar-restaurant located in East Bloomfield. Mason spent a lot time at a Connecticut offsite while in the middle of an undercover assignment. "I'll see you in approximately two hours. I hope you're not looking to borrow money." The FBI agent had no idea of his friend's latest activity.

Mason made up his mind that if the big shot from the corner was seeking information or wanted to beat some rap, the meeting would be short. He thought back to early days on the corner and the completely different directions he and Randinoli had taken. He smiled as he recalled some of the stories of life at 12th Ave. and Bruce Street. For no reason, Mason recalled Randinoli hitting Carmen in the face with a baseball bat. A terrible accident, but nonetheless, he never offered an apology. *Sure, the friendship was strong during the 12th and Bruce days, yet there was no doubt: today Randinoli lived on the dark side.*

Driving by oneself allows the mind to wander. Maybe his old friend is going through a born-again transformation? Is he pissed off enough to do something crazy, even for him? If the topic of discussion centered on something of a personal nature, Mason would listen and decide what to do. Maybe his friend had been thrown out of the big bed again and needed to get his love life in order. Does he want to turn over to the lighter side? Mason smiled again, thinking *"not likely"* to all of the above. One rule never changed: they never discussed business of any kind.

He pulled the FBI vehicle, the "bucar," into a parking space directly behind the restaurant. Mason drove a beat-up 1960 Chevy, unlikely to disappear to a chop shop, even this close to Newark. He glanced at his watch, now twenty minutes after seven. Mason needed to stretch, get inside and use the facilities. He thought, *"It's time to cut back on the coffee."*

In the rear of the restaurant, Randinoli waited alone in a booth. He threw back his second Jack Daniels.

"You look like Kennedy after a bad day at the track. The career not going well?" Mason rightly figured that a little dig never hurt.

Randinoli did look haggard. "Must be the stress of hard work, twenty-four seven. I need to talk."

Mason decided to set the record straight. "No problem. Remember the rules. Do not tell me anything you would not tell another cop." Randinoli knew the guidelines when it came to their conversations but it would not hurt to repeat and reinforce them. As he spoke, Mason looked directly into the eyes of his friend.

Randinoli got quiet, disappointed, as he responded, "You will never be just another cop."

Mason was now uneasy. He ordered a ginger ale from the young waitress. "Gabe, do not put me in a bind. Depending on what you say, I either cover up a crime that's been committed, or initiate an investigation that could...no, would, land you in the joint. Right?"

Not the usual tough guy persona, Randinoli said, "I guess so."

"You know so." He showed a little smile, recalling other times when Randinoli frequently spoke the same phrase. "Be right back." Mason headed toward the men's room.

Randinoli smiled, regained his composure. He felt better just seeing Mason. Waving for another drink, he thought to himself that maybe the Yandola problem will go away. Maybe he'll get another opportunity at the union rat. Maybe he would lay everything on Lombardi. Maybe he will tell the boss he gave specific orders to Lombardi and the associate disobeyed. *Maybe, my foot.* He knew for sure he would not drop a dime on anyone else. *The soldier will take the heat.* Next time he'll work alone and make things right. Now he had lots of stuff going on in his head. He made another decision, now determined to return to the family's growing business in New Jersey. Once he grows the money supply everyone will be happy, and the Yandola screwup forgiven. He would enjoy being with his friend. Randinoli felt better already, and decided to forget his problems for now.

Mason returned to the table. "Now, what is the crisis?"

"It's forgotten. I may have overreacted to a situation. Can you believe that, me overreacting? Really, let's just keep it simple. It's really good to see you looking good and taking care of business. Blackie and Tony would be proud."

Mason was relieved. As always, the two friends manufactured small talk about childhood days. Both were now relaxed and enjoying some quiet time with each other. Two hours flew by. They said their goodbyes and set out in very different directions.

As they reached their cars, Randinoli called out, "And all of it, it's all business. No matter what happens, remember I made my decision a long time ago." He got in the driver's seat before Mason could respond.

Mason did not mind the drive back to New England. He looked forward to the numerous cases the Boston office was investigating. His first stop would be to touch base with "Saucy," his favorite North End pizzeria owner. The pizza guy was one of the best sources of information in the city. He did not like the wise guys. "They threatened my old man when I was a kid. He passed shortly after that. I believe he died from fright."

However, Mason sensed that his Mafioso friend was in the middle of a volcano. What did he say? *"No matter what happens."* Always aware that the wise guy chose a dirty business, Mason sensed his friend might have made a mistake or two, and was now concerned with the consequences. Again, Randinoli's eyes told a somber story.

Chapter Forty-Seven

1983—New York

Acting on reliable source information, the Boston office opened an investigation targeting certain bank officials working in concert with phony borrowers. The officers knowingly released bank funds to people using aliases and furnishing false identification and financial information. Phony *borrowers* from both the New England and New York areas were part of the scheme. Two major Boston banks were the victims of the largest thefts. FBI Boston, the office of origin, received invaluable assistance from the New York squad, which provided the Boston agents with help identifying the Big Apple players.

Supervisor Mason and SAs from Boston's Major White Collar (WCC) and Special Operation Group visited the New York office. Joining forces, Boston and New York personnel initiated a number of joint physical surveillance operations from state to state. After learning the daily habits of the main players, Mason and New York OC supervisor James Wells placed an undercover agent (UCA) into a well-planned scenario. This resulted in immediate beneficial intelligence regarding the plans of the main players.

Before his transfer to New York, SA Patrick Bergin served in the Chicago Office. While in Chicago, Bergin immersed into an undercover role where the targets were bank officials, skimming large sums of cash from dormant accounts. Mason approached his friend to accept the role of the UCA for the big case. Without hesitation, Bergin agreed. "Man, a chance to get back in the game and out of the office, let's do it." They gathered the necessary identification material, plotted the scenario and were off and running. The investigation lasted six weeks and culminated in a huge success.

In Boston, the United States Attorney indicted and successfully prosecuted bank officials and *borrowers* from both the Boston and New York areas. SA Bergin's testimony and tapes of several conversations contributed to the successful guilty verdicts. One of the prosecutors said, "We were lucky, they never had a chance to spend the money. The restitution ordered by the judge amounted to several million dollars." The investigation cemented further the working relationship between the two offices.

While in New York, Mason discreetly inquired about Randinoli's activities. The New York OC supervisor did not have anything new to add. "In summary, Randinoli is a made guy, a capo in the Bonanno family. He is actually a big shot, probably the biggest earner. Gabe's ability to bring in money means he often meets with the Bonanno family boss, Joe Nittoli. While in the company of the Don, on one occasion Randinoli met the big man himself, John "Dapper Don" Gotti, the ruler of one of the five families, New York's Gambino syndicate." Mason knew the LCN commission included one representative of each of the five New York families. Gotti sat atop the commission. Wells said, "Gotti once joked with Nittoli, and said, referring to Randinoli, 'I better be careful, this guy dresses almost as good as me.'" Mason had no interest in hearing more war stories concerning an old friend.

One of the Boston OC agents wanted to hear more. He inquired, "How did Sal Cassando become the family Don?"

The OC supervisor explained. "In July, 1969, one of the strongest positioned of the Bonanno bosses, Salvatore Galenti, bought it in the Bushwick section of Brooklyn. Cassando was a little crazy and, without any authority, ordered the murder and took over as boss without any challengers. Shortly after the Galenti hit, the new boss promoted his friend Joe Nittoli as capo regime. Nittoli allegedly orchestrated the contract to kill Galenti. Reliable informant information later corroborated the fact Nittoli did the actual shooting. He despised Galenti."

"The LCN too creates interesting historical tidbits. A few years prior to his murder, Galenti conducted the induction ceremony in Brooklyn wherein Joe Nittoli and Anthony Spero became LCN members." This account was accurate. Randinoli now bragged, alleging that Nittoli and he were close friends. He always added that Nittoli "is a man who deserves everyone's respect." Once Randinoli became accustomed to wise guy jargon, he used it to impress at every opportunity.

Wells continued. "Before a prospect is given consideration for membership, he must 'make his bones.' We believe that Randinoli killed a guy named Jimmy Zack prior to his initiation into La Cosa Nostra. During the seventies and early eighties, Randinoli stayed immersed in the gambling, loan sharking and union kickback end of the family businesses. Part of good business included the murders considered necessary to keep the peace."

It was all accurate. Whenever he received instruction to kill someone, the kid from the Hilltoppers followed orders. He took seriously the oath of omertà. He viewed the cold-blooded assassinations necessary ingredients for doing business. He came to this conclusion many years ago and continued with this sick philosophy to the present time. Ending a life of someone considered detrimental to family business was part of the tradition—murder a necessity.

The people from12th Avenue and Bruce Street would strongly oppose Randinoli's chosen lifestyle. They could only speculate what Randinoli did on a daily basis.

The New York office received other FBI employees. AD Price flew to many FBI offices with the pretext of official business. During one of his bogus trips to New York, the AD took a chance. After a few drinks at a nearby bar on Franklin Street, he thought if he could meet a real gangster his bona fide reputation as an organized crime fighter would be solidified. His mind made up, Price placed a call to the FBI office and asked to be connected to a particular squad. He was given the line of an OC supervisor.

"This is Assistant Director Todd Price. I am in the city for a few days and I understand you supervise one of the family squads…which one again?"

"The Bonannos." Jim Murray had heard a bigwig from the bureau came to town unexpected and uninvited. Murray was flat out busy and did not want to involve himself with anyone from FBIHQ, an AD or otherwise.

"I want you to set up a meeting with the head of the Bonanno family…what's his name again?"

Murray surmised rightly the caller was full of shit. But he didn't care why the AD wanted a sit down with Joe Nittoli. The New Yorker wanted to rid himself of the AD and get back to his own business.

Murray said, "His name's Joe Nittoli. Are you in the office?"

"That's sir!"

"What?"

"You mean, are you in the office—sir?" The AD now slurring his words.

Is this moron for real? Fuck him! "It sounds like you're in a bar—sir! Is there a number where you can be reached—sir?" *I should have given him a phony name. What's he gonna do, transfer me to New York?*

Price guessed accurately he was no match for the native New Yorker. He read his cell phone number to Murray. "How long will it…?" The phone went dead. *Welcome to New York, big shot.*

Price ordered his fourth Beefeater martini when his cell buzzed, the number displayed not familiar. "Hello."

A voice said, "Where you at?"

Price, who thought he was in charge, asked, "Who is this?"

The voice sounded annoyed, "You wanna meet someone, where you at?"

The AD realized Murray acted fast. "I'm at a place called Cryan's, it's on Franklin Street."

Fifteen minutes later two of Don Nittoli's guns walked into Cryan's and eyeballed the ten customers at the bar as if looking for a friend. They spotted Price sitting alone in a booth near the back of the room. He appeared to be out of place. One nodded to his partner and left without saying anything. The other sat at the bar and looked directly at the AD.

Three minutes later Don Nittoli, now in his late fifties, six-four and weighing near two hundred and fifty pounds, walked into the bar. The bodyguard at the bar nodded to his boss. Nittoli headed directly for the booth in the back and sat down across from Price. Always an imposing figure, before Price said a word, Nittoli spoke, "You wanted to see me. What is your name, and your business?"

The alcohol never failed him. Price did not have to face reality when under its influence, he became a different person. It gave him a false sense of bravado, he said things he would never think of uttering when sober.

Price appeared almost smug. He said, "I don't believe we've met. And you are?" The words came out without any hesitation. Let's hear it for the gin. The booze was doing its job.

Nittoli leaned across the table, his head now ten inches away from Price. "You either answer my question now or I get up and walk away very angry. Then, I have my attorneys bill the FBI for my valuable time. Then, my friends come to Washington D.C. to pay you a visit. Then…"

Price forced a lame smile as he interrupted, "Please, please my friend. You must be Joe Nittoli." He lied, "I've heard so much about you." He motioned to the lone waiter. "Let me buy you a nice drink. What will you have?"

Nittoli's voice now an even monotone. "The last time. Your name, your business." He waved at the waiter with a dismissal motion.

"Of course. My name is Todd Price, and I am with the Federal Bureau of Investigation." Price deftly reached into his inside jacket pocket and presented FBI credentials showing his photograph. Another weak smile, he continued: "At present, I am not the Director, merely a lowly Assistant Director." He thought he would attract the attention of this lowlife mobster.

"I am here out of respect for a friend who asked me to meet with you. So I have another question, what is your business with me?" Nittoli desired an answer.

Price said, "I only wanted to meet the most important man in the Bonanno family. I believe we can help each other. Maybe not now, not today, but some day. You have no reason to be concerned. I'm not here to arrest you or any of your soldiers. Is that what you call your employees?"

"Okay, now you met me. Tell me your business with me." The Don appeared at ease but now felt an urge to hurt the FBI man.

"Have a drink with me, Joe. We can get to know each other better." Price signaled the bartender to bring another Beefeater. Nodding toward the bar, he said, "Let me tell you this guy would never survive in D.C. That's the place to go for a martini—a real martini."

Nittoli realized he sat across from someone under the influence of alcohol. The Don knew nothing of Price's background; perhaps the AD called for the meeting on a lark. It wouldn't be easy to behave as a gentleman but he would control his temper. Price rambled how important a person he was in "the District" and of his goal to become the next FBI Director. After ten minutes Nittoli had heard enough, he would not listen further to an egomaniac, drunken big shot.

Don Nittoli decided he would not waste any more time. He slid out of the booth and stood. "Well I hope you enjoy our little town. And no, I have no doubt you're not here to arrest me or my friends. Soldiers? That's what they called us in the army. Goodbye."

Both guns waited as their leader walked toward them at the front door. The three men were gone before Price could react.

The entire meeting ended abruptly. But Price was already thinking how his version of the get-together would impress others.

After seated comfortably in the limo, the Don turned off the tape recorder as taught to do by the family techie.

The AD ordered another martini.

Chapter Forty-Eight

A rat by any other name

1983 could be best remembered as the year of Price's masterplan in action.

During a recent telephone call Randinoli felt an obligation to share something with his friend, although it could be meaningless.

"For what it's worth, my boss met with one of your FBI big shots, a guy named Price. They may have met more than once. Our people are guessing all kinds of crazy things. They have no idea what it means. The speculation is that whoever it is, your guy is a rat. Ciao." He hung up before Mason could remind him of the rule—no business, never. Mason did not respect Price as a representative of the FBI; yet this was the first time he heard the AD was deep into no good. It wouldn't be the first time FBIHQ personnel, while visiting field offices, met with the well-known people in the area—those considered to be the movers and shakers, the important people. Politicians, clergymen, sports figures, even mobsters would make time for a visiting Assistant Director from the FBI. He was aware the most corrupt politician in Boston, a state senator, would entertain visiting FBI inspectors each year the division was undergoing an annual office inspection. For now, at least, Mason would give Price the benefit of the doubt.

AD Price knew of the longtime relationship between the New York Mafiosi Gabriel Randinoli and the supervisor in the Boston office, Brad Mason. It was just one of the many useful facts he acquired at FBIHQ. The story emanated at the academy during the summer of 1972, when Mason confided in his roommate, Barry Mazalewski, the fact that he and Randinoli were boyhood friends.

The conversations between the roommates in the dormitory seemed innocent enough. Mason described St. Joe's, the Club, Duffy's Tavern, Phillips Bakery, the Hilltoppers, and in greater detail, the infamous Bruce Street crap game that opened for business day and night. The stories would be without interest if they excluded Randinoli and his antics. Himself a Newark native, Mazalewski loved listening to his roommate speak of another part of his city, and reciprocated with a few Mulberry Street tales of his own. The roommates agreed that what they discussed in Room 427 at the Academy stayed in Room 427. A decade passed by before Mazalewski forgot the verbal contract.

For the most part, Mazalewski never chatted with anyone about his private bullshit sessions with Mason. He once said, "They wouldn't understand it. Why discuss Newark stuff with people from Cherry Hill?"

More than a decade passed and Mazalewski was now assigned to the Foreign Counter Intelligence Squad in the New York office. After one particularly long day, he and a few of the agents from the Bonanno OC squad stopped by one of the local cop bars on Corona Avenue in Queens. The twelve-hour day spent following a known Russian mole throughout the boroughs, Mazalewski looked forward to a few cold ones. The agents threw back a few draught Millers, played pool and generally relaxed. Mason's name came up in connection with a recent Boston case and the valuable information the Boston agents developed in New York. The relationship was positive between the two offices, mainly a result of the Special Operations Group teamwork developed on recent New England–New York investigations. As Boston supervisors, Mason and OC Supervisor Mark Ireland spent a great deal of time in the Big Apple. Both sought out and utilized necessary assets that each developed in New England through the years. For different reasons, the sources were relocated in New York.

Mazalewski never required too many beers to get his mouth motored. Slurring his words a little, he bragged that Mason and he were roommates at the academy. He entertained the New York agents with a detailed account of the very brief boxing match while in new agents' training. Mazalewski emphasized how he closely supervised most of Mason's training sessions, forgetting that the sessions never really took place. His account of the brief event would cause his audience to vision a fifteen round epic. Without giving it any thought, Mazalewski commented that Mason grew up with someone who may possibly be a wise guy in the city. "It bothered Brad but the guy's mind was made up at an early age, nothing anyone could do about it. I'll bet he changed his mind and leads a life of poverty and chastity."

Curious, one of the New York agents asked, "What's the guy's name?"

"I can't recall the actual name. It began with an R, something like Racan-elli, Rocatelli, Randoli, somewhere in there. Definitely an Italian surname ending in a vowel—close enough." This got a laugh, coming from someone with the surname Mazalewski. One of the agents commented, "Like a Polack surname ending in 'ski,' I got it. That should be easy to figure out."

The conversation drifted to more important matters. In took a few days for the innocent remarks to reach the New York OC squads. Now the OC agents were interested, hearing of the connection between Mason and Gabe Randinoli, a Bonanno capo. "It has to be Gabe Randinoli. He's a made guy and the only member originally from Mason's home state of New Jersey. We'll look into the Newark aspect."

Unintentionally, one of the New York OC agents who earlier worked in New Haven passed the gossip to one of his old applicant squad members now at FBIHQ. The tidbit found its way to AD Price. Price stored every piece of news and gossip he heard. He once told Mayhew, "You never know when an apparent innocent comment will come in handy." One of his kiss-ass sources of information was a section chief assigned to the highly influential "Special Agent Transfer Section" at FBIHQ. Price sensed a real opportunity. He spoke to his *friend* in confidence, convinced him he could and would do great things for the SC's career. Of the handful of embarrassing characters in the entire organization, Price had a flair for sifting them out and using them to further his campaign.

Price told the section chief to keep their relationship confidential. "I'm in the process of working with a handful of key supervisors whom I'll transfer to the bureau. You keep me apprised of Mason in Boston. I need to know if the Boston office plans to transfer him, or anything altering his location." The SC believed Price had ambition but trusted that the AD's concern rested with the needs of the bureau. He had no idea of Price's sick obsession to sit in the Director's chair.

A year passed since he became an Assistant Director. Price continued with his persistence in gathering information about Randinoli and his role with the Mafia, while keeping a sharp awareness of Mason's whereabouts. Price also made note of the fact Mason had a close ally in AD Max Blaney. He decided both men were expendable and would deal with Blaney at the right time. At one of his watering holes after too much to drink, Price mistakenly expressed his plan to his believed-to-be confidante, Melvin Mayhew.

The alcohol had an effect on his slurred words. "Melvin, the two people who could get in my way are AD Max Blaney and Boston Supervisor Brad Mason. Mark my words, they are both history."

AD Todd Price continued with his mission. He would be the first Ivy Leaguer to occupy the Director's chair. He finished accumulating the necessary political support by threatening weak-kneed politicians with bogus investigations deep into their backgrounds, as well as their office staff and aides. They each were aware of Price's father and his vast financial empire. Added to this, a few empty promises and much ass kissing goes a long way in the nation's capital. His plan would be rock solid when the final action occurred. However, this would be the easy part, dealing with a lowly supervisor assigned to the New England territory. Going back to the days when Price was a mere clerk assigned to the Director's office in Washington to the present time, only his personal ambition counted. He did not waste time educating himself with how the bureau actually functioned at the street level. The AD, possessing an egocentric personality, was now utterly convinced of his importance. *Trivial matters do not concern important people.*

Price knew virtually nothing of Supervisor Mason. Had he paid attention to mid-1983 bureau-wide teletypes, he would be aware that the Boston Division completed a rape/murder case in the Boston territory. The AP and UP as well as the D.C. media covered the case for a two-week duration. A male in his late fifties, arrested by the FBI and Massachusetts State Police, was tried in state court, found guilty of rape and first-degree murder and sentenced to life in prison. When the egomaniac AD perused the newspaper, he never thought to pick up a phone to call the Boston office to get details of the case. Later, all the facts connected with the investigation surfaced at the bureau. SSA Mason and three SAs received fiscal awards as well as personal letters of commendation from the Director. What Mason treasured most came in a personal letter of gratitude he received from the victim's family.

The investigation caught fire when Brad and Ann, with their next-door Framingham neighbors, spent a weekend at the cottage the Mason's had purchased in Yarmouth Port on Cape Cod. The ninety-mile drive was often heavy-going because of Route 495 traffic, but this weekend, as a result of traffic-free roads and Mason's heavy foot, they arrived in record time. It was always worth it when the two couples sat down to cold beer and a homemade New England clambake with lobster, soft-shell clams, mussels and corn on the cob. Mason paid attention and asked a lot of questions when he feasted on his first clambake at the home of a state trooper friend. The first part of the preparation was digging a pit in the ground by the back fence, followed by collecting seaweed at the warm-water Nantucket Sound beach just a few minutes away. The idea was to steam the food over the seaweed and a heat-radiated stone. The garage stored plenty of round, medium-sized stones for this purpose. Finally, a canvas tarp was drenched in water and placed on top of the entire pit and the food steamed for several hours. At six p.m. the feast was "in the oven."

However, on this night Mason would not be around to enjoy the festivities. His son Michael called to say that a cryptic message left on the telephone machine at home sounded important. Michael said, "I wrote it down, Dad." After listening to the message Mason excused himself, placed a call to a road trip agent living in Duxbury and headed towards Route Six and Ashton, Massachusetts.

"I'll try to get back quick." He said the words knowing it was wishful thinking.

A fifteen-year-old high school student, Penny Lacey, was missing and presumed dead. On the second day of the investigation, Mason told the SAC that an individual named Nigel Jackal either was the killer or knew who was responsible. He believed that a useful rapport with Jackal would pay dividends. Now, nine days later, the teenager was still missing when Jackal called and left the message for Mason. "Agent Mason, you know who this is. If you call me back I want to finish our conversation." The taped message would later be played for the jury in the crowded county courtroom.

Mason met SA Jim Montgomery at a Burger King north of Cumberland, just minutes from Jackal's residence. "Jim, I believe he's our guy. I think he wants to get it all out. I'm not going to call him. We're going to see him in person."

Montgomery said, "I hope he's our guy. I was with the parents this afternoon. No family should have to go through what they're dealing with." Montgomery, a teacher before entering the FBI, showed real compassion and would work as long as it took to bring closure for the Laceys.

The agents arrived at the Ashton residence and found Jackal at the front door smiling. "I heard your car. It didn't take you long to get here. Come in and sit down. I'll get you something to drink." They refused the drink offer.

"This is Special Agent Montgomery. What's up, Nigel?" Mason did not want the suspect to have time to change his mind.

Nigel smiled and asked, "Can I still call you Brad? "

Mason said, "Yes."

"I wrote down what you said. You told me a hidden, deep dark secret will eventually choke someone, possibly to death." Nigel spoke these words slowly, speaking Mason's words verbatim.

Neither agent responded. Mason offered a slight nod to his partner who reached in his pocket, producing a small note pad.

"Well, last night I never slept a wink. I felt like I could choke to death." Using a nicotine-stained hand, he crushed what remained of a Marlboro cigarette on the nearby ashtray and immediately lit another.

Mason said, "I understand. Before you go on, yesterday before our discussion I advised you of your rights. I gave you a waiver form that you read and indicated that you understood your rights. Is that correct?"

"Yes."

Montgomery handed a type-written piece of paper to Jackal. "Take this waiver, read it again and if you understand it, sign it before you continue."

Jackal read and signed the waiver containing his Miranda rights—the right to remain silent, to have counsel with him during questioning, offering financial assistance if he wasn't able to afford counsel—and handed it back to Montgomery.

"You said you did not sleep well?" Mason would not waste time.

Jackal moved to the edge of the chair, placed the hand holding the cigarette over the other and began rubbing them back and forth. He looked upward to the ceiling. "I did what you hinted at. I lured her in my car—I choked her." His voice very calm, he appeared to be relieved. He lowered his head and looked directly into the eyes of his interrogator. "I appreciate the things you said."

"We can get back to that later. Where's the body?"

Everything moved swiftly. Jackal described the exact location of the missing girl's remains. Montgomery immediately called in the location to the FBI office and State Police Headquarters and the local police station. The family was notified and although the tragic loss of a child lingered, for them closure was accomplished.

Jackal was immediately placed under arrested and taken in custody.

Walking to their vehicles, Montgomery said, "You had a good feel for this guy from the get-go. You been reading those crazy psycho unit pamphlets sent out by the bu?"

Mason laughed. "No Jim, I think it goes back to a poker game I used to play in Newark. You get a feeling about whether a guy's lying the way he looks at his cards. Thanks for being here."

Mason and Montgomery shook hands and left the area.

Mason drove fast and was back in Yarmouth Port at two-thirty a.m., not surprised to see three people hanging in there. He accepted a cold beer, ate a plateful of the clambake, and talked for another hour before calling it a night. He was grateful that he was not ambushed with questions. *What the hell, they will be reading plenty about it in the next few weeks.* He thought of the grieving family. *There's no death sentence in the state. Was life in prison really just?*

The trial, verdict and sentence concluded in a few months, and the FBI and Massachusetts State Police closed a major investigation. The majority of heavyweights at FBI Headquarters in D.C. were proud of the focus and professionalism displayed by the personnel of the Boston division. Except for one particular Assistant Director who had no interest in the particulars of the case, the amount of resources devoted to the matter, nor the ending. He never gave a thought to the dead girl or the family and friends left behind. AD Price only stored one subject in his sick brain. He was inebriated with his single thought, *"The time is near. I will be the Director."*

Despite his rocket-like rise, AD Price was unaware of the fact that no two FBI offices operated exactly alike. The priorities differed. The use of resources in one office was not the same for another. Had he taken the time to involve himself in a little research, Price would have ascertained that Mason's reputation was genuine as a hands-on supervisor of highly active squads and resident agencies throughout New England since 1978. Now in 1983, Mason's supervisory responsibilities included the South Shore Resident Agency, which was manned by two veterans and responsible for putting away more bad people than any of the other four hundred RAs in the bureau. So instead of picking up little tidbits, such as Mason also wearing the New England coordinator hat, the AD moved forward with his master plan.

"Get Boston on the phone, I need the SAC now," he barked to his secretary.

"Sir, it's Assistant Director Price at the bureau. He sounds more happy, joyous, and free than usual." Bev Carson, a Dorchester native, was personal secretary to many SACs assigned to the Boston office; they each loved her honesty and loyalty.

The Boston SAC was prepared to receive the call. Earlier in the week, a private conference call took place between himself and AD Max Blaney. During a three-year assignment at FBIHQ, Blaney had heard it all. He could judge when the noise was fact or rumor. He definitely supported Mason and was pissed at the way Price used the power of his office to insert pressure on anyone in his way. Gallagher often thought, *"God help the country if that worthless son of a bitch ever sat in the big chair."* From what Blaney gathered, Price's plan included taking advantage of Mason's reputation. He would pressure Mason to take part in a covert operation targeting Gabriel Randinoli and members of the Brooklyn-based Bonanno crime syndicate. Obviously, Blaney was well aware of the relationship between Mason and his friend from Newark. Blaney absolutely understood neighborhood loyalties dating back to his days on the streets of Detroit. Mason, in past talks, informed Blaney of his position regarding AD Price.

Gallagher and Mason sat in the SAC's office and turned on the speaker phone. The AD sounded almost jovial. "Well, two heavy-hitting crime fighters in the office at the same time. The streets of Boston must be in a panic."

"And how's yourself, Mr. Assistant Director?" Gallagher asked with a slight Gaelic lilt.

"Just fine Gene, and our friend is with you?"

"Hi Max, everything is secure. The speaker's on." Mason made clear the circumstances.

"Good, thus commences the conversation that never took place." Blaney focused right in. "We were spot on. He intends to involve Brad in his high-level attack against the Mafia, in particular targeting your friend in New York allegedly in an effort to obtain his cooperation and rat out the bosses. Yesterday I asked two of my OC section chiefs to join me in my office—names not necessary now. As you both know, an AD is a very important position, we even have our very own johns. They did not know I was using the restroom attached to the office. They spoke of Price and one of them said, and this is almost verbatim, 'the crazy bastard is going to play hardball with the guy in Boston. The AD said he goes along or it's adios to his guinea friend in New York.' The other agent could not believe what he heard. He said, 'adios? What's he saying? Price believes he can get the mob guy whacked or worse yet, transferred to Butte?'"

"The other chief did not laugh. Then he said, "I think his visits to New York have given him a sense of real power. He believes he can influence the mob boss to place Mason's friend on the hit list."

They sat in silence. Blaney said, "Brad, these are definitely two employees who will be valuable to the group when we leave the FBI. Anyway, they heard the water running and ended the conversation." Blaney, a former black bag agent while in Pittsburgh, an expert audio-video technician, collected many taped discussions over the past year. The recorder he previously placed in his office *accidentally* picked up the conversation of the two section chiefs.

The listeners in Boston looked at each other. Finally, Gallagher spoke. "Is the sick bastard actually talking of having someone whacked?"

Blaney said, "A jury could arrive at such a conclusion. I think not, however I believe his obsession over the big office is enough to label him certifiably crazy and without a doubt, very dangerous. Remember one of Brad's sources learned that Toddy boy's been observed in the city with Randinoli's big boss. What's that about, for chrissakes? What's his name again?"

"Nittoli—Joe Nittoli." Mason uttered the words slowly, doing his best to stay calm. He remembered his friend saying that Nittoli met with an FBI heavy. It had to be Price, and not, as he first thought, someone from the New York office.

Gallagher looked at his supervisor and spoke of the known facts. "The prick does not know of your intention of leaving the bureau, actually the plans of you both retiring. I think we will hear from him soon. Then we will regroup for the next barrage."

Mason thought of the words of the OC Section Chief: Price *"can influence the mob boss to place Mason's friend on the hit list!"*

Chapter Forty-Nine

No good deed shall go unpunished

SAC Gene Gallagher was expecting the AD's call when it came in early Monday morning. Picking up the receiver, he said, "Gene Gallagher."

"Gene, I want one of your supervisors, Brad Mason, on a plane and in my office on Wednesday."

"Who is this?" Gallagher did not like the AD so why not spread a little angst.

"I heard my secretary announce the call. This is Assistant Director Todd Price calling from headquarters." The AD sounded angry.

Gallagher spent time at headquarters and was well aware of Price's reputation. Some SACs were not impressed with FBIHQ folks bearing impressive titles. Gallagher fell into this category. He asked, "Is there a problem?"

"I hope not. Have Mason in my office no later than noon Wednesday." Price did not intend to give Gallagher too much information. If Price decided to transfer Mason to another office, he knew the SAC could construct a case to keep Mason in Boston by insisting he was in the middle of a priority investigation. Gallagher would obtain the support of the United States Attorney's Office. The AD would be powerless to override this maneuver. Price did not realize that Gallagher could also thwart any order to take a supervisor out of the division for any period of time.

It was unusual for an SAC to be kept out of the loop when it involved one of his supervisors. The line ended before Gallagher had the chance to protest. Gallagher called out to his secretary.

"Miss Carson, as usual you are shooting in the K5 area. The AD is up to no good. If Brad is settled back from the Portland deal, tell him to stop by."

Gallagher and his secretary often alluded to the kill area, the K5 of a firearms target sheet, as analogous to referencing an accurate evaluation of a particular situation.

An hour later Mason walked in the SAC's office and said, "What's up Gene?"

"I understand everything went well in Portland."

Mason and OC supervisor Mark Ireland were in Maine to finalize the preparation of a SWAT team operation, which was a co-investigation with a sister DOJ agency, the Alcohol, Tobacco and Firearms (ATF). A large group of known New England gun dealers expected a substantial delivery of automatic weapons and various other destructive items from the West Coast. Mason and Ireland planned the operation and assigned the manpower, and then stepped back to let the team do what they did best. The team leader, an ex-military special ops veteran, directed the operation. The SWAT agents from both agencies worked like clockwork. The bad guys were surprised and a dozen gun dealers were apprehended without a shot fired. In addition to the firearms, a large quantity of drugs and boxes used to ship rounds of ammunition, filled instead with currency, were confiscated. In total, the successful operation relieved the gang of over eight hundred and fifty thousand dollars.

One of the FBI agents, a native New Englander, surprised the two Boston supervisors with an authentic New England clambake. He earlier placed everything in perfect alignment on top of fresh seaweed and red-hot stones, and covered the spread with a water-soaked and well-used gray canvas. It was a perfect September afternoon. They feasted on homemade New England clam chowder, steamed clams, and corn on the cob with tons of heated butter. A few cold beers topped off a fabulous lunch.

The Boston supervisors said their goodbyes and drove back to Massachusetts with surprisingly little traffic. Ireland remarked, "Sometimes we get pissed at the way things go on the job and in the bureau—then something like an all-agent clambake in Maine makes it all worthwhile." Mason knew exactly what he meant.

The Interim Director would be leaving soon so haste was in order. Price intended to impress the people who have a path to the president, the real influential movers and shakers in the capital. When the plan completed, they would be convinced that Price alone, through his high intelligence and professional expertise, achieved something never before accomplished in law enforcement. The convincing story would go something like, "AD Price created a plan and personally hand-picked and directed one of his subordinates to maintain secret contact with a New York Mafiosi, touted as the mob's golden future, the next *numero uno*." He planned to feed the pols more bull-shit about how he orchestrated and supervised every act of the play. Price hallucinated often when producing and directing his fantasies. Often he would hurry his worksheets to the restroom. Orgasms became regular occur-rences.

Two requirements remained for Price's fantasy to become a reality: *the wise guy must get on board; and Mason must be reassigned to FBIHQ.*

SAC Gallagher brought Mason current on the call from Price. The SAC told Mason, "It has to be in connection with your friend in New York. I'm sure the prick knows we can prevent the trip to D.C. but we need to move on it. I'll get started."

Mason asked his boss, "What can you do?"

Gallagher continued. "I'll formulate the argument to keep you in Boston. When I finish with the supporting documents you will not believe how im-portant you are. We can't spare you, not even for a day. Get me the file numbers for the bureau priority investigations assigned to your squad. And keep those files secure, you never know with this turd. Some of the public corruption cases are near trial. The prosecutors do not want new blood at this late date. When we finish putting it all together you and I will take a stroll down Congress Street. The United States Attorney will join us in our justi-fication to keep you here."

Mason was relieved. "Thanks, chief. Man, you really don't want me to meet with him."

Gallagher repeated his distaste for Price. "You know what I know and how I feel. Brad, it cannot be emphasized enough." Mason's boss smiled. "Remember, my friend, this is the bureau, and no good deed shall go unpun-ished. That would be plural in your illustrious case, no good deeds."

"Thanks for the wisdom, Clare," Mason said, citing the person respon-sible for the SAC's quote, author *Clare Booth Luce.*

Chapter Fifty

We have a long memory

In the fall of 1984, Mason worked on the follow-up investigation and trial preparation for a state senate case involving a high-ranking member of the upper house in Boston.

Randinoli too kept very active in his chosen profession. He stayed busy in New Jersey and was responsible for most of the revenue taken in by the Bonanno crime family. Under the leadership of Don Nittoli, his family rose in power. They had more members and were by far the wealthiest of the five families completing the commission. In a weekend edition of the New York Times, they were referred to as "the most brutal of all crime syndicates in New York." The writer obviously worked with accurate sources. The article pointed to the family's operation in New Jersey and the "ruthless tactics employed against enemies of the Bonannos." Underboss Carmine Cuccio blamed Randinoli for the bad press. In private, he told one of the capos, "Gabe goes overboard with the collection end. He is too wild."

The boss never took his eye off the ball. All aspects of the business required his attention. Nittoli told his underboss, "Carmine, we must consider 'Johnny Boy' Maggio to be a threat to the well-being of the family. The capo has strayed and he's brought shame to us all."

Nittoli re-emphasized his gratitude for the money Randinoli brought in while the boss was inside. He always looked for reasons to overlook any faux pas of his captain. *Now if Gabe does this work without a problem, the heat will be off to get rid of him.* He said to Cuccio, "Gabe got the work done with Alizzio, but not so well with the disposal. He did a good job on the Manzi thing. He has learned to embrace each detail, exclude nothing. Give it to Gabe, he will do it right." He wanted the capo to succeed. Cuccio noted the boss did not comment on the Yandola contract and decided to keep his mouth shut. Cuccio thought it wiser not to upset his Don. He was confident that Randinoli's time would come.

The underboss wasted little time. He sent word to Randinoli and the next day Cuccio met personally with the capo at the same familiar restaurant. Cuccio did not mix words and very clearly delivered the order. "Gabe, Joe made this his personal project. John Maggio is dead, and you make it happen."

He looked Cuccio in the eye and spoke the expected response. "Carmine, please tell the boss I will not let him down. I appreciate this work." Randinoli was pleased that the boss still trusted him to carry out an important contract; he knew he could not fail this time. Getting the order to take out one of their capos—another made guy, a man of honor—was huge.

Randinoli asked Cuccio why the order came down. "I thought Johnny Boy was in good shape, always doing his job?"

Cuccio smiled and quietly responded, "The family does not forget, we have a long memory." As he said this, the underboss was thinking of Gabe's blunders. He explained that Maggio for many years acted as Don Cassando's trusted bodyguard. "He obviously didn't perform his duties in an acceptable manner." Waving his hand in a dismissal manner, he added, "He got very careless. That is more than you need to know—and it stays with you."

Randinoli thought, "*These guys are not very original, 'we have a long memory.' That's what Nittoli said when he assigned me the Allizio contract.*"

He was glad that Buchanan was released from prison recently. Randinoli would have preferred just having Buchanan with him but decided to bring an army for this work. The show of force would impress that he took the work seriously. He chose his accomplices as part of the hit team; Tito Restaino, Dinny "Specs" Buchanan, Louis Polcari, his cousin Richard Polcari, Frank Pizzoti and Manny Anguilo.

He justified the huge crew, reminding everyone that "Johnny Boy Maggio is a captain and street savvy. If Maggio has any idea he made the list he'll hire a few guns from out of town to stay close to him. No excuses this time, every base will be covered."

Randinoli spat out the order. "Specs will do the close work as a welcome home gift." Translated, this meant Buchanan, a longtime associate with a record of accomplishment of killing, would do the actual up-close shooting. He worked with the capo on the Manzi contract and performed better than most. He reminded Randinoli of home, of 12th and Bruce. Buchanan always understood his role and kept quiet about the work. Not of Italian descent, he realized that acceptance as a made man for him was not a possibility but it did not stop him from doing his job. Like the others working with Randinoli, he earned a great deal of money. Buchanan was content being part of the action and never complained of his status. He had been involved in several hits, including two strangulations, and was respected and feared by many.

"The plan's simple. If we all do our jobs the work will be over and done within a few minutes." Gabe discussed the details with the crew and everyone acknowledged his role.

For two hours they waited outside of Maggio's residence. It was dark. At eight p.m., Maggio was on his way to meet some friends at a local bar. He never suspected any problems and was startled when he heard Pizzoti's voice.

"Johnny Boy, do what you're told and everything will be okay." Anguilo and Pizzoti grabbed his arms and forced Maggio to the stolen car they earlier positioned across the street from the bar. They placed him in the passenger seat. Buchanan, already sitting in the back seat, placed a chrome-plated Smith and Wesson 5-shot revolver an inch from the back of Maggio's head and squeezed off all five rounds. It was over in a matter of seconds. The side of Maggio's scalp splattered against the windshield and side door window. It would not require a medical examiner to pronounce the mobster dead. Randinoli earlier expressed the operation in a very clear manner. "Specs, he gets it as soon as he sits in the car. None of this driving around the city looking for the right spot."

Following the pre-discussed plan, the crew worked fast and lifted Maggio's body from the car, wrapped it with heavy plastic rolls and placed it in the trunk. Using two vehicles, Randinoli and his accomplices drove to New Jersey where earlier they planned the disposal of Maggio's remains. Following instructions, they would deface the body, separating the body parts.

Everyone participated in the gruesome mutilation. The Polcaris did most of the dirty work with the use of chain saws. The crew completed the job and considered it successful.

Who would be the next wise guy to spill his guts in order to save his ass? A decade later, Manny Anguilo turned rat and among many other mob secrets he provided the detailed facts about the Maggio murder that included how "we took him in the barrel to Seaside Park at the Jersey shore. The family owned some property off the beaten path, ya know? It was an abandoned lot. It was dark. Me and Louie Polcari dug a hole and dropped him in."

The problems mounted for Randinoli when, on the last day of June, a group of teenagers were using the same lot for a softball game. They smelled something strange and noticed the area where the killers had spread lye. They called the local police who discovered and removed Maggio's remains. Again, the medical examiners were able to make a positive identification with more than enough body parts and dental work.

When the news reached the bosses, Cuccio used it as more ammunition to destroy Nittoli's support for Randinoli. "Joe, this should never happen. Are we becomin' rank amateurs? I mean, you and me will be doin' the work if this keeps up. Gabe is wrong. Right the guy's dead, but that should be the end of it. Am I right?"

Don Nittoli knew of the bad blood between his underboss and his captain. Yet he knew Cuccio echoed the sentiments of many in the family. Randinoli did the work up to a point. Allizio, Yandola and now Maggio. Two were killed but the bodies showed up. How long could the Don protect his bread and butter, his most gifted earner? He thought and after a few minutes he admitted, "Carmine you are right. There will be a time when work will be done…"

"But Joe, how much longer…?" Cuccio never finished with his objection.

Nittoli's voice grew louder. "I just said you were right, did I not? That I agreed with you? And you interrupt me when I am explaining. You question when I will make an important business decision. Do you forget who is still the head of this family? Do not interrupt me again." His voice quieted. "Now is not the proper time to make this decision, to do this kind of work. I tell you, you will be the first to know when the time arrives. Understood?"

"Sure, I didn't mean to question your judgment." He was sorry that he mentioned the subject. Cuccio wanted to end the conversation.

Nittoli knew that he made his point. "Carmine, you are the underboss, and my good friend. You are a good man. We will forget the business for now. We need some food. Call the driver."

Randinoli experienced the same symptoms over ten years ago, after killing Cesare Alizzio. Deathly sick to his stomach, he did not eat any solid food for three days. Most of his associates had forgotten his once infamous nickname. This latest operation resurrected his mob nickname, the "Exterminator"; the cheap shot only said behind his back. He became more paranoid thinking the law watched his every move. In his car he drove circuitous routes, sometimes taking twice the time required to reach a destination. On occasion he would order his girlfriend Mae Yong to drive while he stayed hunched over in the passenger seat.

Over the next few months, Randinoli placed calls to Mason. The conversations were short. "Hi, how are things?" Followed by a little ball breaking and ending with "take care of yourself." The relationship changed considerably from the 12th Avenue and Bruce Street days. Although he did not know specific details, Mason knew what Randinoli had become and prayed for him but somehow understood and accepted the inevitable. His friend would spend his days in prison or worse yet…Randinoli understood fully he could never take advantage of his friend's position in law enforcement to cover his mob activities. His paranoia was growing. *"If only I could get a heads-up when they were closing in. How close are the feds to an indictment, an arrest? Thank God for Big Joe Nittoli, at least I know I will never make the hit parade."*

The capo dreaded the thought of spending the rest of his life in prison. Yet, if he ever attempted to pump his friend for information, he had no doubt Mason would not hold back. He never did in the past and would not start now. 12th and Bruce was a long way off in another life. When Blackie Capone spoke of the corner and "taking care of our own," everyone on the corner was on the same page. When he left his old friends, Randinoli read from a much different play book.

Although neither discussed serious business, Randinoli hinted his career suffered a setback. He never got specific. *It would be a bad idea, telling an FBI agent you screwed up on a murder contract.* Underneath the tough exterior, Randinoli agonized over his life situation. As much as he wanted to lay out his activities of the past decade, he could not speak the words to his friend. When by himself, the man of honor thought of his youth and the mistakes he made and the life he chose. *Hey suck it up. Onward and upward. Things work out. It's all about the bread!*

Then he would rationalize. In spite of a couple of business setbacks, Randinoli believed being the premier earner trumped the mistakes. Being the breadwinner was a guarantee he would remain in good grace with Don Nittoli. Once, after a tough day of collections, he told Buchanan, "Some guys that we clip are never found. Good for them. Others show up, so what? They're dead! Who cares that some are identified and others just stay missing." Now he was near screaming, "I am a busy man. Who cares? Dead is dead, right?" The family associate nodded his agreement and ordered more drinks.

As a capo regime, Randinoli became more aggressive; he organized business unions in New Jersey and received large pay offs from union officials to keep labor peace. He utilized contacts from years gone by. As a result of his initiative, the family's bottom line grew to a record number, the benefit of new unions to include restaurant workers, construction of all kinds and even large grocery chains. The crime family was now the boldest of the New York organizations when it came to controlling union bosses and infiltrating the memberships with their own people. Randinoli specialized in physical violence when it became necessary to make a point.

In Essex County he stayed away from the Newark Roofers Local, the place of his former employment. Several of his old friends still employed as roofers would not tolerate any strong-arm bullshit from anyone, including a neighborhood guy, now a full-fledged mobster. There was more than enough added revenue taken in from the myriad of unions paying tribute. The Bonanno people were ecstatic with Randinoli's business acumen.

"The guy is a money machine." Nittoli said this several times. But things change and the boss recognized that Randinoli's ability to bring in the bread was not enough to cover other inadequacies. Carelessness regarding crucial family business could not go unaddressed.

Chapter Fifty-One

Tell me what is so important

The capo knew exactly the location of the boss. Without fail, Don Nittoli visited his favorite bathhouse on Henry Street in Queens every Monday, Wednesday and Friday. Randinoli figured his news would be of interest to the boss of the family. It would do no harm making the boss happy. Recently Randinoli believed, and rightly so, he had lost favor with Don Nittoli. A couple of contracts did not go exactly as planned.

He opened the door to the steam room and walked toward Nittoli. The captain was confident the boss would be glad to see him and certainly welcome the news he brought.

Nittoli sat on a wooden step and perspired profusely. He loved the way the steam worked on his body. He never exercised and considered this ritual helped him stay healthy. "Cleans all the garbage out, you come out a new man." The time spent in the steam room was possibly the only occasion he was without a big cigar in his hand. He sat with his legs spread, a large cotton bath towel hung over his thighs up to his protruding stomach. On either side of him, about four feet away, sat two guns. In addition to the large towels covering the two bodyguards, each had a smaller towel wrapped around his right hand. Both bodyguards recognized Randinoli. Nevertheless, holding their weapons they looked directly at him, watching his every move.

When Randinoli appeared, still in street clothes, Nittoli did not attempt to cover his annoyance. "Gabe, you were not expected. You are very aware of my feelings toward surprises. You had better have good purpose in being here." The boss, a college graduate, utilized his English grammar education on occasion.

"Joe, I received a phone call today. I think that you should know about it."

The boss encouraged his people to call him by his first name and not always as boss or Don Nittoli. Many of the older members ignored the request and continued to use a title of respect. "Remove your jacket, sit down next to me." Nittoli waved at his protectors to move to the far side of the room. Randinoli noted that when they sat down both moved their towels so they now held their weapons with both hands. The four mobsters were alone. "Here, have some water and tell me what is so important."

Randinoli accepted the bottle of water and spoke. "The call came in about an hour ago. A guy speaking very high-end English says he wants to meet with me. I tell him I do not know who he is, I ask where he got my name and telephone number and tell him I'm not happy to hear from someone I don't know." Randinoli paused for breath. "He says none of that is important, I should just listen to what he has to say. I'm ready to hang up but I figure he knows how to reach me again so I decide to listen to the prick."

Nittoli interrupted. "Before you continue, you did not recognize his voice?"

The capo answered, "No, but he's not from around here."

"Go on."

Randinoli continued. "Then he tells me how important he is. This is almost a direct quote. "I am calling from Washington D.C. I am an Assistant Director with the FBI. We need to sit down and speak." At first, I figure someone's breaking my balls. I said I don't know you. You're a stranger. I don't talk with strangers. Have a good day. I'm just about to hang up and he says a name."

Nittoli now listened carefully. "What name?" He noted his capo's hesitation.

Finally, Randinoli said, "You remember I told you about my friend from Newark."

"Who is now an FBI agent, yes? Mason. That's the name he spoke?"

"Brad Mason. He said he had important information for me concerning Brad. He will be in the city next week. Then he's almost whispering, I could just about hear. He said I could not tell anybody about the call, especially my friend. He says he will cause much trouble for Brad if I tell him this guy reached out. He will call me when he gets in town." Randinoli looked down at his clenched hands. "That was it, he hangs up. Joe, you know I usually know how to handle most situations. This I'm not too sure, I don't know what to make of it. First I feel I should talk with Brad. Then I think if this guy is for real and he hurts Brad, then what? I whack the son of a bitch?"

Nittoli smiled. "Right, you kill an Assistant Director of the FBI. Then I'm sure what I will do with you. You reacted right, now you need to think clearly. He never gave his name. Wait until you hear from him. Let me know, maybe we play cops. We cover the meeting and go from there. We have Mike fix you up with a little device. It is best we do not say one word of this to anyone, understand?"

"Right. Okay, I will reach you as soon as I hear from the guy who says he's a fed." He smiled. "Thanks, I knew you'd have the answer." Another lesson learned at the corner of 12th and Bruce; *always let the chief think he has all the answers.*

"Now, leave me alone to my perspiration. I am sure you have other things you need to address." Randinoli's crew was concentrating on a shylock issue, a heavy bettor from Staten Island now very delinquent on borrowed money. Randinoli already made arrangements to pay a personal visit to the deadbeat's jewelry outlet on 48th Street in Manhattan. The capo knew the area very well. For the past five years Randinoli loaned mob money on the streets of the jewelry district, resulting in lucrative returns. Confident the debt would be paid in full, Don Nittoli closed his eyes.

Randinoli hesitated. "Joe, the Maggio thing…"

The Don waved him off. "One thing at a time. Stay focused on your new friend from the FBI. Now go!'

He did not share another matter with his capo. Last year in Manhattan, at a bar called Cryan's on Franklin Street, the Don met with FBI Assistant Director Todd Price. The discussion turned out to be a disappointment. Price drank heavily and mumbled meaningless garbage. Nittoli wore his trusty recorder to the meeting. Actually, anyone listening would hear the words of a psycho who drank too much, and not anything of a criminal nature.

Chapter Fifty-Two

He can suffer much discomfort

The boss received a call from his capo.

"I would like to meet with you." Nittoli recognized the voice and knew the purpose of the requested meeting.

"Sure, I'll be at the library at six." Nittoli hung up. Always alert for phone taps, the message was clear to both parties. Randinoli and the Don would meet at a popular Italian bar and restaurant in Brooklyn at eight p.m.

The restaurant was still filled with the dinner crowd staying for conversation and a few drinks. The two men occupied a private booth in the rear of the restaurant. The boss's protection detail occupied seats at the bar. Nittoli, not one to waste time, asked, "When did he call, what did he say and how did it end?"

"I contacted you the minute I hung up. He said the same stuff as the first call. He will be in the city on Wednesday. He wants me to meet him. He will call when he gets in and we will meet. I will pick out where, a good restaurant where he can get good Italian food. Joe, the guy is one cocky son of a bitch. I wanted to go through the phone and choke the rat bastard."

The boss always gave Randinoli a wide berth, in part because he liked him, but in particular because from the beginning his capo brought in the money. "Did you hear what I said the last time? You must relax and think clearly. We have two days to prepare for your meeting. Have Mike Iovita provide you with a suitable miniature recorder. He will not expect someone in our line of work to be recording a conversation. However, if he should want to search you or you suspect anything at all, you act insulted and you leave. *Comprendere*? No conversation, you just leave. We'll have our people there to insure you make a clean exit."

Randinoli was happy the boss stayed involved in the latest developments. He thought to himself, "*I was right, the Maggio problem not really a problem. It's all good.*"

Assistant Director Todd Price believed his position of importance was now on the rise. From the moment Price learned of Mason's close relationship with a made Mafiosi, he prepared to pressure the supervisory special agent to convince his friend to cooperate with the AD. Price's motive had never been for the benefit of the law enforcement community but purely his self-aggrandizement. His objective never wavered. He would rise to the lofty position of FBI Director. His grandiose plan required Randinoli to turn on his wise guy associates. He will convince the mobster there is no option. Either he cooperates or both he and Mason feel pain.

The obsession never left him. Price would take credit for bringing New York organized crime to its knees almost single-handedly. He believed by ingratiating himself with the top wise guys in New York, Price's bona fide moved in an upward direction. The gist of his strategy was still on the shelf. Today his covert meeting with Gabe Randinoli will get things rolling. The capo will agree to cooperate and furnish information and ultimately testify against alleged members of organized crime. The AD still had a trump card to play, a guarantee in his back pocket. He would pressure the supervisor from the Boston office. His sick brain now full speed ahead. If necessary, his next meeting with Nittoli will literally bury Randinoli. *There is no chance Randinoli will not cooperate. I will make sure he understands his options. He will join with me or he will die.*

On Wednesday evening, Randinoli sat alone in Forcella's Bistro in Brooklyn. Before he left his car, he reached in his jacket and activated the recorder. The AD recognized the mobster from an arrest photograph he obtained before he left FBIHQ. When the stranger approached the booth, the capo reluctantly shook hands with the mystery man who smiled as he introduced himself.

"My name is Todd Price. I appreciate your promptness." Randinoli quickly sized up the stranger as over six feet tall, soft in the belly and someone who wants to appear in charge.

Price said, "I am famished. What do you suggest for dinner? I understand this restaurant offers excellent seafood and pasta dishes." The AD picked up this gem of information from the yellow pages and not any firsthand experience.

Randinoli forced himself to heed the warning of his boss about control-ling his temper. "If you like seafood, try the shrimp scampi and a side of penne arrabiata." He counted on the pure hot sauce to burn Price's throat. When he arrived at the restaurant he told the maître d' to "go heavy with the red pepper on the pasta dish."

"Sounds delicious, if you would order for me I would appreciate it."

Randinoli did not intend to spend more time than necessary with the FBI official. He motioned the waiter and ordered for both himself and Price, and included a bottle of Chianti.

Price appeared nervous. "I will not waste your time. You may have an idea why I called for this meeting." He lied as he said, "I am here on official business. Your dear friend Brad Mason works for me, as well as a few hun-dred other FBI agents."

Randinoli said, "I knew a Mason a long time ago. What has your official business to do with me?"

The AD smiled. "I think you still know him. But we won't debate that point. You can help him immensely, and help yourself."

A bottle of wine and a huge bowl of antipasto appeared at the table. The waiter poured the Chianti into both glasses and left the table.

Price took a long pull of the wine. "Brad can go a long way up the ladder. Alternatively, he can remain stagnant. Or worse, he can suffer much discom-fort." Price waited for a reaction that never came.

If ever Randinoli wanted to physically injure another human being, this was one of those times.

"I will be more direct. You, my friend, can make the difference. You can help Special Agent Mason and at the same time help yourself. You know where I am going with this, of course?"

He dragged on his cigarette, and Randinoli said, "No."

The AD expected more response and became irritated by the wise guy's apparent uninterested demeanor. "Okay, I will lay it out so even someone like you will understand. I want you to cooperate with me, to work with me. The FBI will debrief you concerning your associates and their activities since you have been a member of an organized criminal enterprise. Of course I refer to the Bonanno family of which you are an officer and a rising star. In return, you will not be prosecuted for any of your past illegal activities, to include murder. More important, your friend will survive. He will be given a position of responsibility enabling his rise in the bureau. Rather than a severe demotion, he will be promoted and receive an increase in salary. He and his family stay in civilization, with no transfer to some godforsaken part of the country."

Randinoli tired of listening to the threats but remembered the recording of each word. He picked at the antipasto.

"Well, do you have any questions of me?" Price displayed the phony smile. "I have been doing all the talking. What say you, my friend?"

Randinoli placed his fork on the salad dish. *My friend?* "I have been listening. I think I know what you're demanding of, me. I admit I'm confused."

"Of course this is all new to you. All your questions will be answered in due time. I will guarantee that…" The AD experienced the first interruption.

"No, I have no questions. I don't believe you're dealing with accurate information. You want me to cooperate with you regarding my membership in…I believe you said, 'an organized criminal enterprise?'"

"That's correct."

"And my what? 'Illegal activities?'" The AD now nodding in agreement and feeling optimistic the way the wise guy quoted the proffer.

Randinoli looked directly at Price. "I don't know what you smoke in that funny-looking pipe of yours, but I have no idea what you're talking about. You obviously have me confused with someone else. It's none of your business but I will fill you in anyway. I am in sales, which is certainly not an illegal activity in this great country or a dishonest way to make a living." He started to stand. "Now if you will excuse me."

Price near screamed, "Hold it right there you worthless son of a bitch. If you say no to me and walk away, I will make both of you dregs sorry you ever left New Jersey. You will pay big time. You will suffer more than you can imagine. I want your answer. I will…"

Randinoli stood and dropped a crisp fifty-dollar bill on the table.

The 12th Avenue and Bruce Street product completely forgot the live microphone. "Two things. First, I'm not your friend," he said, now nose-to-nose with the federal big shot. "And second, you want my answer? Good, here it is. Go and fuck yourself Mr. Prick, or Price, or whatever your fucking name is. Enjoy the arrabiata."

His right eye now teared in waterfall fashion, the AD could not conceal an uncontrollable tic. As Randinoli neared the exit door, the meals arrived. Price stared at the delicious-looking arrabiata, his appetite non-operational.

It took forty-five minutes for Randinoli to arrive at the Bonanno headquarters. He telephoned Nittoli immediately after leaving his meeting with Price. He handed the recorder to his boss. "The guy is nuts. I hope the tape's clear."

"Mike has never had a problem with the clarity of his product." The boss gave the tape to Mike Olivita, who examined the small device.

"Looks okay." Looking at Nittoli, he asked, "You want to hear it now, boss?"

"Yes, by all means. Let us hear if Mr. Randinoli has a future in show business."

At the conclusion of the recorded conversation no one spoke. Finally, Nittoli smiled and said, "Gabe, 'Go and fuck yourself?' Apparently, you have little respect for such a high-ranking federal official. Just kidding. A good job, my captain. Perhaps someday Mr. Price will listen to his voice uttering very embarrassing things." The Don reminded them to remain silent regarding the tape. They understood and the meeting ended.

Gabe thought, *"Brad 'can suffer much discomfort.' I wonder if Price even tried the arrabiata."*

Chapter Fifty-Three

The seat of government

Many people assigned to federal positions in Washington D.C. believe they occupy powerful positions. Some do indeed. Whatever branch of government they work for, they recognize the District as the "seat of government." This description does wonders for the ego of a government lightweight.

The alleged important meetings in New York did not come cheap. Price wasted taxpayers' money flying roundtrip as a first-class traveler, ostensibly investigating a top-secret, need-to-know operation. One of the highest-ranking people in the entire FBI, an organization of ten thousand quality agents and twenty-five thousand loyal support personnel, lied, cheated and stole on a daily basis.

In spite of what Price perceived to be solid preparation, the AD struck out with Randinoli. Not a problem, the ruthless AD always used his gofer whenever he tested a new lie. He relayed to Mayhew his version of "my successful face-to-face conversation with Mr. Randinoli." His story included how the wise guy feared going to jail for several murders in which he played a part. He told Mayhew he met with Randinoli at a secret meeting place in New York. According to Price's account, which he would use to impress and threaten the Boston supervisor, he pressed Randinoli for his cooperation and ordered Randinoli to furnish him information and later testify against members of the Bonanno crime syndicate and other La Cosa Nostra representatives. In return, Price would go to bat for Randinoli, helping obtain a reduction to his sentencing. Sounding like a bona fide OC investigator, he said Randinoli "faced hard time for the Maggio murder."

Mayhew asked Price, "If by chance the Director presses for more specifics, how do you handle him?"

Always able to wing it, Price said, "Simple. I say Randinoli reached out for me when he heard of my visit to the city. He didn't trust our people in New York. He told me the New York FBI wanted him put away for life. He knew I outranked all of them and was desperate to cut a deal."

The AD would announce he would "declare war against the Mafia," starting with the most powerful group, the Bonanno family. The plan includes staffing a section at FBIHQ consisting of the best and most experienced field supervisors. After much deliberation, Price would personally select Boston supervisor Brad Mason to implement the master plan. Price correctly reasoned Mason had the respect in the field and was a natural choice to head up the super squad. The press will love Price when he assures them all Bonanno family members will answer for their crimes. Nothing could prevent Price's rise to the big office with this accomplishment as the hallmark of his resume.

Mason spent thirteen years of his career in the New England area, with intermittent assignments in New York and New Jersey. Now well aware that AD Todd Price would soon make his move, Mason and his friend AD Max Blaney were making plans of their own.

His cell phone rang. SSA Mason ascertained the call came from an old friend, someone he had not heard from in some time. Mason could only guess at the reason for the call.

He closed the office door and picked up the phone. "This is a surprise."

Randinoli said, "Yeah, well I thought it was time to say hello." His voice did not reflect the self-confidence of a big shot. The stark reality hit: Mason's boyhood friend from the corner had become a hit man, a cold-blooded killer. *There's always hope—maybe not.*

Mason did sense a real problem. All past conversations were strictly on a personal level. Neither of them ever discussed their respective business nor questioned the other's activities. Mason intended this call to remain with those spoken and unspoken guidelines. "Good to hear your voice, you're okay?"

Randinoli attempted to regain his composure. The edge in his tone was still present, "I'm not sure when..." His voice broke off.

"Whoa pal, what is it, what's happening?" Mason was now confident of his assessment. His friend was in a spot where he had no control. Was someone with Randinoli now?

"Nothing." Randinoli paused a moment. "Shit, can't I catch up with my main man from 12th and Bruce? Not sure when we get together again, that's all. You know me. I make decisions. I made a decision to give you a jingle." Randinoli attempted to sound upbeat.

Mason now believed to be true what he recently picked up from a reliable source. Convinced his friend hurt inside, it could be anything. The FBI agent guessed Randinoli had ample reason to be concerned. Was his life on the line? Whenever the OC people discussed the Bonanno family they would say the capo earns so much money he would never make a hit list. Going back to the early days, whenever a problem surfaced Randinoli always came up smelling like a rose, no matter what the downside potential. Could he escape from this impending danger?

Mason said, "I'm recalling a conversation that took place in my apartment."

Randinoli barely whispered, "I remember." Now an awkward silence before he asked, "And the world of law enforcement? I hear you have been a busy fed. There's not many empty accommodations left in the jails."

That's it Gabe, keep it light.

"I suppose everything is pretty much status quo here. And the business world, how's that going?" Mason regretted what Randinoli had become but accepted the realization that he was powerless over the actions of his friend. Randinoli understood fully he could never use his friend's position in law enforcement to influence his mob activities. If he ever tried, Randinoli had no doubt that Mason would not hold back, he never did in the past and would not start now. They could both feel the reality, 12th and Bruce now far off in the distance.

"You know business is business." He sounded almost sad. "A lot like the gas station at the Five Corners. Some days busy, other days quiet. The difference is at the station I ran the show. Now I kind of work for somebody else." Randinoli was sorry he said this. He did not want to come across as a complainer. "But at the end of the day I still run my end of things. Hey, sales is sales." He said more than he intended.

Randinoli always sounded as though he was proud of Mason and his career. Although neither discussed serious business, Randinoli hinted his career suffered a setback. He never got specific. It would be a bad idea, telling an FBI agent you screwed up on a few murders. Underneath the tough exterior, Randinoli agonized over his life situation. He wanted to lay out his activities of the past decade. However, why dump his garbage on someone he considers a brother and place Mason in more than awkward situation?

There's always some good news, though. The Bonanno people were very pleased with Randinoli's extraordinary knack for bringing in money. In spite of a couple of business setbacks, Randinoli had the respect of the members. Maybe not all, but the ones that mattered. He increased the family's presence in a few newer unions, the restaurant workers, and fast food store employees. He tried to convince himself that Don Nittoli would not place his name on any hit contract. A respected capo for ten years, he wanted to believe the mistakes were viewed as minor. He figured Nittoli was satisfied when the Don gave Randinoli assurance in private conversation.

What Don Nittoli did not say was that he, too, was under pressure from within his family as well as others sitting on the commission. One of his longtime allies on the commission made it clear: "Don Nittoli, I do not have to tell you. It is bad business to ignore contracts gone sour. The solution is simple. Someone must be held accountable for the serious errors." The Don listened without comment. He is still boss and will decide if anything needs to be done.

The friends from 12th and Bruce touched on small, irrelevant stuff before ending the conversation. As usual, Randinoli lied. "Whoops, gotta go—still a busy man. You take care. I'll catch up."

Don Nittoli tired of all the input regarding his capo and whether Randinoli should live or die. The Don thought long and hard and concluded he would shock many people but it would be his decision. Randinoli would be given another opportunity to right the ship.

The Don made another business decision. Family associate Robert Mamoli blatantly ignored the Don's edict dealing with the business of drugs. The boss summoned the underboss to a meeting.

After he poured two cups of cappuccino, Don Nittoli said, "Carmine, you are my most trusted friend and advisor. You will disagree with what I have decided. No, more than that my friend, you will be angry."

The underboss of the Bonanno crime family, Carmine Cuccio, appeared confused. He said, "This sounds like a big deal Joe, what's the problem?"

The Don smiled. "First, I don't see it as a problem. We have a situation and we will deal with it." His look turned serious. "Then it will be gone and forgotten. So listen carefully." The boss sipped his cappuccino. "First, we have someone who disrespects the family and ignores my rules…"

"That would be…" Cuccio began to interrupt.

Don Nittoli waved him off. "I asked that you listen carefully." Cuccio nodded, recognizing his error.

"You were about to say the name Robert Mamoli—and you would be correct. He must go as yet another reminder that we are not in the business of drugs. Now more than ten years have passed since Frank Manzi paid with his life. Everyone else received the message and acted accordingly. We have stayed respectable and out of that dirty industry. It exploits children and poor people. Now we have Mamoli. He disgusts me and he goes. Now that part of the equation solved, we study the second part. Who will do the work? Again, I know you have strong feelings on this but I have gone over the situation and obtained the counsel of the consigliere."

Cuccio dared not speak. In spite of the commission's recommendation, the underboss realized the Don had arrived at a decision. It was a done deal.

Nittoli looked directly at Cuccio. "Gabe Randinoli will do the work. Before you speak, my decision did not come easy, not without a great deal of thought. My choice would be opposed by the commission, by our own members and especially by you, Carmine. I am well aware of this. Yet I am the head of our family and I must do what I believe to be in the best interest of us all. Most of you will say it is because of Gabe's earning power. You would be wrong. I believe he deserves this opportunity, this final chance to prove he can deliver the goods. You are more familiar with his past performance as well as anyone. Not the best but not the worst either. This will decide his fate. You give him the order to get rid of Robert Mamoli." This ended the conversation.

Randinoli was elated when the order came. So long as Don Nittoli headed the family, Randinoli believed he was invincible. The boss always liked Randinoli and would continue to protect him. Now he was giving the captain important work to reinforce his support.

On this Friday afternoon in May of 1986 the weather was rainy and cloudy, the streets near empty. Robert Mamoli entered a Manhattan bookmaking joint on the corner of 85th Street and 10th Avenue. Positioned across the street, Randinoli, Charlie Sassano and Stevie Lombardi watched him go inside. Unfortunately, Mamoli's friend and known drug pusher, Alfonse "Bats" Tato, waited in a car outside the building.

Lombardi said, "That's Bats Tato. Maybe we should wait for another time."

Sassano was impatient. "Why wait? The boss wants it done. Let's do it."

Randinoli agreed. "Don Nittoli will not be bothered if another lowlife drug scum buys the farm. If we have to, Bats goes too. Time to go."

The three gunmen walked across the street and arrived just as Mamoli exited the book parlor. Without saying a word, Randinoli punched the unsuspecting drug dealer in the face, crushing his nose. Randinoli had some minor dealings with Mamoli and had made up his mind to beat the victim to a pulp before killing him. "You like drugs. All the drugs in the world won't help you." He punched and kicked until Mamoli lay motionless. The capo fired several shots into Mamoli's limp body. Randinoli never forgot the Yandola screw up so he made certain Mamoli died.

As the three killers turned from their victim's lifeless body they saw Tato jump from the car and begin running south on 10th Avenue. Randinoli wasted little time. Tato was an eyewitness to his friend's killing and could testify against the three Bonanno family members. Randinoli pointed at Tato as the terrified onlooker ran for his life. "He has to go. Take him, Charlie." Sassano, an expert marksman, shot Tato repeatedly as Tato attempted to run up 10th Avenue. He had been hit with four rounds from a Glock revolver.

Both bodies were found and identified by the NYPD. Officials recovered Tato's lifeless body twenty-five yards from the entrance of the gambling parlor. It was no surprise that there were no witnesses to the brutal murder. Mamoli was immediately outside the front entrance. During a cursory examination of Tato, one of the medical technicians remarked, "This one died instantly. A tight group, any one of the four rounds was enough to do the job. 1986 starts off with a bang. New York is on its way to a record year."

Chapter Fifty-Four

Where's Gabe going?

Now July 1986, Assistant Director Todd Price was running out of options. He failed to convince Randinoli to cooperate and furnish information about the LCN and its operations. He needed the matter cleared so there would be more time to spend lining up support with the politicians on the hill.

At a routine staff meeting, the FBI Director questioned Assistant Director Price regarding the trips to the New York Office. Price immediately lied.

"Sir, I was contacted by one of the leaders of the Bonanno crime syndicate. I convinced him to cooperate with us or be prosecuted for a number of federal violations. The bum wants to accept my offer. I will shore up the details when I see him again." Price manufactured a lengthy relationship with the Bonanno captain, when in fact he met Randinoli on one occasion. He purposely omitted disclosing the covert meetings with Joe Nittoli, the boss of the Bonanno family.

Time for Plan B. Price held no doubt that Mason would play ball especially since the supervisor would advance his own career in the process. If not, the AD would force him to cooperate.

The call came the following week. The SAC wanted to see him.

Mason drove in to the city and met with his friend SAC Gene Gallagher.

Gallagher handed him the paper. "This teletype just got here from FBIHQ." He handed it to Mason. "It's quite clear. You're instructed to meet at headquarters with Assistant Director Todd Price. The teletype makes it clear; we cannot diffuse this order as we did with the last one. You need to meet with Price tomorrow."

Mason finished reading the official document. "I bet he heard I would be retiring from the FBI and wants to talk me out of it."

Gallagher answered, "Ya think?" They both knew why the command performance was ordered.

His boss said, "Here I go again. I know I sound like a broken record. And again, you know I was at the bureau with the prick. So again I emphasize, do not let your guard down. The guy is more cunning and ruthless than ever and becoming desperate."

Price never comprehended the possibility of an FBI agent and a Mafiosi as close friends. Price believed he learned something from his meeting with Randinoli. The AD underestimated the gangster; he expected Randinoli to possess street smarts but the AD did not anticipate the capo's casual demeanor. Price realized his threats were viewed as weak, without substance. He wrongly imagined he played in the little leagues. In truth, Randinoli would never be fearful of facing indictments for unsolved murders. The mob bosses received the legal ramifications from their lawyers. Finally, Randinoli was comfortable with the knowledge that the Maggio incident was history. The high-priced mob law firm issued a guarantee that indictments were not an issue. At that instance, Randinoli told the AD what to do with his threats.

One issue remained. Would Randinoli speak with his boss of their meeting? Not very likely. If personally contacted by an FBI heavyweight, a wise guy would keep the meeting quiet. Should Randinoli report such a meeting to his boss, the capo would be viewed as someone stepping out of line, too ambitious. If Plan B failed, then Price would speak with Don Nittoli and fill the Don with his version of the meeting.

There would be no obstacle today. The supervisor would be out of his element in Price's territory, FBIHQ, the seat of government. He had prepared well for his face-to-face with Mason. Price harbored no doubt. Now certain he held all the cards, he'd dangle the carrot in front of the kid from the ghetto explaining the benefits of a transfer to headquarters and make clear the severe downside of a refusal.

He warmly welcomed the Boston supervisor to "the seat of government, Brad, where it all happens." Mason politely refused the offer of a drink. The AD wanted to look and sound as an executive getting right to the point. He would explain why he ordered Mason's presence at HQ. "My friend, I am glad we finally get to meet. I will not mix words. I can help you—really help you."

Without pause, he offered Mason a lucrative, newly-created position at headquarters. The AD amplified all the benefits. "Brad, headquarters is the place to be, everything worthwhile happens here. It's where a smart person prepares for life after the bureau, for retirement, connects with the right people and all the rest." He loved to hear his own voice. Now confident he convinced the supervisor, he said, "I am offering you the opportunity of a lifetime."

What's the catch? Price displayed his very convincing bureaucratic scowl and continued. His scheme required Mason to prepare a detailed report of his lifelong relationship with Gabriel Randinoli, the New York Mafiosi. "I want you to recall everything—conversations beginning with your first day as an agent, every meeting, the whole enchilada that ever took place between you and the worthless hood, minute details. My friend, I think you understand. This means a great deal to us—to you and me."

"Listen," Price continued, "so you two grew up together, so what. You're not anything like him. He's a piece of crap. Let me tell you, I really hustled his rotten ass, Brad my friend, I gave him the bullshit about how much smarter he was than the rest of those bums. I even exaggerated a little." Price smiled.

Mason held back his anger. Price just told him Gabe met the AD. "You exaggerated sir, about what?" Mason said.

Price offered the phony smile and said, "I didn't want to ask you to approach him so I made the connection. You know, more muscle behind the contact. I let Randinoli believe you, his boyhood friend, supported the headquarter plan for the mobster to work with the FBI. I told the greasy guinea you and I talked often of how we wanted him to work with us." Mason's stomach muscles tightened thinking of Cuban Pete and his many Italian-American friends from the neighborhood and co-workers in the FBI.

Price now resembled a Cheshire cat. Mason read Price for a naive person, a jerk who didn't comprehend what it meant to come from 12th and Bruce and still call someone a friend no matter what road he traveled. "What did Gabe say, sir?"

The obese AD lifted his huge body from the extra-large beige leather chair and walked in front of the huge oak desk, still smiling. "The piece of shit told me to go and fuck myself. Can you imagine?" Price had no clue as to the relationship with "the piece of shit" and the man sitting before him. Price sat on the edge of the desk, the smile intact. "We both know that no one really cares about the likes of Mr. Gabriel Randinoli. When he goes, it'll be good riddance."

Mason's mind raced. "How do you mean 'when he goes'? Where's Gabe going?"

Price recovered and said, "Just a figure of speech. Enough about him. We're here to discuss your future, so let's continue."

Mason thought of the agreement he and Gabe had, "no discussion of business." *Gabe never told me of his meeting with Price. He kept his part of the bargain.*

Mason figured when Randinoli refused the offer he didn't consider Price a threat to anyone. His friend read Price like a book. Mason reflected back to the corner and Randinoli's decision-making faculty. If any such conversation actually took place, Price is not revealing the entire truth. *I wonder if Gabe dropped him.* Mason wondered how Price knew of the relationship between him and the LCN capo. The late night heart-to-heart conversations with his roommate at the academy never entered his mind.

At this juncture, Mason saw no benefit in showing his hand or, worse yet, dropping the fat bureaucrat. Although growing more impatient, Mason decided to follow Gallagher's advice. He would feign interest and listen to the rest of Price's fabrications. "If you'll fill me in I will…"

He never finished.

Price fantasized over his plan. He excitedly told the supervisor, "When the time comes to make my final pitch to the influential decision makers, I will impress with meticulous details. Of course, I will affix my signature and take credit for your detailed report. After my latest conversation with my friend Don Nittoli, I consider Randinoli's death a forgone conclusion." Price, now wide-eyed, was on a roll. "This will be the first-ever treatise of its kind. The wise guys will kill Gabriel Randinoli, a capo in the Bonanno crime family, when they learn he cooperated with me. I convinced him he had no choice. I made that crystal clear."

Price believed that the pols and presidential aides would have no choice but to recommend him for the big chair. Why allow any truth into the equation? He would lie about his meetings with the mobster, and insert untruths never said by Randinoli. He would insert the names of real mobsters, naming them responsible for the unsolved mob killings. Price would attribute all of his information to his personal informant, Gabriel Randinoli. At one time, he mistakenly told Mayhew, "Hearsay is infrequently challenged when its source is the Assistant Director of the FBI. He added, "No one checks the word or the work of an AD. We are infallible, not capable of making mistakes."

Mason made note Price never mentioned his clandestine meetings in New York with the big boss himself, Joe Nittoli.

Plan B was now moving along as Price planned. When Mason caves and accepts the transfer, the rest will be easy. All of FBIHQ will listen in awe as

Price speaks of how he convinced a high-ranking member of the Mafia to outline how the LCN is organized and its operation on a day-to-day basis. If the recent scuttlebutt on the Hill is true, the new Director will come from within the ranks and Price is certain to make the short list. He would step up the campaign to his cronies in the media, selling his ingenious strategy, his unparalleled plan to bring a cadre of highly successful and productive agents back to FBIHQ. Transferring Mason to headquarters would be another glowing example of his strategy. The detailed explanation will include his long thought-out conclusion that headquarters required more street talent to insure the field offices operated in the best interest of the bureau and the country.

At one time, the FBI denied the existence of a Mafia. Director Price will make organized crime his number one priority, his personal "attack against the mob." The press will devour the story.

Price relit his newly acquired and quite expensive Rinaldo pipe and took a long pull, speaking as the thick smoke elevated straight up. "I told you it's not my intention to mix words with you. I expect everything to move along without obstruction." A repeat of the phony smile. "You know I can make it happen, you would have no choice." The gloves were off. The Boston supervisor could feel the sting of the oft-spoken, unofficial government pressure.

"Sir, I feel threatened. Is that a threat?" Mason sounded concerned, perhaps somewhat frightened.

Now the attempt at sincerity disappeared, as did the smile. "Not at all. Consider it reality." There lay the black and white of the situation. The Boston supervisor must agree to drag his family from a home they love, the kids from great schools, and move to Washington D.C. where he would pose as the head of a sham Bonanno family investigative unit, or he would be forced into it. Price dictated the inevitable.

A lifetime flashed before him; Mason experienced a myriad of emotions.

Later in the day, recalling the entire meeting with Price, he placed a call to his friend. "You know Max, some of the stuff I used to hear at Saint Joseph's now makes sense."

Blaney asked, "Like what?"

"Sister Francis used to quote from somewhere in scripture, "and a man's enemies will be those of his own household."

"Amen, brother." Max Blaney recalled the reading from his early days in Bible study classes in Detroit. "My memory is that it is from Matthew, Chapter ten, verse thirty-six."

Despite Randinoli's business errors regarding his duties, Nittoli always forgave and allowed him to continue earning—and living. Mason, mindful of the oath sworn by his friend and mindful he may have broken a few rules, still believed Randinoli would survive. He always did. The man sitting in front of him admitted he spoke with Nittoli and put pressure on the boss to get rid of Mason's friend. He wanted to vomit. AD Price submitted bogus travel vouchers in support of his frequent visits to New York. He misrepresented his justification for the expensive travel. His travel in no way related to bureau business. Mason now held no doubts. One of the purposes of the law-breaking bogus trips was to end the life of the former tenor drummer.

It was clear that the AD did not identify with Randinoli, and he certainly had no idea who Mason was. No question, yes, he was inept, but AD Price wielded much power in the FBI and the entire national law enforcement community. He may be the most hated bureaucrat in the bureau, not because of his meteoric rise to power, but because of his actions. A few minutes passed. Price was now confident he would hear the compulsory answer he expected and demanded.

Mason thought of the kid volunteering at the shelter. *Time for a decision Brad my man.*

Mason knew his time in the bureau was near over; he and Blaney and the others would be retiring in a few years. If he stayed in the AD's company one minute longer Mason would act out something he would regret. The time came to end the meeting. The thought going through his mind would not scatter. Mason could not rid his brain of one important fact: Price wanted his friend from St. Joe's dead.

Mason asked very quietly, "Sir, when Gabe told you to go and fuck yourself?"

Price, feeling excited, said, "Yes, yes exactly, that's just what he said."

Mason continued, "Was he sitting or standing?"

The big man appeared confused, "Why, standing, what…?"

Mason said, "Well, in that case." He got up from his chair, stood eye to eye with the Assistant Director, lowered his voice and said, "Go and fuck yourself—Sir."

As Mason slowly turned and walked to the door, the AD's mouth appeared unable to close. His right eye twitched rapidly.

Price recovered and as the big door closed screamed a series of obscenities and threats. "And you will never know when it's coming or where it comes from."

The door closed on the elevator. Mason reached in his jacket and disengaged the recorder.

Chapter Fifty-Five

But a squealer?

For the present, AD Price had no choice other than to face the hard facts. He struck out with Randinoli first and now Mason. His approaches to both of them failed miserably. The wise guy told him what to do with the perceived threats. Then the FBI agent reinforced the idea. Now they will be dealt with so they fully understand their mistakes. The AD will personally handle Mason's punishment and will convince the head of the crime family to address a problem he is unaware of with Randinoli.

Mason's refusal to play ball resulted in the expected chain of events. Price told Mayhew, "The Boston supervisor better buy a vast supply of sunscreen. He'll be applying it year round. Mason will rot in the Deep South and no one will know who orchestrated Randinoli's demise. No one will learn of my meetings with Randinoli and Nittoli."

Thirty days after his conversation with Price at Headquarters, Mason received the official orders transferring his assignment from the Boston office to the Tampa, Florida, division. He learned that Price called SAC Gallagher before the transfer papers were cut. The actual office of assignment transfer reached Boston a week later. No guesswork about who caused it, the transfer emanated directly from "the office of AD Todd Price." Mason was more disappointed than anything else, knowing that a great organization let someone like Price slip between the cracks, into its ranks, and allowed him to climb to the position of Assistant Director. Price bragged at headquarters about how he gets things done. He giggled as he remarked to Mayhew about how "the sunny climate will do wonders for Mason's Irish, light skin condition. Skin cancer is rampant, a real money machine for an old classmate, the dermatologist. Florida is a great place for skin cancer, right?" A sinister smile—it appeared he won a major battle. Mayhew thought, "*He deserves his reputation as a coward and a ruthless bastard.*"

SAC Gallagher, not a newcomer to the ways of the bureau, had been around the block more than a few times during his career. He spent three years at headquarters prior to his promotion as SAC Boston. Gallagher learned a few facts concerning administrative matters, especially connected with transfers. The street agents were not privy to little known facts. An SAC possesses authority to preclude transfers out of his office for any number of justifications and for long periods of time. The usual reason included citing a particular priority investigation requiring the transferees' personal attention. A completed case readying for presentation to an AUSA would meet the standard. The SAC merely imposed the boilerplate "the needs of the bureau" into justification for any delay of transfer. He succeeded once before when Price ordered Mason to a meeting at the bureau. Gallagher used all the right words on the proper documents and with the support of the United States Attorney's Office justified Mason's contributions to the Boston office.

Gallagher, with Blaney's assistance, intended to thwart Price's attempt at the transfer by officially attesting it compulsory for Mason to remain involved in several ongoing investigations in New England. Once a transfer is postponed it's usually forgotten, and ultimately cancelled. The pending investigations in Boston supported Mason's delay and ultimate cancellation.

Price nursed another of his frequent hangovers. Mayhew listened to more of Price's grand plan. "I'm angry. But Mason's transfer will solve any further problems with him. The mobster is a different case. I'll convince the boss, what's his name?" Now his sarcastic self, "Oh right, Giuseppe Joe Nittoli. I met him several times when I was in New York. A typical mobster. I read him like a book. This time I'll convince the Don that Randinoli has been unfaithful to the Bonannos and during our meeting, requested by him, Randinoli furnished me with enough information to destroy the family. The boss will be forced to cut a deal and like magic, Mason's dear friend is finished for good. I believe the accepted term with these scum is he will "sleep with the fishes."

Price shouted to his secretary, "Get me on the early flight to Kennedy, first of course."

Nittoli agreed to the meeting. "Let's see what this moron has to say this time."

The boss had no intention of picking up and transporting Price to a meeting place. "I'll meet you at one o'clock at Wood Ibis restaurant in the

Bronx." The Bonanno-owned restaurant was operated by friends who lived part time in Florida, thus the name of the business. "Tell the cabbie it's on East 181st Street." Mason and Randinoli were not the only recorders of interesting conversations; Nittoli always remembered to bring his miniature along. He maintained the cassette containing their first meeting. He relished having the so-called good guy "on the record," and he'd take advantage of the AD's motor mouth.

After giving drink orders, Nittoli asked, "Todd, what brings you to New York this time?"

The AD gave his best conspiratorial look. He wanted to sound like a legitimate member of the world's preeminent law enforcement organization. "I will not waste your time or mine. You have a squealer in your organization."

Squealer? Nittoli withheld his smile. He thought, *maybe a rat or a problem—but a squealer? Too many 1930 Jimmy Cagney movies for this gavone.*

"One of your people is too close to one of my agents." Price used his practiced conspiratorial voice.

Already irritated, Nittoli thought, *"This man does not use first names when he speaks. He talks down to people."*

Nittoli appeared amused. "Todd, it has been such throughout history. The good guys talk to the bad guys and vice versa. Of course, we know who the real good guys are. Like right now, you and me, it's a game. We play each other, one outsmarting the other today and the other gets a turn tomorrow. It usually ends in a tie." Nittoli let this sink in. "I am well aware some of my people are on speaking terms with law enforcement. I myself have many friends in your business. The agents refer to this as working an informant or a necessary asset. My people call it bullshit or covering your ass."

Price sensed he needed to be more convincing; he must persuade Nittoli his captain is cooperating with the bureau, he must raise a specific problem with Nittoli. "You think this is a harmless game?" He would play his trump card. "I'm sure one Gabriel Randinoli has told you of his meeting with me?" Price was ready for a yes or no. If yes, he would lie about the meeting and say that Randinoli spilled his guts.

Nittoli was ready for such a question. He had listened carefully to the recording of the meeting his capo had with Price. He feigned surprise, "No, he did not, and I don't believe you."

Price smiled. "I didn't think so. And of course he will deny it if you confront him. So I will get to the point. He wants a deal for himself.

Randinoli does not want to spend one day in prison. Your employee is furnishing the FBI with valuable information, and as a result we will successfully prosecute members of your organization as well as other families."

Don Nittoli, the head of the most feared criminal enterprise in the country, went speechless. He stared at Price, concealing his true feelings, and realized the AD wanted to have Randinoli killed. And he expected the family to make it happen.

Price hid his joy, as he seriously misread the Don's reaction. "So, we understand each other. As I stated, Randinoli is very close to one of my agents. The two go back to their days in New Jersey. You can check it out."

"Who is your agent?" The Don probed, to see how far this despicable creature would go.

"I have no intention of giving up the names of any of my people." *No rush! It's important to come across as a strong yet fair leader.*

Nittoli insisted. "Not good enough. You say Gabe is a rat, who says so— you? And why are you telling me this garbage?"

The AD, ignoring the last question, spat out, "The agent's name is Brad Mason, a thorn in my side who will pay dearly for his behavior."

Nittoli pushed aside the half-filled glass of wine. He was aggravated. The Don would finish with this narcissist and return to running his business. It's common knowledge, Randinoli and the FBI agent were both born and raised in Newark, stayed in touch and reunited from time to time. Randinoli never attempted to hide the relationship; he spoke to his boss of the meetings. Nittoli never feared the two friends discussed business. Nittoli never discussed business with his personal law enforcement acquaintances. He decided he would someday meet Mason. The capo said that his friend was a baseball nut. The Don would enjoy discussing his favorite sport with another lover of America's pastime.

Why was this *uno strattone* dropping both names? The boss rightly figured that Price wanted Randinoli dead. The "I" in FBI stood for Integrity. *This worm has none.* Nittoli concluded AD Price had no honor. The Bonanno boss believed Price, for a second time, attempted to ingratiate himself with a Mafia boss and at some future date, the AD would expect a favor. The crime boss was certain Price did not care one iota how Nittoli and associates earned their living. Price wanted something more than his present position. The next comment from the AD supported the Don's reasoning.

"Of course, when I am in complete control of the FBI's so-called war against organized crime, it will be a war in name only. The propaganda will satisfy the media and the citizenry. You personally will not be troubled."

Price attempted a conspiratorial smile. "I understand business is business. It will have no impact on your life."

Nittoli heard more than enough. He listened to the ranting of a sick person. *Perhaps he's mentally unbalanced. Yet still dangerous if allowed to continue in a prominent position within the FBI.* "I must get back to my work. We will conduct our own investigation and act accordingly." He purposely avoided setting up another meeting. The Don did not offer to shake hands.

Not yet finished, Price said, "I'm sure you will see what I say is true. I know you will never divulge what I have said here today. As for Mr. Mason, I will personally take care of him and his career. I will not fool with him, he will pay." Price figured these words would add to his bona fide. He attempted to impress with his spoken toughness. Nittoli would later discover that this too was a lie. Price had already ordered Mason relocated against his wishes.

Nittoli left the restaurant and walked directly to the curbside where his driver waited in the new Lincoln. The Don delayed until safely in the vehicle before turning off the recorder.

Price satisfied, motioned for the waiter. His performance deserved a strong drink. It took a while but now, February 1987, he finally smelled victory.

Chapter Fifty-Six

Business is business

The first week in December 1987, Joe Nittoli made a personally painful yet necessary pronouncement. He reluctantly issued the order. Gabe Randinoli, a caporegime of the family, "must die." The order to kill his favorite captain came with a heavy heart, yet Nittoli justified the hit to himself. Randinoli, in spite of his dedication to the family and the money he earned, botched more than one assigned contract. Over a decade had passed since Cesare Allizio was killed and his mutilated body found and identified. Five years ago, Stevie Lombardi never emptied his weapon when he and Randinoli and others fouled up another hit. In 1982, Teamster official Anthony Yandola made the hit parade, and after taking nine rounds throughout his obese body, lived to testify about family business. In 1984, John "Johnny Boy" Maggio was killed by Specs Buchanan and his body was later located by law enforcement. Finally, Don Nittoli assigned Randinoli a bad rap for the Robert Mamoli and Bats Tato screw-up earlier last year.

The Mamoli contract took place during inclement weather in May of 1986, when members of the Bonanno family murdered family associate Robert Mamoli. The Don's order called for one assassination, not two.

Randinoli's explanation was short and simple. "The drug pusher was a surprise. I gave the okay because he would have been around to testify against the four of us."

True, Bats Tato turned up at the wrong place at the wrong time but paying with his life could not be justified. At the time, underboss Carmine Cuccio argued that killing Tato in broad daylight was stupid. "Who says he would have testified? We would have been given the opportunity to talk to him and convince him that testifyin' against us was a bad idea." Randinoli held the Mamoli contract and he and members of his crew, Stevie Lombardi and Charlie Sassano, were responsible for both murders. He placed the blame squarely on the capo, Gabe Randinoli.

No matter Randinoli's justification for killing Tato, the Don considered it bad business. The required permission attached only to Mamoli and not to an innocent civilian. The elderly consigliere Richard Poli reluctantly agreed with the boss. He offered a simple explanation. "Once Mamoli was hit, unfortunately Tato had to go. That said, if Gabe had to do it over he would wait until Mamoli was alone and get the work done close up and personal."

Randinoli's scorecard read seven at bats, five hits, and four errors to include hitting the wrong ball. This was considered a very good batting average for a major league baseball player, but very mediocre for a seasoned hit man.

The boss always valued the financial contribution of his capo. He recalled a decade ago, giving Randinoli a pass for the Allizio work strictly a result of the money. Now he thought, *"We will miss the inc*ome*, but business is business."*

The Don reached the underboss Carmine Cuccio and advised him of his decision. "Carmine, this is an important piece of business. It will upset a lot of people but it must be done. I will let you know who will do the work." Don Nittoli recognized that his underboss was pleased to hear the news.

Nittoli summoned a top-secret meeting at a little-known coffee and donut shop on Staten Island. On the Tuesday evening requested by Nittoli, the owner posted the "closed" sign on the front door of the business. At the meeting he told the underboss and the other attendees, "Gabe spends time talking to the feds although there is no reason to believe the discussions are business-related. Gabe told me personally that growing up in Jersey his best friend was now a fed, but the two never discussed business. I have no reason to mistrust a sworn man. I believed what he said. I still do. Yet as you know, he failed more than once carrying out our work." He let his reasoning sink in. "I will let Carmine know who will do the work. It will be soon."

Nittoli did not disclose that an upper-echelon FBI person, Assistant Director Todd Price, during one of the surreptitious meetings between the two leaders, dropped the dime that Randinoli lied to his boss. Don Nittoli rightly figured Price to be a lowlife, but retaining a position as Assistant Director in the FBI lent at least some credibility to the story. Randinoli's mishandling of specific contracts and pressure from family members, coupled with Price's accusations, were all enough to order the hit.

When he was alone, the boss again played the tape. Price told Nittoli, "Through the years, Randinoli passed valuable information to his FBI friend later used to prosecute cases against several people in your family and other mob individuals." Price told the boss that his capo spent a great deal of time with his FBI friend since Randinoli's promotion as the family's principal representative in northern New Jersey. Nittoli did not like nor trust the man, an Assistant Director in the FBI. Price appeared more calculating than many of his mob associates. Nittoli's impression of the AD never wavered. He said, "Those who sneak around dropping dimes on associates are as bad as any who kill and commit other crimes. Price is proof that the so-called moral people are anything but... I'm happy his words are a matter of record."

Price, the perfect example of someone using words and rank to destroy lives, released false information knowing the result could cause the ruthless termination of another human being. Why would such a high-ranking bureau official say such things? He recalled that Price initiated the first contact with the Bonanno boss. At that time, Price leaked a bogus story that he possessed valuable information that could benefit Nittoli. The boss of the Bonanno family saw no down side to meeting with the fed. Price's valuable information turned out to be lies.

It became obvious that Price's heavy drinking led to more drivel. Price thought that Nittoli trusted him and the two could share close secrets and personal objectives without any compunction. Nittoli learned two undisputable facts about his source. The AD despised Randinoli's friend in the FBI, and Price, the big number two, would do whatever necessary to become the next Director of the FBI. Nittoli thought, *"That is his business, it will not influence or have an effect on my family. If this 'nome importante' becomes the Director of the FBI, someone will be interested in playing back a few tapes for this 'bugiardo.'"*

Nittoli finally put aside his personal feelings for Randinoli. He had reconciled himself to his dictum to have the capo murdered. Further, he never doubted the reason for Price's hatred of Mason. The agent refused to use his friend's position in LCN to help a rat like Price become the Director of the FBI, and at the same time boost his own career. The crime boss understood loyalty. It was no contest choosing between the two FBI men. When the contract completed, he would take steps to help his capo's friend. Nittoli shared with his consigliere. "Brad Mason will think fondly of his friend when he hears how Gabe stood up to the powerful FBI man while keeping a promise to Mason. The tapes speak volumes. Gabe never discussed business."

Chapter Fifty-Seven

I hope your guy is wrong

Mason said, "What the hell are you saying?" The phone call came from an FBI agent, a close friend.

The call originated from the Newark FBI office. The voice at the other end repeated the message. "I hear from a source that our friend may be whacked by his own people. He apparently made some major blunders. Don Nittoli is under pressure to take him out. The source owes me and sees this as a way to pay back. Brad, we both know that these rumors come and go but if the info is accurate and the contract signed, there is nothing to be done about it, right?"

Mason ignored the query. "I leave for Jersey tomorrow afternoon. Can we meet someplace?"

Mazalewski answered, "Absolutely, how about the place in Belleville. Six work for you?"

"I'll be there. Be safe."

The connection ended. Neither man found it necessary to talk further.

The next evening, a few minutes after six p.m., Mason walked through the front door of the Belleville bar and restaurant. He waved to the owner, Billy Bambrick, an old friend. Mazalewski, already seated in the corner, nodded as Mason moved toward the booth. "I ordered a couple of Dewars, you good with that?"

"Scotch is fine. You just get here?" Mason could never figure out how his roommate from the academy always managed to arrive first for any engagement or assignment.

Mazalewski caught the drift of the inquiry and laughed. "Right, I've been here for at least a half hour. I thought you might be a little early for a change."

Mason welcomed the shot. "Maz, if you stayed busy like normal people you wouldn't have so much time on your hands." They both smiled as a young woman set the drinks in front of them. "So, you were saying?"

"But before I begin. Congratulations, I heard of your transfer to the Tampa division. I'll bet AD Price took a personal interest in that move."

"Absolutely, Max and Gene Gallagher are working on getting it killed. No matter, we could be gone before all the paperwork gets resolved. Now, your informant?"

"The source is not a made guy," Mazalewski said. "That said, he is close to the action. He gives me more credit than I deserve. A few years back he reached out for me. Now he believes I went to bat for him on a robbery beef involving hot televisions and computers moving interstate. Actually, I could not have helped him even if I wanted to. The case was weak and he walked with a misdemeanor and no jail time. To this day, I let him think whatever he wants."

Mazalewski described the conversation with the source as close as he recalled. "I never mentioned your friend. It came unexpectedly, or as our roommate Ray Mendez always said, 'Right out of the freakin' blue.' The bottom line is, he offered the information to show how important he is and how much he knows. I can't vouch for its veracity."

"What exactly did he say?"

"First thing he says is it is highly unusual for this stuff to get out. The family does not want other members to know the name of someone making the hit list. The name is always a top secret. Then he says that loose lips sink ships and that kind of thing. Anyway, he says a big shot captain named Randinoli could make the hit parade. Apparently, through the years Gabe got careless and made too many mistakes. The source didn't know what the specific problems were. Whatever, he surmised Gabe never saw them as mistakes. The source acted surprised because Gabe is recognized as a huge earner. He turns in a great deal of scratch to the family, more than anybody." Mazalewski sipped his drink and thought of something. "Oh, and at the end, he added that there's talk of information about Gabe coming from one of *our* guys. He called the unknown guy a quote 'heavy hitter' with the feds. He didn't have any specifics about this, meaning the outside information. That part is more likely bogus."

Mason discarded the last comment. He believed the source's information was real. During one of their conversations, Gabe said the same thing. At the time, Mason incorrectly thought the individual to be one of the New York OC heavyweights. He intended to speak with Supervisor Wells but never found the time.

"Maz, I hope your guy is wrong." Mason searched for more to say but couldn't find the right words.

Mazalewski was one of the few people familiar with the close relationship between his friend and Randinoli, both growing up in Newark. "We both know there is categorically not a thing we can do. Look at the facts. These things are always kept top secret. No one knows of anyone making the list until the deed is done. So, it's more likely all bullshit. If there's any truth to what this guy heard then Gabe probably has the same info. Let me repeat, a contract to whack someone stays absolutely quiet. You don't hear of it until the body is found or someone goes missing. That said, it's not unusual for the wise guys to break each other's balls. 'Hey, I hear you made the list' or, 'keep messin' with me and you go to the top of the hit parade.' That kind of stuff. Anyway, Gabe will do what he needs to do. Maybe he goes to Nittoli and asks him flat out, pleads his case or whatever. If the story is all bullshit, as is more likely the case, he ignores it and then, no harm no foul. I wanted you current on the latest rumor mill, that's all."

Mason challenged the information. "Maz, you're sure Gabe would have the same information? Maybe I should call him."

"No question on that score. My source says Gabe would definitely hear the same story. And no, I don't think you should call. Besides, you two never discuss business, right? This is business." Mazalewski sounded sure of himself.

"Okay, call if anything else comes up. You're going back to New York tomorrow. Maybe there's some new news circulating." Mason finished his drink.

Mazalewski had more to say. "You know I have a relationship with Don Nittoli. This would be a first—even for me. If you think I should…"

Mason interrupted. "Thanks Maz, I appreciate that. Let's wait and see what shakes out."

"Okay, I'll be in touch. In the meantime, relax. You are the shortest of the short timers. It's not far off; we're only a few years away. Then we can handle the stuff the bureau can't. After you retire and then Max, we have Judy, Joe and Dennis, and of course, your roommate and trainer. Ya know, I don't think I'll miss the bu as much knowing we'll be working together."

"You're right on, roomie. It looks like the void will be filled with some interesting overseas investigations. You take care of yourself."

The two friends embraced. "Thanks buddy, a few more years and the bon voyage extravaganza."

Mazalewski spoke of plans in the mix for months. In a couple of years the group would retire within weeks of each other. Plans for the new entity, Global Private Investigation, Inc., were in play. Mason and Blaney, the two principals of GPI, would leave the bureau followed by Judy Nassan, Dennis Moore, Mike Reagan and Mazalewski. He kept it quiet for the moment, but Mason recently spoke with friends from Chicago who could possibly be joining the new venture. An old friend from the corner, a most important part of the new organization, already gave the thumbs up to the new venture.

On the return flight to Boston, Mason could think of nothing else. He last spoke with Randinoli two weeks prior. There was nothing said to raise any flags. His friend sounded the same, everything was great and his career on the rise, the predictable wise cracks and no more. As per the rules, the friends didn't discuss business. *Yet Gabe sounded different. Maybe he heard what Maz heard.*

He wondered how Randinoli would act if he heard he made the hit list. What choices did he have? Mason smiled as he pictured his friend wrestle with his options. *How about the witness protection program, Gabe? "No thanks, no time for that, I'm a busy man. Besides, I'm nobody's witness and I don't need protection.'*

Mason would call the capo when he landed in Boston.

Chapter Fifty-Eight

My way

Mason left a message each time he reached out for his friend.

It turned out to be the real thing—no rumor. Nittoli assigned the contract to kill Randinoli to his underboss Carmine Cuccio, a ruthless, well-tested assassin. The boss shared minimal information with Cuccio. He kept his instructions simple. "In New Jersey, Gabe met up with an old friend, now a fed, and got careless. The Don never mentioned the conversations that he himself held with FBI Assistant Director Price. Nittoli, never really troubled with the way Randinoli handled the Allizio and Yandola contracts, was still very much aware that many believed that someone should pay. He halfheartedly used Price's information to justify the hit.

"You know all you need to know, Carmine. You are the underboss of the family and I give you this work because of its importance. Just get it done right, understand? No ad-libs, no suffering! Boom, over and done with! Understand?" Now the boss was not able to hide his emotion. "I mean it. No suffering—not even a little."

Cuccio nodded in agreement. "I will take care of it," he quickly responded. They embraced, kissing on both cheeks. The underboss did not share the Don's sentiments for the named target. Jealous of the capo for years, Cuccio discreetly campaigned within the family to get rid of Randinoli.

Reliable assets later communicated to law enforcement personnel that Nittoli instructed him to "make absolutely sure, no screw-ups." Cuccio earned his reputation. He was one ruthless son of a bitch, a psychopathic killer. The two-inch purple scar on his left cheek added to his tough guy façade. This he received as a young leg-breaker, prior to making his bones. Cuccio genuinely enjoyed the killing aspect of his chosen profession.

Cuccio selected hardened killer capo James "Jimmy" Palmeri, longtime family associate Dinny "Specs" Buchanan, and capo Charlie Sassano to form the hit team. All three were at one time part of Randinoli's crew. Buchanan, another psychopath, was closer to Randinoli than any member of the family and Cuccio would enjoy watching him suffer as his friend died. Buchanan was upset and bewildered by the order. The associate wanted to refuse the work, maybe feign sickness, but figured he did not have enough information regarding the reason for the hit. Buchanan felt grateful that the assignment of doing the main work went to Palmeri. He did a lot of work with the intended victim and was not looking forward to the job. He thought, *"I won't enjoy this. Thank God I'm not doin' the close up and dirty work."*

Sassano and three selected guns were responsible to serve as follow-up, insuring no tails were in place and providing security for the lead car. The ruse set up by Cuccio included telling Randinoli there was a sizable debt overdue and the collection required a large, experienced crew. "Gabe knows these things happen in our business. He will not be suspicious. Jimmy, you tell him it's the guys from upstate and we expect opposition. On more than one occasion, he became involved with large collections from those people." Randinoli's violent approach always resulted in family debts favorably resolved.

Randinoli's girlfriend, Mae Jong, told him Mason called a few times and left short messages on the answering machine. She didn't sound concerned and said, "He said to call him when you receive the message."

"I'm running late, I'll get back to him after I finish some work. It won't take long." Randinoli rushed from the apartment and hurried to his car.

The capo accepted Palmeri's reason for the meeting. He had no cause to doubt his old friend and fellow capo. Randinoli exceeded the speed limit and was punctual for the meeting. At the 4th Street headquarters, he found a parking space across the street from the store. He pulled his overcoat up, shielding his ears from the December cold. He leisurely waved to a few members as he walked in the building and approached the table where the underboss sat alone.

He was surprised to see the underboss. "Carmine, how goes it?" It happened quickly. Palmeri and one of Sassano's guns quickly came from behind a counter and forced Randinoli to the back section of the store. Cuccio threatened, "You know the drill Gabe, no struggle. Just let it happen—make it easier." The scene mirrored a Hollywood movie script. The hit team forced him to lie face down on the worn linoleum-tiled floor. Palmeri deftly covered

Randinoli's head with a clean, black cotton towel while Sassano tied his wrists behind his back using thin shade strings. Cuccio reached in and removed Randinoli's revolver from inside his breast pocket and handed it to one of the guns. "Here, hold on to this. He won't need it where he's goin'." The loaded weapon, a Smith and Wesson .38 Special Revolver with a two-inch barrel, was now Randinoli's favorite, better known on the streets as a "38 Special."

Randinoli did not speak. His brain would not quiet, it spun in circles. Could this be happening? Randinoli often thought of how he would feel knowing his life would be over. He forced a slight smile. Everyone in the business knew a hit list existed. But the Godfather liked him; the kid from the corner never anticipated anything like this. Surprised and upset with himself that he was caught off guard, now he would take what came and make the best of it. Blackie said it many times: "You roll the dice, you take your chances."

As they rehearsed, Palmeri and Buchanan each held an arm and led Randinoli through to the back entrance where the stolen 1972 Oldsmobile sedan waited with the engine running. Earlier, the car was lifted from a used car lot in the Bronx. Palmeri said, "The last thing I need is my old lady complaining about blood stains in the Caddy."

In the back seat, Cuccio sat directly behind Randinoli who was strapped into the passenger seat. Buchanan settled in behind Palmeri, the selected driver. Four individuals followed close in a year-old Lincoln Continental. Earlier, Cuccio had emphasized repeatedly: "There will be no mistakes. At the completion of the job, we want the big man to be happy. We make the hit and immediately we bury the body. Gabe's remains must never be located." He spoke these words again, showing total disregard for the victim, once a highly-respected member of the Bonanno family. Cuccio enjoyed others' discomfort. Randinoli remained quiet; he never spoke a word.

Gabe surprised himself. He was nervous but not afraid of the inevitable. Was he actually surprised, or had he been expecting this for some time? Did he really want to die? He smiled to himself, his mind wandering. "*Would that be something, Brad stopping the vehicle, and placing everyone under arrest. He could charge me with anything, maybe 'failure to do right.'*" His mind drifted back to the days at 12th and Bruce. He recalled his friend saying, "I pray. I don't know—it works for me."

The exit road off Jones Parkway travelled in a large loop around a huge billboard sign that read, "Wheaties, Breakfast of Champions." It depicted a big-league pitcher throwing a baseball. Buchanan spoke, softer than usual, "Hey Gabe, you go see the Red Sox/Yanks play at the stadium, right?" There was no answer. "You won't miss much this year, a bad season comin' up." Buchanan resigned himself to the inevitable. He did not want this to happen, and was the only one actually trying to make light conversation to help relax his friend. Palmeri too considered Randinoli a friend, but took the work in stride, business as usual.

Cuccio said, "Anuffa that. I'll do the talkin'." He dominated the conversation during the ride from mob headquarters to the warehouse on Commercial Wharf in the Red Hook section of Brooklyn. He pontificated that his heart was not in the contract. The underboss leaned over the seat to place his mouth close to Randinoli's ear and spoke quietly, for effect. "You know I always liked you, Gabe." He smiled at Palmeri, who was watching through the rear-view mirror. "I mean, smart, tough—we all benefited, you made a bundle of money for all us guys." Randinoli made one of his decisions. Going back to one of the first lessons he learned at the corner he remained quiet. From prior experience, he was familiar with Cuccio's reputation for sheer ruthlessness. Randinoli used to admire the brutality but now he refused to show any feelings. On more than one occasion, Cuccio enjoyed watching and listening as a victim begged for mercy. He sought that reaction from Randinoli. Will it come? Cuccio roughly removed the blindfold from the target's face. Again, he placed his mouth next to his victim's ear.

The underboss persisted. "Hey Gabe, you might as well take your last look at the world. What's today anyway? Oh yeah, December 13, 1987. Number thirteen, not a good sign."

The kid from 12th Avenue and Bruce Street stared straight ahead, never whispering a sound.

The psycho gangster became angry. He was about to end this guy's life and no display of emotion—nothing. The others were not happy with the way things were going. Cuccio wanted a reaction of some sort. Most guys about to buy it cried or begged, attempted to cut a deal, some wet themselves. Randinoli would not give him the satisfaction.

"Jimmy, turn on the radio, maybe some music will help." Cuccio looked ecstatic when Sinatra's "My Way" was introduced.

"Gabe, I wish I could stop this, you know that, eh, right? I mean you fucked up and the man says you go, right? So you go. What can I do?" He acted as though he was truly sorry. Ol' blue eyes continued, "*And now the end is near and so I face the final curtain.*"

The others in the car were not enjoying Cuccio's taunting words or the funeral music. They were anxious to finish the job and return to one of the bars. Buchanan especially looked forward to getting hammered at the bar he and Gabe frequented. Palmeri thought the same as the others; this maniac could be the next boss, *God help us.* The car arrived at the warehouse and Palmeri deftly pulled up to the door and waited.

"Yes, there were times, I'm sure you knew when I bit off more than I could chew."

The overhead garage door opened very quietly. An elderly man dressed in greasy mechanic's overalls nodded recognition and immediately disappeared to the back end of the building.

Sassano's back-up car arrived a few seconds later and parked directly in front of the garage door. The heavy metal overhead door then closed, creating a loud thud. As the plans called for, Randinoli was quickly removed from the front seat by Palmeri and one of Sassano's men. They steered him and placed him face first to a sidewall filled with bathing beauties. Now Cuccio felt assured he would hear what he expected, especially with Sassano and his people as interested observers. Sassano and the others waited and watched.

Cuccio went over the planned killing several times during the previous two weeks, detailing exactly how the contract would be accomplished. Everything was now in place. The underboss, with Nittoli's approval, previously ordered Jimmy Palmeri to carry out the actual execution. There would be no screw-ups, at close range, one shooter only. Cuccio repeatedly gave the explicit instruction. "Three in the back of the head, over and out."

Cuccio desperately needed to hear the skipper beg or at least show some sign of fear. "Gabe, I meant what I said, I really like you." He again lowered his volume and spoke almost in a whisper. "As your good friend, how do you want it?"

Buchanan, the only associate present, had heard enough. "The boss was clear Carmine, no ad-libbing. Do the work!" Underboss or not, the others had enough of Cuccio's sick theatrics.

In a moment, the garage became still. In his last moments, Gabriel Randinoli's silence offered a message. Later one of the hit team would say he thought he saw Randinoli moving his lips, as though in prayer. Randinoli, in his last living moments, received some of the respect he always craved. His mind raced, returned to the happy days at 12th and Bruce. He could hear the near perfect execution of Saint Joe's crisp drum line. He very clearly pictured the homeless shelter, and a smiling Sister Francis. He smiled as he thought of his father and his friend. He relaxed as he prepared for the end of whatever was coming. He smiled as he remembered a conversation with his friend—and he prayed.

Cuccio was near anger. He glanced toward Sassano, and then nodded to Palmeri.

Cuccio muttered, "Merry Christmas, captain." Before any more taunting, Palmeri, the first made guy Randinoli met, fired three quick shots from the .22 caliber revolver. Randinoli never heard Sinatra's ending.

"To think I did all that; and may I say – not in a shy way, no, oh no not me, I did it my way."

Buchanan mouthed, "Sláinte, my friend."

Standing next to him, Sassano asked, "Specs, what'd you say?"

Buchanan looked callously at the capo without responding. For a brief moment he thought of putting a round between Cuccio's eyes.

Years ago, Randinoli followed up on one of his decisions. More than anything else in life he ached to be a real wise guy, someone respected because of his association with La Cosa Nostra. His chosen family today carried out a decision of its own. Randinoli's life reached a violent conclusion. Fifteen years ago he swore, while speaking an oath, that he would live and die by the rules and regulations defined by La Cosa Nostra. Now 1987, the Christmas season, at age fifty, a mob rule ended his life.

Cuccio, with plenty of experience disposing of bodies, earlier conducted his own research. His first choice was "The Hole" in Ozone Park, Queens, but recent activity in the area changed his mind. "Put him in the trunk of your car. Bring him to the Staten Island burial grounds. No one must ever find the body, or we will join him very soon." Palmeri and Buchanan could never claim they misunderstood the orders received from Cuccio. There was no ambiguity. Don Nittoli insisted on a clean murder, saying, "Leave nothing for the cops to identify and investigate."

The two guns wrapped the body in thick clear plastic and placed their recently deceased friend in the trunk of the stolen car. They drove to Staten Island to the well-known dumping area. Working with new spades, they dug out a grave, dropped the body in, and filled the grave. It was all in a day's work.

Loyalty? Omertà? How long does it last? Certainly not forever with some people. The whippoorwills continued to chirp. A few years later, one of the most ruthless members of the Bonanno syndicate, Carmine Cuccio, fully cooperated with the feds, furnishing specific, well-coached testimony. He testified that he "carried out the ordered hit in 1987 when, during the Christmas holidays, we lured Gabriel Randinoli to a warehouse in Brooklyn where he was shot three times in the head—he died instantly." During testimony, he sucked up to the news reporters when he described the actual shooter, Jimmy Palmeri, as "the best in New York." At the trial, the new whippoorwill lied that he and his associates buried Randinoli in a Staten Island warehouse. He swore that he could not point out the exact spot. The prosecutors were not at all concerned about such a minor issue. The body would remain missing.

Although he earned millions for the family, Randinoli ended up penniless, discounting a few thousand dollars his girlfriend found in a dresser drawer. There was no "golden parachute," no stock savings, 401-K or IRA to leave to any family members, not to mention his harem of female friends. An informant correctly stated, "There's no retirement package in this business. You take care of your own pension plan or you don't get one."

The crapshooters from the 12th and Bruce schoolyard, Blackie Capone and Tony Quinn, organized a collection among the old neighborhood people. They quietly garnered the contributions. Following the Mass as Saint Joseph's, Don Nittoli also left an envelope at St. Joe's club. Inside was ten thousand dollars in cash and the outside was marked, "Gabe's father." Cuban Pete Randinoli gave the envelope to Mason. "Please see that this is returned. We don't take charity, especially when it's blood money." The aging tailor started to weep, "the blood of my son." Mason later gave the envelope to Mazalewski who returned it without comment to the head of the Bonanno family.

The properties signed for and in the name of Gabriel Randinoli were immediately transferred by mob attorneys to blind trusts. The trustees listed included several shady law firms. The assassins even assumed ownership of Randinoli's year-old Caddy. It was not the first time Palmeri took possession of a victim's assets. "Finders keepers, losers weepers."

Chapter Fifty-Nine

They got our friend

It became official in January 1988. Boston SAC Gene Gallagher was successful in suspending SSA Mason's transfer to Tampa. Familiar with the bureau agent transfer system, the SAC placed the right wording on the right forms and AD Price's command became history.

Once again, Gallagher proved he knew his way around the FBI bureaucracy. "Supervisor Mason, I think you need to get out of Boston until you make your official exit. I have just the place to utilize your idle time. We won't need to field calls from our friend at FBIHQ." Gallagher ordered the interdivision transfer.

The following Monday, Mason was named supervisor of an undercover special operations group (SOG). He now spent his time at an offsite west of Boston. He welcomed the relaxed dress code, tired of suits and ties. The particular assignment dictated what the SOG agents wore. They were all trained in UC work and fit in with most scenarios. One day they were dressed as longshoremen on the docks waiting for a stolen shipment to arrive; the next day might find someone posed as a bank teller aiding in a bank fraud and embezzlement investigation.

The SOG stayed busy with cases emanating from Boston headquarters. Each supervisor worth their salt requested some kind of assistance from the SOG; either surveillance or a court-approved installation, or whatever tasks the suits could not perform. For many years, the Boston and New York SOGs were acknowledged as the best in the bureau. They worked together as so many bad guys traveled between New York and New England. Every day the squad worked OC, WCC or foreign counter intelligence priorities.

SOG air and ground teams were undeniably necessary weapons. The ability to deprive a target of an alibi as to his whereabouts aided the prosecutors preparing indictments. The half dozen SAs involved in the technical operations kept a full schedule, as well, performing the covert entries requiring installation of court approved audio and visual assets. The agents moved in and out of the offsite space around the clock. Mason juggled cases, agent schedules and his own sparse personal life. Each Boston headquarter supervisor or "suit" viewed his squad's mission as one requiring priority attention. The steady request for undercover assistance, ground and air surveillances, and covert audio and video installations were all handled—albeit not in the time span wished for by the individual squads.

The SOG secretary became quite comfortable with the mantra. She would tell the requesting supervisor, "You are on the list. We will call when your turn comes up." They didn't like the rule but accepted it as a facet of doing business.

His friend went missing at Christmastime and now, a week into the new year of 1988, the word came late in the afternoon. In the garage, Mason and one of the pilots planned a request for coverage of an active counterfeiting ring. The United States Secret Service (USSS) considered the matter a priority. USSS had spent all of their sparse manpower on the investigation for the past eighteen months and prepared to make arrests. The bureau provided the air and ground support. The speaker clicked on. "Brad, you have a call on six." Mason, thinking it was yet another urgent need of the "suits," picked up the nearest phone in the garage.

Into the worn-out receiver, he said, "Mason."

"I thought you'd want to hear it from me." Mason immediately recognized the voice and picked up on the fact that the caller's voice sounded uncharacteristically soft. The caller said, "They got our friend."

Mason swallowed hard, and hesitated. "When? How?"

Mazalewski did not want to answer.

"Maz, talk to me."

"Okay, sometime around Christmas week, actually it would be…let's see…I have a calendar here…December 13… right, Sunday December 13. The word is three in the back of the head. I'm pulling out all the stops. If I learn more I'll call immediately. If that works for you."

"I guess so, thanks—thanks for the heads up, you take care. I'll be in touch." The phone went silent. He placed the handset in the cradle and sat motionless. Brad Mason was confused. Maz said around Christmas week. He smiled to himself as he heard Gabe saying, *First I do a little more Christmas shoppin' Ho, Ho, Ho!*" He would keep the date in his head for a long time—December 13, 1987. He heard Maz's voice, *"three in the back of the head."*

There's a big difference between knowing something could happen and learning it actually took place. His mind ran to clear recollections of the corner of 12ᵗʰ Avenue and Bruce Street. Mason often thought it may end for Gabe in an awful way, and now he struggled to convince himself that it was real. The friends learned something in Saint Joe's: *"We do not pick or choose the outcomes, they happen exactly the way God chooses."* His mind continued racing. The order had to come from Nittoli. That's right, but with help from another organization? *Anything is possible when one recalls the garbage littered by one individual at FBIHQ. Maybe he didn't pull the trigger but…someone will pay.*

Mason would confirm Maz's story. He left the building and walked to the local coffee shop. After an hour, he left his untouched coffee and returned to the SOG. It could be a rumor, not unusual in Gabe's business. True, Maz worked OC in the Big Apple for years and maintained a close acquaintance with the Bonanno boss, Joe Nittoli. Maz always obtained accurate intelligence. Still, this needed to be verified.

He placed a call to New York. "He'll know why I'm calling. Tell him I'll wait to hear from him." Max Blaney was now running a special at the New York Office. Within the hour he returned Mason's call. "Maz is right on. It's all speculation regarding the shooters but no discrepancy with the informant feedback. No surprise, nothing out there about the location of the body."

Mason walked out of the building without saying anything to anyone. He drove aimlessly around the city and then parked in an empty lot next to the town library. His eyes reddened as he pictured his friend after one of his adventures and heard his voice: *"Hey, I got it figured, no problem."*

News travels fast, especially bad news. Friends from the old neighborhood called to offer condolences and vent their anger. Tempers were rising. Never a person to hold back, Johnny Zatz said, "I think a quick visit to the city settles the matter. I talked with Blackie, Tony, and a few others. They asked me to call you first. We think you need to stay out of this one. As those people like to say, we will do the work." Zatz always stored a supply of weapons of mass destruction. "I just got a new order. The military just came out with these grenades…"

Mason did his best to dissuade the plan. "Zatzie, what say we hold up on that? Officially, he's missing. Yeah, we know what that means but maybe some more information will come out." He did his best to sound convincing.

He added, "Zatzie, this is not a 12th and Bruce get-even thing. We both know Gabe made decisions years back and never drifted from his choices."

Zatz said, "True, if this was business and he died as a direct result of the career... like Blackie always said, business is business. If it turns out to be a whole new ball game and retaliation is in order, then we give it our attention. You good with that?"

Mason gave his word, "My man, we give it some time. I'll get back to you."

Zatz lightened up. "Ya know Brad, I was remembering how the little shit talked about the mafia. Gabe said, 'It sure beats being a politician or something really dirty. They are the real dangerous ones.'"

Mason forced a laugh. "You're right about that. He said the big difference was that the politicians lie and cheat every day, the wise guys only once in a while."

Zatz wanted to talk. "But you're right about Gabe and his decisions. His mind was settled on being a wise guy from day one. At times Gabe thought he was invincible, almost untouchable. I remember Zebep warning him 'you can't keep drinking from the same well.' Brad, say hello to...whoever. You take care of yourself." He wasn't finished, but now it was difficult to hear his voice—he was thinking out loud. "Three in the back of the head. "

Mason choked and said, "It was quick Zatzie." The conversation ended.

Was Gabe taken by surprise? He sometimes sounded different but then he would be right back to being Gabe. Everything was great.

Mason could not get Price out of his mind. He wondered what Price said to his friend and to Nittoli. Mason tried to relax and think of how he and Blaney and the other GPI employees would deal with Price as private citizens. Will the Assistant Director's father involve himself and his financial empire?

The majority of the New Jersey media coverage reported Randinoli missing and presumably dead. The Newark papers, in particular 12th and Bruce alumnus Martin Hatlas writing for the Newark Star-Ledger, offered a new twist. Few people knew of Hatlas's connection to 12th and Bruce; growing up he lived on Morris Avenue and occasionally would hang out on the corner. He was unique, and knew want he wanted to do with his life. As a youngster, he was a bookworm and determined to work and write for a newspaper. He also knew how to sell his product. Hatlas had balls, and his story hinted that the bureau and not the New York mob was responsible for the missing gangster. The readers loved the twist but wondered where the hell he came up with such a variation. He wrote as though he was in possession of first-hand information, fact or rumor. His friend Mason had no trouble with Hatlas's interpretation.

The Hatlas story, with the headline "Local Mobster Gonzo; FBI Happy? Responsible?" questioned why law enforcement would benefit from Randinoli's death. Its main message said that the FBI was embarrassed because Randinoli was a "successful mobster" who could never be caught, never served hard time and went about his business in New Jersey making millions while avoiding interference from the feds. Hatlas reported, "Gabe Randinoli was not an ordinary wise guy gangster." He portrayed Randinoli as a local kid who made good, someone who gave back to the old neighborhood where he grew up.

The old crapshooters enjoyed the hoopla. Tony Quinn said, "A genuine Robin Hood, Gabe?"

Blackie Capone laughed as well. "I don't know much about that Hood guy, the dude with the knickers and the bow and arrows. Did he like to kick people too?"

The wise guys in New Jersey did not know what to make of the story. Therefore, they took advantage of it by attempting to gain public support, reaching out for sympathy because such a great humanitarian met an untimely end. Numerous calls made, anonymous letters written, all crying foul. A woman from Hazlet, in a letter to the Newark News editor queried, "What did the government do with the poor man's body?"

It was a different story in New York. A contract is usually a complete secret, at least for a short time period. The newspaper reported that the Bonannos, especially, were well aware of who was responsible. The members were certainly cognizant of how things worked in the family. It was simple, no secret that Randinoli messed up some important work. Maybe he personally did not make the mistakes but it was his commitment. He was in charge. No surprise he paid the price.

Chapter Sixty

Tell him his friend did not suffer

Gabe had much potential but business is business.

A year prior, Christmas 1987, these words justified the action of Don Nittoli, when he approved the contract to end the life of Gabriel Randinoli.

A year had passed. The memorial Mass in Newark was over and now, in the middle of January 1989, Nittoli decided it was time to release the recordings. The Don kept an inventory of useful knowledge concerning relationships—good people and bad. The boss issued an order he wanted to see a friend, FBI Agent Barry Mazalewski. "Tell him it's personal."

Brad Mason was not the only FBI agent to have a friend on the other side. Mazalewski met the boss of the Bonanno family when he first transferred to the New York office of the FBI and the two men quickly liked each other. They would often play checkers and argue baseball while drinking cappuccinos. For both men, it played out as a game. Nothing of importance was discussed. Mazalewski recalled the words of his roommate at the FBI Academy when he spoke of his mob friend. "Gabe and I talk of the old days and keep current on each other's health. We have a rule, no business."

When the request came from Nittoli, the agent did not hesitate. He drove to the 69th street café and entered the front door. The FBI agent walked to the back room of the newly-renovated Bonanno headquarters, noting the modern furniture, a new, rich looking bar, carpeting and fresh paint and wallpaper on the walls. Don Nittoli sat alone at a corner table.

"Joe, how goes it?" Mazalewski made note of the two guns seated at the booth across from where Nittoli sipped his cappuccino.

"Good Barry, and you?" The Don stood and embraced the agent.

An extremely large man appeared and without speaking placed a fresh cup of cappuccino in front of the visitor. The boss smiled. "My memory is that you enjoy a good cappuccino even more than I."

"Your memory is excellent," Mazalewski said as he raised his cup in a toast. "To your health."

"Grazie, bello verder ti!" The tapes lay concealed under a cloth napkin.

The two acquaintances filled a half hour with innocuous chatter, enjoying each other's humor and laughing at funny incidents they shared in the past. Mazalewski looked around at the refurbished surroundings and smiled as he commented, "This is very nice. Business must be good."

"Barry, you know the joint was falling apart. This is a change of pace, a new look. We all need change now and then. I thought of applying for a federal building loan but decided against it. You have no idea. Those people require piles of paperwork."

The agent smiled. "I can imagine. Uncle never seems satisfied." The time went by fast. Mazalewski figured the Don would get to business when he was ready. The agent figured right.

"I have something for your friend from Newark. I would appreciate it if you delivered it personally." He pushed the small package, neatly wrapped with brown paper, across the table. It contained two cassettes; one of Price's conversations with Randinoli and the other with Nittoli.

Mazalewski hesitated; he appeared concerned. "My friend from Newark? I came to pay a visit and say hello, not to involve myself in an exchange of possible evidence."

Nittoli almost laughed aloud. "I guess once a cop always a cop. There is no exchange, no evidence. I see a small gift, nothing else. He accepts or rejects—his choice. We are just two friends enjoying cappuccinos. I believe this will be of interest to your friend, and he does with it whatever he pleases."

Mazalewski looked over at the two bodyguards and placed the package containing the gift in his pocket. "It will be my pleasure to deliver your good wishes. Thank you for the delicious drink."

Nittoli placed his hand on the younger man's arm. "Tell him his friend did not suffer. He committed serious errors yet I still keep second thoughts that perhaps someone overreacted." His mind wandered and he waved his arm in no particular direction, adding, "Or maybe Gabe was never meant for this business."

Mazalewski, another person who came from the streets, disagreed with the way some things get accomplished, yet he understood the explanation expressed by the head of a large criminal enterprise. To summarize the

Don's words, *He may have misgivings now but perhaps "someone" overreacted? Not someone. Joe Nittoli gave the order to kill Mason's friend. And it was carried out.*

The Don offered a weak smile. "My friend, give Brad my best. Lately I tire easily. We have finished our visit for now." The Don would not discuss the matter any further. He ended the meeting.

The two men stood, hugged and shook hands. As he walked away the agent turned and said, "I almost forgot. Happy New Year, Joe. Stay healthy."

Nittoli raised his cup of cappuccino and said, "Grazie, my friend. Buona fortuna." The bodyguards remained attentive, their eyes never wandering from the FBI man. They watched as he exited the building.

The boss was in a happy frame of mind. "You two can relax. That was the FBI, for God's sake."

Mazalewski's farewell remark reminded Don Nittoli his full medical checkup was long overdue.

Chapter Sixty-One

We look out for our own

Mason submitted his retirement notice on December 2, 1990, citing "personal reasons" on his official resignation. There would be no mention of Price's misuse of power and position. Without question, he and Blaney and the others would address the Price matter as private citizens. While dealing with the former AD, the name of the organization would be protected. They all believed that one bad apple should not blemish the FBI's reputation as a premier body of law enforcement.

While in D.C. at breakfast one morning, Mason spoke with his confidante and soon to be partner in a global private investigative firm, AD Maxwell Blaney. The two men held a mutual unique respect for the other since May 1972 when Blaney, substituting for the ailing Director, administered the oath to Mason's new agent class. During their bureau careers, Mason and Blaney worked together on many widely-publicized investigations and became close friends. Now eighteen years later, they would be private citizens in business together. Blaney was from the streets of Detroit, and like Mason, understood the wise guy mentality. Earlier, he had warned Mason of the devious moves Price was making to force Mason out of New England. "That bum wants revenge. He will not accept the fact that he is not God and does not call the shots. He'll never forgive you."

Mason did not doubt his partner. "Max, I hold him at least partly responsible for the death of…okay a bad guy, who happened to be my friend from 12th and Bruce. Tony Quinn used to say, 'When you pick up the dice one of two things happens. You win, you lose.' Price has crapped out."

Blaney agreed. "He will be the number one priority of GPI. We move on him first, get him out of the way and have the time available for the overseas work." Blaney would not wait for Price to inflict more damage on good people. "We'll deal with him first. Okay, we're agreed the group will meet with him at FBIHQ." Blaney thought of something, he was beaming. "By the way, I almost forgot to share some good news with you. As we discussed, I spoke with our mutual friend in Chicago. The retired FBI employee agreed to watch over our Chicago office. Of course, she sends her very best to her favorite FOA and insists on a fancy title."

"You've made my day. That's great. Judy will bring much more than loyalty to GPI. She has that sixth sense when it comes to sifting through mountains of investigative information and pinpointing the essential stuff and dumping the rest. Most important, she reads people. No one ever fooled her with bullshit. If not for her I might still be a green first office agent."

Blaney said, "I think I'm going to enjoy our business. And who knows, we may even make a few bucks to live on. Okay then, we just reached our first major business decision. Deputy Director for Chicago Operations, that is DD.C.O, is Judy Nassan." He stopped and thought, "How much does someone with such a lordly title get paid?"

"Not my job. You're the financial expert of Global Private Investigations, LLC. I'm sure you'll figure it out."

The conversation returned to Price. Blaney said, "We've planned life-after-the-bu for a long time. For certain, we couldn't make things right if we stayed with the FBI. This is the right way. We vamoose now at the top of our game with our reputations in the law enforcement community intact." They reached the decision as a group, now ready to retire from the bureau and pursue most of the same objectives following a different venue, and with fewer restrictions. During their careers, the group witnessed too many evil people falling between the cracks and escaping punishment.

Mason agreed. "I have retired and you, Assistant Director Maxwell Blaney, will follow next week, then Maz, Moore and Reagan."

Blaney said, "My papers are ready to go."

Blaney could say anything he wanted to Mason, they were that close. Earlier, when Mason blamed himself for his friend's chosen lifestyle, Blaney said, "Hold on man, you took an oath to investigate violations of the laws of the United States. More important, I, sir, administered said oath. Your friend's allegiance was a little different. His oath was to kill anyone who messed with La Cosa Nostra—a slight disparity wouldn't you say?" Maxwell Blaney never minced words. "I think we both knew how his life would end."

Mason said, "I think I get your drift, anything else?"

"I have to ask you and I'll only say it once, okay?" Blaney rose through the ranks the hard way and was well aware of AD Price's well-deserved reputation as a treacherous individual. Blaney endured first-hand experiences with Price when the AD did nothing to conceal his despicable prejudices toward blacks, women and other minorities in the bureau. His bias went as far as education. If one graduated from anything less than an Ivy League college, then that person did not count for much in Price's warped world.

Price once opined, "L. Patrick Gray should have stayed in the military. We need minorities in the FBI like we need another pecker." Gray succeeded Director Hoover in May 1972. Soon after his appointment, Gray hired the first two female FBI agents, an ex-marine and a former nun. Blaney remarked, "Both women served with honor in spite of the ever-present microscopic surroundings. I know what it was like." Blaney enjoyed a well-deserved reputation as a perceptive street agent, a fair and qualified supervisor who moved upward in the FBI, worthy of every promotion. AD Price was a scumbag and Blaney looked forward to the day when he answered for his intolerable behavior.

"Well, since you have not Mirandized me, let it out." Mason smiled at his friend.

During the previous ten years, the two men spent many hours and days together. Blaney was aware that Mason and Randinoli were companions in Newark during the fifties. He also was knowledgeable of the reputation of Newark's Central Ward. His aunt, uncle, and three of his cousins lived on Hunterdon Street for many years. In those days, the AD and his family often visited with relatives in Newark to celebrate birthdays and other occasions. Blaney witnessed what Mason went through after hearing of Randinoli's murder and brought him much comfort. Notwithstanding, his friend was an FBI agent and Randinoli was a member of La Cosa Nostra, a criminal who broke laws. Blaney knew Randinoli's criminal activities included the full gamut, including murder. Blaney believed for certain Mason never discussed any business with Randinoli. He was sure neither of them knew any of the specifics the other was involved in through the years. Yet Mason was still an FBI agent, and a good one. Blaney wanted to clear the air.

He began, "You were friends in spite of..." Mason interrupted.

"Let me make it easier for you, Max. I believe the query is, "How could they remain friends through the years when they were so different concerning the things that truly mattered?" He looked directly at Blaney, who nodded agreement.

"My friend, the only plausible answer I can come up with would be to quote a gentleman by the name of Blackie Capone, who more than once stated emphatically: '*you remember the law, at 12th and Bruce we look out for our own.*' The translation is simple, no matter what happens we don't aid and abet but we don't turn away from our friends."

Blaney understood perfectly. Their careers paralleled: married with three children; college degree after years at night school; late entry in the bureau; and most of all, a dislike for individuals with power taking advantage of others. This last commonality directed at the so-called good guys as well as the bad. Post-bureau they always planned to remain partners as private investigators. They often discussed how as private citizens, particularly with their experience and contacts, and now as PIs, they could obtain results that "by-the-book" law enforcement people could not achieve. Undoubtedly, former AD Price would receive the required attention of the newly formed company. Blaney noticed his friend frowning. He seemed to be in deep thought. "That finishes it, right?"

Mason, looking perplexed, recalled a conversation with Randinoli after his friend had too many drinks.

"You thought of something?" Blaney asked.

"I think we were at the roofers' hall in Newark. He had had one too many drinks. I believe his exact words were 'Who is your guy who meets with my boss?' We never discussed business. I stopped him, chalked it up to the booze and that was it. When we parted, I guessed I sluffed it off. I thought about what he said but couldn't tie anything together." He continued, "I may have thought that one of our New York OC guys had a sit-down with Nittoli. Gabe had to know it was Price meeting with Don Nittoli but didn't give up a name. I can't say it enough, we agreed from the beginning never to discuss business. We both lived up to the agreement. Now it fits; Price started with Gabe and struck out. Next, he threatened me and got nowhere. Finally, out of desperation he goes to the top of the family, and takes a shot at Joe Nittoli. At this alleged top-secret discussion, it's a good guess that Price related contrived stories about Gabe's relationship with me. We know exactly what he said to me. You and Moore and Reagan listened to the tape enough."

Blaney picked up on the explanation. "So in summation, my friend, Price left D.C. several times and made bogus trips to New York. He furnished a phony reason for each trip, thereby committing a federal crime each time he submitted false justification on his signed vouchers. Toddy never visited the New York office or met with any of our people. Gabe was spot on. It certainly was one of "our guys." It was the man with the ego as big as the Empire State. I will make further inquiries and add this to the group's already solid case against the prick." His mind wandered and he added, "Man, would I love to know exactly what Price said to Gabe."

Mason noticed and appreciated that Blaney called his friend by his first name. *I know Gabe was not without flaws but he did volunteer at the shelter.*

Not surprisingly, Ann was happy when her husband finalized his decision. She had her own personal reasons: the worry he would not come home some night; that the phone would ring and someone from the FBI would have distressing news. "Whatever we do, wherever we go, we'll be together, like always." Hearing these words from the person he loved more than anyone or anything in the world made Mason's decision easier.

Ann shared the news with family members, happily telling her brothers and sisters, "Brad won't be facing bad people with real guns anymore." They all remembered the day in Chicago's West Side when he and his partner and Sergeant Vito Bianco narrowly escaped death during a violent gunfight with drug dealers.

Mason valued the people and the work in Boston. He would leave the bureau without fanfare. SAC Gene Gallagher organized what started out as a small get-together at Ryan's, a favorite cop pub and restaurant in Everett, a few miles north of Boston.

The gathering included the entire Mason clan. The room grew louder as the war stories ran wild.

His friend and roommate at the academy drove up from New York. Barry Mazalewski asked to see him in private. Mason didn't expect to discuss business and was curious about the request. "I won't waste time my friend. I have something for you from Gabe's boss, the guy who approved the hit in '87."

Mason showed his surprise. "Maz, what are you talking about? From Don Nittoli?"

"Right, no one knows anything about this, and I didn't listen to them. He asked me to deliver them personally, so here you go." He extended his hand, clutching the two cassettes.

"Hold on Maz, time out. Get Max in here." The ex-roommate hurried to locate the AD.

"Max, could you come in the back for a minute? Brad is back there."

"What is it? Bill Reagan is in the middle of a great story slash lie." Blaney relished Reagan's monologues, especially spiced with a Jewish, Irish, Indian, Italian or whatever dialogue.

"Brad needs you to look at something. It's important, it won't take long." Blaney reluctantly followed the New York agent to the back of the restaurant.

As the big man approached, Mason saw the frown on Blaney's face. "Maz has something for me from Nittoli."

"Nittoli?" AD Blaney clearly caught off guard. "What the…"

Mazalewski produced the small package. "He asked me to deliver it to Brad in person. I have no idea of its contents. It's the size of two cassette tapes."

"I think you should take custody, nothing official of course." Mason was smiling as he spoke.

Blaney smiled right back. "Custody, my sweet black ass. You are speaking of evidence, my good man—you who ain't no 'mo a federal agent."

"Right on, and which of the two of us is still in the evidence business? Certainly not *moi*, a tax-paying, private citizen." He pointed an index finger at the package. "I believe you are still on the job as they say. Pointing to Maz's package, he said, "That, whatever it is, does not exist."

Blaney, Moore, Mazalewski and Reagan, also known as the *group*, would be exiting government service the following week. Judy Nassan was already a private citizen doing preparation work while waiting for GPI to open for business.

"Do not go there, Brad," Blaney answered. "It may describe a mob secret, a serial killer, a terrorist cell, or some such thing. We could be talking a chain of evidence issue here." Mazalewski suppressed delight and enjoyed this exchange.

Mason said, "I believe we both have a good idea of what it contains and none of it is good for Toddy boy."

Blaney nodded in agreement. Now looking at Mazalewski, the AD asked, "Who else knows of the tapes?"

"Sir, to my knowledge, we three and Nittoli." Maz attempted to sound business-like.

The room went quiet for a minute.

Blaney frowned at them both. "I shall take the tapes that do not exist. The group will listen to the content, and then decide how to proceed further, if at all. Agreed?"

Mason waved, indicating he was on board. A jubilant Mazalewski hurried out of the room. "We still have time to catch the punch line."

In less than a minute, Mazalewski rushed back yelling, "No rest for the weary. You won't believe who just walked in."

Todd Price would not quit. Uninvited, he appeared at the bon voyage party. It was obvious he already consumed enough alcohol, which provided the nerve to make an appearance. He intended to behave in a normal manner, as if among friends. He socialized with people he never met. "Hello, I'm Todd Price, an AD with the bureau." At the bar in the back end of the large room he ordered a vodka and tonic. He sat at a table occupied by a few state troopers. He stopped a waiter and asked for another drink, saying "always be prepared, have one at the ready."

The group worried Price would spoil a happy occasion or, worse yet, someone would seriously hurt the AD.

Blaney spoke up. "Don't pay any attention to him. Let him have a few drinks and be on his way." The others agreed.

Moore added, "The Price file is getting bigger. I'll check out this visit, another bogus trip paid for by the taxpayers."

After he quickly finished four vodka and tonics, he demanded to be one of the speakers. Paddy Platten, the master of ceremonies du jour, said to those at his table, "If he even gets close to the microphone, someone will shove it up his fat ass." Platten politely denied the AD's demand, telling Price there were time constraints and a prearranged program.

As requested, the speeches were brief. The speakers comprised of the United States Attorney, the OC supervisor, and the SAIC of the United States Secret Service, all gracious and complimentary.

Price drank more and whined about not having the opportunity to speak. Platten introduced Blaney as "the person representing the FBI, and our featured and last speaker." After a few light war stories, his words were in the true tradition of the FBI. Mason listened, most grateful. Only a few close friends in the room were aware of the global PI firm that was already off and running. The group recognized how important these friends and associates would be as sources in the world of investigations.

Price was relentless, especially after several strong drinks kicked in, all gratis for the Washington D.C. big shot. He behaved as if the function took place in D.C. and he was the head honcho. He sauntered up to the guest of honor and Blaney, who were enjoying proceeding down memory lane, along with a few of the agents they both knew and worked with in Chicago, Boston, New York and elsewhere.

True to form, the interruption was typical, and rude to say the least. Price, now slurring his words, said, "What a shame you two will be leaving us. Too bad I won't be able to extend an invitation when I am sworn in as the new Director of the FBI." Smiling broadly now, the courage coming from the alcohol, he continued, "You two will be lowly regular citizens. In addition, you, Max my friend, from an Assistant Director to a what? Perhaps you'll land a position as a security guard in the heart of Detroit. It's such a pity."

Blaney could not restrain himself and, now in Price's face, said, "I told you once before, only my friends call me Max." He moved even closer. "And if you consider yourself one of the good guys, we leave the bureau with smiles on our faces knowing we did our best. You've disgraced a great organization. We look forward to dealing with you in the future." Blaney and Mason discussed often their plans for the PI firm, especially for Price. At best Price's future appeared dismal. The sixty-four dollar question remained. How far would Price, Sr., go to keep his son out of prison?

Most of the agents and support personnel present heard Price's remarks. One of Mason's roommates at the academy, Joe O'Dea, relished the anticipation of Price getting a genuine ass whipping. "Let the games begin."

Most folks in the Boston office knew of Price's underhanded attack against Mason. The attempted biased transfer and the forged threats spread throughout the FBI. Bureau people for the most part take care of other employees. Mason recognized this trait from day one. In addition to fidelity, bravery and integrity, bureau personnel exhibited compassion for other employees and their families, especially in times of need. He heard it said often, "Remove the few assholes and everything would be fine."

Now Mason moved in as close as physically possible, nose-to-nose with the AD. He spoke very slowly and never allowed his eyes to move off target. "One, you are here uninvited. Two, unfortunately for you, we will never be *regular* citizens, nor regular anything. And three, leaving 'us'? As for you, an 'us' never existed."

Awaiting a response, he mused, *what say you Gabe? I drop this turd?*

The AD was finished for the evening. Now unable to conceal the look on his face, it revealed genuine fear. It was an epiphany; he now grasped a stark reality, the man in front of him was no longer employed by the FBI. Price had lost his sword. He turned away and slowly walked toward the main section of the lounge, trying to remove a terrifying fact from his brain. The alcohol could not block the inevitable. Everything was coming apart for the would-be Director of the FBI. He recalled the times he threatened Mason, believing he could influence the FBI supervisor to do his bidding. Price wanted Mason to take advantage of the relationship with Randinoli and force the wise guy to turn on his own people. Price never comprehended loyalty, especially the kind nourished on the corner of 12th Avenue and Bruce Street.

AD Price left Ryan's in desperate search of another bar. His mind dulled, he forced a short-lived thought. *"And at least I still have my position and power in the FBI. Time moves on and people forget the past."*

The group prepared to introduce the steps required to oust Price from his employment with the bureau. They documented everything in writing although nothing of evidentiary value ever reached the inside of an official investigative file. Blaney's small unit now was satisfied that what they had in their possession would get the attention of Assistant Director Price.

The plan included focusing on two main issues. The tapes provided by Don Nittoli would make for interesting listening. Everything was recorded. Second, they were current on Price's threats against Mason and his efforts to facilitate an illegal transfer out of Boston.

After months of covert investigation, the group readied to confront Price. Mason and Blaney earlier agreed the strategy would remain simple. They would force Price to retire without criminal charges brought against him and let the newly formed GPI firm deal with him from their Washington D.C. office. No one spoke it, but the group was pleased Price's repugnant actions would not be made public.

Maz said it best. "Are we brainwashed or what? The 'don't embarrass the bureau' mantra lives on."

Blaney said, "He's much more than an embarrassment. He's worse than some of the people we helped put in the joint."

Chapter Sixty-Two

Remember Fats Waller

In January 1991, now three years since his friend went missing, Mason heard of Nittoli's illness. Mason and Blaney were busy with meetings in New York and monthly intercontinental flights. A group of clients hired GPI to conduct major due diligence inquiries in the U.S. as well as several other countries, including a few situated in the Mideast. The two senior partners of GPI did not discuss the nature of the inquiries with anyone outside of the inner circle. Even the other four officers knew only what was necessary to their particular duties, and not given the entire objective.

When Mazalewski informed Mason of Nittoli's possible incurable sickness, Mason said, "I think I'll pay him a visit and check it out for myself." He wanted to inform the former Don that although some time had passed, Gabe's murder was not forgotten. He and Blaney had read the latest court papers regarding the Bonanno crime family. In particular, they focused on the section dealing with Don Nittoli's surprising testimony:

Footnotes: Government's Motion for Downward Departure Pursuant To Section 5K.1 and 18 U.S.C. 3553 (s). Motion filed on 02/01/1990 on behalf of Giuseppe Nittoli in United States District Court Eastern District of New York. Motion filed because of Nittoli's "substantial assistance in the investigation or prosecution of another person who has committed an offense."

Blaney said, "We never know which of them will fold next. I must say, this one shocked a lot of people on both sides. Nittoli impressed me as someone who viewed the omertà oath as sacred. That New York cop was right on; when the heat is turned up, the whippoorwill's race to the prosecutor's office to sing the first song."

Maz added, "I used to sit with the guy at the Bonanno headquarters, we drank cappuccino and solved the problems of the world. I tell you, I couldn't believe it. But when the word came of his sickness, I guess it makes more sense. You said it, what it comes down to is cover your ass and make the best deal. They utilize the FIFO method of accounting for inventory, first-in-first-out."

During the Don's testimony, the New York newspapers were brutal. The readers loved the story. The Daily News was especially relentless, with headlines that screamed, "Don Nittoli, What About Your Oath?"

Mason said, "I'm more surprised he's still alive. He must have an army around him. Gabe never ratted on anyone. Look how he finished."

Blaney said, "Don't go there, Brad. No matter what you feel about this guy, yes, he ordered the hit. That stuff has been part of the Mafia for a few hundred years. It's what happens, what's expected, it goes along with the turf. Remember what Gabe told you, "it was business."

The massive Manhattan apartment was furnished with expensive décor. Mason recognized one of the bodyguards as part of the delegation of capos that paid respects at the funeral Mass held at St. Joe's. He waved to Mason, "Hey, how ya doin?"

Mason said, "Good, thanks. Everything good with you?"

"Well, I'm one of the few left. Most of the people that worked with Gabe are either dead, in the slammer or..." he smiled, "or in the witness protection program." The former agent gained immediate entry to the Don's tastefully-furnished bedroom. On the wall facing the bed hung a twelve-by-twelve black and white photograph of Joe DiMaggio swinging the bat at Yankee Stadium.

Nittoli perked up when his visitor entered the bedroom. He waved a nurse away. "It's nice to see Gabe's good friend." He was obviously happy to see the ex-FBI employee.

Mason immediately noticed the physical change in the former powerful head of the Bonanno crime syndicate. He had aged considerably since his visit to Newark when he led a contingent of family members to Saint Joseph's Catholic Church. His arms now covered with black and blue smears caused by the many needle punctures. There were tubes attached to his nostrils to enhance breathing. His face covered with crusty flakes of dead skin. Nittoli now appeared a sickly old man, no resemblance to the dominant LCN icon of three decades.

After the usual greetings, Mason got to the point, "Joe, it was not totally unexpected. Still, I lost a friend. Someone made a bad call on that one."

Nittoli said, "I agree. I remember hearing someone saying that we are all responsible for our actions."

"I recall that as well." He noted the hoarseness in Nittoli's voice and the red teary eyes.

"Also, we all pay in the end." Nittoli said this slowly.

Mason answered, "That's right."

Nittioli looked sad as he repeated to Mason what he said at St. Joe's Club in Newark. "I really liked Gabe."

Mason recalled what Blackie Capone used to say on the corner: "Sometimes we need to make tough decisions. Always remember, business is business." The message here: Nittoli was never at ease with his decision but business is business and the Don saw no alternative to his order to end Randinoli's life.

The aging boss smiled. "I know we elderly wise guys are always on our death beds. We are too sick to stand trial and all the rest. However my friend, to the point, I have less than a few months. It must have been those beautiful cigars. I have esophageal cancer. Incurable. I will give the doctor permission to speak with you so you can verify what I say."

"That's not necessary. I'm sorry. You lost a few pounds?"

The Mafiosi coughed and reached for a tissue. "Yes, I am no longer that big, beautiful robust man. Please recall what I told your associate. Gabe did not suffer. Sometimes, in spite of his successes, I think Gabe was not meant for our business, the wrong DNA or something."

Earlier Mazalewski told Mason that the Don admitted he gave the order and the hit on Randinoli was justified. Now Nittoli reinforces it. Maybe he feels better telling the former agent his friend did not suffer. Mason nodded, he would remain positive. "Sometimes things happen, things change and even doctors are proven wrong."

"You need to be a 'don't' bettor on this one. All the x-rays, tests, even a second opinion show the inevitable. Do not take the odds. Anyway, if the cancer does not do the job then… " He forced another smile. In an instant, the Don looked weary, ready to get some rest. Mason recognized that the once influential mobster referred to his testimony against many LCN members. He did stay out of jail. However, his days were numbered. His fatal sickness allowed him a short time more to live. His visitor thought, "*If this is living, you can have it.*"

Don Nittoli excused his act of treason. "Brad, the so-called information I gave in court was old stuff. Your people knew who was dead and who did the work. I simply verified it without adding any useful information. My kids convinced me to do it. I'm dying and they felt I would go out as one of the good guys. I did it to satisfy my sons. Thank God none of my children followed in my profession. They are all good citizens and even pay taxes."

Mason listened to Giuseppe "Joe" Nittoli, who spent close to three decades associated with the Bonanno organized crime family and rose to leadership positons in that enterprise—from a young thug to capo regime, from an underboss to the top of the heap—to become the boss of the entire criminal enterprise. The man before him sat on the five-family commission. Speaking of his testimony, Nittoli sounded like he did a noble thing, but he broke a cardinal rule. The people in his business would spit on his grave. The former Don was now confessing, giving reasons for turning on his own people. Nittoli failed to mention that if he did not cooperate, the feds were ready to strip him of every nickel he possessed. Nittoli's worldly possessions were vast; he was a very wealthy man. His testimony allowed for his children and grandchildren to enjoy the benefits of comfortable life styles.

Nittoli moved to another declaration. "I tell you this; do not doubt Price's responsibility. His lies were as ruthless as if he did the work himself. The skunk deserves worse than what I hear you have planned. Getting fired by the FBI is the coward's way out. So he leaves the FBI in disgrace. What then? He's fat and comfortable in one of his wealthy father's companies? You and your friends are letting him off easy. If someone like Specs Buchanan could get to him, Price would suffer a whole lot more."

Mason ignored this latest comment. He had heard the name before. Mason believed Nittoli held Price even more responsible for Randinoli's death than himself, the man who gave the order. He thought, "*This guy may have given orders to kill more men than General Patton.*"

Mason, about ready to leave, said, "I wouldn't be too concerned with Price. His worse days may be ahead. I may see you again Joe. You hang in there just as you once told me." Mason started for the door, then turned back and said, "Remember Fats Waller."

Nittoli's face beamed. "I do remember, I do. 'One never knows, do one?' Go Yanks."

This was the last time Mason saw the longtime boss of the Bonanno crime syndicate alive. Three weeks later Nittoli died in bed at his home. His death received a small amount of media attention. Few of his former friends and associates attended the funeral; no parade of limousines was present. A young soldier of the family remarked, "He broke his oath. Let him rot." This young wise guy never met nor saw the former Don. Like Mason's old friend, the young wannabe made a decision. The young thug obviously believed the omertà ceremony meant something more—that it was a sacred pledge, and never violated.

When Blaney heard the news, he told his partner, "I think your visit was the right thing to do. Anyway, we know he told the truth at the end. He died when he said he would."

Mason answered, "Right, another closed case. He also understood that if he was feigning the sickness, and his own people did not take him out then..." Blaney finished the thought.

"You're correct, partner. We had more than necessary to feed the bureau. Don Nittoli would be in prison for the remainder of his golden years." Blaney added, "Not a good place for a former big shot turned stoolie."

Mason picked up a thick manila folder from the desk. The label read TODD PRICE. "We now can move our GPI resources in another direction."

Chapter Sixty-Three

His right eye twitched uncontrollably

They gathered a mountain of information and referred to it as "the report." It included the names of bureau personnel ready and willing to testify, all with personal knowledge of Price's quest to force Mason to wear a wire against his boyhood pal, absent the required court order. The group responsible for the work detailed Price's actions that had one objective only, placing AD Price in a most powerful standing and closer to his goal, that of FBI Director.

AD Maxwell Blaney and the other members of the group, ADs Mike Reagan and Dennis Moore, surprised Price on a Friday morning in May 1991.

Blaney called Price. "Todd, Maxwell Blaney. Any plans for lunch today?"

Thrown off guard by the call and naturally suspicious, Price answered, "This is a surprise. Let me look." He feigned shuffling a few papers on his desk. "No, nothing important on my calendar. What's the occasion?"

"We are both so busy and never really see much of each other. I know things did not go well at the bon voyage party in Boston, but that's history. Reagan and Moore will be joining us. Lunch at Maynard's, and we'll meet in the lobby at 12:15 and walk over together."

The four were punctual.

Not surprisingly, the popular restaurant enjoyed a brisk, noon hour clientele. Blaney's 12:30 reservation turned into a smart move.

"Good job with the reservation." Moore, always the hungry one, looked forward to the huge salad bar and house lunch specialty; a bowl of Manhattan clam chowder and "the best Reuben sandwich in the District." Reagan, of Irish-Italian descent, considered himself a food connoisseur and earlier suggested Il Canale in Georgetown, but they were time restricted. Besides, the three ADs did not want to be in Price's company any longer than necessary. They would visit Il Canale at a later date and celebrate his retirement.

The host escorted the four men to the corner booth previously requested by Blaney. Price attempted to give the appearance of someone in complete control. He was aware that Moore and Reagan were present at Mason's party and witnessed his encounter with Blaney and Mason. AD Price was still riding high, now the top seed to be the next Director of the FBI. Present company would shake when hearing his name. Whatever game Blaney had in mind, he would be playing with the master.

The plan was to go with small talk until after they finished eating. The carefully orchestrated seating plan positioned Moore and Reagan on either side of Price. Now, with lunch consumed, Blaney slowly reached across the table and grabbed and squeezed both of the surprised ADs wrists. "Todd, are you wearing anything?" Simultaneously the other two members of the group thoroughly searched his chest, back, crotch and legs.

"What the hell are you do...?" asked Price, who was caught completely off guard.

Reagan then swiftly rubbed his hand through Price's scalp. Onlookers likely would think that the grown men were behaving as mischievous boys. The professional search was over in a matter of seconds.

Price, determined to act and look professional, straightened his tie and arranged his hair in place.

Price sipped Perrier water and smiled. "Max, I have a distinct feeling we are here for something more than the wonderful food." He glanced at the other two, both wearing well-rehearsed poker faces.

From here on it would be strictly business and the group would relish every minute. Blaney decided for the time being to ignore the "Max" part. Looking directly at Price, he said, "We discussed some things and decided it would be a generous gesture on our part to buy your last meal as a member of the Federal Bureau of Investigation."

Taken back by the statement, Price managed to stay cool. "Max, I never realized what a funny man you are. Now what happens, a little slapstick comedy, a few more jokes, perhaps an old song?" Again, his quick look to both sides found two very somber looking agents.

Blaney leaned across the table, closer to his subject, and now spoke very slowly. "Now what happens, you ask? It's what we say happens, and it happens when we say it happens, and nothing will happen to prevent it from happening." Moore, now forced to cover the grin on his face, would later remind Blaney of the effective but way-too-long sentence.

Blaney continued. "First, when you get back to your office you very politely request your secretary to prepare a letter with your signature outlining your immediate resignation from the FBI."

"You must be…" Price tried to protest. His right eye was now visibly twitching. Moore leaned forward as he placed his index finger to his lips in the typical "keep quiet" gesture.

Strictly business, Blaney continued, "Do not interrupt. Your letter of resignation will include whatever personal reasons you care to illuminate. There's no need to delineate your crimes, all within the federal jurisdiction of the Department of Justice and the FBI. It would not surprise me if you discuss these dastardly acts later, possibly with FBI agents or even private investigators." Now Blaney stole a glance at his co-conspirators, who were struggling to hide the joy they were experiencing.

Price, whose grandiosity remained with him, thought, *"Whom do they think they are dealing with? Soon I will be the Director of the FBI. They will be lowly citizens scratching out a living."*

Quickly composing himself, Price said, "Threats against an Assistant Director of the FBI, Max, I am surprised. You can talk all you want. I'm not leaving the bureau but you three can certainly follow Mr. Mason, your mob-connected friend. That is your choice." Price was still thinking himself untouchable. *"They cannot know of my meetings with Randinoli and Nittoli. The stupid mob boss certainly will not talk."*

Blaney removed the mini-recorder from his inside jacket pocket. He looked at the AD and slowly placed the device on the table. He now spoke slowly. "Listen closely, you piece of shit," Blaney said. "The first voice you will recognize as that of Giuseppe 'Joe' Nittoli, boss of the New York Bonanno crime syndicate." He pressed the *play* button.

"Todd, what brings you to New York this time?" Blaney, a master of the *pause* button, then said, "And of course the next voice is none other than…"

"I will not waste my time or yours. You have a squealer in your organization. One of your people is too close to one of my agents."

Pause. Blaney continued, "Again, we have Mr. Nittoli."

Price sat in fright listening, not moving a muscle.

"Todd, it has been such throughout history. The good guys talk to the bad guys and vice versa. Of course we know who the real good guys are.

Like right now, you and me, it is a game. We play each other, one outsmarting the other today and the other gets a turn tomorrow. It usually ends in a tie. I am well aware some of my people are on speaking terms with agents. The agents refer to this as working an informant or a necessary asset. My people call it bullshit or covering your ass." *Pause.*

Moore could not hold back, he let out his sinister Richard Widmark laugh. "This part is really great."

Reagan added, "I think they call it juicy courtroom entertainment."

Price's complexion now ashen, he remained perfectly still, his eyes glued to the mini recorder. Blaney pushed the *Play* button. "Again, we have the high level representative of the FBI."

"You think this is a harmless game. So you are aware that one Gabriel Randinoli is furnishing the FBI with valuable information, and as a result we will successfully prosecute people in your family as well as others."

"Who is he speaking with?"

"So we understand each other. I have no intention of giving up names of any of my people." *Pause.* Moore could not hold back. He looked at Price and punched his fist in the air in an "atta boy" gesture towards the AD. "Integrity! That's the stuff."

Play. "Not good enough, you say Gabe is a rat, who says so? You?" And why are you telling me this garbage?"

"The agent's name is Brad Mason. Check it out and you will find that they go way back. I never intended to give you the reason but I will. Mason is not following my orders and needs to grasp a meaningful lesson. Like you, I must run my business with a rock-solid degree of discipline. What you do with your man does not matter to me whatsoever. Mason must be free of doubt. He must realize that I can get things done—on both sides."

Price sat in silence. His right eye twitched uncontrollably. *Pause.*

"Toddie, what happened to good old fidelity?" Moore acted very serious.

Play. "I must get back to my work. What you have spoken is not enough. I can assure you that I will conduct my own investigation and act accordingly. I thank you for your interest."

"I am sure you will see that what I say is true. I believe you take your business serious. I believe Randinoli broke an oath. I know you will never divulge what I have said here today."

The recording ended. Reagan, now on a roll, said, "I love the part about the rock-solid degree of discipline. We have a special copy with musical background. The quality is top-notch." He followed with his Peter Sellers' special, "The case, it is solved." He spoke the last word in two distinct syllables—*sol-ved*—a perfect impersonation of the actor. Blaney waved him off and spoke.

"Now, you understand the situation. I will not waste time playing your meeting with Randinoli, especially since you contributed to and bear a responsibility for his death. You remember how you impersonated a US Attorney and told Gabe that he would not be prosecuted for any of his crimes, even murder. All original tapes and copies stay with us." For the second time, Blaney leaned across the table and, emphasizing each syllable, said, "As I stated earlier, now what happens is what we say happens, and it happens when we say it happens, and nothing will happen to prevent it from happening. I repeat, you return to your office and you very politely request your secretary to prepare a letter with your signature outlining your immediate resignation from the FBI."

Price opened his mouth to speak, but Reagan said angrily, "Did you not hear the man? Shut the fuck up. Again, do not interrupt."

Moore chimed in, "We will immediately scrutinize your letter of resignation."

Reagan added, "Your letter need only explain your reasons briefly, personal reasons, acute hemorrhoids, whatever."

Still strictly business, Blaney continued, "There is no need to delineate your crimes. Your resignation will suffice for the present."

Moore then asked, "Max, have you covered *everything*?"

"Thanks, Dennis," Blaney said. He looked directly at Price and displayed the recorder with both hands. "Knowing how your sick mind works, you are thinking your own words are not enough to bury you. You are mistaken. We possess signed, sworn statements of hard-working, dedicated FBI Headquarters' personnel detailing everything pertaining to your alleged business trips to New York. The accounting folks in the voucher section have captured and scheduled the fraudulent expense vouchers you submitted and signed, all in support of the fraud against the government violation."

"We are aware you have little experience as a lead agent in cases even similar to this. You realize that your position is one of power and prestige. The record will show that you used your position of rank and power to influence others for your benefit. We are sure that your father's expensive defense lawyers will explain the various violations to you. The biggy of course is U.S. Code, Title 18, Section 1031, to wit Fraud Against the Government and a few others. Each count punishable by several years in prison depending on the guidelines. I am certain the indictment charging you with numerous violations of federal criminal law will take into account each of your New York trips as a separate count."

Moore, reminded of another issue, said, "Brad's transfer?"

Blaney nodded and said, "Thanks again, so much to absorb in so little time. Briefly, the responsible people at headquarters will swear under oath that you, without cause, perpetrated SSA Brad Mason's transfer to Florida, fully cognizant that you had no justification and that the climate could cause severe skin cancers. Further, there is sworn testimony that you openly bragged of your meetings and close relationship with Nittoli and Randinoli. And last but certainly not least, some citizens believe that your disgraceful conduct resulted in the death of a U.S. citizen, one Mr. Gabriel Randinoli. Citizens on both sides." That was enough. Blaney glanced at his co-interviewers. "I would not want to be in such a position."

Moore and Reagan nodded their agreement, and Reagan said, "No, not at all, not a good position to occupy. Allow me to mention one other recording, another small piece of evidence. We have allowed you to hear one of several recordings of your conversations. You may remember threatening SSA Mason. I believe one of your threats was as follows." Reading from an index card, Reagan said, "'And you will never know when it is coming or where it comes from.' Your media friends will love that one."

Moore took one parting shot. "And the sworn statements? One will stand out. I always thought your friend Mayhew was quiet, a man of few words. Some might even say, no balls. Man, did I misread that lad. You may recall bragging that Messrs. Blaney and Mason...let me check." He too produced an index card and then continued. "'Mark my words—they are both history' is the way you phrased it. Well, that person vividly remembers your every word, especially the quid pro quo stuff to get to the big chair." Moore, who truly disliked the man in front of him, could hardly contain himself as he put his face an inch away from Price. "By itself, it's enough to terminate your FBI employment and put your sorry fat ass behind bars." Price's actions were more personal to Moore who was an ASAC in Cleveland when Mason interviewed for the job.

Reagan was not quite finished. "During our talk with Mayhew, he informed us of his conversation with you regarding your family. When he asked you where dear old dad made all his money, you said if you disclosed that information you would have to kill Mayhew. He believed you meant it. Well, be assured that the life and adventures of one Mr. Redley Price will continue to be thoroughly examined."

Blaney removed a credit card from the restaurant bill pouch and signed the check. The three satisfied investigators rose in unison. Blaney looked down at a broken man, his right eye now tearing and twitching in staccato fashion. "One more thing, say your goodbyes today and make it your last visit. Do not return to headquarters or to any FBI office—ever." As they walked from the table, Blaney turned back one last time. "And yes, we will be in touch."

Chapter Sixty-Four

Global Private Investigations, LLC

Former FBI Supervisory Special Agent Brad Mason and recently retired FBI Assistant Director Maxwell Blaney did join forces after leaving the FBI. Barry Mazalewski came on board as the director of investigative operations. Three other key people would join as team leaders: Judy Nassan, Dennis Moore and Mike Reagan were proven team players and added precisely what the partners sought—experience and ability.

The newly formed Global Private Investigations (GPI), LLC, headed by Blaney and Mason, included offices in Boston, Chicago, New York and Washington D.C.. Word of the new company traveled fast, and the rapidly-building client list already included well-known corporations and individuals. Judging from retainers received, money would not be an issue. The partners agreed to take on pro bono cases as well.

During a discussion, Blaney recalled their careers with the FBI. "The few bad actors who escaped without a scratch, that's what I remember." Blaney looked forward to targeting corruption, especially crooked politicians and law enforcement individuals shielded by the system. The new partners also were bothered by the quality cases dropped by prosecutors before reaching a judge and jury. Too often, prosecutors declined prosecution for bogus reasons, perhaps in deference to political pressure or a quid pro quo.

Mason recalled a public corruption case that occurred in northern Michigan. "I saw the film. My memory is the state police ran a sting operation that included video and audio coverage of several meetings. The evidence showed a local bankruptcy judge and two or three individuals representing the governor accepting money from an undercover cop. In return, the public officials provided the contractor with sweetheart building contracts."

Blaney remembered. "Right, and no indictments. The case was abruptly dumped with little fanfare. The official bullshit came out as not having enough evidence to prosecute and the same crap about possible entrapment, and so on. We'll put at least a dent in that type of bullshit."

The partners' business plan for the new organization was to assist in bringing to justice those entities that appear to be beating the system, slipping through the cracks. GPI would select projects on an individual case basis.

Moore said, "Another example would be the matter in Pennsylvania all over the TV. It looks like the locals can use a hand. There's only one suspect for a brutal double murder and the suspected perp has a real bad sheet. The cops want to search the guy's house but the state attorney won't give the okay for a search warrant. The chief of police is screaming he has ample probable cause, but it's no go. The FBI tech guys believe they can help out so they're heading for Philly as we speak. Maybe GPI will be able to bypass a lot of the so-called legal blockades and just get the job done."

Blaney added, "It's rare, but law enforcement is included. We know of a dirty cop still hiding behind the protection of his union lawyers. He avoided facing responsibility for improper and sometimes criminal behavior. He received minimal administrative punishment and eventually was released from duty—taking with him an undeserved pension and benefits at the expense of the taxpayers."

In addition to the myriad of criminal and civil cases, GPI would assist individual state and federal agencies experiencing "inside" problems.

"Of course, GPI will be operating within the confines of the law." Blaney added.

From time to time with the FBI, Mason and Blaney may have taken some chances and overstepped their authority. On a kidnapping case that concluded with happy results, one of the now incarcerated kidnappers sued Mason, another agent and a state trooper, accusing them of using physical force to learn the location of the gang hiding the two abducted teens taken from their home. The plaintiff gave up the location of his accomplices and the children were safely returned to their parents, who tearfully praised the work of law enforcement. It took round-the-clock police work for the case to end on a happy note. Federal prosecutors opined that the kidnapper's suit would go nowhere, the work of a jailhouse lawyer.

Blaney said, "GPI resources will be available to victim departments and communities on a gratis basis. Our law enforcement contacts will show their gratitude by assisting with useful information on other GPI cases. A win-win for both sides. But for now, it appears our resources will be spent out of the country. When you consider the enormous fee we're getting, the client really wants us over there."

The entire team of six now prepared to travel to the Mideast, specifically Tel Aviv, to explore an unusual offer made to GPI. Early indications pointed toward a busy exposure overseas as well as domestically. The GPI agent list swelled as specific contacts were in place in several overseas locations.

One priority still loomed with the two partners. At the proper time, GPI would visit Centreville, Virginia, the new residence of former Assistant Director Todd Price, now employed as an executive vice president with Comtech Global Corporation (CGC), the largest industrial conglomerate in the world.

After his sudden departure from the number two spot in the FBI, private citizen Todd Price found life treating him better than he deserved. However, he wrongly figured his early departure from the FBI would be enough to satisfy Blaney and Mason and the rest of the group. He assumed Randinoli's death would surely be forgotten, no loss there, nothing more than a lowlife hood. Price never heard from them, so the former big-shot AD believed he now could enjoy the remnants of his meticulous planning. *Let those two save the world as they play at being private investigators.* No surprise, due diligence research remained a shortfall in Price's repertoire. He did not know who comprised GPI, the principals, the clients, or the reputation already earned by the new company. Had he done his homework, Price may have learned much about GPI's impressive growing client list and possible targets.

In August 1991, three months after his sudden departure from the FBI, Price was hired by CGC, a Fortune 500 company with a seat on the New York Stock Exchange. Rated by the Wall Street talking heads as the wealthiest company in the world, CGC's modus operandi included hiring people with the right connections and the potential to increase the business bottom line. CEO Saul Mendelsohn was fond of saying, "I am more than willing to pay top dollar for such candidates. I expect to get back the salaries many times over." Mendelsohn paid Price a handsome salary, a more than generous 401K, stock options in excess of the norm, health and other lucrative benefits.

Price's old money and well-established family connections aided him in his job search. His father, Redley Price, called in a chit and offered future high-end client referrals as an incentive. The elder Price was clear with Mendelsohn. "When Todd is on board with CGC, you can expect very lucrative client referrals. Of course, without him I can't promise anything."

Price, Sr. sat on the boards of the major banks and several Fortune 500 corporations with offices in the District of Columbia. His sojourns overseas remained a mystery.

Todd Price sustained his ability to persistently deceive people, a knack mastered during his long tenure as a high-ranking government employee. This ability was now ingrained in Price's persona. He lied even when there was no need. Less than honest when employed by the FBI, he continued hiding the truth when he interviewed with CEO Mendelsohn. "I am burned out at the bureau, no more challenges. I started at the bottom of the ladder and rose to the top. I have accomplished everything I set as goals and objectives. Saul, I didn't want to sit around waiting, for God knows how long, to become the Director. You can rest comfortably that my contacts within the FBI are solid and will benefit CGC in the future."

Price's former associate at the FBI, Melvin Mayhew, often said, "The bum came from a ton of money, yet he still lies about coming up the hard way. Price cannot be truthful."

Before hiring Price, Mendelsohn sought feedback from both Max Blaney and Brad Mason. Neither hesitated; both unequivocally denounced Price and advised Mendelsohn not to hire him. Without going into detailed explanations, the former FBI agents were emphatic. In spite of this, Mendelsohn made a selfish business decision based on greed. The appeal of the almighty dollar outweighed common sense and the counsel of informed contacts.

Not particularly impressed with the man in front of him, Mendelsohn was swayed by the position Price held in the FBI and his political contacts. The Price family connections were what cinched Mendelsohn's decision. He wasted little time and hired the former FBI employee. He figured that he would simply get rid of him, as he had others, if Price did not perform and bring additional prosperity to CGC. Mendelsohn's hiring offer included a stern caution to Price. "If you cause media coverage of us, it better be favorable. You talk a good game. I will give you an opportunity to back up your ambitious goals." The CEO, not yet finished, added, "Remember my number one rule: Never embarrass CGC—or you pay."

"Of course, Saul," Price answered confidently. The new giant of the business world turned and left the impressive office. He smiled as he thought of that same caution he heard as a member of the FBI. He ignored the paradigm as a member of the bureau and would continue to follow his personal code of conduct. Still craftier than all others, he figured his new boss felt it his duty to say such things. After all, Saul is the CEO, he must appear sincere. Mendelsohn's genuine forewarning left Price's mind before he stepped into the elevator. The important executive had things to do, places to go and people to see. He would now use his valuable time to solidify his political connections. For now, his father would guide enough business to CGC to satisfy the CEO.

Price's first stop was at a familiar bar on F Street NE. He owed it to himself. It was a time to celebrate.

Chapter Sixty-Five

The guy is killing us

It took less than four months. Now December 1991, Saul Mendelsohn's phone call came in first thing on a Monday morning.

"I better take it. We know what he's calling about," Blaney said as he picked up the phone. "Hello Saul, Max Blaney."

The caller got right to the point. "Max, the guy is killing us. It's my fault. I trusted him to be at least honest. He spends his time ingratiating himself with people he believes can help his political career. He spends company money like it was his own. He..." Blaney heard the angst in the CEO's voice.

"Saul, remember the old ticker, you need to slow down. Have your driver get you over to our office. We can sit and talk. Brad is here as well. Between us maybe we can figure out a way to help."

Ever since he was put on the CGC payroll, Price had been making the rounds of Washington D.C.'s reputable law firms. He would say his success at opening doors was due to his impressive credentials, but the truth was that no one dared to say no to the son of Redley Price. His message was the same during his visits to each firm. Todd Price was establishing residence in the state of Michigan where he expected to be elected to the United States Senate. The pitch expanded with each presentation. "I am sharing this with you because I'm well aware of the influence your firm has in the state of Michigan. When I was at the FBI, I was encouraged by many to seek the office." He would show his artificial smile and continue. "Of course, your firm will benefit with additional clientele hoping to gain favor with their U.S. senator and a strong lobbyist."

He did not stop with the legal profession. Price still believed the members of the news media truly admired him. He took advantage of what he perceived to be an unlimited expense account and entertained reporters with lavish meals. To this group, he spewed a slightly different story. "I will let you know when the time is right to announce my candidacy and you will have exclusive rights to the breaking story." Not yet finished, he feigned the sincere smile. "I know I can depend on you to acquire the dirt of my opponents, whoever they may be. And of course, print each word."

Redley Price, who controlled the family's enormous fortune, accepted as fact the lies his son told when he left the FBI. To this day, the father assumed it was his son's personal decision to end a distinguished career with the FBI.

The father remained totally immersed in the security of his vast holdings. He stayed busy with his dubious overseas dealings, and chose to be proud of his son without having to involve himself in his life. The elder Price viewed his son as a former, highly respected senior official of a prestigious law enforcement agency, and now as a high-ranking executive with a world leading global corporation. So it was an easy undertaking for Price to convince his father he expected the sponsorship of the Price dynasty, especially the necessary financial support.

The son remained delusional. "Father, I will bring honor to our family." Price continued to be an expert at deceiving people, including those close to him.

His father burst with pride. "I am so proud of you. Imagine how we will boast about you, United States Senator Todd Price. I tell you there will be more than financial backing. I will twist arms and legs and do whatever it takes to insure your election."

Along with his personal visits around the District, Price always included stops at his favorite bars. The smell of liquor permeated his many appointments. While his goal was to impress the movers and shakers of the nation's capital, Price's inflated ego needed the false courage provided by the excessive use of alcohol.

Word travels quickly. Mendelsohn heard the bad news from several sources. His high-salaried executive was embarrassing CGC on all fronts. In his travels, Price never mentioned the goals or objectives of his employer. It was all about his ego and self-centered plans.

When he arrived at GPI, Mendelsohn was directed to the conference room where Blaney, Mason and Nassan were waiting. Mendelsohn was offered a drink, which he refused. The CEO was obviously stressed out. As he sat down, he said, "The guy is crazy. I don't know what to do. You knew him when he was at the bureau, what the hell happened?"

Blaney offered his best shot. "Saul, I will repeat what we said when you asked about bringing him on board. I will go over it. Our experience with Todd Price has not been good. He…"

Mendelsohn could not wait, he interrupted, "Crissakes Max, I…"

Max Blaney did not often lose his temper. When he did, things could get ugly. He raised his right arm in a stop motion and stared directly at the powerful business tycoon.

"Saul, hold it until I finish." He looked around the table and gestured toward Mason and Nassan. "We here still deal with facts. I started to say, you came to us about Price. We told you all we could about Price. We finished our discussion with you by saying that under no circumstances would we have anything to do with Price." He looked at his partner.

Mason added, "That should have been enough. You ask what happened to him since he left the bureau. We never told you everything was as it should be when Price was at the bureau. We didn't share everything we knew of him. That would be unethical. We were clear on one thing: We did tell you we could not and would not recommend him for any position. We believed after listening to us, you would stay away and have nothing to do with him. You ignored our advice. You sought our opinion, we gave it, and you still hired him. Your reasons are your reasons. It was business and strictly your business decision."

The GPI board members had discussed the reason for the visit before Mendelsohn arrived and were in total agreement on their position. Mendelsohn was indeed a giant of business, but Blaney did not intend to pull any punches. "Perhaps you thought with his family connections, Price would be an asset to your company. I don't know what you were thinking, but as Brad said, you made a business decision. Now it appears to be a serious mistake. We discussed the matter before you arrived. Judy, Brad, Dennis, Maz, Mike and I are in total agreement. In your place we strongly recommend you get rid of the son of a bitch now. And that's a free assessment, no charge."

The CEO did not appear to be in control of his emotions. "But Max, the guy's family is so powerful. You have no idea how far his father reaches. They could put a huge dent in our company." Mendelsohn looked at Mason and said, "You could speak to Price and at least slow him down. Brad you could do that, right?"

Mason heard enough. He replied, "Sure Saul, I could speak to him. But it would be a short talk. I would probably put him in the hospital before the conversation ended. Listen, you just heard what Max said. It really is that simple. We and Price do not mix in any way. If you keep him on, then as before, the choice rests with you. GPI is here to help you but never ask us to get in bed with Todd Price. One of the finest crapshooters I know always says, "Do not chase bad money with good." Mason showed his obvious annoyance with the CEO. Both he and his partner understood what must be done. Mendelsohn cannot make a previous bad call better by overlooking what is mandatory. He and Blaney decided Price, Sr. would not be discussed. They all noted that Mendelsohn erred when he assumed GPI had *no idea how far the father reaches.*

The meeting ended with Mendelsohn near in tears agreeing he caused a business catastrophe when he hired Price. But one of the most influential figures in American industry balked when faced with what his friends said was a simple decision. He would think long and hard before making such a move. Like so many others, he truly feared Redley Price.

When Mendelsohn left the meeting, Nassan said, "We need to catch the flight to New York in an hour or so. Wednesday it's wheels up for Tel Aviv. The other three have left. Maz has a car and a driver waiting in front of the building."

Blaney said, "Okay, let's do it. Put Saul out of our minds, on the back burner. The flight out tomorrow will be a long one. We can sleep."

As they hurried out of the conference room, Mason said, "Sleep? Some of us need quiet. We all can't fall asleep on a picket fence. I hope you brought along those snore killers. You'll have the entire plane screaming for double shots."

Blaney actually looked forward to flying. Overseas trips did not faze him. He never found it difficult to sleep, anywhere, anytime.

"I told you many times. Sleeping is an art. It takes training. It…"

Mason and Nassan were already heading for the elevator.

Saul Mendelsohn had every reason to fear Price, Sr. One of the richest men on the planet, among his multiple holdings he owned manufacturing companies of every description all over the world. At present, his arms and high tech munitions conglomerate in the Mideast brought in more money than all of his other holdings combined. He told his comptroller, "The approaching peace talks in East Jerusalem could do us much harm. We need to make sure they do not happen. I will continue personally to apply pressure."

This was not the first time he hired thugs and killers to enforce his objectives. Throughout his menacing existence, Price, Sr. has taken whatever steps necessary to advance his vast empire. Now he would deal with the so-called peacemakers.

Chapter Sixty-Six

The visit

The New York office of Global Private Investigations was located on the fifth floor of a high-rent office building on Fifth Avenue in Manhattan.

In early March 1992, three months after the second trip abroad, the GPI officers were in New York preparing for the week-long trip overseas to meet with a mysterious client. Not one to tread lightly, Judy Nassan called out on the intercom, "Brad a guy calling himself Mr. Smith for you. You want I should get rid of him?"

"No, send it in." Mason made it a practice to accept most calls. It annoyed him when someone would either not accept calls or worse yet, forced you to listen to a long-winded greeting on an answering machine. The message usually ended with the lie: "Leave a message and I will get back to you as soon as possible."

He answered, "Mason."

The male caller sounded surprised to hear a voice. "Oh…yeah…I'd like to see you. I read where you guys are in the city. So I thought I could talk to you." The voice was difficult to hear, almost too soft, although the caller sounded very polite.

"Sure, your name is Smith, right?"

No hesitation this time. "Yeah, that's right."

Mason said, "Well tell me what it's about. Do we know each other?"

"Yeah, well no, not really. I'll give you the dope when we meet if that's okay." The caller never raised his voice but appeared anxious to end the call.

"Okay, we're busy getting ready to leave the city soon." His curiosity took over. "How about nine tomorrow morning? Do you know where the office is?"

"Yeah I do. Okay, thanks. I'll be there at nine. Take it easy." Mr. Smith hung up.

The partner of the firm left his office and walked down the hall, stopping at a huge door with gold lettering marked, "BARRY A. MAZALEWSKI, Director of Operations." Mason opened the door and entered the office.

He glanced around at the opulent surroundings. "Man, look at this place. You've come a long way from Mulberry Street. If the FBI could only see you now."

The smiling DO looked up. "You may not believe this roomie. The bureau calls here on a daily basis. It's the same old embarrassing song. Please Maz, come back. We need you. Crime is rampant, blah, blah and blah."

The boss quickly terminated the direction of the conversation. "I just got off the phone. I've a nine a.m. meeting scheduled here tomorrow. The unknown male caller is a Mr. Smith. I didn't recognize the voice. He sounded almost too quiet. He said he read, and I quote, 'where you guys are in the city' and wanted to talk. Period."

Maz looked concerned. "So what're you thinking?"

Mason answered, "Not much. You take a peek. If he turns out to be someone of interest, let me know before I sit down with him. If not, I'll see him and we go from there. He could be anyone, I have no idea."

"I was planning on being in extra early anyway. The machine will be operational. If he's carrying, we'll handle it." Mazalewski returned to his project.

"Good stuff. Do you really need that picture of Henny Youngman hanging in the middle of the wall?" Mason enjoyed taking a few shots at his roommate from the academy.

"We all have our heroes. As Henny always said, 'If my mother knew what I did for a living, she'd kill me. She thinks I'm selling dope.'"

Mason laughed. He turned and headed out of the office and opened the door, "For sure, the middle initial on your name plate does not stand for Anthony."

Morning came quickly. After speaking earlier with Maz, Mason sat alone in his office.

At nine a.m. on the button, his door opened and Nassan showed her face. "A Mr. Smith for you, sir."

"Sir? Thank you, Judith." He called her by her given name when they both were sounding as professional as possible. "What's he look like?"

"He's not someone I recognize from the bureau. Never saw him around here. I'd have to say I never saw the man. First thing I noticed was the thick glasses. He has huge hands. About fiftyish, just under six feet, brown grayish hair, blue eyes appear bigger behind the glasses. Those peepers look right through you. He has definitely seen stuff. Looks, you know, physical. I didn't get a chance to grab some DNA, but if you want me to…"

Mason smiled and raised his arm, "No, you did fine. Where's Maz?"

"He said the visitor is clean. He and Mike are available."

"Okay Judith, please show Mr. Smith in. Do I smell fresh coffee?"

"Someday you'll get to the point and not beat around the bush when you'd like a cup. I'll bring in a pot, and maybe your friend Smitty will join you." Nassan loved her job.

The big man entered the office and stood next to one of the soft leather chairs. Nassan's physical description was accurate. Mason offered his hand and instantly become aware of the size and strength of Mr. Smith's hand. Mason gestured to the soft leather chair. "Take a seat. Judy's bringing us some coffee."

She set down the tray with a pot of coffee and two large cups on the edge of Mason's desk. Nassan said, "Help yourself. Watch out, it's hot." She smiled at her boss. "Will you require anything else, sir?"

"That should do it. Thank you." The multi-tasked employee walked out and closed the office door. She would assemble the itineraries for the long trip overseas.

Mason smiled at his visitor. "We're usually not so mannerly. We've been friends a long time and we take advantage of our friendship. I'm Brad Mason." Pointing to a chair, he said, "Have a seat." Mason poured out two cups of coffee.

The big man accepted the cup and looked around the room. A generously-sized oak desk, two chairs and a side table with a small unlighted lamp were the extent of the furniture. A photograph of President Ronald Reagan shaking hands with Senator Walter Mondale during the 1984 presidential debate hung on the wall behind Mason's chair. He noted a few smaller frames, presumably family photos, displayed on the desk.

"I thought there would be some FBI stuff around." The stranger surprised his host.

Mason's curiosity aroused, he said, "No that was then, now is now. You know something about me. What about you, have we met before? Is Smith your real name?" Mason had a good idea of the visitor's identity.

"Naw, I figured you may have heard my real name. I said Smith so's you'd see me. I didn't wanna take a chance of not gettin' in."

Mason liked the visitor right away. "Fair enough. What's your name and why are you here?"

The visitor lied. "I ain't really here for anything. I mean, I just wanted to see you and tell you…I mean I know you were a friend of a friend…anyway my name is Dinny, it's Dinny Buchanan. They call me Specs." He smiled as he touched his thick glasses.

Mason indeed had heard a few tales of Specs Buchanan. He smiled back. "I guess you've been wearing those babies for a long time."

"Right, since I was a kid. They said I was born with real bad eyesight. I forget just what they called it, but I always needed the coke bottles. The older I get the thicker they get."

Mason thought, "*You can never tell about people. He seems like an alright guy, yet the stories…*"

"So what mutual friend are we talking about here?" Mason asked.

Buchanan lowered his voice. "Gabe. Gabe Randinoli and me were good friends. Well I worked for him. We did a lot of work together."

Mason said, "Okay Specs, so you know that I knew Gabe. Gabe told you?"

Buchanan felt relaxed. "Yeah. Near the end he said your name a lot. Ya know, just the two of us talkin.' We were havin' a few drinks and he said you guys went way back and you were his best friend. He only talked about when you were young. I figure that a few times when he left for a few days he touched base with you. He never talked about any of that. He really liked to go back and remember a lot of stuff when you were kids. I know he said you were in a church marchin' band. You all hung out on 12th Street or somethin' and some other street…"

Mason helped out. "12th Avenue and Bruce Street." He smiled, "and it was a drum and bugle corps, not a band." *Gabe punched a few people who called it a band.*

"Yeah, that's what he said, 12th Avenue and Bruce Street. He talked about the big crap game he worked at. Let's see, what else? Oh yeah, how you helped him get into business, a gas station I think. Just lots of stuff. I could tell you guys were tight."

"Specs, I don't recall seeing you at the service we had for Gabe. I may have missed you."

Buchanan's demeanor changed. "Nah you didn't miss me. I wanted to be there. You don't know how much. It was by invitation only. You had to be a certain guy, have a certain name if you know what I mean. I can't tell you what I felt when the rest of them left the store and headed for Jersey."

Mason never gave a thought to the people who accompanied Don Nittoli to the Mass at St. Joseph's. Now it dawned on him, they were considered important people in the Bonanno family. *The man in front of him sipping coffee, last name Buchanan, could never be a made guy. Specs said "we did a lot of work together." I can only imagine.*

"I think I understand." Mason thought it time to change the subject. "So Specs, is there anything you want? Anything I can do for you?"

"I can't believe that Gabe's gone two years. I know you're not on the job anymore. And I know that the FBI big shot got away with a pass. He lost his job or some such crap."

"You're speaking of…?" Mason did not finish his thought.

Now louder, Buchanan said, "I'm talkin' about the guy who came to the city and talked with Gabe and with the boss. I'm talkin' of Mr. Price, the other rat responsible for what happened to Gabe. I think about him a lot."

Mason asked, "The other rat? Specs, I finally accepted that Gabe is gone. Although it's not official until the medical examiner says so. But he can't do that without a body. You know it was never located. I don't get what you mean. You say Price and someone else is responsible for Gabe's death?"

"Mr. Mason…Brad, you're a hundred percent right about that. Okay? You can take it to the bank. You want officially? Okay, here it is. Officially Gabe is gone. Don't doubt it. So let's say that someone had to give the order. I consider the guy made a bad call. Now let's say the guy who gave the order is gone too—right? I mean the guy who ordered the work. Nothin' I can do about that, right?" Buchanan was not waiting for an answer. "The guy that gave the order listened to Price say things about Gabe. He knew that Price lied but he needed more excuses to get rid of Gabe. The bottom line is that Price convinced the boss…or whoever gave the orders, that Gabe betrayed the family. The FBI big shot can't be ignored. Price's lies is what was used to whack Gabe—end of story."

The two men sat in silence.

Finally, Mason spoke. "You have no doubt Gabe is dead. I believe you. What about his body?"

Buchanan answered, "Look, we both liked Gabe. He was the only one who…Gabe was good to me. We both were friends of Gabe, maybe in different ways but I won't lie to you." Buchanan placed his coffee mug on the table and stared directly into Mason's eyes. "I have no doubt he's gone. And the body will not be found."

The former FBI agent felt his stomach tighten. "Were you wi…?"

Buchanan stopped the question from being asked. "You just have to trust what I say on that score." He lied again. "No, I wasn't there. And no, I don't know who did the work. I know that the boss liked Gabe. Not only for the dough his crew brought in, but Don Nittoli trusted him and…well, he just liked him. But in the end Don Nittoli caved. He took the word of a scumbag like Price. I talk to you like this because Gabe always said that he learned his loyalty at 12th and…"

Mason helped him remember. "Bruce Street, 12th Avenue and Bruce Street."

"Right, and you bein' from the same place understands what that means."

"So this is why you came to see me. To tell me you believe Price is responsible for our friend's death and you believe he got away with murder." Mason understood that Buchanan missed his capo.

"That's it. Price didn't pull the trigger but he got away with murder. He got a slap on the wrist. I know you worked to have him thrown out of the bureau but that's not enough. Every time I think of him breathin' the air I…"

"Hold it Specs. I know where you're going with this. I believe we both know we're here remembering and talking about our mutual friend and nothing else, right?"

Buchanan understood the meaning. "That's the way I see it."

"Okay, then if I were to say Mr. Price will probably be spending the rest of his life in a federal institution, how would that sound?" Mason and Blaney were sure that the company's investigation of Price's activities while on the federal payroll would be enough to put the former Assistant Director behind bars. They were close to turning over the results to the United States Attorney's Office.

Buchanan had given the subject much thought. "You know the system. Lawyers, judges, juries, witnesses…who knows? It could still take years. He could spend the rest of his life on a big boat sailin' around someplace. Like I said, the maggot still breathes."

"You're right. More than likely it will take no less than a year. He's already lining up the best law firms in D.C. But for what it's worth, I think a year of waiting will get to him. He's a coward and a weak human being. We can be certain he won't be in Virginia living the good life. My suggestion is let the thing play out. Prison would be the best solution."

The big man relaxed. "I guess you know better than me. But with a jury, who knows, he could walk." Buchanan heard what he came to hear. Now he would say enough to appear like a reasonable person accepting Mason's answer.

"I've been involved in many cases. The evidence against Price is overwhelming. He goes away for life." Mason surprised himself for confiding in his guest.

Buchanan stood up from the chair. "Okay, I appreciate that we could talk. I just wanted you to know that he always talked real good about you." He showed a wide grin. "Oh yeah, the club. He said that was a great place to hang out. He said he played pool downstairs by the bar while you were upstairs sweatin'. Anyway, good luck to you."

"And to you, Specs. I'm sure Gabe enjoyed the times you spent together." From stories Mason heard of the man with the thick glasses, he did indeed enjoy his work. Mason came around to the front of his desk. He and Buchanan shook hands. Mason tried to camouflage the pain. The Bonanno associate did indeed possess a powerful grip.

Sitting alone, Mason wondered if he saved Price from a vicious beating, or worse.

Walking to the elevator the big man thought, *"That's for sure, we did spend some crazy times together."* Now Specs heard his friend saying, *"Specs my man, I made a decision. What's the weather like in Virginia?"*

Chapter Sixty-Seven

Sorry Specs

At ten a.m. on a Friday morning, one month after his visit to Brad Mason, Specs left the Bonanno headquarters in Brooklyn without revealing his destination to any of the crew. He lied to Jimmy Palmeri. "I need to see my cousin for a few days. He's upstate so I'll put the AC on and drive up. He's in bad shape so what the hell, I'll get to see him before he goes."

After he left the store, Palmeri said to no one in particular, "Ya know, Specs ain't been the same since Gabe bought it. I didn't even know he had a cousin upstate. I guess maybe he needs a change of scenery."

After his visit with Mason, Buchanan spent his time making plans. First, he made the necessary phone call to Philadelphia. He checked and rechecked the street maps of a particular area of D.C. and Virginia. The psychopathic killer even followed one of Randinoli's old routines. Using the Farmers' Almanac, Specs researched the weather forecast for the time of his visit the following week. Not unlike his old boss, Specs made a decision. Fearful of heights, he did not like to fly. He would drive the two hundred and fifty miles in his low-mileage 1978 green Ford 350 pickup truck. The hot August weather was not an issue—the air conditioner worked as well as any unit on the road.

Randinoli once said, "Specs, you spend more money on that truck than the Congress does on pet projects." Specs took excellent care of his truck. Money no object, he spent whatever necessary to keep the engine and the body in prime condition. It stayed dependable and he loved everything about it, particularly the extended bed. "If you treated your ladies like the truck, you wouldn't have to keep looking for new ones." The truck was comfortable enough to stop along the way and grab a few winks. He didn't want to risk using an unreliable rental, plus why leave paper trails all over the place? In an earlier phone call, Buchanan told his former cellmate that he would contact him when he reached the destination.

The drive down the major highways turned out to be pleasant even for the month of August. Traffic was not a problem, except for a half hour delay as he exited the New Jersey Turnpike to I-95. A tractor trailer rolled over leaving a single lane opened southbound. Buchanan used the time to visualize his mission. If other drivers looked at the bespectacled man driving the obviously well-kept Ford pick-up, they'd guess he just remembered a funny joke or was listening to a comedian on the radio. He gripped the steering wheel so tight he couldn't steer. How he wanted to feel *it* again—the *something* he could never explain. A car horn blasting got his attention and he abandoned his fantasy.

Not one to waste time, years of experience taught the killer not to confuse things, to keep it simple. For twenty-five years Buchanan worked on murder contracts for the Bonanno family. A few did not turn out so good. Poor planning was always the culprit. He and Randinoli worked well together, and most jobs were fulfilled without any complications as a result of simple planning. He also remembered that the fewer people in the crew, the better chance of success. *Me and Gabe worked like clockwork.* He stopped for gas, used the restroom and made his call.

Buchanan spent many days and nights in prison. He did not make many friends on the inside but, Sid Lufkin, age forty-one, was the exception. Lufkin stood five foot nine, and was one hundred and seventy-five pounds of muscle. While in prison he worked out every day and his heavily-tattooed body did not show an ounce of fat. Buchanan and Lufkin were cellmates for two years, both serving time resulting from gambling and aggravated assault convictions. They were feared by the other inmates and ruled the roost in jail. Both enjoyed well-deserved reputations for their brutality. While serving time, the two cellmates borrowed two thousand dollars from Ishmael, a new arrival to the prison. Then they proceeded to beat the prisoner half to death. Ishmael thought he would enter the loansharking business while serving time. He neglected to ask if that business was already spoken for.

The two ex-convicts remained in touch on the outside. Lufkin was now in the lucrative business of selling drugs to college students in Pennsylvania. They met at a predetermined location, Armstrong's Triple Ale, a biker bar outside of Centreville.

After downing two Jack Daniels each and some small talk about his flight, Lufkin asked, "So Specs, how's the whatchamacallit business, the Mafiosi, that's it, right?"

Buchanan answered, "Still makin' a nice livin'. You look like you're not hurtin.' Those rich college kids got lots of bread, I guess."

"You got that right. Mommy and Daddy send them to school to get smart. Instead they get stoned. But nothin' I can do except give 'em what they want and make a ton of dough. Oh, before I forget, Greg the nut job sends his best. He finished his stretch and got out last week. I told him I would be seein' you. He said to tell you that if we need him, he's available. But you said it was somethin' for only the two of us. I told him I'd be in touch if you needed another gun."

Buchanan got along well with his former cellmate. They both got to the point without unnecessary conversation. Buchanan discarded the offer. "Yeah, okay, but you and me are plenty for this job. You thank Greg for me. It's simple, a hit. I do the work. You drive and keep the peace. You okay with that?"

Lufkin did not hesitate. "No problem. Give me what I need."

"The target is a guy named Price. He works in the District and lives in Centreville. He sometimes spends nights in D.C. and gets home late. We want him at night on the way home. We boost a car in the District. We keep it simple. You drive the hot car, I'm in my truck. We stop him and have him think it's a robbery. You get in his passenger seat with him. You keep your piece next to him, force him to follow me. He needs to feel safe so he don't pull somethin' crazy on the busy road. He needs to believe it will be over in a hurry and he'll be on his way. We go to our location. I get in the back seat. Like I said, I do it myself."

Lufkin said, "I guess I'm gettin' his blood all over my new shirt."

"No blood." Buchanan looked down as he turned the palms of his huge hands upward and spread open his fingers. "I got my favorite scarf. The one I got from my mother. It's red silk."

Lufkin forced a smile. "Specs, this sounds personal."

Buchanan nodded, "I lost a good friend. Just say this is payback." He took a long swallow of his drink. "We start tomorrow. We follow him back and forth for a week or so. He doesn't know us so we can be a little aggressive. I don't want to lose him if he makes an unexpected turn off the highway. On our off time, we can pick out a spot to bring him for the work." He did not disclose the information he received from Mason that Price would soon face a federal indictment. Buchanan would handle this without waiting for help from the law.

The surveillance worked even better than expected. The August weather stayed predictably hot and without rain. Each day the skies cleared and the forecast called for more of the same. Traffic between the twenty-three storied Comtech Global building in D.C. and Price's massive estate in Centreville was extra heavy at rush hour but, surprisingly light otherwise. Price avoided the early morning traffic, leaving his home at ten a.m. On this particular Monday and Tuesday, he left Comtech early and stopped at a few bars along the route, obviously familiar with the taverns. Lufkin fit right in at the bars and watched as the target drank heavily. Price drove drunk but made it home each evening without killing himself or anyone else.

Thursday evening, after a full week of close surveillance, Buchanan observed, "The guy makes a truck full of dough. He drinks like a fish every day. Some days after he ties the load on, he drives home drunk. He looks like shit. Yesterday he spent an hour with a shrink. The nights he doesn't go home he stays at a motel in town and drives back to the office in the morning." He handed his partner a magazine and said, "I picked up this fancy magazine that shows pictures of his office, bedrooms and all."

Lufkin read aloud, "The accommodations are every bit as luxurious as a five-star hotel. Is this a great country or what?" Not usually a jokester, Lufkin offered a weak attempt at humor. "It makes me want to return to the soft mattresses in the joint." He did not relish the daily driving excursions. Lufkin was anxious to get back to his drug business.

The two ex-convicts were satisfied with the results of the preparations. They had the exact times and routes taken by Price. On Friday, Price returned home at about seven-thirty and never left the house. Early Saturday morning, a block from Price's house, Buchanan said, "We stay until noon. If he goes, we go with him. If not, we knock off and spend the time checkin' the spot we picked out. Then we start again on Monday. If he repeats the stayover, we do it on Wednesday on his way home." Buchanan thought of Randinoli and how precise he was when giving orders for a hit. He missed his boss.

He'd been away from the city for over a week. In the evening, Buchanan called the store. A familiar voice answered, "Hello."

Buchanan said, "Just the voice I wanted to hear. How're things?"

Jimmy Palmeri was surprised. "Specs, where the hell you at? We thought maybe you was dead. Where you at, man?"

"Geez, I didn't know you guys loved me so much. I'm still at my cousin's place. He's not doin' so good. I'll be back by next week. Start plannin' my comin' home party."

"You should call. Really, Carmine's been asking." Palmeri sounded concerned.

He lied, "I did call. Charlie was the only guy around. I know I told Charlie. He was supposed to let the guys know." Buchanan knew he was on safe ground using Charlie Sassano's name. Not only slow, but his memory was getting worse the older the wise guy got. Buchanan ignored the "where" part of the question.

Palmeri said, "Charlie? You know Charlie. He can't remember his own name anymore. Anyway, I'll need you next week. I got some carpentry work and I want you to help me with it. I'm buyin' the material now. So call the minute you get back."

"Sounds good. I don't wanna get rusty." Buchanan returned to his notes.

Buchanan got the message. Palmeri had a collection to make and needed Specs to convince the deadbeat to pay the debt. Palmeri was taking care of the preparation work. It would be just another day at the office.

Monday night Price stayed in the District. Not engaged in CGC business, he continued the same pattern of gaining political support for himself. His phone calls to lobbyists, congressional aides and the press consisted of lies, threats and whatever he believed necessary to further his political career. Tuesday was the same routine. He did not go home.

Buchanan was decided. He told Lufkin, "Tomorrow's show time."

On Wednesday, Price's Mercedes was positioned in the usual spot in the parking garage used by CGC for its select executives. He never noticed the stolen, late model Lincoln as he drove out of the garage. Lufkin drove the Lincoln and stayed within a reasonable distance behind Price. As part of his careful precaution, Buchanan told Lufkin that on the day of the work, Buchanan would stay in the background. He did not want to take the chance that Price would recognize the pickup with New York plates that had been tailing him for the past week. The walkie-talkies would stay quiet. Buchanan had repeated to his accomplice that they stick to complete radio silence once the scenario began. "No distractions. Don't say a word unless it's life or death."

Both appeared to be businessmen of sorts. They were clean shaven, dressed in suits, with white shirts and ties. Traffic on I-66 moved along at a brisk pace. Buchanan pulled in close behind the Lincoln. The three-vehicle entourage drove twelve miles of what would have been a thirty-mile trip to Price's residence. The spot picked out earlier for the actual work was an additional mile in front of them.

Lufkin beeped the horn lightly and pulled alongside the new Mercedes. Buchanan moved forward and now was directly behind Price. By now

Lufkin had his window opened, he smiled and shouted, "Excuse me sir, Mr. Mendelsohn wants you to…" His voice faded. Buchanan tapped his horn lightly, slowed down feigning fear of causing an accident. They both waved Price to the side. "Mr. Price, would you pull over so…" Lufkin, holding a leather attaché case in his right hand and smiling in a friendly manner, shouted something at Price…"yours, yours." He appeared to be indicating the case belonged to Price. Buchanan continued to sound the horn of the truck.

Price was confused. He never thought through what was happening. If Mendelsohn wanted him would he send someone to yell on a busy highway, and what's with the pick-up truck? Both drivers appeared to be well-groomed. What the hell was the attaché case all about? No big deal. He would see what they wanted and be on his way. He needed a drink.

Price slowed down, signaled for a left turn and brought his vehicle to a safe stop on the shoulder of the highway resting directly behind Lufkin's Lincoln.

He earlier wiped the stolen car clean and now Lufkin, still smiling broadly, turned off the engine, exited the car, and waved the mystery bag as he walked hurriedly towards Price's vehicle. He wore the new leather gloves.

Price watched Lufkin open the passenger side of the Mercedes and, still smiling, he sounded almost friendly. "This is a robbery. We only want your car and your money." As Lufkin sat in the passenger seat as planned, he forgot the part about keeping Price at ease. His voice changed as he added, "This gun is pointed directly at your head. We're desperate men. If you don't do exactly what I tell you, I'll spread your brains all over your new car. I mean our new car."

Price tried to talk, "Why…"

Lufkin was emphatic. "Keep your mouth shut. I won't tell you again. Now you're gonna follow that green truck pullin' in front of you. We go down the road a little ways. When I tell you, bring this beauty behind him and leave it runnin'. We take your car and money and say goodbye. You can keep the truck. Nobody gets hurt." His gun stayed pointed at Price's head.

They left the stolen Lincoln on the side of the road. Price followed instructions and drove his Mercedes close behind as Buchanan turned south toward Falls Church.

Price's mind raced, he tried to speak. "You said Mendel…?"

"I won't tell you again. Keep your fuckin' mouth shut!" Lufkin pressed the Glock hard against Price's neck.

Near choking, Price said, "Okay, okay. Just don't hurt me."

After traveling nearly three miles, Buchanan pulled in to what appeared to be an abandoned piece of property on the outskirts of Falls Church. They had checked it out thoroughly along with the vacant garage sitting in the middle of the lot. Price followed instructions and pulled to a stop directly behind the truck.

His thoughts were all jumbled. Price was cognizant that Mason and Blaney and the other GPI investigators were still working to put him in jail. Although his powerful father was doing everything to thwart the investigation of his son, maybe they would be successful and Price would be indicted, found guilty and sentenced to prison. Aside from that, Price was always fearful of being killed. The nightmares would awaken him in the middle of the night, in a cold sweat. He could not identify whom or what he feared. In his case, it could come from anywhere. Was it the bad guys, or maybe the good guys? The disgraced former FBI executive was convinced he would suffer and be punished for all his sins. His psychiatrist was no help.

The Mercedes idled and Price stared at the figure exiting the truck and walking toward him. Price immediately recognized the big man wearing the thick glasses. In an instant, he understood the reality of situation. It was crystal clear in his brain. He identified Buchanan as "Specs," the man sitting at the bar in New York when Price met with Mason's friend Gabe Randinoli. It could only mean one thing. This was to be settlement for Randinoli's death. Buchanan opened the back door and sat in the back seat of the luxury sedan. He placed his huge hands on top of Price's seat and looked hard at the back of the terrified man's head.

Price had already removed the pill from his jacket pocket as Buchanan entered the car and Lufkin was slightly distracted.

Buchanan stared through the thick glasses and began his brief homily. "Todd Price, you remember my friend Gabe. He's dead and it's your fault. Now it's your turn, you worthless piece of garbage." Buchanan held his favorite scarf and stretching it taut with both hands, moved it toward the executive.

"Sorry Specs, I go my way." Price swiftly tossed the pill in his mouth and before either killer could react, he bit down hard.

"Sid, grab the son…" Lufkin was too late.

Price, the complete coward, would never allow himself to go to prison. As a former law enforcement official, his fate was without doubt. Although somewhat surprised at current events, he was not unprepared. Seconds after biting down on the cyanide tablet, the potassium was in his system. He would be brain dead within minutes, followed by the stoppage of his heart.

The two former cellmates were familiar with people in prison on death row taking such a way out. Rather than face the electric chair or a hanging, they chose the pill. Some inmates could not face the brutality of their fellow prisoners. There were even a few that found the unbearable living conditions to be too much. Whatever the reasons, they all made a decision.

Buchanan, an experienced killer, reached forward and placed two fingers over the carotid artery. The former Assistant Director of the FBI was dead. He said, "Time to go Sid. This guy is startin' to piss me off. I still want to strangle the son of a bitch."

Lufkin put his weapon back in his pocket, opened the car door and exited the vehicle. He removed his gloves. "I'm outta here Specs. These Virginia people are nuts. I need to get back to civilization."

Chapter Sixty-Eight

The group

August in New York was a nice time of the year. Each had arrived early Wednesday morning. The flight on El Al Airlines out of JFK was scheduled for take-off at eleven fifty-five a.m. The GPI group sat around the shiny, twenty-four-foot redwood conference table. The company principles, Max Blaney and Brad Mason, occupied either end. Barry Mazalewski and Judy Nassan sat on one side, and Dennis Moore and Mike Reagan on the other.

Newspapers lay strewn all over the room. They had each read the morning accounts and now discussed the contents dealing with the apparent suicide of Todd Price.

Blaney sipped the hot coffee. "Far be it from me to appear cynical." He paused as the others stared in disbelief. "But this does take the pressure off GPI. It would have required a great deal of our time to finish off Todd ourselves. Of course, I don't really mean finish him off as in you know, finish him...although a life sentence would have cost the taxpayers a fortune. And, with lawyers involved, a possible early release, all very complicated. He took the easy way out. I say goodbye and good riddance."

Moore despised the recently deceased man. "He did get away easy. But you're right Max, Goodfuckinriddance!"

Mason said, "Before we leave, I'll let some old friends know what happened. They keep current on national news but may have missed the name. They'll be happy to learn that the two responsible for Gabe's death are now history."

Maz added, "So true. Don Nittoli, a terrible cancer and now Price, not the most pleasant way to go. The public sees it as a good guy and a bad guy.

We know better. A few of the so-called good guys can be as bad as or worse than the bad guys. They both ended poorly. In the end, it's called street justice."

Everyone was aware of Maz's opinion regarding coffee and donuts, so Moore started in. "Hey Maz, are these the best or what"?

The director of operations bit. "The coffee is hot and it's good. The donuts too, very tasty. I'll bet all the other executives in town are having eggs benedict or some such thing. Coffee and donuts! I feel like I'm back in a bucar in New York watching the bad guys wreak havoc on the streets. I can hear my partner now: 'Looks like we'll be tailgatin' this mug for a few more hours. More coffee, more donuts.' It was like mandatory to live on this stuff. I went crazy for the stale crap we used to get at that flea hole on West 44ᵗʰ Street. The badges always got a discount so nobody complained."

Reagan's lips filled with red as he chewed on a second jelly donut. "Maz, had you read the small print when you accepted your appointment as a special agent, you would know that the daily donuts and coffee were indeed mandatory. You complained then, you complain now. Eggs benedict? You used to think that was the long-haired trumpet player with 'Chicago.'"

The entertainment was interrupted. The front desk agent walked in and placed a phone in front of Blaney. "It's Mendelsohn, the Comtech CEO. He will speak with either of you. Sounds important."

"We know what he wants. I'll take it."

Blaney picked up the phone and said, "Saul, its Max."

Saul Mendelsohn went livid. "Jesus Christ, did you hear the late news? Now it's all over the TV, radio this morning. The whole world is hearing this shit. Already we're bombarded with inquiries. The crazy son of a bitch will ruin me. CGC is being crucified. The questions, why, who, what happened. What is CGC involved in? What happened? It's fucking simple. What happened is the crazy bastard committed suicide…he just went out and…"

Blaney heard enough. "Saul, Saul, you need to quiet down. You're heading for the big one. Listen, we are all here. For information, we'll be airborne in an hour or so. I'll put you on speaker so don't use any foul language. Take a deep breath and relax, you…"

"Max, are you shitting me, relax? Have you any idea what this means? The FBI son of a bitch was supposed to be a stellar representative of Comtech Global Corporation, a company I've given my blood, sweat and tears too all my life. First I learn that he is the worst of the worst. He is building his political future and doing nothing to earn the big chunk I am paying him. Now, when I am ready to can the no-good shit, what happens? He takes a fucking pill, goes to sleep for good and fills the newspapers with questions. You hear what is asked? Did he really commit suicide or did someone force the pill down his throat? Is there a connection between his former employment with the FBI and Comtech? What exactly are they working on at Comtech, some heavy shit with people in the Mideast? The questions are endless. This will kill a reputation that took years to build. My secretary placed several calls to his old man. He won't take my calls. You have no idea what a ruthless son of a bitch Redley Price is."

No one in the group felt poorly for the Comtech CEO. Blaney told him, "You do what you think is best. We told you before that we would never hire him, nor ever work with him for any amount of money." They figured correctly that Price would hide the truth from potential employers and conceal the actual reason he left the bureau. Apparently, the Comtech due diligence people did not take the extra step. Inquiry would have divulged that Price was never considered for the position of FBI Director. Mendelsohn was greedy. He believed that with his FBI background and old money family connections, Price would benefit CGC in spite of himself. Now the CEO desired to place the mistake elsewhere. He made the decision and now searched for sympathy from the former FBI employees. As for his comment concerning Price, Sr., he was mistaken. The people at GPI were certainly aware of Sr.'s ruthlessness.

"Saul, I'm sure things will settle. Time has a way of dealing with this stuff. When we return from our trip, come over and we'll see where things are then." Blaney looked at Mason, who nodded affirmatively. "Brad is here. Do you want to add anything?" He knew his partner was more than upset with Mendelsohn for hiring Price in the first place.

"Hello, Saul."

"Yeah Brad."

"I agree with Max." He added, "If your business is clean and has nothing to hide, then there's little else to be done. That said, to insure that Price was straight and not engaged in criminal activity while representing you, I think you should have your people dig into every action, every move he made on behalf of CGC. Learn your culpability, if any, and have your legal people deal with it now—before anyone else does." Mason didn't add that knowing Price's background, a fair amount of dirt will likely surface.

Moore pointed to the phone and signaled that Mendelsohn was near vomiting at this point.

Mendelsohn barely got it out. "You think...criminal activity, my God. I never considered that a..." The CEO gasped for breath.

Blaney pointed to his watch. "Saul, we need to go. Listen closely. Bottom line, at this point the only thing we know is Price is dead. He may have committed suicide. I underline what Brad said in a nutshell. It makes sense to scrutinize the activities of a former officer of the business. He was your agent. He spoke for you. Learn of any bad shit before anyone else does. Period."

"Can you have your people…?" Mendelsohn wanted the former feds involved now.

"I don't want to appear insensitive, but I have to end our connection. No, our people cannot do anything now. When we six return you can stop by and we'll talk. By that time things may look much better. Good luck." Blaney stood as he ended the call.

As they hurriedly walked through the lobby, Blaney stopped short as a familiar figure walked toward him. A well-dressed, distinguished looking man in his late fifties put out his hand and smiled. "Max, I am aware that you are short for time." He then shook Mason's hand. "Brad, I won't take the time now, but this is important." He looked at the others and continued for all to hear. "A situation has come up. Could be similar or worse than former AD Price. Do you have time to help us out?"

Blaney said, "Jack, I'm confused. As to Price, we know that he's dead. That's all we know. What's the rest of it?"

Jack Silkworth lowered his voice in the crowded building. "He was in serious stuff. As you know, his father has made an enormous amount of money through the years. People will be more than shocked to know where the bulk of his money came from. Mendelsohn and the rest at CGC will be upset to say the least. The bureau needs you on this since the law restricts us from doing what needs to be done. I'll wait until you return from your trip, although it would help if you assign one of your people to get started with some preliminary work."

Blaney and Mason glanced at each other. Each knew the other well enough to be on the same page when it came to business. Without speaking, they jointly decided to withhold the latest news from the FBI official. They had received as yet uncorroborated accounts of Price, Sr. and his activities in the Mideast. The sketchy information indicated that he may be responsible for deaths and bloodshed in the area. One source referred to the powerful head of the financial empire as "the mystery man" of the Mideast.

A common piece of intelligence came from more than one source. Without alerting the news media, there were to be covert peace talks. Operatives from Israel and Palestine were working toward this end for several months. GPI would play an important part in bringing the parties together and insuring the secrecy of any talks.

Mason said, "Mr. Silkworth, you certainly have our attention. Are you sure it can't wait a week or so?"

He smiled. "Brad, I distinctly remember asking you to call me Jack. And no, a week is a long time. Having one of your agents with me now would help a great deal. There are important details to be worked out immediately. Anyway, you and Max give it some thought on the flight out. If you can spare a body now, that's great. If not, I understand. I'll bring you up to speed when you return."

Assistant Director Jack Silkworth without question was one of the most respected men in the FBI. If the president decides to break with tradition and appoint the next FBI Director from within the ranks, the smart money was on Silkworth. It made sense for GPI to cooperate with the AD.

Blaney and Mason looked at each other. Together they turned to the director of operations, who whistled softly and pretended to be staring in space. Mazalewski accepted the inevitable. "That's right, sirs. Especially first class with great food and booze. I couldn't handle it." He looked at the FBI executive. "I'm all yours, sir."

Mason said, "You know you and flying, Maz. But you'll have help. Remember I told you about my partner in the Chicago office?"

"Yeah, Norman, right? Tim Norman?" Mazalewski's memory served him well.

Blaney said, "Brad and I have spoken with him. He'll be here this evening." He said to Silkworth, "That's it then, you can fill them in and they'll do whatever's necessary."

Moore looked at Blaney then said to Mason, "Them, they? How many are we talking about here?"

"Two good friends and great coppers retired from the Chicago PD. Vito Bianco and Bill Jeffries will be with Norman. I will call on the way to the airport and bring them up to date. They'll call you when they get in. Okay with you?"

Mazalewski was delighted. "Absolutely, the more the merrier."

Silkworth was happy the way things turned out. "May I call you Maz? I think you should call me Jack."

Before the groups parted, Silkworth said, "I believe you will be most interested in the other targets."

Walking swiftly toward the door, Reagan added, "Maz, be a good host. Share the donuts, for God's sake."

Chapter Sixty-Nine

That's life

Two weeks after his trip to Virginia, Buchanan was back in Brooklyn. The Friday night before Labor Day, the popular mob bar was packed with wise guys, wannabe wise guys and neighborhood regulars. As always, the action was in full swing in the back room. Two high stakes poker games and a crap game were going full steam. The cigar and cigarette smoke was thick, the booze flowed and the music from the sound system was louder than usual.

Seated at the bar, a few of the crew celebrated a big payday. The week turned extra profitable when a well-heeled Texan visited one of the family's crap games. The visitor rolled enough sevens to drop forty-five thousand in one night's action. The conversation strayed from the sports betting to the weather, even to politics. Buchanan could hold his alcohol with the best of them and the Jack Daniels came at a fast pace. The *Jackie D's* were going down as fast as the bartender could refill his glass. Tonight, he acted melancholy and talked more than usual.

Buchanan motioned to the bartender with two fingers.

"Whoa Specs, they'll be carryin' us outta here." Jimmy Palmeri recognized that few could keep up with Buchanan when it came to consuming alcohol. However, since he was not buying, he made room for the bartender to place the new drinks in front of them.

Palmeri lit a cigarette. "So Specs, your cousin's doin' better, that's good."

"Yeah, the Buchanans are a hardy lot. That's what my old man used to say when he was whackin' us kids around." He changed the subject. "Look at the action back there. Before Gabe moved us in here, it was a ghost town.

Now we make scratch like its goin' outta style. Gabe always treated his friends with respect." He held his head with both hands. "Jimmy, it was wrong to whack Gabe. You know I worked with him on more than one job. He always did the right work. So a body shows up now and then. Who gives a shit?"

Palmeri looked around to make sure no one was listening to the conversation. Everyone knew Specs and Randinoli were tight. Palmeri thought of the capo. "Specs, I knew Gabe longer than anyone. I think we all miss him. We did what we did. We followed orders, right? Gabe would be the first to say it, right? He always said we had rules. I don't think he would expect us to do anything different, right?"

"I'm not sayin' don't follow rules. I don't know. I still say the boss listened to a no-good rat. That never happened before, not since I've been around. I mean, since when does an outside piece of shit say who goes and who stays?" Buchanan looked toward the front of the bar and smiled broadly. "I still expect Gabe to walk through the door. He'd say to me, "So Irish, how's it goin'? Ya know, he'll be gone four years this Christmas."

"That's right." Palmeri remembered something. "I almost forgot. Did you catch today's Daily News, the guy who bought it down in Virginia some place?" He looked around before whispering, "It was the same big shot FBI guy who come from D.C. and met with Joe. The story is he killed himself. I can't think of his name it's…let's see…I read it today, what the hell was it…?"

Buchanan stared straight at his own image in the mirror behind the bar. "Price, Todd Price. Yeah, I heard." He appeared to be daydreaming. "Right off the highway, I-66." He showed a wild look on his face. "Probably couldn't live without his buddy the Don."

"That's it, Price. Good goin' Specs, you got a good memory. You're right, he's the same fed that Joe listened to. Who knows, Gabe might still be here."

The juke box played Sinatra, who else? Buchanan adjusted his thick glasses and said, "Listen to that, you just can't get away from 'old blue eyes.' Right on Francis, that's life. Not for Mr. Price though. Al, turn the volume up a little." He threw back the double shot. The music got louder, Sinatra singing another big hit,

That's life, that's life and I can't deny it.
Many times I thought of cutting out
But my heart won't buy it
But if there's nothing shakin' come this here July

I'm gonna roll myself up in a big ball and die.

Palmeri listened and smiled. "Gabe loved to listen to Sinatra's music. You can always count on the man from Hoboken to have the lyrics for every occasion."

I-66? Where'd that come from? I didn't read that shit. Naw, he's not a pill guy... Specs would've used the scarf.

Epilogue

The New York office of Global Private Investigations, LLC, was located on the fifth floor of a skyscraper building on Fifth Avenue in Manhattan. The team officers were preparing for what was expected to be at least a week-long trip overseas. Max Blaney thought of little else except the upcoming trip. The purpose of the trip, to meet with a very special client, remained a mystery to four of the officers. Blaney and Brad Mason had maintained a tight lid on the details. In the conference room, two of the officers found folders containing the necessary documents and reports.

Blaney, Mason and the other former FBI agents, Mazalewski and Nassan, assembled in a conference room. Mike Reagan and Dennis Moore were expected shortly. Blaney started the discussion. "If things get crazy over there, GPI will be in the crosshairs of more than a few pissed off people— and possibly countries."

Mason agreed. "It's been handled well so far. If we shared everything we knew from the start a lot of valuable time would have been wasted with unnecessary speculation."

Mazalewski said, "I stole a quick look at the material. This trip will be more challenging than any of the investigations we were involved with as FBI agents. Bill and Dennis spent all of yesterday with the original source. They should be here soon."

Judy Nassan smiled. "I knew that the bureau was loads of fun for us all but this sounds like a blast. I can smell the explosives, hear the gun shots, and the blood…the blood makes it all worthwhile. You people are sick…"

She was interrupted when the door to the conference room swung open and the two remaining GPI principles walked in. Nassan, always glad to see her co-workers, said, "Well speak of the devil, and look who stops by."

Moore replied, "And the very same to you, Ms. Nassan." He helped himself to a cup of coffee from the double pot sitting on the nearby table. Reagan followed suit and said, "Have we missed anything of interest?"

Mazalewski answered, "Not a thing. Our little ray of sunshine was just sharing one of her entertaining commentaries."

Moore was serious, "I can't believe what could actually happen with this stuff. We're talking the biggest treaty ever. I mean secret peace talks in the Mideast. It's almost as if…"

"Whoa, hold it a minute Bill." Blaney wanted to stay as organized as possible. "Listen up people." He looked at Brad.

Mason sat up straight. "We need to sit tight. Max and I have something to share." He glanced at Moore and Reagan, "Then we can pick it up from your contact with the source. We have known for a while about the possible involvement of Redley Price and we've received sparse unverified info regarding possible peace talks. We decided that both subjects were nothing more than that, unsubstantiated talk. After listening to Assistant Director Jack Silkworth, we now think there is definitely something to it. GPI is being asked to do everything possible to insure that the talks happen. That's why we're going over and that's what we'll do. After we have a clear picture, we'll figure out what needs to be done and do our best to allow the parties to negotiate."

Blaney added, "On the flight over we will explain in detail the material in front of you. Pay close attention to the section dealing with Redley Price's profits from his military investment in weapons of mass destruction. The charts are clear; for him, peace in the area equates to losing a ton of dough. We'll compare the stuff we have with what you got yesterday from the source. Then we can address any questions or concerns." As an afterthought, Blaney said, "We're almost guaranteed some fireworks. If Price's people interfere, then we have a contingency plan ready for that scenario and people already in place." Blaney spoke in his serious monotone. The others understood his meaning.

The El AL flight took off from JFK airport on time and ten and a half hours later arrived in Tel Aviv without incident. Moore was the last to walk off the plane with Mason. "Brad, the contact we're meeting, the international arms dealer, what's his name again?"

Mason kept walking straight ahead and smiled as he answered, "The citizen's name is Zatz, Johnny Zatz."

The GPI team taxied to their headquarters.

Acknowledgement

A SPECIAL THANKS to Jim Ring, my longtime friend and colleague from the FBI, unquestionably the ultimate authority on the history of La Cosa Nostra. Jim was my number one reader, allowing me to take full advantage of the experiences he nurtured writing two popular books: the fast-moving international thriller *Necessary Assets* and *784 Broadway*, a reach-back to memories of his childhood and how his immigrant family lived and worked and loved. Our get-togethers and correspondence began shortly after I started *12th and Bruce*. His encouragement and timely reminders that each word was precious prevented me from falling off the cliff.

Other readers offering valuable insight and counsel: Ken O'Brien, Todd Randinelli, Moe Courchesne and John Svirsky.

My publisher and doer of everything-else-it-took to keep this neophyte's head in the right place, Henry Quinlan of Omni Publishing Company, remained patient and his expertise and experience carried the project over the hurdles of planning and publishing. Editor Theresa Driscoll proved once again that she grasps the things that matter. She never tired of dealing with the author's multitude of questions. Thanks, Theresa, for your patience and understanding as we worked through the book cover issues.

Pat, my bride, my friend, provided the constant encouragement necessary for this labor of love to complete. As an occasional reader, her supporting mantra usually concluded with, "That sounds just right, I like it." Always a source of strength, while writing I recalled my children, Tom, Tim, and Maureen's lively presence during our family's early days in New Jersey, Ohio, Illinois, and Massachusetts. Their steady phone calls of encouragement, "How's it coming Dad?" made the trip back to *12th and Bruce* much smoother. Tim also applied his talents as the essential computer expert, photographer and website designer.

I have been blessed with a loving family. Once special boys, our six grandsons are extra-special men: Thomas, Patrick, and Colin MacGeorge; Ryan, Daniel, and Alex deMartin. They—along with Tom's wife Celeste, Tim's partner Paul Hatlas, Maureen's husband Bill deMartin, Ryan's wife Anna-Maria and their daughter, God's latest gift, great-granddaughter Giana—each provided motivation to push forward.

The following people, in no particular order and for no particular reason, contributed to this lengthy project: Bill Erickson, John McLaughlin, Ed Fitzpatrick, Jim and Barbara Critchley, Judy Murphy and Charlie Vogt.

The author extends a sincere thank you to friends who allowed their surnames to appear in the manuscript. There are too many to mention—you know who you are.

About the Author

TOM MacGEORGE, while serving in the FBI's Boston office, supervised the special operations group's participation in the first-ever electronic interception of a La Cosa Nostra/Mafia induction ceremony, to include the oath of *omertà*, the code of silence. During this age-old ritual, individuals were inducted as "made" members of a large criminal enterprise.

The author also served as the Boston Division's White Collar Crime Supervisor and Coordinator for the New England region. In these positions he testified in federal and state court criminal trials to include kidnap/murder, public corruption and bank fraud and embezzlement. In addition to his assignment in Boston, Tom served in the FBI's Chicago and Tampa offices and later at the Fort Myers resident agency investigating drug violations and voter fraud.

Following his retirement from the FBI, Tom founded and served as president of a private investigation company. Born in New Jersey, Tom and his wife Pat reside in southwest Florida. At present, Tom is planning his next novel.

MacGeorge may be contacted by email at: tjmpi@outlook.com or through his website: www.tommacgeorge.com.

Praise for 12ᵗʰ and Bruce

"In 12th & Bruce, MacGeorge details the economic and social disintegration of Newark through unique, compelling, and memorable characters—life-long friends. Rough and often humorous, they understand the love and respect upon which their friendships are based. It is sometimes hard to tell the good guys from the bad. Brad Mason becomes an FBI agent. His best friend Gabe Randinoli chooses life in a New York crime family. Their friendship is no secret, but can it survive?"
—JAMES RING, Author of *Necessary Assets* and *784 Broadway*

"Tom MacGeorge equips and allows his characters to tell their story of the disintegration of a way of life, a community, and the bonds of friendship and loyalty that served as the foundation of life in the Newark neighborhood of 12th & Bruce. This story touches our emotions in the most unexpected of ways. Humor, pathos, anger, and kindness are all present as two boyhood friends fight to maintain their friendship. It is fitting the story begins with an unforgettable funeral."
—GEOFF MASON, Mainstay Communications

"12th and Bruce is not a whodunit, yet I quickly turned each page wanting to know more about two friends growing up in the 1950s in an inner city environment. The author takes the reader from the early days in the neighborhood through the very different paths the two friends traveled. It was my first time experiencing an actual Mafia induction ceremony as Tom Mac-George brought me inside the Brooklyn apartment to witness the centuries-old tradition of omertà, the code of silence. The language is so real, the result of the author's experience that comprised a long law enforcement career. I look forward to the movie. *Grazie!*
—BRIAN BEASLEY, Beasley Broadcast Group Inc.

82665804R00239

Made in the USA
Columbia, SC
19 December 2017